ROGUE SQUADRON

ROGUE SQUADRON

BOOK 1 OF THE
ROGUE SQUADRON SERIES

MICHAEL A. STACKPOLE

NEW YORK

2021 Del Rey Trade Paperback Edition

Copyright © 1996 by Lucasfilm Ltd. & ® or ™ where indicated.
All rights reserved.
Excerpt from *Star Wars: Rogue Squadron: Wedge's Gamble*
copyright © 1996 by Lucasfilm Ltd. & ® or ™ where indicated.
All rights reserved.

Published in the United States by Del Rey, an imprint of Random House,
a division of Penguin Random House LLC, New York.

Del Rey is a registered trademark and the Circle colophon is a trademark of
Penguin Random House LLC.

Originally published in paperback in the United States
by Bantam Spectra, an imprint of Random House, a division of
Penguin Random House LLC, in 1996.

ISBN 978-0-593-35979-2
Ebook ISBN 978-0-307-79621-9

Printed in the United States of America on acid-free paper

randomhousebooks.com

4 6 8 9 7 5 3

Book design by Edwin Vazquez

To George Lucas

The universe he created is so vital and magical that
I remember not only when and where I first saw the film,
but when and where I first saw the trailer for the film.
If someone had told me then I'd be writing in
that universe now, I'd have told them they were insane.

Once again, Mr. Lucas, you make dreams come true.

THE ESSENTIAL
LEGENDS COLLECTION

For more than forty years, novels set in a galaxy far, far away have enriched the *Star Wars* experience for fans seeking to continue the adventure beyond the screen. When he created *Star Wars*, George Lucas built a universe that sparked the imagination and inspired others to create. He opened up that universe to be a creative space for other people to tell their own tales. This became known as the Expanded Universe, or EU, of novels, comics, videogames, and more.

To this day, the EU remains an inspiration for *Star Wars* creators and is published under the label Legends. Ideas, characters, story elements, and more from new *Star Wars* entertainment trace their origins back to material from the Expanded Universe. This Essential Legends Collection curates some of the most treasured stories from that expansive legacy.

DRAMATIS PERSONAE

ROGUE SQUADRON

COMMANDER WEDGE ANTILLES (human male from Corellia)

CAPTAIN TYCHO CELCHU (human male from Alderaan)

LIEUTENANT CORRAN HORN (human male from Corellia)

OORYL QRYGG (Gand male from Gand)

NAWARA VEN (Twi'lek male from Ryloth)

RHYSATI YNR (human female from Bespin)

BROR JACE (human male from Thyferra)

ERISI DLARIT (human female from Thyferra)

PESHK VRI'SYK (Bothan male from Bothawui)

GAVIN DARKLIGHTER (human male from Tatooine)

RIV SHIEL (Shistavanen male from Uvena III)

LUJAYNE FORGE (human female from Kessel)

ANDOORNI HUI (Rodian female from Rodia)

ZRAII (Verpine male from Roche G42)

M-3PO (Emtrey; protocol and regulations droid)

WHISTLER (Corran's R2-D2 astromech)

MYNOCK (Wedge's R5-D2 astromech)

ADMIRAL ACKBAR (Mon Calamari male from Mon Calamari)

GENERAL HORTON SALM (human male from Norvall II)

GENERAL LARYN KRE'FEY (Bothan male from Bothawui)

CAPTAIN AFYON (human male from Alderaan)

CREW OF THE *PULSAR SKATE*

MIRAX TERRIK (human female from Corellia)

LIAT TSAYV (Sullustan male from Sullust)

IMPERIAL FORCES

YSANNE ISARD, DIRECTOR OF IMPERIAL INTELLIGENCE
(human female from Coruscant)

KIRTAN LOOR, INTELLIGENCE AGENT
(human male from Churba)

GENERAL EVIR DERRICOTE (human male from Kalla)

ROGUE SQUADRON

1

*Y*OU'RE GOOD, CORRAN, *but you're no Luke Skywalker.* Corran Horn's cheeks still burned at the memory of Commander Antilles's evaluation of his last simulator exercise. The line had been a simple comment, not meant to be cruel nor delivered that way, but it cut deep into Corran. *I've never tried to suggest I'm that good of a pilot.*

He shook his head. *No, you just wanted it to be self-evident and easily recognized by everyone around you.* Reaching out he flicked the starter switches for the X-wing simulator's engines. "Green One has four starts and is go." All around him in the cockpit various switches, buttons, and monitors flashed to life. "Primary and secondary power is at full."

Ooryl Qrygg, his Gand wingman, reported similar start-up success in a high-pitched voice. "Green Two is operational."

Green Three and Four checked in, then the external screens came alive projecting an empty starfield. "Whistler, have you finished the navigation calculations?"

The green and white R2 unit seated behind Corran hooted, then the navdata spilled out over Corran's main monitor. He punched a button sending the same coordinates out to the other pilots in Green Flight. "Go to light speed and rendezvous on the *Redemption*."

As Corran engaged the X-wing's hyperdrive, the stars elongated themselves into white cylinders, then snapped back into pinpoints and began to revolve slowly, transforming themselves into a tunnel of white light. Corran fought the urge to use the stick to compensate for the roll. In space, and especially hyperspace, up and down were relative. How his ship moved through hyperspace didn't really matter—as long as it remained on the course Whistler had calculated and had attained sufficient velocity before entering hyperspace, he'd arrive intact.

Flying into a black hole would actually make this run easier. Every pilot dreaded the *Redemption* run. The scenario was based on an Imperial attack on evacuation ships back before the first Death Star had been destroyed. While the *Redemption* waited for three Medevac shuttles and the corvette *Korolev* to dock and off-load wounded, the Imperial frigate *Warspite* danced around the system and dumped out TIE fighters and added bombers to the mix to do as much damage as they could.

The bombers, with a full load of missiles, could do a *lot* of damage. All the pilots called the *Redemption* scenario by another name: the *Requiem* scenario. The *Warspite* would only deploy four starfighters and a half-dozen bombers—known in pilot slang as "eyeballs" and "dupes" respectively—but it would do so in a pattern that made it all but impossible for the pilots to save the *Korolev*. The corvette was just one big target, and the TIE bombers had no trouble unloading all their missiles into it.

Stellar pinpoints elongated again as the fighter came out of hyperspace. Off to the port side Corran saw the *Redemption*. Moments later Whistler reported that the other fighters and all three Medevac shuttles had arrived. The fighters checked in and the first shuttle began its docking maneuver with the *Redemption*.

"Green One, this is Green Four."

"Go ahead, Four."

"By the *book*, or are we doing something fancy?"

Corran hesitated before answering. By *book*, Nawara Ven had referred to the general wisdom about the scenario. It stated that one pilot should play *fleethund* and race out to engage the first TIE flight while the other three fighters remained in close as backup. As long as three fighters stayed at home, it appeared, the *Warspite* dropped ships off at a considerable distance from the *Korolev*. When they didn't, it got bolder and the whole scenario became very bloody.

The problem with going by the book was that it wasn't a very good strategy. It meant one pilot had to deal with five TIEs—two eyeballs and three dupes—all by himself, then turn around and engage five more. Even with them coming in waves, the chances of being able to succeed against those odds were slim.

Doing it any other way was disastrous. *Besides, what loyal son of Corellia ever had any use for odds?*

"By the book. Keep the home fires burning and pick up after me."

"Done. Good luck."

"Thanks." Corran reached up with his right hand and pressed it against the lucky charm he wore on a chain around his neck. Though he could barely feel the coin through his gloves and the thick material of his flight suit, the familiar sensation of the metal resting against his breastbone brought a smile to his face. *It worked for you a lot, Dad, let's hope all its luck hasn't run out yet.*

He openly acknowledged that he'd been depending quite a bit on luck to see him through the difficulties of settling in with the Alliance forces. Learning the slang took some work—moving from calling TIE starfighters "eyeballs" to calling Interceptors "squints" made a certain amount of sense, but many other terms had been born of logic that escaped him. Everything about the Rebellion seemed odd in comparison to his previous life and fitting in had not been easy.

Nor will be winning this scenario.

The *Korolev* materialized and moved toward the *Redemption*, prompting Corran to begin his final check. He'd mulled the scenario over in his mind time and time again. In previous runs, when he served as a home guard to someone else's *fleethund*, he'd had Whistler record traces on the TIE timing patterns, flight styles, and attack vectors. While different cadets flew the TIE half of the simulations, the craft dictated their performance and a lot of their initial run sequence had been preprogrammed.

A sharp squawk from Whistler alerted Corran to the *Warspite*'s arrival. "Great, eleven klicks aft." Pulling the stick around to the right, Corran brought the X-wing into a wide turn. At the end of it he punched the throttle up to full power. Hitting another switch up to the right, he locked the S-foils into attack position. "Green One engaging."

Rhysati's voice came cool and strong through the radio. "Be all over them like drool on a Hutt."

"I'll do my best, Green Three." Corran smiled and waggled the X-wing as he flew back through the Alliance formation and out toward the *Warspite*. Whistler announced the appearance of three TIE bombers with a low tone, then brought the sound up as two TIE fighters joined them.

"Whistler, tag the bombers as targets one, two, and three." As the R2 unit complied with that order, Corran pushed shield power full to front and brought his laser targeting program up on the main monitor. With his left hand he adjusted the sighting calibration knob on the stick and got the two fighters. *Good, looks like three klicks between the eyeballs and the bombers.*

Corran's right hand again brushed the coin beneath his flight suit. He took a deep breath, exhaled slowly, then settled his hand on the stick and let his thumb hover over the firing button. At two klicks the heads-up display painted a yellow box around the lead TIE fighter. The box went green as the fighter's image locked into the HUD's targeting cross and

Whistler's shrill bleat filled the cockpit. Corran's thumb hit the button, sending three bursts of laser bolts at the lead fighter.

The first set missed but the second and third blasted through the spherical cockpit. The hexagonal solar panels snapped off and spun forward through space while the ion engines exploded into an expanding ball of incandescent gas.

Corran kicked the X-wing up in a ninety-degree snap-roll and sliced through the center of the explosion. Laser fire from the second fighter lit up his forward shields, making it impossible for him to get a good visual line on the TIE. Whistler yowled, complaining about being a target. Corran hurried a shot and knew he hit, but the TIE flashed past and continued on in at the *Korolev*.

Time to write a new chapter for the book *on the* Requiem *scenario*. Corran throttled back almost all the way to zero and let the X-wing decelerate. "Whistler, bring up target one."

The image of the first TIE bomber filled his monitor. Corran switched over to proton torpedo target control. The HUD changed to a larger box and Whistler began beeping as he worked supplying data to the targeting computer for a missile lock.

"Green One, your velocity is down to one percent. Do you need help?"

"Negative, Green Two."

"Corran, what are you doing?"

"Making the *book* a short story." *I hope.*

The HUD went red and Whistler's tone became constant. Corran punched the button and launched the first missile. "Acquire target two." The HUD flashed yellow, then red, and the pilot launched the second missile.

Numbers scrolled away to zero as the missiles streaked in at their targets. Two kilometers away the first missile hit, shredding the first TIE bomber. Seconds later the second missile hit its target. A novalike explosion lit the simulator's cockpit, then melted into the blackness of space.

"Acquire target three."

Even as he gave the order he knew the rate of closure between the bomber and his ship would make the last missile shot all but impossible. "Cancel three." Corran throttled up again as the third bomber sailed past and brought his ship around. He switched back to laser targeting and climbed right up on the bomber's stern.

The dupe's pilot tried to evade him. He juked the double-hulled ship to the left, then started a long turn to the right, but Corran was of no mind to lose him. He cut his speed, which kept the bomber in front of him, then followed it in its turn. As he leveled out again on its tail, he triggered two laser bursts and the targeting computer reported hull damage.

The bomber's right wing came up in a roll and Corran did the same thing. Had he continued to fly level, the X-wing's lasers would have passed on either side of the bomber's fuselage, giving the bomber a few seconds more of life. Keeping the bomber centered in his crosshairs, Corran hit twice more and the bulky craft disintegrated before him.

Pushing his throttle to full, Corran scanned for the fighter he'd missed. He found it two klicks out and going in toward the *Korolev*. He also found five more TIEs coming in from the other side of the corvette, eighteen kilometers away. *Damn, the bomber took more time than I had to give it.*

He brought the torpedo targeting program back up and locked on to the remaining fighter. The HUD seemed to take forever before it went red and acquired a lock. Corran fired a missile and watched it blast through the fighter, then turned his attention to the new TIEs.

"Green One, do you want us to engage?"

Corran shook his head. "Negative, Two. *Warspite* is still here and could dump another flight." He sighed. "Move to intercept the fighters, but don't go beyond a klick from the *Korolev*."

"On it."

Good, they can tie the fighters up while I dust these dupes.

Corran studied the navigational data Whistler was giving him. The *Korolev*, the bombers, and his X-wing formed a shrinking triangle. If he flew directly at the bombers he would end up flying in an arc, which would take more time than he had and let them get close enough to launch their missiles at the corvette. That would be less than useless as far as he was concerned.

"Whistler, plot me an intercept point six klicks out from the *Korolev*."

The R2 whistled blithely, as if that calculation was so simple even Corran should have been able to do it in his head. Steering toward it, Corran saw he'd have just over a minute to deal with the bombers before they were in firing range on the *Korolev*. *Not enough time.*

Flicking two switches, Corran redirected generator energy from recharging his shields and lasers into the engines. It took the acceleration compensator a second to cycle up, so the ship's burst of speed pushed Corran back into the padding of his command seat. *This better work.*

"Green One, the *Warspite* has hyped. Are we released to engage fighters?"

"Affirmative, Three. Go get them." Corran frowned for a second, knowing his fellow pilots would make short work of the TIE fighters. They would deny him a clean sweep, but he'd willingly trade two TIEs for the corvette. *Commander Antilles might have gotten them all himself, but then he's got two Death Stars painted on the side of his X-wing.*

"Whistler, mark each of the bombers four, five, and six." Range to intercept was three klicks and he had added thirty seconds to his fighting time. "Acquire four."

The targeting computer showed him to be coming in at a forty-five-degree angle to the flight path of his target, which meant he was way off target. He quickly punched the generator back into recharging lasers and his shields, then pulled even more energy from his quartet of Incom 4L4 fusial thrust engines and shunted it into recharging his weapons and shields.

The resource redirection brought his speed down. Corran pulled back on the stick, easing the X-wing into a turn that brought him head-on into the bombers. Tapping the stick to the left, he centered the targeting box on the first of the dupes.

The HUD started yellow, then quickly went red. Corran fired a missile. "Acquire five." The HUD started red and Whistler's keen echoed through the cockpit. The Corellian fired a second missile. "Acquire six."

Whistler screeched.

Corran looked down at his display. Scrolling up the screen, sandwiched between the reports of missile hits on the three bombers, he saw a notation about Green Two. "Green Two, report."

"He's gone, One."

"A fighter got him?"

"No time to chat . . ." The comm call from the Twi'lek in Green Four ended in a hiss of static.

"Rhysati?"

"Got one, Corran, but this last one is good."

"Hang on."

"I'll do my best."

"Whistler, acquire six."

The R2 unit hissed. The last bomber had already shot past the intercept point and was bearing in on the *Korolev*. The pilot had the wide-bodied craft slowly spinning, making it a difficult target for a missile lock. The *Korolev*, being as big as it was, would present a large enough target that even a rolling ship could get a lock on it.

And once he has that lock, the Korolev *is so much space junk.* Corran switched back to lasers and pushed his X-wing forward. Even though two klicks separated them, he triggered a couple of laser blasts. He knew his chances of hitting were not good at that range, but the light from the bolts would shoot past the TIE and give the pilot something to think about. *And I want him thinking about me, not that* nerf-vette *grazing there.*

Corran redirected all power back into the engines and shot forward. Two more laser blasts caused the TIE bomber to shy a bit, but it had pushed into target-acquisition range. The ship's roll began to slow as the pilot fixated on his target, then, as Corran brought his lasers to bear, the bomber jinked and cut away to port.

The Corellian's eyes narrowed. *Bror Jace has got to be flying that thing. He thinks it's payback time.* The other pilot, a human from Thyferra, was—in Corran's opinion—the *second best* pilot in the training squadron. *He's going to kill the Ko-rolev and I'll never hear the end of it. Unless . . .*

Corran pulled all his shield energy forward and left his aft as naked as the shieldless TIE bomber. Following Jace through a barrel roll, he kept the throttle full forward. As they leveled out again Corran triggered a snapshot at the bomber. It caught a piece of one wing, but Jace dove beneath the X-wing's line of fire. *Here we go!*

Corran shoved his stick forward to follow the bomber's dive, but because his rate of speed was a good twenty percent faster than that of Jace's ship, the X-wing moved into a broad loop. By the time Corran inverted to finish the turn off, Jace's bomber came back up and banked in on the X-wing's tail.

Before the bomber could unload a missile or two into his aft, Corran broke the fighter hard to port and carved across the bomber's line of fire. *Basic maneuver with a basic response.* Without even glancing at his instruments, and paying no attention to Whistler's squealed warning, Corran cut engine power back into recharging his shields. *One more second.*

Jace's response to Corran's break had been a reverse-throttle hop. By bringing the nose of the bomber up in a steep climb, then rolling out in the direction of the turn, Jace managed to stay inside the arc of the X-wing's turn. As the bomber leveled off, it closed very quickly with the X-wing—*too quickly for a missile lock, but not a laser shot.*

The TIE bomber shrieked in at the X-wing. Collision warning klaxons wailed. Corran could feel Jace's excitement as the

X-wing loomed larger. He knew the other pilot would snap off a quick shot, then come around again, angry at having overshot the X-wing, but happy to smoke Corran *before* taking the *Korolev*.

The X-wing pilot hit a switch and shifted all shield power to the aft shields.

The deflector shield materialized as a demisphere approximately twenty meters behind the X-wing. Designed to dissipate both energy and kinetic weapons, it had no trouble protecting the fighter from the bomber's twin laser blasts. Had the bomber used missiles, the shields could even have handled all the damage they could do, though that would have been enough to destroy the shields themselves.

The TIE bomber, which massed far more than the missiles it carried, should have punched through the shields and might even have destroyed the fighter, but it hit at an angle and glanced off. The collision did blast away half the power of the aft shield and bounced the X-wing around, but otherwise left the snubfighter undamaged.

The same could not be said of the unshielded bomber. The impact with the shield was roughly equivalent to a vehicle hitting a ferrocrete wall at sixty kilometers per hour. While that might not do a land vehicle much damage, land vehicles are decidedly less delicate than starfighters. The starboard wing crumpled inward, wrapping itself around the bomber's cockpit. Both pods of the ship twisted out of alignment so the engines shot it off into an uncontrolled tumble through the simulator's dataspace.

"Green Three, did you copy that?"

Corran got no response. "Whistler, what happened to Three?"

The R2 unit gave him a mournful tone.

Sithspawn. Corran flipped the shield control to equalize things fore and aft. "Where is he?"

The image of a lone TIE fighter making a strafing run on the *Korolev* appeared on Corran's monitor. The clumsy little craft skittered along over the corvette's surface, easily dodging its weak return fire. *That's seriously gutsy for a TIE fighter.* Corran smiled. *Or arrogant, and time to make him pay for that arrogance.*

The Corellian brought his proton torpedo targeting program up and locked on to the TIE. It tried to break the lock, but turbolaser fire from the *Korolev* boxed it in. Corran's HUD went red and he triggered the torpedo. "Scratch one eyeball."

The missile shot straight in at the fighter, but the pilot broke hard to port and away, causing the missile to overshoot the target. *Nice flying!* Corran brought his X-wing over and started down to loop in behind the TIE, but as he did so, the TIE vanished from his forward screen and reappeared in his aft arc. Yanking the stick hard to the right and pulling it back, Corran wrestled the X-wing up and to starboard, then inverted and rolled out to the left.

A laser shot jolted a tremor through the simulator's couch. *Lucky thing I had all shields aft!* Corran reinforced them with energy from his lasers, then evened them out fore and aft. Jinking the fighter right and left, he avoided laser shots coming in from behind, but they all came in far closer than he liked.

He knew Jace had been in the bomber, and Jace was the only pilot in the unit who could have stayed with him. *Except for our leader.* Corran smiled broadly. *Coming to see how good I really am, Commander Antilles? Let me give you a clinic.* "Make sure you're in there solid, Whistler, because we're going for a little ride."

Corran refused to let the R2's moan slow him down. A snap-roll brought the X-wing up on its port wing. Pulling back on the stick yanked the fighter's nose up away from the original line of flight. The TIE stayed with him, then tightened up on the arc to close distance. Corran then rolled another ninety degrees and continued the turn into a dive. Throttling back, Corran hung in the dive for three seconds, then hauled back hard on the stick and cruised up into the TIE fighter's aft.

The X-wing's laser fire missed wide to the right as the TIE cut to the left. Corran kicked his speed up to full and broke with the TIE. He let the X-wing rise above the plane of the break, then put the fighter through a twisting roll that ate up enough time to bring him again into the TIE's rear. The TIE snapped to the right and Corran looped out left.

He watched the tracking display as the distance between them grew to be a kilometer and a half, then slowed. *Fine, you want to go nose to nose? I've got shields and you don't.* If Commander Antilles wanted to commit virtual suicide, Corran was happy to oblige him. He tugged the stick back to his sternum and rolled out in an inversion loop. *Coming at you!*

The two starfighters closed swiftly. Corran centered his foe in the crosshairs and waited for a dead shot. Without shields the TIE fighter would die with one burst, and Corran wanted the kill to be clean. His HUD flicked green as the TIE juked in and out of the center, then locked green as they closed.

The TIE started firing at maximum range and scored hits. At that distance the lasers did no real damage against the shields, prompting Corran to wonder why Wedge was wasting the energy. Then, as the HUD's green color started to flicker, realization dawned. *The bright bursts on the shields are a distraction to my targeting! I better kill him* now!

Corran tightened down on the trigger button, sending red laser needles stabbing out at the closing TIE fighter. He couldn't tell if he had hit anything. Lights flashed in the cockpit and Whistler started screeching furiously. Corran's main monitor went black, his shields were down, and his weapons controls were dead.

The pilot looked left and right. "Where is he, Whistler?"

The monitor in front of him flickered to life and a diagnostic report began to scroll by. Bloodred bordered the damage reports. "Scanners, out; lasers, out; shields, out; engine, out! I'm a wallowing Hutt just hanging here in space."

With the X-wing's scanners being dead, the R2 droid couldn't locate the TIE fighter if it was outside the droid's scanner range. Whistler informed Corran of this with an anxious bleat.

"Easy, Whistler, get me my shields back first. Hurry." Corran continued to look around for the TIE fighter. *Letting me stew, are you, sir? You'll finish the* Korolev *then come for me.* The pilot frowned and felt a cold chill run down his spine. *You're right, I'm no Luke Skywalker. I'm glad you think I'm not bad, but I want to be the best!*

Suddenly the starfield went black and the simulator pod hissed as it cracked open. The canopy lifted up and the sound of laughter filled the cockpit. Corran almost flicked the blast shield down on his helmet to prevent his three friends from seeing his embarrassed blush. *Nope, might as well take my punishment.* He stood and doffed his helmet, then shook his head. "At least it's over."

The Twi'lek, Nawara Ven, clapped his hands. "Such modesty, Corran."

"Huh?"

The blond woman next to the Twi'lek beamed up at him. "You won the *Redemption* scenario."

"What?"

The grey-green Gand nodded his head and placed his helmet on the nose of Corran's simulator. "You had nine kills. Jace is not pleased."

"Thanks for the good news, Ooryl, but I still got killed in there." Corran hopped out of the simulator. "The pilot who got you three—Commander Antilles—he got me, too."

The Twi'lek shrugged. "He's been at this a bit longer than I have, so it is not a surprise he got me."

Rhysati shook her head, letting her golden hair drape down over her shoulders. "The surprise was that he took so long to get us, really. Are you certain he killed you?"

Corran frowned. "I don't think I got a mission end message."

"Clearly you have too little experience of dying in these simulators because you'd know if you did." Rhysati laughed lightly. "He may have hit you, Corran, but he didn't kill you. You survived and won."

Corran blinked, then smiled. "And I got Bror before he got the *Korolev*. I'll take that."

"As well you should." A brown-haired man with crystal blue eyes shouldered his way between Ooryl and Nawara. "You're an exceptionally good pilot."

"Thank you, sir."

The man offered Corran his hand. "Thought I had you, but when you shot out my engines, your missile caught up with me. Nice job."

Corran shook the man's hand hesitantly. The man wore a black flight suit with no name or rank insignia on it, though it did have Hoth, Endor, and Bakura battle tabs sewn on the left sleeve. "You know, you're one hot hand in a TIE."

"Nice of you to say, Mr. Horn—I'm a bit rusty, but I really enjoyed this run." He released Corran's hand. "Next time I'll give you more of a fight."

A woman wearing a Lieutenant's uniform touched the TIE pilot on the arm. "Admiral Ackbar is ready to see you now, sir. If you will follow me."

The TIE pilot nodded to the four X-wing pilots. "Good flying, all of you. Congratulations on winning the scenario."

Corran stared at the man's retreating back. "I thought Commander Antilles was in that TIE. I mean it had to be someone as good as him to get you three."

The ends of Nawara Ven's head tails twitched. "Apparently he *is* that good."

Rhysati nodded. "He flew circles around me."

"At least you saw him." The Gand drummed his trio of fingers against the hull of Corran's simulator. "He caught Ooryl as Ooryl fixed on his wingman. Ooryl is free hydrogen in simspace. That man is very good."

"Sure, but *who* is he?" Corran frowned. "He's not Luke Skywalker, obviously, but he was with Rogue Squadron at Bakura and survived Endor."

The Twi'lek's red eyes sparked. "The Endor tab had a black dot in the middle—he survived the Death Star run."

Rhysati looped her right arm around Corran's neck and brought her fist up gently under his chin. "What difference does it make who he is?"

"Rhys, he shot up three of our best pilots, had me dead in space, and says he's a bit *rusty*! I want to know who he is because he's decidedly dangerous."

"He is that, but today he's not the *most* dangerous pilot. That's you." She linked her other arm through Nawara's right elbow. "So, Corran, you forget you were a Security officer and, Nawara, you forget you were a lawyer and let this thing drop. Today we're all pilots, we're all on the same side"—she smiled sweetly—"and the man who beat the *Redemption* scenario is about to make good on all those dinner and drink promises he made to talk his wingmates into helping him win."

2

W EDGE ANTILLES SALUTED Admiral Ackbar and held the salute until the Mon Calamari returned it. "Thank you for seeing me, sir."

"It is always my pleasure to see you, Commander Antilles." Without moving his head, Ackbar glanced with one eye toward the other man standing in his office. "General Salm and I were just discussing the impact of having Rogue Squadron back in the fleet. He feels you are all but ready to go. The unit roster is impressive."

The brown-haired fighter pilot nodded. "Yes, sir. I wanted to speak to you about the roster, if I could, sir." Wedge saw Salm's face close up. "There have been changes made to the roster without my consultation."

Salm turned away from the floating blue globe hanging in the corner and clasped his hands behind his back. "There are circumstances beyond your control that made those changes necessary, Commander Antilles."

"I'm aware of that, sir. Lieutenants Hobbie Klivian and Wes Janson will do well bringing new training squadrons along." *I didn't want to lose them, but that was a battle I lost a* long *time ago.* "And I understand why half the slots in my squadron are going to political appointees . . ."

Ackbar's head came up. "But you do not approve?"

Wedge bit back a sharp comment. "Admiral, I've spent a good deal of the two and a half years since the Emperor died touring worlds new to the Alliance because someone decided our new allies needed to see we had heroes—that we weren't all the bandits the Empire made us out to be. I gave speeches, I kissed babies, I had holograms taken with more world leaders than I ever knew existed. I was there as our propaganda machine built Rogue Squadron up into the needle that exploded the Emperor's Death Star balloons."

The human General in command of the Rebellion's starfighter training center at Folor smiled coolly. "Then you *do* understand why it is important that our allies have representatives within our most celebrated squadron."

"Yes, but *I* know the difference between a real fighter squadron and the monster you've made Rogue Squadron out to be. The Empire isn't going to lie down and die just because they see a dozen ships jump into a system."

"Of course not."

"But, General, *that's* what our diplomatic corps is suggesting. The Bothans want a pilot in Rogue Squadron because *they* found the second Death Star and *we* killed it. And I understand why having *two* Thyferrans is important—we have to appease the two conglomerates that control bacta production . . ."

Ackbar held up a webbed hand. "Commander, a question to the point is this: Are the pilots selected inferior to other candidates?"

"No, sir, but . . ."

"But?"

Wedge took a deep breath and let it out slowly. *Luke would be telling me that anger isn't good. He's right, because anger won't get me any closer to what I want.* "Admiral, I'm commanding a fighter squadron. We're an elite squadron and the only thing I want to change about it is our survival rate. You've let me have the pick of the new pilots coming over to us, and I've got a fine group of them. With some more training I think I can make them into the sort of unit that *will* strike terror into Imperial hearts. And," he added, nodding at General Salm, "I concur with the selection of all the pilots listed on the roster you have, except for two—Rogue Five and my Executive Officer."

"Lieutenant Deegan is an excellent pilot."

"Agreed, General, but he's from Corellia, the same as me and Corran Horn. It strikes me that having Corellia overrepresented in Rogue Squadron is not politically wise."

One of Ackbar's eyes shifted slightly. "You have someone in mind to replace him?"

Wedge nodded. "I'd like to use Gavin Darklighter."

Salm shook his head adamantly. "He's just a Tatooine farm boy who thinks the ability to shoot womp rats from a speeder can make him a hero."

"Begging your pardon, sir, but Luke Skywalker was just a Tatooine farm boy whose ability to shoot womp rats from a speeder *did* make him a hero."

The General snarled at Wedge's riposte. "You can't mean to suggest this Darklighter has Commander Skywalker's control of the Force."

"I don't know about that, sir, but I *do* know Gavin has every bit as much heart as Luke does." Wedge turned toward the Mon Calamari. "Gavin had a cousin, Biggs, who was with Luke and me in the trench at Yavin. He stayed with Luke when I was ordered to pull out. Biggs died there. Gavin came to me and asked to join *my* squadron."

"What Commander Antilles is *not* telling you, Admiral, is that Gavin Darklighter is only sixteen years old. He's a child."

"You couldn't tell it by looking at him."

Ackbar's barbels quivered. "Forgive me, gentlemen, but determining a human's age by visual clues is a skill that has long since eluded me. General Salm's point is well taken, however. This Darklighter *is* rather young."

"Is the Admiral suggesting that someone, somewhere within the Alliance, *won't* take Gavin in when we need to put someone in an X-wing cockpit? I don't think Commander Varth would balk at bringing Gavin on board."

"That may be true, Commander Antilles, but then Commander Varth is far more successful at keeping his pilots alive than you are." Ackbar's even tone kept the remark away from being a stinging rebuke, but not by much. "And, yes, I know Commander Varth has never had to face a Death Star."

Rogue Squadron's leader frowned. "Sir, Gavin came to me because Biggs and I were friends. I feel an obligation to him. Even General Salm will agree that Gavin's test scores are very good—he'll do his *Redemption* scenario in three days and I expect his scores there will measure up. I want to pair Gavin with the Shistavanen, Shiel. I think they'll work well together." He opened his hands. "Gavin's all alone and looking for a new home. Let me put him in Rogue Squadron."

Ackbar looked at Salm. "Aside from this nebulous age problem, you do not disagree with this selection?"

Salm looked at Wedge and bowed his head. "In *this* case—if Darklighter does well in his *Redemption* trial—I see no problem with letting Commander Antilles have his way."

Which means my choice for XO gets opposed fully—not that I expected less. "You are most kind, General."

Ackbar's mouth opened in the Mon Calamari imitation of a smile. "Spoken with General Solo's degree of sarcasm, I believe."

"I'm sorry, sir." Wedge smiled, then clasped his hands at the small of his back. "I would also hope the General would see his way clear to letting me choose my own Executive Officer."

The Admiral looked at his starfighter commander. "Who is presently in that position?"

"Rogue Squadron's XO is Captain Aril Nunb. She is the

sister of Nien Nunb, one of the *other* heroes of Endor. She is every bit as skilled a pilot as her brother and worked extensively with him during his smuggling days. Sullust is providing us aid and having her in Rogue Squadron would definitely increase support from the SoroSuub government."

"Commander, do you quarrel with this assessment?"

Wedge shook his head. "No, sir, not at all."

"Then the problem is . . . ?"

"She's a wonderful pilot, Admiral, and I'd love to have her in my squadron, but *not* as my XO. In that position I need someone who can help train my pilots. What Aril does, what her brother does, is intuitive to them. They can't teach it to others. As my XO she'd be frustrated, my pilots would be frustrated, and I'd have chaos to deal with."

"And you have another candidate in mind?"

"Yes, sir." Wedge looked at General Salm and braced for his reaction. "I want Tycho Celchu."

"Absolutely not!" The explosion Wedge had expected from Salm did not disappoint him. "Admiral Ackbar, under no circumstances will I allow Celchu to be anywhere near an active duty squadron. Just because he isn't in prison is no reason for me to want him in my command."

"Prison!" Wedge's jaw shot open. "The man hasn't done anything that warrants confinement."

"He cannot be trusted."

"I believe he can."

"Come on, Antilles, you know what he's been through."

"What I *know*, General, is this: Tycho Celchu is a hero— much more of a hero than I am. On Hoth he fought as fiercely as anyone and at Endor he piloted an A-wing that led a bunch of TIE fighters on a merry chase through the Death Star. He took them off our backs while Lando and I went in and blew the installation's reactor. He fought at Bakura and went on subsequent missions with the squadron, then volunteered, General, *volunteered* to fly a captured TIE fighter on a covert mission to Coruscant. He got captured. He escaped. That's it."

"That's all you want to see, Antilles."

"Meaning?"

"You say he escaped." Salm's face hardened into a steel mask. "It could be they *let him go.*"

"Sure, just like they let him go at Endor." Wedge grimaced, doing his best to banish the anger he felt growing in him. "General, you're fighting ghosts."

Salm nodded curtly. "You're right, I'm fighting to prevent you and your people from becoming ghosts."

"Well, so am I, and having Tycho with us to train my people will give them the best chance of survival possible."

Salm tossed his hands up in disgust and looked at Admiral Ackbar. "You see, he won't listen to reason. He knows Captain Celchu is a threat, but he won't let himself see it."

"I'll listen to reason, sir, when I see the product of some reasoning."

Ackbar held up his hands. "Gentlemen, please. Commander Antilles, you must admit that General Salm's concerns are valid. Perhaps if there were a way to alleviate some of them, an accommodation could be reached."

"I thought of that, sir, and I've spoken with Captain Celchu about it." Wedge started ticking points off on his fingers. "Tycho has agreed to fly a Z-95 Headhunter in our training exercises, with the lasers powered down so they can only paint a target, not hurt it. He's agreed to have a destruct device installed in the starfighter so that if he goes to ram anything or goes outside spacelanes to which he is assigned, he can be destroyed by remote. When not flying he has agreed to remain under house arrest unless accompanied by Alliance Security or members of the squadron. He's agreed to undergo interrogation as needed, to have all his computer files and correspondence open to examination, and is even willing to have us choose what he eats, when, and where."

Salm marched over and placed himself between Wedge and the Mon Calamari Admiral. "This is all well and good, and might even be effective, but we can't afford the risk."

Ackbar blinked his eyes slowly. "Captain Celchu has agreed to these conditions?"

Wedge nodded. "He's no different from you, Admiral—he's a warrior. What he knows, what he can teach, will keep pilots alive. Of course, there's no way General Salm will ever let him fly in combat again."

"*That* can be etched in transparisteel."

"So serving as an instructor is the only way he can fight back. You have to give him this chance."

Ackbar activated the small comlink clipped to his uniform's collar. "Lieutenant Filla, please find Captain Celchu and bring him to me." The Mon Calamari looked up at Wedge. "Where is he currently?"

Wedge looked down at the deck. "He should be in the simulator complex."

"He's *where?!*" Salm's face went purple.

"You'll find him in the simulator complex, Lieutenant. Bring him here immediately." Ackbar turned the comlink off.

"The simulator complex?"

"It was Horn's turn leading the *Redemption* scenario. Tycho knows how to fly a TIE better than most pilots, so I decided to have him fly against Horn."

Ackbar's lip fringe twitched. "You've taken certain liberties concerning Captain Celchu already, it seems, Commander."

"Yes, sir, but nothing that isn't necessary to make my pilots the best. I'm being prudent in this, I think."

"The most prudent course, Commander—if you cared to protect the rest of the trainees here, not just your own—would have been to keep Captain Celchu out of the simulator facility entirely!" Salm crossed his arms over his chest. "You may be a hero of the New Republic, but that doesn't give you any authorization to jeopardize our security."

Perhaps having Tycho fly today *was a bit premature.* Wedge glanced down penitently. "I stand corrected, sir."

Ackbar broke the uneasy silence following Wedge's admission. "What is done is done. Now using Captain Celchu in the scenario would have made it that much more difficult, would it not?"

A smile creeping back on his face, Wedge nodded. "Yes, sir—which is what I wanted. Horn is good, very good, and the trio of pilots flying on his side in the exercise are not bad, either. Overall, Horn or Bror Jace, the Thyferran, are the best pilots in the whole group. Jace is arrogant, which gets under Horn's skin and keeps him working hard. Horn, on the other hand, is impatient. That'll get him killed and the only way to make that apparent to him is by having someone shoot him up in exercises. Tycho can do that."

The door to Ackbar's office opened and a female Rebel officer led a pilot in a black flight suit into the room. "Admiral, this is Captain Celchu."

Tycho snapped to attention. "Reporting as ordered, sir."

"At ease, Mr. Celchu."

Wedge gave the slightly taller man a reassuring smile.

The Admiral eased himself out of his chair. "You may leave us, Lieutenant." The Mon Calamari waited for the door to close behind his aide, then he nodded toward Wedge. "Captain Celchu, Commander Antilles has told me that you have agreed to a remarkable number of restrictions on yourself and your activities. Is this true?"

Tycho nodded. "Yes, sir, it is."

"You realize you will be flying a defenseless bomb, you will have no privacy and no freedom."

"I do, sir."

The Mon Calamari closed his mouth for a moment and stared silently at the blue-eyed pilot. "You will be treated no better than I was when I served as a slave to Grand Moff Tarkin. You will be treated worse, in fact, because General Salm here believes you are a threat to the New Republic. Why do you agree to such treatment?"

Tycho shrugged. "It's my duty, sir. I chose to join the Rebellion. I willingly froze on Hoth. I followed orders and assaulted a Death Star. I volunteered for the mission that got me in all this trouble. I did all those things because that's what I agreed to do when I joined the Rebels." He glanced down. "Besides, even the worst you can do to me will still be better than Imperial captivity."

Sweat gleaming from his bald head, Salm pointed at Tycho. "This is all noble, Admiral, but would we expect anything less from someone in his position?"

"No, General, nor would we expect anything less of a noble son of Alderaan." The Mon Calamari picked up a datapad from his desk. "I am signing orders to make Captain Celchu the Executive Officer for Rogue Squadron, and to put this Gavin Darklighter in the squadron as well."

Wedge saw Salm's expression sour, so he suppressed his own smile. Even so he winked at Tycho. *Two flights, two kills.*

Ackbar glanced at the datapad's screen, then looked up again. "Commander Antilles, I expect to be informed about any irregularities or problems with your unit or personnel. An M-3PO military protocol droid has been assigned to your office to help you make out reports. Use it."

The Corellian rolled his eyes. "As you wish, sir, but I think that droid could be more useful elsewhere."

"I'm sure you do, Commander, but those decisions are made by those of us who haven't refused promotions time and time again."

Wedge held his hands up. "Yes, sir." *I surrender, but you don't fool me, Admiral. You like mixing it up in battle the same as I do, but you work with the big ships while I like the fast ones.*

"Good, I am glad we understand each other." Ackbar nodded toward the door. "You're dismissed, the both of you. I imagine you have things to celebrate."

"Yes, sir."

"One last thing."

Wedge looked up and Tycho turned around to face the Admiral. "Sir?" they asked in tandem.

"What did you think about the pilots in the *Redemption* scenario?"

Wedge looked over at his XO. "Did you get Horn?"

Tycho blushed. "Oh, I got Horn, but just not as much of him as I would have liked." Smiling proudly, he added, "Admiral, if the pilots I flew against are representative of the rest of the people we have to work with, Rogue Squadron should be operational within a couple of months, and the scourge of the Empire not very much longer after that."

3

K IRTAN LOOR STRUGGLED to keep a self-satisfied smirk from ruining the stern expression he had worked hard to culti-vate. He wanted to appear implacable. He *needed* to be merci-less.

He feared he would fail on both counts, but laid the blame on his eagerness to confront an old nemesis finally brought to heel. What had been a blot on his record would soon be ex-punged. More importantly, people who had ridiculed him would learn they had grossly underestimated him. And in doing so they had doomed themselves.

Kirtan held his head erect as he marched down the com-panion way on the *Expeditious*. The *Carrack*-class light cruiser had not been built to accommodate people of his height, so he felt some of his black hair brush against the ceil-ing. A more cautious man would have slumped his shoulders slightly and lessened the chance of bashing his head on a light fixture or bulkhead support. Kirtan, having once been told that he looked every inch a taller, younger Grand Moff Tarkin—from thinning widow's peak and lanky frame to sharp features in a cadaverously slender face—did his best to emphasize the resemblance.

Even though Tarkin was nearly seven years dead, the resemblance still earned him some respect. On an Imperial naval vessel, respect for an Intelligence officer such as himself was in short supply, so he took what he could get. The military arm of the Empire clearly resented having the government being run by the Emperor's former Intelligence chief, and they took their displeasure out on the least of her servants.

Kirtan ducked his head and entered the antechamber of the *Expeditious*'s brig. "I am here to interview the prisoner you took off the *Starwind*."

The Lieutenant in charge glanced at his datapad. "He just got back from medical."

"I know, I've seen the report." Kirtan glanced at the hatchway leading to the detention cells. "He has been told nothing about the results?"

The soldier's face darkened. "I've been told nothing about the results. If he has a disease, I want him out before he infects the . . ."

The Intelligence operative held a hand up. "Calm yourself, you'll bounce your rank cylinder out of your pocket in a moment."

The Lieutenant raised a hand to check his rank badges and when he found them in place he blushed. "Play your little games with Rebel scum, not me. I have serious work to do."

"Of course you do, Lieutenant." Kirtan flashed a smile that was more predator than comrade, then turned toward the detention cells. "Which one?"

"Holding cell Three. Wait here while I get you an escort."

"I won't need one."

"You may not think so, but he's listed as rating a four on the Hostility Index. That rating requires two officers to accompany an interrogator."

Kirtan shook his head slowly. "I know, I gave him that rating. I can handle him."

"Remember that when you're in a bacta bath washing away his fingerprints."

"That I shall, Lieutenant." Kirtan grasped his hands at the small of his back and started off through the hexagonal companionway. His black boots made a solid clanking sound on the metal grating and he measured his steps carefully to keep the sound rhythmic and daunting.

The hatch to cell Three opened with a hiss of pressurized gas. Yellow light spilled out into the corridor and Kirtan folded himself halfway to double to fit through the opening. He paused inside the cell and stood tall. He narrowed his eyes, then immediately thought better of it. *He always said it looked as if I were wincing in pain.*

The older, heavyset man swung his legs around off the cot and levered himself up into a sitting position. "Kirtan Loor, I thought it would be you."

"Did you?" Kirtan injected sarcasm into his voice to cover his own surprise. "How could that be?"

The old man shrugged his shoulders. "Actually, I rather counted on it."

What? The Intelligence officer snorted. "You mean you thought no one but me would be able to puzzle out your whereabouts."

"No, I mean that I thought even *you* could figure out how to find me."

Kirtan rocked back slightly from the venom in the prisoner's voice, bumping the back of his head on the top of the hatchway. *This is not the way this is supposed to be going.* Narrowing his eyes, he stared down at the old man. "You, Gil Bastra, are going to die."

"I figured that the moment your TIEs started shooting at me."

Kirtan slowly crossed his arms. "No, you don't understand how desperate is your situation here. You thought you outsmarted me and the Empire. You were cautious, but not insurmountably so. You are dying even now."

Bastra's bushy grey eyebrows met in a frown. "What are you talking about?"

"When we took the *Starwind* I ordered a medical evaluation for you. You may have forgotten that I always remember what I have seen and heard, and in doing so you have forgotten how you ridiculed me for using *skirtopanol* to interrogate a smuggler working for the Rebellion. You told me then that he died during interrogation because his boss, Billey, had his people dose themselves with *lotiramine*. It metabolizes the interrogation drug and can induce chemical amnesia or, in some cases, death."

Kirtan gave Bastra a cold smile. "Your medical scan shows elevated levels of *lotiramine* in your blood."

"I guess you'll just have to kill me the old-fashioned way, then." Bastra smiled openly, flashing white teeth in a thick, stubble-coated face. "Since Vader was the last Jedi, I guess you'll even have to get your hands dirty doing it."

"Hardly."

"You never were one to break a sweat doing any work on Corellia, were you, Loor?" Bastra slumped back against the bulkhead. "I don't think you would have fit in even if you'd made an effort. You were always your own worst enemy."

"I wasn't meant to fit in. You were Corellian Security, I was Imperial Intelligence attached to your office." Kirtan forced himself to calm down a bit and unknotted his fists. Lowering his hands to his sides, he tugged on the hem of his black tunic. "And now *you* are your own worst enemy. You have accelerated *blastonecrosis*."

"What? You're lying."

"No, no I'm not." Kirtan let pity slip into his voice. "The *lotiramine* is very effective in masking the tracer enzymes for the disease. Here, on this ship, our medical facilities are far superior to those you would find among Rebels. We were able to pick out the enzymes."

Gil Bastra's shoulders slumped and his grey head bowed. His hands came together around his bulging stomach. "The fatigue, loss of appetite. I thought I was just getting old."

"You are. *And* you are dying." The Intelligence officer idly stroked his sharp chin with a long-fingered hand. "I can do nothing about the former problem, but there *are* ways to cure *blastonecrosis.*"

"And all I have to do to be cured is turn in my friends?"

Looking down upon the grey lump of a man across from him, Kirtan felt momentarily embarrassed by memories of having feared Gil Bastra's judgment of him and his work. Bastra had not been his direct supervisor, but he had been the one to assign officers to work with Intelligence, and Bastra's lack of respect had been reflected through the personnel sent to work with Kirtan. Every time that Kirtan had felt in control and superior, Bastra had managed to undercut him and shame him.

Is this another of those times? Kirtan caught himself and nodded slowly. "There is more fight in you than you would want me to believe there is. I know you fashioned the new identities for your confederates and did a very good job of it, too. In fact, you only made mistakes in your own cover. Still I knew that you'd find yourself a freighter and hop around the galaxy, as your heart pleased. You were too old to change your lifestyle to something totally alien to avoid detection. You decided to gamble and now you have lost."

The old man's head came up slowly. Kirtan saw fire still smoldering in the blue eyes. "I'll give you nothing."

"Yes, yes, of course you won't." The Intelligence man laughed lightly. "You forget, I learned interrogation from a number of very good people, including yourself. I will get information from you. When I do—and you know I will—Corran Horn, Iella Wessiri, and her husband will be mine. It is inevitable."

"You're overestimating your abilities, and underestimating mine."

"Am I? I think not. I know you well enough to know you'll only break under extreme pressure. I can and will take you to the edge of your endurance, then float you in bacta until you are ready to continue interrogation." Kirtan folded his hands together. "However, you are just one relay in the network that will bring the others to me. Corran Horn is too volatile to stay confined in any role you create for him. And I know that role had to be very constricting for him."

Bastra's chest heaved mightily with a sigh. "And how do you know that?"

Kirtan tapped his temple with a finger. "You think I have forgotten the falling out the two of you had? You decided to protect him because his father had been your partner when you started out, but you are a vengeful man, Gil Bastra. Whatever role you created for Corran would squeeze him every day, just to remind him he owed his life to a man he hated."

Fat rippled beneath the prisoner's grey jumpsuit as he laughed. "You do know me."

"I do indeed."

"But not well enough." Bastra gave him a grin that was all teeth and defiance. "I am vengeful—vengeful enough to engineer things so a disgraced Intelligence officer would spend the rest of his career dashing around the galaxy trying to capture three people he once worked with. Three people who escaped out from under his hooked beak, and were able to do so because his nose was so up in the air all the time that he couldn't notice the most obvious of mistakes they made."

Kirtan used scorn to smother his surprise. "I caught you, didn't I?"

"And it took you the better part of two years to do so. Ever wonder why? Ever wonder why, when you were about to give up, a new clue would surface?" Bastra surged forward and stood. Though the prisoner was nearly thirty centimeters shorter, than Kirtan, the Intelligence officer felt somehow dwarfed by him. "I wanted you following me. Every second you were on *my* trail, every moment *I* looked easier to catch than the others, I knew you'd come after *me*. And while you were coming after me, you wouldn't be going after the others."

Kirtan pointed a trembling finger at the old man's face.

"That doesn't matter because you *can* and *will* be broken. I will have from you the things I need to find the others."

"You're wrong, Kirtan. I'm a black hole that's sucking your career down into its heart." Bastra sagged back down onto the cot. "Remember that when I'm dead, because I'll be laughing about it for all eternity."

This cannot continue. I will not be humiliated any longer! "I'll remember your words, Gil Bastra, but your laughter will be a long time coming. The only eternity you'll know is your interrogation, and I guarantee—personally guarantee—you'll go to your grave having betrayed those who trusted you the most."

4

CORRAN MADE A VAIN grab at the hydrospanner with his right hand as the tool slipped from the X-wing's starboard engine cowling. His fingertips brushed the spanner's end, sending it into a spin toward the ferrocrete deck of the hangar. A half second later, when his right knee slipped and unbalanced him, he realized having failed to catch the tool was the least of his problems. He tried to hook his left hand on the edge of the open engine compartment, but he missed with that grab, too, leaving him set to plummet headfirst in the hydrospanner's wake.

Still trying to prepare himself for the agony coming from a fractured skull, he was surprised to find pain blossoming at the other end of his body. Before he could figure out what had happened, his flailing left hand caught hold of the cowling it had missed before, aborting his long fall to the ground. He hauled himself back onto the S-foil and lay there on his belly for a moment, considering himself very lucky.

As the pain in Corran's rump lessened, Whistler's scolding gained volume. Corran rubbed a hand back over his left cheek and felt a small tear in the fabric of his flight suit, prompting him to laugh. "Yes, Whistler, I am very lucky you were quick enough to catch me. Next time, though, can your pincer catch a little less of me and a bit more of my flight suit?"

Whistler blatted a reply Corran chose to ignore.

The pilot twisted around onto his seat with only mild discomfort. "So, do I still need the tool, or did the last adjustment do it?"

The droid's tone ran from high to low in a fair imitation of a sigh.

"No, of course I still need it." Corran frowned. "You should have caught it, Whistler, not me. I can climb back up here by myself. It can't." Even as he said that and slid toward the S-foil's forward edge, it occurred to him that he'd not heard the hydrospanner hit the ground. *That's odd.*

Peering over the edge of the wing, he saw a smiling, brown-haired woman holding the hydrospanner up in his direction. "This belongs to you, I take it?"

Corran nodded. "Yeah. Thanks."

She handed it to him, then climbed up on the cart he'd used to get up on top of the S-foil. "Need some help?"

"No, I've pretty much got it handled, despite what the droid says."

"Oh." She extended her hand toward him. "I'm Lujayne Forge."

"I know, I've seen you around."

"You've done a bit more than that. You flew a dupe against me in the *Redemption* scenario." She leaned her slender body against the side of his fighter, bisecting the green and white wording that indicated the X-wing was the property of the Corellian Security Force. "You put the *Korolev* down."

Corran tightened the hydrospanner over the primary trim bolt on the centrifugal debris extractor and nudged it to the left. "That was luck. Nawara Ven had already taken the shields down with his missiles. It was more his kill than mine. You still did well."

Her brown eyes narrowed ever so slightly. "I guess. I have a question for you, though."

Corran straightened up. "Go ahead."

"The way you took that bomber after me, did you do that just as part of the exercise, or was there something more to it?"

"Something more?"

Lujayne hesitated, then nodded. "I was wondering if you singled me out because I was from Kessel?"

Corran blinked in surprise. "Why would that make any difference to me?"

She laughed and tapped the CorSec insignia on the side of the fighter with a knuckle. "You were with CorSec. You sent people to Kessel. As far as you're concerned, everyone on Kessel is either a prisoner or a smuggler who ought to have been a prisoner. And when the prisoners and smugglers liberated the planet from the Imps, well, that didn't change anything in your eyes, did it?"

Setting the hydrospanner on a safe spot, Corran raised his hands. "Wait a minute, you're jumping to a lot of conclusions."

"Maybe, but tell me, you didn't know I was from Kessel?"

"Well, I did."

"And tell me that didn't make a difference to you."

"It didn't, honest."

"I bet."

The firm set of her jaw and the way she folded her arms across her chest told Corran she didn't believe him. There was a fair amount of anger in her words, but also some hurt. Anger he could deal with—there wasn't a smuggler or criminal who hadn't been angry when he was around. The hurt, though, that was unusual and made Corran feel uncomfortable.

"What makes you think I hold your coming from Kessel against you?"

"The way you act." Lujayne's expression softened a bit, and some of the anger drained away, but that just let more anxiety and pain bleed into her words. "You tend to keep to yourself. You're not associating with the rest of us—beyond a narrow circle of pilots you think are as sharp as you are. You're always watching and listening, evaluating and judging. Others have noticed it, too."

"Ms. Forge, Lujayne, you're making meters out of microns here."

"I don't think so, and I don't want to be judged for things over which I had no control." Her chin came up and fire sparked in her eyes. "My father volunteered to go to Kessel under an Old Republic program where he taught inmates how to move back into society upon their release. My mother was one of his students. They fell in love and remained on Kessel—they're still there, along with most of my brothers and sisters. They're all good people and their work with inmates was designed to make your job easier by giving criminals other skills so they'd not return to crime when they were released."

Corran sighed and his shoulders slumped. "I think that's great, I really do. I wish there were thousands of people like your parents and kin doing that sort of work. The fact is, though, that even if I'd known that, I'd still have gone after you in the exercise."

"Oh, my being from Kessel had *nothing* to do with it?"

He almost dismissed her question with a glib denial, but he caught himself and she clearly noticed his hesitation. "Maybe, just maybe, it *did* have something to do with my flying. I guess I decided that if you were from Kessel and could fly, you had to be a smuggler, and it was important for me to fly better than you could."

She nodded once, but her expression did not shift from one of concern to smug triumph as he had expected it would. "I believe that, and I can understand it. Still, there's something more there, right?"

"Look, I'm sorry if what I did made you look bad in the exercise, but I really don't have the time to talk about this now."

"No time or no inclination?"

Whistler hooted something in an utterly carefree manner.

"*You* stay out of this." Frustration curled his hands into fists. "You're not going to let this go, are you, Ms. Forge?"

With a smile blossoming on her face, she shook her head. "If you'd gotten this far in an interrogation, would you give up?"

Corran snorted a laugh. "No."

"So, explain yourself."

He definitely heard a request for more than an explanation of his conduct in the *Redemption* scenario in her voice. For a split second he flashed on the times at CorSec when his human partner, Iella Wessiri, had made similar demands of him. *Iella had been a conciliator—always the one to be patching up the disagreements between folks in the unit. That's what Lujayne is trying to do, which means I've managed to alienate a number of the other pilots trying to get into the unit.*

"Concerning the exercise, I really just wanted to see how good you were. I'd been able to figure out where some of the other pilots stood in relationship to me, but I'd not flown against you. You know, you're not bad."

"But I'm not in a class with you and Bror Jace."

Corran smiled quickly, then covered it with a frown. "True, but you're still very sharp. I'd like to think the rest of the pilots are going to be at least that sharp. I'd even be set up to fly against that Gimbel kid in his *Redemption* scenario tomorrow but Jace volunteered before I could."

"His name is Gavin, Gavin Darklighter."

"Gavin, then."

"And you didn't want to be following Jace's lead?"

"Would you?"

Lujayne smiled. "Given a choice, no, I guess not. Next to you, he's the most standoffish person in the group."

Corran felt uneasy inside. "I'm not as bad as he is."

"No? At least he has the good graces to deign to join us in DownTime for some recreation. He's a sliced and blown datafile compared to you."

Corran turned to the left and pointed his finger at the astromech droid. "Don't even start."

Lujayne raised an eyebrow. "So your droid thinks you should get out more, too?"

Something halfway between a snarl and a growl came from Corran's throat, but it lacked the power to make it menacing. "Whistler has the ability, from time to time, to be a nag. His problem is that in the time since I left CorSec I've been in situations where I've had to be very careful. I moved through a number of identities that didn't allow me to be very open with people. For example, most recently, I spent over a year as the confidential aide to a succession of incompetent Imp officials governing a Rim world. One slip, one crack in my identity, and I'd have been caught. And when you get out of the habit of trusting folks and relaxing around them, well . . ."

"I understand."

"Thanks." Corran gave her a grateful smile. "On top of that, I'm learning a lot of new things here and I've been trying to concentrate on my flying. That's not easy—there's a whole new set of slang to get used to and people from species I barely knew existed that I now have to work with and even share living quarters with."

"That *is* difficult—my roommate is a Rodian."

"That's rough, but I'll bet she's less idiosyncratic than my roommate." Corran whistled at the Gand pilot entering the hangar. "Ooryl, come over here, please."

The pilot's grey-green flesh clashed with the bright orange of his flight suit, and the knobby bits of his exoskeleton poked bumps in odd places from beneath the fabric as he walked. "May Ooryl assist?"

"I've been curious about something since we were assigned the same quarters, but didn't think to ask you about it until right now." Corran frowned. "I hope you don't mind—you might take it personally and I don't mean to embarrass you."

The Gand just watched him with multifaceted eyes. "Qrygg would hope to avoid embarrassment as well, but you may ask."

Corran nodded in what he hoped was a friendly manner. "Why do you speak of yourself in the third person?"

"Qrygg is embarrassed by not understanding your question."

Lujayne smiled. "You do not seem to refer to yourself with the pronoun 'I.'"

"And you alternate the names you use."

The Gand's mouth parts clicked open in what Corran had decided was a Gand's best approximation of a human smile. "Ooryl understands."

"And?"

Ooryl crossed his arms, then tapped his trio of fingers against his body's deltoid armor plates. "On Gand it is held that names are important. Any Gand who has achieved nothing is called Gand. Before Ooryl was given Ooryl's name, Ooryl was known as Gand. Once Ooryl had made a mark in the world, Ooryl was given the Qrygg surname. Later, by mastering the difficulties of astronavigation and flight, Ooryl earned the right to be called Ooryl."

The woman frowned. "This still does not explain why you do not use pronouns to refer to yourself."

"Qrygg apologizes. On Gand only those who have achieved great things are permitted to use pronouns for self-designation. The use of such carries with it the presumption that all who hear the speech will know who the speaker is, and this assumption is only true in the case where the speaker is so great, the speaker's name *is* known to all."

Corran found the system curious, but somehow satisfying. *It always does seem that those who use* I *the most are the ones who have the least in the way of accomplishments to justify it. The Gands have formalized a system we should have come up with long ago.* "So Ooryl is the equivalent of Corran, and Qrygg is the same as Horn for me?"

"Exactly."

"Then why do you sometimes refer to yourself by your family name, and sometimes by your own name?"

The Gand looked down for a moment and his mouth parts closed. "When a Gand has given offense, or is ashamed of actions, this diminishes the gains made in life. Name reduction is an act of contrition, an apology. Ooryl would like to think Ooryl will not often be called Qrygg, but Qrygg knows the likelihood of this is slender."

Whistler tootled jauntily at Corran.

"People would know my first name was Corran even if we did use this system." He rolled his eyes. "And any droid who wanted to keep his name would have run his little diagnostic program and told me if the extractor was adjusted correctly or not by now."

Lujayne glanced over at him. "Trouble with the engine?"

"Nothing major." Corran pointed down into the hole. "I had to replace an extractor a while back and keeping it trimmed up over the first fifty parsecs is important."

Lujayne nodded. "Until it seats itself properly. Looks like you're working on the housing when you really ought to be just putting a spacer on the axle."

"You know about fixing these things?"

She shrugged. "Landspeeder repair was one of the trade skills my father used to teach. The T-47 uses virtually identical debris extraction systems for the engine. What you're doing will work, but you'll keep making adjustments for another six months. I can measure up a spacer and have it ground down to size for you in a half an hour or so."

"Really?"

"Sure, if you want the help."

Corran frowned. "Why wouldn't I?"

"You'd owe me a favor and you'd have to trust me."

Trusting someone he did not know did feel odd to him, but not so much so that he could not do it. "I see your point. I think, though, I can trust you."

"We have a deal then."

Ooryl looked up at Lujayne. "You will need a spacer and laser calipers? Ooryl will obtain them, if you wish."

"Please."

Corran leaned back on the S-foil. "I appreciate this help."

She smiled slyly. "I hope you think that after you hear what my favor is."

"Name it."

"After we fix up your X-wing, you come with me to Down-Time and get to know some of the others who are likely to make it into the squadron. We've all got the thing pretty well figured out—Gavin's a wild card, but Bror Jace thinks he will probably knock him from the running. A few of us are at the lower edge of what we assume will be acceptable scores, but we hope to make it. Anyway, we congregate down there, swap stories, and get to know each other. Since you'll undoubtedly be in, you should join us."

Corran nodded. "Okay, I'll do that, but that's not the favor I owe you."

"If that's the way you want it."

"Definitely." Corran smiled at her. "I owe you for more than just helping with the engine. Asking me to become friends with folks I should already be getting to know isn't a favor I'd be doing you, but one I'll be doing myself. One thing though, I'm not going to have to get along with Bror Jace, am I?"

"Why should you be the first?"

"Good." As Ooryl returned with the part and the tool, Corran winked at Lujayne. "Well, let's get this engine working, then we can see if there's a way to fix up my relations with the rest of Rogue Squadron."

5

CORRAN HORN TRIED to kill his smile as he entered the white briefing amphitheater, then he saw all the other pilots who *could* smile were absolutely beaming. *Not a one of the nervous expressions we were all wearing the other night in DownTime.* The first message in the queue on his datapad had informed him that after breakfast he was to report for Rogue Squadron's first briefing. The message itself had been neutral and routine in wording—even though it was the first official notification that he'd made it into the squadron.

He'd had a pretty good idea that he'd make it, but despite assurances from the other candidates, he'd never allowed himself to *assume* he would make it. In the past he'd been burned by making unwarranted assumptions. Granted those assumptions had eventually led him to join the Rebellion, which was not a wholly bad thing, but it took him well away from where he had imagined he'd be at this time in his life.

Even though he'd not allowed himself the luxury of believing he'd make the cut before he actually made it, he was proud of his being selected for the squadron. Corran had never been one to hold back. He'd gone into the Corellian Security Force Academy straight out of secondary school and continued the

Horn family tradition by establishing new records in the training there. One of the last marks he surpassed had been set by his father, Hal, twenty years earlier, and Hal had beaten the record set by Hal's own father.

And now I'm a Rebel, an outlaw. What would my father and grandfather have thought? A cold sensation raised goose bumps on his skin. *Whatever, they would have thought much worse things if I'd become an Imp.*

Rhysati Ynr waved Corran over to the bench where she sat. "We made it, we actually made it."

"It was nice of Commander Antilles to agree with our group consensus." He mounted the steps up to Rhysati's row and slid in next to her. "It hasn't sunk in yet in some ways."

The Gand, sitting behind them, leaned forward. "Ooryl learned your *Redemption* run had the highest score of our training cycle."

Corran flashed the Gand a big smile—he'd found exaggerating his expression did indeed help Ooryl catch its import. "Who came in second? Bror Jace, I bet."

The Gand shook his head. "Gavin Darklighter beat the Thyferran."

"The kid beat Jace?" Corran glanced over at where the tall, brown-haired pilot from Tatooine sat talking with the black-furred Shistavanen wolfman, Shiel. Corran, with years of experience in the spaceports and stations on Corellia, had spotted Gavin as being young despite his size. *It's in the eyes—the years just aren't there but apparently the piloting skill is!*

The Twi'lek sat down next to Ooryl, looping one of his brain tails back over his left shoulder. "Jace isn't any happier about it than he was about losing to you. He volunteered to fly in an eyeball in Gavin's exercise and got hit with a missile at range. He never had a chance."

Corran nodded his head and looked up toward the front of the room where Bror Jace stood. Tall, slender, and handsome, the blond-haired, blue-eyed pilot had proven himself to be very good during the selection exercises. The Corellian thought he might even have liked Jace, but the man's ego was as big as an Imperial Star Destroyer and likely to be just as deadly. The ego-cases Corran had known in CorSec had always burned bright but burned out early. At some point they got themselves into a situation they could have just as easily avoided had they been thinking clearly.

Corran smiled in Jace's direction and caught a return nod from the black-haired woman to whom Jace was speaking. "Ooryl, how did Erisi Dlarit do in the exercise?"

"Middle of the hunt, after Nawara Ven and ahead of Ooryl. Lujayne Forge came in at the back of the group, with the others in between. The scores were still very good, but competition is stiff here."

Wedge Antilles entered the room and marched down front to where the holographic briefing display grew from the floor like a mechanical mushroom. Joining him at the front of the room Corran saw the mystery pilot from the day before and a black 3PO droid with a nonstandard head. It looked more like the clamshell design seen on flight controller droids, where the concave upper disk overlapped the lower one, but left a facial hole. The unusual construction made sense, both given the lack of spare parts for droids and the fact that this droid was assigned to a fighter squadron. The little bit of a sagittal crest on its head made it look somewhat martial.

"People, if you would be seated. I'm Wedge Antilles, the commander of Rogue Squadron." The green-eyed man smiled openly. "I'd like to welcome you here and congratulate you on being chosen for Rogue Squadron. I want to go over with you the basic criteria we used in making our selections and let you know what will be expected of you as your training continues and missions are assigned to us."

Wedge looked out at his audience and Corran felt a bit of a shock run through him as their eyes met. *His eyes have seen the years—have seen more than they should have.* Corran knew of Wedge's background because Hal Horn had been one of the investigators trailing the pirates who killed Wedge's family at Gus Treta. Hal had kept his eye on Wedge and had pronounced him a lost cause when he started smuggling weapons for the Rebellion.

Wedge exhaled slowly. "You all know the history of this squadron. Even before we were formally created, we were given the job of killing the first Death Star. We did it, and lost a lot of fine pilots in the process. All of them were and are heroes of the Rebellion—they'll be as famous as some of the old Jedi Knights in the years to come. Rogue Squadron saw a lot of action guarding convoys and raiding Imperial shipping after that. We covered the evacuation from Hoth, fought at Gall, and a year later, at Endor, we killed another Death Star. From there we went to Bakura and fought the Ssi-ruuk.

"After seven years of nonstop fighting, the leadership of the New Republic decided to rebuild and revitalize this unit. This was a wise choice because all of us—those who had survived had seen a lot of new pilots come into Rogue Squadron and get killed in Rogue Squadron." Wedge looked over at the mystery pilot. "All of the veterans wanted to see Rogue Squadron continue, but also wanted to see the pilots in it get the training they needed to survive."

The TIE pilot nodded in agreement with Wedge's statement. Wedge looked back at the new pilots. "About a year ago Admiral Ackbar, at the behest of the Provisional Council, presented me with the plans for re-forming Rogue Squadron. Rogue Squadron had become a symbol for the Alliance. It needed to live up to its legend and become once again an elite group of pilots who could be called upon to do the sort of impossible jobs Rogue Squadron has always managed to complete. As you know, we have interviewed and tested a lot of pilots—nearly a hundred for each of the dozen positions you now fill.

"The reason I mention all this to you is so that you'll be aware of something that might not have sunk in during your selection process. You *are* elite pilots and you are *more* than just that, but no matter who you are, or how good you are, you'll never be considered as good as Biggs Darklighter or Jek Porkins or anyone else who has died in service to Rogue Squadron. They are legends, this unit is a legend, and none of us are ever going to be able to be more than they are."

Except for someone like you, Commander, who already is *more.* A grin blossomed on Corran's face. *And I can dream, can't I?*

Wedge opened his hands. "Truth be told, most of you are already better pilots than a lot of the men and women who have died in this unit. You are an eclectic bunch—two of you had death marks against you before you joined the Alliance and the rest of you will earn them as soon as the Empire learns who has been assigned to this unit. You were chosen for your flying skill *and* for other skills you possess because Admiral Ackbar wants this unit to be more than just a fighter squadron. He wants us to be able to operate independently if necessary and perform operations that would normally require a much larger group of individuals."

Rhysati leaned over to Corran. "Baron-Administrator Calrissian had his own group of Commando-pilots back home. The idea's got merit, even if they couldn't stop Darth Vader from causing trouble."

Corran nodded. "CorSec had its own Tactical Response Team. Wanting to make Rogue Squadron into something similar explains why some of us made it when others didn't." Corran still wondered what special skills Gavin was going to bring to the group, but he was willing to wait for an answer instead of assuming there wasn't one.

The Commander continued his briefing. "Over the next month you'll get the most intensive training you've ever had. Captain Celchu will be in charge of it. For those of you who do not know him, Captain Celchu graduated from the Imperial Naval Academy and served as a TIE pilot. He left Imperial service after his homeworld of Alderaan was destroyed. He joined the squadron shortly thereafter and participated in everything from the evacuation of Hoth to the Death Star run at

Endor and more. He is a superior pilot, as some of you have already learned, and what he will teach you will keep you safe from the best pilots the Empire can throw at us."

Wedge nodded toward the droid. "Emtrey is our military protocol droid. He will deal with all requisitions, duty assignments, and other administrative duties. You will be moving to a separate complex here to continue your training—Emtrey has your room assignments and initial craft assignments and will give them to you at the end of this meeting.

"So you're all now part of Rogue Squadron. What you can expect of the future is this: endless amounts of boredom and routine punctuated by moments of sheer terror. As good as you are, statistical studies of fighter pilots indicate most of you will die in your first five missions. While survivability goes up after that, the odds are still not good that you will live to see the complete destruction of the Empire. The reason for that is that you *will* be there to see bits and pieces of it being lopped off. Rogue Squadron will be given tough assignments and will be expected to complete them, specifically because we *are* the best there is."

Wedge rested his hands on his hips. "That's it for now, unless you have any questions."

Jace stood. "Will our training consist of more simulator work, or will we be given actual X-wings to fly?"

"That's a fair question. Emtrey has informed me that our squadron has been assigned a dozen X-wings. We have possession of ten at this time, with two more expected inside the week. When those ships arrive we'll start training in them. Until then, and as a supplement to flight training, we will use a lot more simulator exercises."

The Commander smiled. "And, yes, we could have been assigned A-wing or B-wing craft, but we're using X-wings. You may debate the merits of the various ships among yourselves, but Rogue Squadron has always been primarily an X-wing squadron, and shall remain so. Any other questions? No? Then you're dismissed until 0800 hours tomorrow at which time we'll meet again and begin molding you into a true fighting unit."

Corran stood, intending to head down to thank the Commander for picking him for the squadron, but Jace approached Wedge first, and Corran refused to do anything that gave the impression he was following Jace. *Later, I can thank him later.*

Nawara Ven stroked his chin with his left hand. "So, two of us are already under death marks. I wonder who?"

Rhysati poked him in the ribs with her elbow. "You mean you aren't, Nawara? You were a lawyer, after all."

"Yes, and there are doubtlessly some of my clients still on Kessel who would love to kill me, but I'm not aware of having a death mark." His red eyes narrowed. "The Shistavanen is a rough customer. I could see him as being wanted by the Empire."

The blond woman frowned. "I'd taken his being one of them for granted. What about Andoorni Hui? She's a Rodian and most of them tend to work with the Empire. Did she do something to anger her old employers?"

Ooryl blinked his big compound eyes. "Not her. Rodians are hunters who live and die by their reputations. Andoorni is a huntress who decided that joining the most celebrated hunting band in the galaxy—Rogue Squadron—is a way of furthering her reputation. Ooryl does not think she did anything to bring the wrath of her past patrons down on her head."

Rhysati looked over at Corran. "What do you think?"

"Me? I don't know. I don't think I ever ran into her when I was in CorSec, but I have trouble telling one Rodian from another and I can't speak their language. I do know she wasn't on any apprehension lists I ever saw, so she didn't have a death mark before I left the service." He shrugged. "Shiel probably *does* have a death mark on him, on the other hand. A lot of the wolfmen were put out of the scouting business because of the Emperor's restrictions on exploration. Some of them turned around and sold their services to the Rebellion and found havens like Dantooine and Yavin. I don't think the Empire appreciates that sort of activity."

"More correctly, Mr. Horn, Riv Shiel earned his death mark when he slew a stormtrooper team that tried to apprehend him, thinking he was Lak Sivrak." The black protocol droid carefully ascended the stairs. "Forgive me for interrupting, and please allow me to introduce myself. I am Emtrey, human-cyborg relations and regulations with a military specialty. I am fluent in over six million languages and familiar with an equivalent number of current and historical military doctrines, regulations, honor codes, and protocols."

The ends of the Twi'lek's brain tails twitched. "As well as being familiar with the personnel files of everyone in the squadron?"

"Why, yes." Golden lights glowed deep in the dark hollow of the droid's face. "My primary function requires me to carry such data around with me. Without it . . ."

Nawara held a hand up. "So you could tell us who the other individual is with a death mark on him or her."

"I could." Emtrey's head canted at an angle. "Shiel has made no attempt to conceal his death mark, but the other person has said nothing about it. Would revealing his identity be wise, Mr. Horn?"

Corran shrugged. "I stopped being a law enforcement officer a bit ago, so I don't know if revealing that information would be a violation of the law. Counselor Ven might."

The Twi'lek half closed his eyes. "Hardly. Death marks imposed by the Empire are meant to be a matter of public record. And, in this company, it is hardly a disgrace."

"Who is it?" Rhysati asked.

"Nawara's right, it's more a badge of honor here than anything else." Corran crossed his arms. "C'mon, Emtrey, say what you know."

The droid looked at Corran carefully. "Are you sure, sir?"

Why ask me? "Of course."

"Very well." The droid righted its head again. "The other death mark was issued after the brutal murder and vivisection of a half-dozen people."

Corran's blood ran cold. "Who did that?"

The droid's eyes burned bright. "You did, sir. You're wanted on Drall, in the Corellian Sector, for the murder of six smugglers."

6

LAUGHING SO HARD he had to hold his stomach, Corran sat down abruptly. He only partially landed on the bench, and ended up on the floor at Emtrey's feet. "That's nothing." He swiped his hands at the tears streaming down his face. "I'd forgotten all about it."

The Gand looked down at him. "Ooryl was not aware murder was seen as mirthful."

Nawara Ven folded his arms. "It isn't."

About the time Rhysati stepped back, imposing Emtrey between herself and him, Corran realized he'd quickly destroyed what his previous socializing had accomplished. He scrambled to his feet and composed himself. "I can explain this, I really can."

The Twi'lek lawyer twitched a brain tail at him. "I've heard that before."

"Yeah, well, this is the truth, unlike what your clients were probably saying." Corran looked at the droid. "Can you tap into registry files from here?"

"I am fully capable of a whole host of functions in that regard . . ."

"Good. See if you can pull up the death files for the names

in the reports about the murders, then match them up with birth bytes." As the droid's eye-lights started to flicker, Corran turned back to his squadron mates. "The short form is this—at CorSec, in my division, we had an Imperial Liaison officer who had enough ambition to dream about being a Grand Moff, and just enough talent for dealing with regs and bureaucracy to be a severe problem. He wanted us to bear down on all Rebel smuggling in the system, but we were more concerned about hunting down the kind of pirates who actually hurt folks—glit smugglers and the like. Loor—that was the Intelligence officer's name—threatened to bring us up on charges of aiding the Rebellion. The Imperials fleeing to Corellia after the Emperor's death gave the Diktat a lot of support, and that meant Imperial officers suddenly had the muscle to back up their threats.

"My boss, Gil Bastra, decided to make up new identities for himself, my partner Iella Wessiri, her husband Diric, and myself, but he knew Loor would be suspicious of time we all spent together outside the office. Gil and I made up the records for these smugglers, put hints out that they existed and were very bad, and then put out reports that they'd been murdered. Loor saw all the reports—and reading them was the closest he ever got to a field investigation. In a staged scene in the office, Gil accused me of having executed the smugglers and I said I hadn't and that he couldn't prove it anyway. We had a public falling out and Loor assumed we never met with each other after that. We did and set things up so we could head out and away from the Empire."

Corran sighed. "Loor and I did not get along at all. He threatened me with a death mark for those deaths if I ever got out of line. When I took off—when he set me up and failed to kill me—he followed through. That's where the death mark comes from."

The Twi'lek opened his hands and looked at the droid. "Do you have the records, Emtrey?"

"I do. They have birth bytes."

"Gil did good work. Convert the time of their births to military time. Reverse values for minutes and hours, then compare that to the birth date of the next person in alphabetical order—using Basic, of course."

The droid tilted his head to the right. "There is a progression. The birth time of one is the month and day of the birth of the next, but the pattern does not loop all the way around."

"It does if you add in my birthday and birth time." Corran smiled. "On top of that, the hospital where they were born doesn't exist—nor does the town where it's supposed to be."

Rhysati emerged from behind the droid and patted Corran on the shoulder. "I'm happy to know you're innocent, but couldn't you have found something aside from death to use to fool your Imp?"

"Well, when you're in CorSec, you see enough death that you have to joke about it or it grinds you down. Besides, watching Loor read the fictional reports and react to them was funny."

"Then he would find Gil Bastra's death file amusing, I take it?"

Corran's jaw dropped open. "What?"

The droid's head became level. "There is a notice of Gil Bastra's death. It came when I asked for the data on all the names with the report."

"That can't be."

"Oh, I'm afraid it is, sir." Emtrey's head tilted to the left. "It was appended to Imperial holonet transmission #A34920121."

The pilot shook his head, wishing he didn't feel so hollow inside. *Gil, dead?* "No, I don't believe it. Gil can't be dead."

The Twi'lek eased Corran down onto the bench. "How reliable is the report of his death?"

The droid's eyes flickered for a moment. "Answering that question could compromise intelligence-gathering operations."

"What difference does it make, Nawara?" Corran rubbed

both hands over his face. "It was reliable enough to be put out on the holonet."

Nawara smiled carefully, though the sight of his sharp peg teeth carried with it a hint of menace. "No, Corran, the *report* of a death went out on the holonet. That says *nothing* about the reliability of the information upon which the report was based. That report could have been based on something your Gil did, or even something this Loor did to get at you."

He's right. "You must have been one grand lawyer to spot that sort of inconsistency."

The Twi'lek slapped Corran on the shoulder. "You would have hated me if you were trying to make a case against one of my clients—whether he was lying about his innocence or not. So, Emtrey, how reliable is this report? Are there other reports that corroborate it?"

"I have no related reports."

"It wouldn't make any difference if you did, at least not any that came out of Corellian Security Force files. Gil had full access to the database. The same way he created new identities for my partner, her husband, himself, and me, he would have entered everything to make it look good. He really went all out—we had temporary identities that let us travel to the worlds where he had created solid identities we could hide behind. At my last destination he had me working as an aide for the local Military Prefect."

Rhysati gave Corran a hard stare with her hazel eyes. "So are you saying you aren't Corran Horn?"

"No, I *am* Corran Horn. I used the identities Gil made for me when I ran and hid, but I joined the Rebellion as myself." Corran took a deep breath and sighed heavily. "Look, what I've told you about myself is true, but I haven't told you everything. It's not that I haven't trusted you, but a lot of it I didn't want to talk about. I . . ."

The blond woman reached out and squeezed his shoulder. "Hey, we all have bad memories."

"Thanks, Rhys." Corran's chest felt tight, but as he spoke

he could feel some of the tension ease. "There was a lot of bad blood between Loor and me, and knowing I was going to head out, I really started defying him. He decided to have me dealt with. On what I thought would be my last assignment I drew an X-wing from the pool of craft we'd captured and converted to CorSec use. I was supposed to pull a surprise inspection on small-time smugglers who were coming in-system. Whistler and I mounted up—the R2 had served as my partner in the field and had all the new identity files Gil had made up for me. Unbeknownst to Loor, Whistler also had already computed a number of jumps from Corellia since I had planned to take him with me when I left.

"Where the smugglers were supposed to be I found debris and two flights of TIEs looking for trouble. I *illuminated* a couple with my lasers, then jumped out. That's the start of a long story about how and why I'm here now."

Emtrey looked down at him, his eyes glowing like stars in his black face. "Sir, do you have copies of the identity files for Mr. Bastra and the others?"

"Nope. Gil was the only person with a complete set and I'm sure he destroyed them. I've only got mine and they're stored in Whistler's memory."

"Perhaps, sir, if you could provide me with *your* files, I can search our databases and see if I can locate other files that were similarly sliced, thereby determining if Mr. Bastra's new identity is known to us."

"Ooryl sees the wisdom of this."

Corran smiled over his shoulder at the Gand. "So do I. I don't see how it can hurt."

"Sir, if you will permit me then, I will make inquiries of your R2 unit and try to solve this mystery."

Corran nodded. "Do what you need to do."

"Yes, sir, which reminds me." The droid passed each of the pilots a narrow piece of plastic with an embedded black magnetic strip on the back. "These are your room assignments. Mr. Horn and Mr. Qrygg will continue to be billeted together.

Mr. Ven, you will room with Mr. Jace, and Mistress Ynr will share a room with Mistress Dlarit."

The Corellian looked back at the Gand. "At least I know you don't snore." *Heck, I don't even know if you breathe.*

The soft tissues just inside Ooryl's mouth wobbled around for a second. "Ooryl does not believe you do either. Ooryl does not sleep in the same manner as most others, so your occasional production of rhythmic nocturnal sound is not a problem. Ooryl finds it somewhat soothing, in fact."

"First time I've heard it described as 'soothing.' "Corran blushed, then stood and patted the Twi'lek on the arm. "I don't think you can describe anything about your roommate as soothing, my friend."

Nawara's red eyes darkened slightly. "Since I won't be fighting with Jace for mirror space to preen, I think our conflicts will be minimal—I shall take solace in that fact. Rhysati, on the other hand, will have more trouble with the other Thyferran."

"Why? You think I'm going to worry about my looks to impress the lot of *you*? No chance." Rhysati folded her arms across her chest. "I'm going to be spending my time becoming the best pilot there is in this squadron, so romance is not high on my list of priorities."

Corran smiled. "Besides, you don't need to work to be beautiful, Rhys."

"Sure. Just you remember that when I turn your X-wing into slag."

"Oh, I hope you would not do that, Mistress Ynr." A plaintive tone warbled through Emtrey's words and his arms flailed. "The forms I would have to fill out, the court-martial and requisitions for new parts—the work would be endless."

"Easy, Emtrey, I was joking."

"Ah, oh, yes, of course you were." The black droid's arms settled back down to his sides. "If you have no further need of me, I will find this Whistler of yours, Mr. Horn, and see what I can do to learn more about the fate of your friend."

"Thank you, Emtrey." Corran suppressed a smile as the droid turned about with tiny steps, then headed for the door. "Nawara, did you have to deal with protocol droids in court?"

The tips of the Twi'lek's head tails recoiled. "They functioned as paralegals, but none were allowed into court without restraining bolts. A judge once threw a gavel at one."

"Not your droid, I take it?"

"No. *I* was not a welcome sight in Imperial courts, so any droid I could have afforded would not have been allowed in."

Rhysati frowned. "But then there was no chance that the defense you offered your clients would be as strong as it should have been. That's not just."

"Law and justice are seldom served at the same time." Nawara shrugged. "The quest for justice has brought us all to the Alliance, has it not? Rhys, you want justice for the dislocation of your family when the Empire made them flee Bespin. I am looking for the justice I could not get for my clients. Corran wants the justice denied to innocent people oppressed by Imperial officials."

Nawara stopped and turned toward the Gand. "And you, my friend, what is the justice you seek?"

Ooryl's armored lids closed for a second over his multifaceted eyes. "Ooryl does not believe you would fully understand what it is Ooryl seeks. The acceptance Ooryl has known here is indeed a welcome relief from the prejudice of the Empire. This shall suffice as Ooryl's justice."

"A noble quest indeed, Ooryl," Nawara assured him.

Corran led the quartet from the briefing room. Their route to their new homes took them out of the main complex through a tunnel to a smaller warren of rooms and suites. The Rebel base had once been an extensive mine complex on Commenor's largest moon, Folor. The Commenor system had been chosen because of the high level of shipping traffic that passed through it and because of its proximity to Corellia and the Core worlds.

Corran let his right hand trail over the smooth surface of

the tunnel walls. "Are we really after justice, Nawara, or do we really want revenge?"

"Or is this a case, Corran, where revenge and justice are two aspects of the same thing? We are all committed to seeing the Empire brought down. The Emperor's death advanced our cause, but not enough to bring the conflict to the conclusion we want. Three in ten worlds are in open rebellion and perhaps another twenty percent are nominally supportive of our fight, but half the worlds are still firmly allied against us. When the Emperor dissolved the Senate he gave the Moffs control over their provinces. While I do not believe Palpatine saw that action as a hedge against disaster, that is, in effect, what it has become."

"I know. If not for some of the Moffs playing power games against each other, we'd be hard-pressed to keep from being driven away from the Core." The Corellian frowned. "Then again, with Vader and the Emperor dead and the Death Stars destroyed, I wonder if the Rebellion hasn't lost some of its fire."

"I agree with that." Rhysati moved to the front of the quartet, then turned to walk backward down the hallway and face them. "Vader was a symbol, just like the Emperor, and when they died the relief was palpable. I think a lot of folks believed the whole Rebellion was won there. I'm taking the revitalization of Rogue Squadron as a sign that at least Commander Antilles and Admiral Ackbar don't share that belief."

The Twi'lek looped one of his brain tails back over his left shoulder. "By defeating the Emperor at Endor, the Rebellion proved itself a legitimate power in the galaxy. Within a month after Endor the Alliance's Provisional Council issued their Declaration of a New Republic. The Rebellion became a government—albeit one with very little in terms of real assets—and it presented an alternative to the Empire. Worlds joining the New Republic are doing so on their own terms, and those negotiations are far from joyous things. Destroying the Emperor did bring a lot of nations into the fold, but primarily those who felt most oppressed or most threatened."

Corran thought for a moment. "What you're saying is that the victory at Endor transformed a military insurgency into a political entity."

"Not exactly, but close. Politics was always part of the Rebellion, but it remained largely dormant while the war was being fought. With the death of the Emperor it became more important because it allowed the Rebellion to bring in more worlds without having to resort to military conquest." Nawara pointed vaguely back behind them with a taloned finger. "Commander Antilles's victory tour shows how important politics was and is to the Rebellion—a key military leader was taken out of service and forced into diplomatic duty."

"And there are all the stories about Luke Skywalker and the possibility of reestablishing the Jedi Knights." Rhysati smiled. "Even though the Jedi had been wiped out by the time I was born, my grandmother used to tell me stories about them and the Clone Wars."

"My grandfather fought in the Clone Wars."

The Twi'lek stared at Corran. "Your grandfather was a Jedi?"

"No, just an officer with CorSec, like my father and me. He knew some Jedi Knights, and fought alongside them in a couple of actions near Corellia, but he wasn't one. His best friend was, and died in the wars, but Grandpa never talked about those times very much." Corran glanced down. "When Vader started hunting down all the Jedi, CorSec resources were used to find them and my grandfather didn't like that at all."

"The sort of resentment such Imperial action engendered among the people is precisely the means by which the Alliance is able to bring worlds in to join it. Princess Organa and the host of diplomats working for the Alliance have done more to strengthen the New Republic than the whole *Katana* fleet could do, *if* that legend were true and we had control of it. Even so, there is a limit to what the diplomats can do."

"Hence the reconstitution of Rogue Squadron."

"I think so, Corran."

Rhysati frowned. "What am I missing?"

Corran jerked his head toward Nawara. "He's saying that the diplomats have pretty much mined all the ore they can find. The worlds who want to join us have; those who don't, haven't; and those who aren't sure will need some convincing. Thyferra, for example, is the source of ninety-five percent of the bacta in the galaxy. They're neutral right now, and making grand profits selling to all sides, but we want them in our camp. Putting two of their people in Rogue Squadron sends a message to the Thyferrans that we value them. The same goes for having the Bothan in the squadron."

"And the unit *is* commanded by a Corellian and has another Corellian pilot in it." Nawara tapped himself on the chest. "I'm either a token Twi'lek or a token lawyer."

Rhysati laughed. "I'm a token refugee, I guess."

Ooryl snapped a trio of fingers against his billet datacard. "Ooryl is token Gand."

"So, if this unit is a symbol that's filled with symbols, the supposition is that we have to do something very symbolic to get more worlds to join the New Republic." Corran smiled. "As long as that means I get to bring justice to a bunch of Imperial pilots, I'm all for it."

"Oh, I think you'll have that opportunity, Corran." The Twi'lek's rosy eyes darkened to the color of dried blood. "I'd guess Rogue Squadron will have the greatest of that sort of opportunity."

"You think you know what target will be coming up next, Nawara?"

"It's only logical, Corran." Both of the Twi'lek's head tails twitched in tandem. "Before too long we'll be going after the biggest symbol of all. Let's hope they train us very well because Rogue Squadron is bound to be the tip of the spear the Alliance stabs into the heart of the Empire."

A chill ran down Corran's spine. "Coruscant?"

"The sooner it falls, the sooner the Empire falls apart."

"I never wanted to go to Coruscant." The Corellian pilot smiled. "But if I have to go, doing it in the cockpit of a Rebel X-wing will make the visit just that much more memorable."

7

WEDGE ANTILLES KILLED his proud smile as he began his walking inspection of his X-wing. He brushed his fingers along the underside of its smooth nose cone. "Newly refinished, good." He emphasized this judgment with a firm nod of his head so those who could not hear him could determine what he was saying and thinking.

Throughout the cavernous hangar the pace of work had slowed as he came to inspect his ship. His squadron had already cleared the area and waited for him on the dark side of Folor, leaving him alone with the technical staff. Aside from his X-wing, three other X-wings being worked on, and a scattering of other broken-down fighters, there was little to occupy the attention of the crews. While they made a show of rolling up cables and sorting tools, they watched him and his reaction to their work.

He continued on around to the starboard side of the craft, noticing how clean the crew had gotten the proton torpedo alleys. Another nod. The background hum of conversation picked up in volume and speed, but Wedge ignored it and continued his walk-around.

He could have cited dozens of reasons for doing a preflight

inspection of his fighter, and all of them would have been good and right and militarily proper. The starfighter had seen him through seven years of pitched battles with a minimal amount of failure. The inspection allowed him to spot anything that might be trouble before he got out into space—and *that* would save him a long cold wait for a rescue crew.

More importantly than that, his taking a tour around his ship set a good example for the rest of Rogue Squadron. He wanted to fight the belief that because they were elite pilots they were above the mundane sort of duties all other pilots had to endure. Most of his people weren't like that, but he didn't want laziness by one person to slowly spread to the rest of the squadron. While they weren't there to see him, he knew news of his inspection would get back to them. *And if I do this right, they'll be sorry they missed the show.*

He paused for a moment and looked at the rows of TIE fighters, bombers, and Interceptors painted on the side of the ship. Big Death Stars bracketed the collection of smaller ships on either side, and Ssi-ruuk fighters had started a new row, right at the top of the red stripe bisecting the fuselage. *It has been a long fight. And will be longer still.*

Behind him Wedge heard some chittering that Emtrey translated. "Master Zraii apologizes for not being able to fit all your kills in the space allotted. The ships rendered in red are meant to represent a squadron worth of kills—meaning a dozen."

Wedge frowned as he turned to face the droid. "I have a vague idea how many ships there are in a squadron, you know."

"Yes, of course, sir. I know that, but given that the Verpine normally count in base six and humans use base ten, twelve, which to a Verpine is known as 'four fists,' the potential for confusion warranted explanation."

The human held his hands up in surrender. "Fine. Just tell him that he can group kills by dozens or gross lots. It makes no difference to me."

"Gross lots, sir?"

"A dozen dozen, Emtrey."

"One hundred and forty-four? Four wings?"

"Yes, forty-eight fists in Verpine."

Emtrey looked from Wedge to the brown insectoid trailing behind them. "Sir, if I knew you were fluent in Verpine . . ."

"Enough, Trey. I'm not fluent in Verpine, but I have a head for figures. Let me finish this inspection." Wedge took in a deep breath and slowly let it out again. *I'm going to have to talk to Luke and find out how he puts up with his 3PO unit— wait, that won't work. I don't have a sister around here to foist the droid off on.*

He walked back to the starboard engines and inspected the cooling vanes and what little of the centrifugal debris extractor he could find. After looking over the engines he examined the lenses for the deflector shield projectors and saw new ones had been installed. Shields gave the X-wing its major advantage over TIE fighters and contributed to the X-wing's reputation for being able to take a lot of damage before it went down. Even though the lasers were being powered down for the training exercises, seeing the deflector shield equipment in good repair pleased him.

He paid very careful attention to the twin laser cannons mounted on the ends of the ship's stabilizer foils. He pulled down on the bottom one and felt a slight shift before the unpowered actuator prohibited movement. That was good— more play than a couple of centimeters meant the lasers might shift out of alignment during use.

"Emtrey, ask Zraii what range he zeroed these lasers at?"

A click-buzz exchange took place between tech and droid. "He says he zeroed them at 250 meters, Commander."

"Good." When they had flown against the Death Star the X-wings had been reconfigured so their zero—the point where the four beams converged—was nearly half a kilometer. That allowed them to be employed very effectively in knocking out stationary ground targets. In space combat, where ranges shrank and targets moved quite a bit, keeping the focal point closer increased the chances of scoring lethal hits on the enemy. While the lasers could still hit another fighter at a range of more than a kilometer, the lasers were at their most powerful at the close ranges common in dogfights.

The cannons' barrels, flashback suppressors, gate couplers, and lasing tips seemed in good shape. Ducking beneath the cannons, he swung around to the aft of the X-wing. Power couplings, deflector generators, exhaust ports, and power cell indicators all seemed in order. The inspection of the port S-foils and cannons showed them to be in good repair.

His inspection ended with his return to the nose of the craft, he bowed his head to the Verpine tech. "It looks as good as new, if not better."

Emtrey translated and the Verpine started buzzing. Wedge couldn't figure out what was being said, but the friendly pat on the arm by the insect-man told Wedge the enthusiasm he heard was positive. "Emtrey, what did you tell him?"

"I told him that you think this ship is superior to what it was in its pre-molt stage. That is high praise. He is saying that he has a passion for restoring antiques like this and has taken the liberty to make minor adjustments that will enhance performance."

"Oh, wonderful." Wedge smiled and kept his tone light. The Verpine, with their fascination for technology and with eyesight that allows them to spot microscopic details—like stress fractures—without magnifying equipment, made for some of the best tech support in the galaxy. They were also known, however, for tinkering with the ships for which they cared. Wedge had never had a problem in that regard, but stories abounded about ships where the controls had been reconfigured into what a Verpine found would be a much better alignment—not realizing most pilots did not have microscopic vision or didn't think in base six.

Continuing to smile, Wedge mounted the ladder an assistant tech ran up against the side of the X-wing. Poised on the edge of the cockpit, the pilot looked at his astromech. He didn't recognize it beyond realizing it was one of the flowerpot-topped R5 droids. Though the R5 *was* a newer model astromech droid, Wedge actually preferred the dome-topped R2 astromech droids like the one Luke used because of the lower target profile they offered an enemy. "Then again, if they're close enough to hit you, you'll take the shots before they hit the cockpit, won't you?"

The droid's panicked hooting brought a smile to his face. "Don't worry, the shooting is not going to start yet."

Wedge dropped into the pilot's seat and got a pleasant surprise. One of Zraii's improvements had been a refurbishing of the padding in his ejection seat. *This will make those long hyperspace jumps more comfortable.* He strapped himself in, then brought his systems up. All the monitors and indicators came to life as expected. "Weapons are green and go."

The R5 unit reported all navigation and flight systems were working, so Wedge pulled on his helmet and keyed his comm unit. "This is Rogue Leader requesting departure clearance from Folor Traffic Control."

"Rogue One is clear for departure. Have a good flight, Commander."

"Thank you, Control."

With the flick of a switch he cut in his repulsorlift generators and feathered the throttle so his fighter rose from the hangar deck in a deliberate and firm manner. Using the rudder pedals to keep the lift generators in tandem, he killed roll and yawing. He wanted there to be no doubt in the minds of anyone in the hangar that his was a steady strong hand on the controls. His performance, he knew, would be pulsed out through the base's rumor network and become fodder for every idle conversation until something truly worthy of discussion displaced it.

Adding some forward thrust, he moved the X-wing into the magnetic atmospheric containment bubble and through it to the airless exterior. Once outside, he kicked the Incom 4L4 Fusial Thrust Engines in at full power and rocketed away from the craggy grey lunar surface. He rolled the X-wing and brought the nose up slightly, sending the fighter into a gentle arc toward the horizon.

The datascreen in front of him reported the engines were working at 105 percent of efficiency—an increase he put down to Verpine tinkering. Throttling back to 70 percent, then 65 percent, he dropped his speed and flipped a switch above his right shoulder. The stabilizer foils split and locked into the cross pattern that had given the X-wing its name.

He glanced at the upper left corner of the screen and saw his R5 unit had been designated "Mynock."

"Are you called Mynock because you draw a lot of power?"

Urgent whistles and tweets were translated to a scrolling line of text at the very top of the screen. "A pilot once said I screamed like a mynock when we were in combat. A slander, Commander."

"I can understand that. No one likes to be thought of as a space rat." Wedge shook his head. "I need you to adjust the acceleration compensator down a bit. I want .05 gravity."

The astromech droid complied and Wedge immediately began to feel more at home in the cockpit. To combat the effects of negative and positive gravity because of maneuvers, the starfighter had a compensator that created a gravity neutral pocket for both the craft and pilot. It prevented a lot of problems with blood flow and black- or red-outs in pilots, but Wedge felt it insulated him from the machine and left him out of touch with his situation.

Flying with all gravity negated felt, to him, like trying to pick up grains of salt while wearing heavy gloves. It might be possible, but it would be a lot easier without the interference. Flying required use of all the senses and the compensator cut out most kinesthetic sensations.

And that kills pilots. Wedge was convinced that some pilots had died unnecessarily because they couldn't feel where they were. Jek Porkins, a heavyset man who *always* had his compensator on at full, had plowed into the first Death Star while trying to pull out of a dive. His repeated assurances of "I can hold it, I can hold it" died in a burst of static as his X-wing slammed into the Emperor's toy. Had Porkins not been compensated, he could have realized he wasn't pulling up and he might have had time to do something else.

Flying without full compensation is just one more thing we need to teach these kids. Wedge laughed at himself. Aside from Gavin the whole crew in Rogue Squadron was almost his own age or older. He thought of them as kids because they hadn't seen the sort of duty he and Tycho had. *And with what we'll teach them, maybe they'll survive longer than the rest did.*

Wedge rolled the X-wing again as he hit the terminator line and daylight flopped into darkness. Punching a console button he changed his screen over to a tactical scanner and picked up a dozen other traces. The screen reported and tagged eleven X-wings and one Z-95XT Trainer—the benign version of the X-wing's little brother.

He switched his comm over to the tactical frequency he shared with Tycho. "Everyone green and running, Tycho?"

"Affirmative. Systems are go. There's been some grumbling about feeding at the pig trough, however."

"No surprise there. Shifting to Tac-One."

"I copy."

Flipping the comm over to the frequency shared by the rest of the squadron, Wedge caught the last of a comment by Rogue Nine, Corran Horn. ". . . blind, wallowing pigs, and slow."

"I'm sure, Rogue Nine, your comrades who fly Y-wings will be pleased to know what you think of their ships."

"Sorry, sir."

"Good." The unit commander throttled back and fed his repulsorlift generators enough power to counter the moon's gravity. The reference to Y-wings, their slow speed and the underpowered nature of their sensors, had been heard in Rebel camps since the earliest days of the fight against the Empire. The B-wings had been developed to counter the flaws with the Y-wing and replace it in service, but production had yet to meet demand, so plenty of Y-wings still saw service.

Their reputation as "wallowing pigs" had led to the naming of the Folor gunnery and bombing range the "pig trough." Alliance command had originally designated it the "Trench" as a memorial to the pilots who had died running the artificial canyon on the Death Star, but pilots saw no reason to stand on ceremony. Y-wings practiced their bombing runs in the twists and turns of the lunar canyon while fighter pilots preferred the rolling and looping demanded of them in the satellite field circling the moon.

"Today I want you all to do some basic work on the gunnery range. Laser targets have been set up to provide you a number of flying and targeting challenges. Your run will be graded for accuracy and speed, and if you get hit, you'll lose points. If you suffer an equipment failure, pull out and you'll get another run after things are fixed. We don't want to lose you or the equipment, so try not to do anything stupid. Any questions?"

Horn's voice squawked through the helmet headset. "Sir, our lasers are zeroed at 250 meters, which is a little short for ground attack missions."

"I guess, then, you'll have to be very good and very quick in shooting, won't you, Mr. Horn?"

"Yes, sir."

Wedge smiled. "Good, then perhaps you'd like to go first. Mr. Qrygg will fly your wing."

"Yes, sir." The enthusiasm in Horn's voice matched the energy in the roll and dive his X-wing executed. "Shifting to ground attack mode."

"Good luck, Mr. Horn." Wedge killed his comm unit. "Mynock, pull a sensor feed from Horn's R2. Shoot it to Captain Celchu on Tac-Three." He popped his comm over to

Tac-Two. "Captain, you'll be getting a datafeed from Rogue Nine."

"It will be interesting to watch. He's going in hot."

"That he is, Tycho, very hot. He wants to set a mark the others can't possibly hit." Wedge nodded slowly. "I think he needs to get a different lesson today. Here's what we'll do . . ."

8

CORRAN PULLED OUT of his dive and skimmed the surface of Folor. He aimed the nose of his snubfighter at the paired mountains that marked the opening of the pig trough. A line of red lights burned on and off in sequence, seeming to send the light from the plains to the peaks of the grey mountains. Below him the rough rims of countless craters flashed past.

"Nine, should Ten shift shields forward?"

"Negative, Ten. Even them out. We'll probably have targets at our backs." Corran glanced at his datascreen. "Whistler, can you boost my forward sensors? Screen for background formations and pick out what's anomalous. Yes, yes, take care of your communications link first, but just do it. Thanks."

After a couple of seconds the astromech droid complied with the request and the image on the datascreen refined itself. The mountains appeared in a light shade of green and likely targets—in this case the lights on the mountains—were translated into red circles that began to blink when he had a clear shot at them. From past experience he knew Whistler would turn the circles into diamonds if they proved to be hostile.

The fighter shot forward into the trench. Tall, jagged walls rose tall on either side of him. Unlike canyons carved through stone by the relentless flow of water, this one boasted sharp walls that would grind a fighter into dust. *It seems as if I'm flying between teeth, not stones.*

He guided the fighter up over a small rise and then down into a valley where two red circles became diamonds. His cannons tracked left and lit up the first target while laser fire from the Gand hit the second. "Nice shooting, Ten."

"Ooryl was anxious. Ooryl will wait for clearance to fire in future."

"Not at all. Two more targets. I've got them." Corran let his fighter drift to the right. "Pick up what I drop."

"As ordered."

Corran pulled back on his stick and climbed sharply to get at the first target. He shot it before its laser could depress enough to shoot back at him. Rolling his ship to the left, he moved back to the center of the canyon, then finished the roll with an inside loop that brought him down to target the second diamond. It hit him once before he took it out, but the shot from the target did not penetrate his shields.

Climbing back up, Corran stood the fighter on its right S-foil and arced around a corner in the trench. Coming up to let his sensors read the valley beyond a steep rise, he took laser fire from two bunkers nearly a kilometer distant. He pushed the stick forward and brought the X-wing down to the deck, then worked his way back up to the rise. "I've got the one on the port side, you take starboard."

A brief, high-pitched whistle came through the comm to signal Ooryl's understanding of the order.

The X-wing streaked over the ridgeline and immediately started taking fire from the target on the left. Corran dipped below it, intending to repeat his steep-climb run from before when Whistler started wailing. A threat light burned in the aft position. "Full shields aft, Whistler!"

Laser bolts shot past the X-wing as Corran jinked to the left. He punched the right rudder pedal, vectoring thrust to kick the tail of his fighter into a bit of a skid to port. Doing that took him out of line with both guns, while allowing him to keep his nose on his intended target. He triggered four bursts of fire, hitting with the second and third.

He rolled the fighter to present its belly to the mountain wall that had housed the gun he'd silenced, then he cut in his repulsorlift generators. They created a field that bounced him off the wall and pushed him back toward the center of the canyon. Rolling back down to starboard, he killed the repulsorlift generators and dove to pick up a little speed. In doing so he came out beneath Ooryl and still had laser bolts popping past him.

Whistler shifted views of the canyon for a moment and showed Corran what had been happening in that section. An emplacement had been located on the reverse slope of the rise. Had Corran not ducked his ship back down when he took fire the first time, his sensors might have picked up its location.

I would have come up, looped, hit it, then rolled out and picked up the right side target. Ooryl could have nailed the left target and we'd have been set. "Forward view again, Whistler." Seeing the array of targets upcoming, Corran trimmed his speed back to allow him more time on target. "It's going to get busy."

Whistler hooted something about understatement.

Targets came fast and seemed to get more accurate the deeper he ran into the trench. Corran tapped his lucky charm once, then forced himself to concentrate. He analyzed target locations and plotted angles of attack. Rolling his fighter, diving and climbing, he wove his way through the gunnery course. He didn't get every target he shot at, but fewer of them hit him.

Two thirds of the way through the course Corran and Ooryl approached another ridge like the one that had hidden a gun position on its back slope. "Drop back, Ten. Let me draw fire from any back slope guns, then you can roll in and nail them."

A squeal answered him. Corran sailed up over the rim prematurely and snapped a shot off at the guns to the left. Rolling wide to the right, he sideslipped out of fire from below. "Midslope down, Ten." Without waiting for confirmation Corran corkscrewed his X-wing around and lased the starboard target. The port target still fired at him, but he dove below its line of bolts and cruised farther into the canyon.

"Ooryl got it, Nine."

"Congrats, Ten."

Coming around the last sweeping turn Corran saw a narrowing of the canyon down toward the deeper part of it. Above that crevasse four laser targets had a perfect field of fire for blowing any X-wing out of the sky, but they couldn't shoot down into the split in the rocks. "Whistler, give me the width of the crevasse."

The droid mournfully reported it was 15 meters on average, 12.3 meters wide at the most narrow point.

"Good. The walls will cover me." Behind him, anticipating him, Ooryl had already rolled his X-wing up on its starboard S-foil. Corran smiled and dipped toward the crevasse while keeping his wings parallel to the ground.

"Nine, you need to roll."

"Negative, Ten. It's wide enough—a meter to spare on each side."

"If you go dead down the middle."

"If I don't I'll be *dead*." Taking a deep breath, Corran focused on an imaginary point about ten meters off the nose of his fighter. He kept his hand gentle on the stick and steered for that point. He kept it in the middle of the crevasse, floating left and right as sections of the wall jutted out from one side or the other.

The choke point closed with him. *Easy, easy*. He drifted to port for a half meter and suddenly the tight spot was behind him without his having left any paint on either side of it. The walls streaked by, black and grey blurred together. Corran found himself steering the ship almost effortlessly. He knew he could have handled the run at full throttle and not had a problem.

It almost feels as if I have kilometers off each S-foil, not a meter or two. The bright line marking the end of the crevasse yawned open before him. *And now I've got targets.*

Swooping up and out of the rock slit, Corran's X-wing spat fire. He started with the lowest target, hit it squarely with the first shot, then tracked his fire up and to the starboard with a roll and climb. He blasted the second target, then continued his roll until he was inverted. Firing two controlled bursts got him the third gunnery station and Ooryl, threading Corran's loop, tagged the last one.

Corran came down, around, and shot past Ooryl as they headed out of the range. Hauling back on the stick, he stood his X-wing on its tail and rocketed away from Folor. Rolling out into a long loop, he traded distance for time and pulled up on Ooryl's wing as they both headed in toward where the rest of the squadron orbited.

Commander Antilles's voice filled Corran's helmet. "Very impressive flying, Mr. Horn. Your score is 3250 out of a possible 5000. Quite good."

Corran smiled broadly. "Hear that, Whistler? Rogue Leader was impressed." He activated his comm unit. "Thank you, sir."

"You can head back to base now, Mr. Horn. Your participation in this exercise is at an end. Consider yourself at liberty for the rest of the day."

"Yes, sir. Rogue Nine heading home."

YEAH, I WAS at liberty—liberty to be humiliated. Muscles bunched at the corners of Corran's jaw as he ground his teeth. He'd waited in the hangar for the others to come back to base, hoping to hear his mark had stood through the rest of the exercise. He knew he was looking for congratulations on his great flying, *but not in the egotistical way Bror Jace would have been.* He didn't want to lord it over the others, but he did want to know they thought he was good.

The others had come back in pairs and, for the most part, had tried to avoid him. Lujayne Forge and Andoorni Hui had been the first to return. As he saw their ships come in his smile became broad. He knew he had blown past any score they could set. *They're good pilots, but I was really flying out there. They couldn't touch me today.*

Andoorni had remained silent, possibly brooding—but who could tell with Rodians? Lujayne had been almost apologetic. "I got 3300, Corran. Andoorni hit 3750."

"What?"

Lujayne hesitated, tucking a strand of brown hair behind her left ear. "It was just our day to fly well. You inspired us, really."

"Inspiring, Horn." The Rodian's ears rotated toward him, then back again as Andoorni wandered away.

Lujayne gave him a sympathetic smile. "Want to head to DownTime and get something to eat?" The tone of her voice suggested strongly that he wanted to take her up on her offer to spare himself from what was headed in his direction.

Despite the unspoken warning, he'd shaken his head. "Thanks. Maybe I'll see you at the tapcafe later."

Corran continued to wait for the rest of the squadron to return. Peshk Vri'syk and Ooryl came back together. The ruddy-furred Bothan took great delight in reporting a score of 4200. The Gand had been very quiet and when he finally spoke he said, "Qrygg scored 4050."

That answer told Corran something very strange was going on. In reverting to calling himself by his family name Ooryl had shown himself to be ashamed of his score, but Corran knew he should have been ecstatic about it instead. The fact that Ooryl clearly didn't want to speak with Corran, and only relented after Corran insisted, meant that whatever Ooryl was ashamed of had to do with Corran.

The others in the squadron didn't say much of anything

except to report their scores. Each pilot had scored better than Corran and most had done so by over 1000 points. That didn't seem possible to Corran. *He knew he had flown that course as best as he could. On subsequent runs I might score up in that range, but not first time out. That's not possible. Unless . . .*

Corran jogged over to where Whistler had plugged himself into a recharging outlet. "Whistler, at the start of our run, you set up a communications link with someone. Who?"

The droid's holographic projector began to glow. A miniature image of Wedge Antilles floated between them.

"You sent him my sensor data, right?"

Sharp scolding whistles followed an affirmative tone.

"I know I didn't prohibit it."

A curt squawk made Corran wince. "Yes, Whistler, I *did* approve your action. Never again give out that sort of data without my permission, got it?"

The little droid piped demurely, then shifted to the singsong tone he had used to warn Corran when Loor had entered the CorSec office. The pilot turned and saw the Headhunter Trainer come through the magcon bubble, followed closely by Rogue Leader. Purposely ignoring Whistler's bleats, Corran watched the ship land.

"Time to get some questions answered."

Corran felt a tug at his flight suit leg as Whistler's pincer attachment closed on the cloth. He pulled away, tearing the material. "You betrayed me once here, Whistler, don't compound the problem."

The droid's mournful tones played out in time with a funeral march as Corran closed with Wedge's X-wing. He ducked beneath the nose and snapped to attention as Wedge descended the ladder. His throat thick with anger, Corran saluted and held his quivering hand in place until Wedge returned the salute.

"Do you want to speak to me about something, Mr. Horn?"

"Yes, sir."

Wedge tugged his gloves off. "Well?"

"Permission to speak frankly, sir?"

"Knock yourself out, Mr. Horn."

Corran's hands convulsed into fists. "You gave everyone else *my* targeting data. I flew my heart out and flew that course as good as anyone possibly could on his first time through. You turned that data over to the others, so they were making a run based on the things I had done. You gave them my score as a base and they built on it."

Wedge's brown-eyed gaze did not waver as he met Corran's stare. "And?"

"And? It's not fair, sir. I'm one of the best pilots in this squadron, but it looks like I'm the worst. The others appear better but they're not. I've been robbed."

"I see. Are you finished?"

"No."

"Well, you should be, or you *can* be. Do you understand me?"

The icy tone in Wedge's voice filled Corran's guts with frozen needles. "Yes, sir."

Wedge nodded past him toward the exterior of the base. "You need to examine why you're here, Mr. Horn. You're part of a team and have to act like it. If I need you to shoot a trench like that and feed your data back to a Y-wing squadron coming through, I'll have you do it. How good *you* are means nothing if the rest of the people in the squadron get killed. You might be the best pilot in the squadron, but the *squadron* is only as good as the worst pilot in it.

"Today the others learned to use data from a reconnaissance flight to help them through deadly territory. You learned that you're not more important than anyone else in this squadron just because you're a gifted pilot. I'm pleased with those lessons having been learned by my people. If you're not, I'm certain there are other squadrons who would love to have Rogue's washouts."

Corran's cheeks burned and his stomach turned itself inside out. *He's right—he saw the same thing Lujayne did and found a way to point out how serious a problem it can be. I've been an idiot.* He swallowed hard. "Yes, sir."

"Yes, what, Mr. Horn?"

"I'm happy learning what I learned, sir. I want to stay with the squadron."

Wedge nodded slowly. "Good, I don't want to lose you. You've got the makings of a superior pilot, but you aren't there yet. You have the skills you need, but there is more to being part of this squadron than flying well. The training you get will be a bit different from the others, but your need to learn is just as great. Do you understand?"

Corran nodded. "Yes, sir. Thank you, sir."

Wedge handed his helmet and gloves to an astrotech. "And just so you know, you're right to be angry. Remember this, though, giving in to that kind of anger in battle will get you killed. I don't think you want that any more than I do." The leader of the squadron tossed him a sharp salute. "You're dismissed, Mr. Horn."

Corran returned the salute, spun on his heel, and marched stiffly away, deeper into the hangar. He threaded his way through the fighters, stepping over power cables and around tool carts. He purposely steered himself away from where Whistler was recharging—the little R2 unit had perfected an "I told you so" whistle that Corran realized he'd heard far too often since his father's death.

"Mr. Horn."

Corran stopped and blinked away the gathering clouds of dark memories. His hand rose in a salute. "Captain Celchu."

The blue-eyed man returned the salute, then crossed his arms over his chest. "Still walking and talking?"

"Sir?"

"Either Commander Antilles is losing his touch in dressing down recruits or"—Tycho smiled lopsidedly—"you're made of sterner stuff than I might have otherwise imagined."

9

C ORRAN'S GREEN EYES narrowed. "I don't think the Commander cut me any slack, sir."

Tycho held a hand up. "Forgive me, Mr. Horn, that did not come out the way I wanted. From your CorSec record and the way you tend to excel in scenarios where you act alone, you have struck me as a loner. Loners don't tend to like it when they're made to be a team player."

But that's not how I am. Is it? Corran frowned. "I can work with others, but I know I can only rely on myself when things fall apart. I can't help that attitude because it kept me alive in tough times."

Tycho pointed toward the passage deeper into Folor base and Corran fell into step with him. "The problem with that attitude, Corran, is that it keeps others away. It makes it more difficult for them to help you when you need it. It keeps them uncertain that you will help them when the time comes that they need you."

"Hey, I'll never leave a buddy in trouble."

"I don't doubt that, but you define buddies on *your* terms. Others may not see themselves as your friends." The taller man pressed his lips together in a grim line. "It's clear that being here is not easy for you."

That's an unwarranted assumption. I've adjusted as well as anyone. Corran glanced to the right at Tycho. "Why do you think that, sir?"

"You were with the Corellian Security Force and spent a good deal of your time hunting down people who are now your allies. That transition isn't something you can make overnight."

"It couldn't have been any easier for you, sir. You were an Imperial pilot."

Tycho did not reply immediately and Corran sensed a window of vulnerability that had opened, then slammed shut almost immediately. He knew it with the certainty he'd known when he'd hit on lies suspects told him during interrogation. He wanted to pounce and push, but the hint of pain he saw flash through Tycho's eyes stopped him.

"Let's just say, Corran, that my situation was quite different from yours." Tycho's face slackened into an emotionless mask. "Different time, different circumstances."

Corran heard pure honesty in Tycho's words and decided against pushing. That honesty cleared his mind and punched through walls he didn't realize he'd erected. "You may be right, sir. Looking around here I see the sort of smuggler's hideaway my father and I ached to bust wide open. Just looking at this place I know it had to have been used by smugglers before the Alliance turned it into a base. If I'd known then what I know now . . ."

"You would have been even more convinced that the Rebellion was wrong."

"Yeah, I guess I would have." Corran slapped his own belly with his right hand. "I remember being in the CorSec Academy when the Imperial warrants for Han Solo and Chewbacca were issued. They were charged with the murder of Grand Moff Tarkin—no word about the Death Star, of course. I remember thinking that if I were already in CorSec I'd have gotten Solo. I thought he was a blot on Corellia's honor."

The hint of a smile tugged at the corners of Tycho's mouth. "And you still do."

Corran winced. "He smuggled spice for a Hutt. I understand that he made some choices that made his life fall apart. I can sympathize with his freeing Wookiee slaves—no one on Corellia liked the idea of slaves—but he sank pretty low after that."

Tycho nodded. "When your life disintegrated, *you* didn't sink that far, so *he* shouldn't have?"

"Something like that." Corran stopped just before they entered the corridor out of the hangar. "Is that your assessment of my opinion, or your assessment of Solo in relationship to your leaving Imperial service as he did?"

Tycho's smile broadened. "Interesting insight. I think there was a time that Solo, who had bound his conception of honor to his service to the Empire, forgot that honor could exist outside Imperial service. This seems to be a misconception that has been corrected."

"And correcting it won him fame, glory, and Princess Organa."

"True, but what's important is that he knows honor exists inside you and can only radiate out. What goes on outside can't change it or kill it unless you abandon your honor. Too many folks give it up too easily, then do whatever they can to fill the void in their hearts." Tycho shook his head. "Forgive me this little lecture. I've had an unfortunate amount of time to think about this sort of stuff."

Two Alliance Security officers walked over to where Corran and Tycho stood. The female Lieutenant spoke with a calm, even voice. "Captain Celchu, are you ready to return to your quarters now?"

The taller man suddenly looked very fatigued, as if his skeleton had just become one size smaller so his flesh hung loosely from it. "Yes, I believe so. Thank you for this conversation, Mr. Horn."

"You're welcome, sir."

Tycho nodded to the woman. "After you."

"No, sir," she said, "after *you*."

Her tone struck Corran as all wrong. He had assumed she had been offering to escort Captain Celchu to his quarters as a courtesy, but the edge in her voice transformed her words into an order. *Why would they be forcing him to return to his quarters? I don't understand. She's treating him like a criminal.*

He stared after them, trying to reconcile the Security officer's action with a need to protect Tycho from some threat. He couldn't imagine anyone in the Alliance base who would begrudge Tycho actions taken before he joined the Rebel cause. Becoming a Rebel was like starting over—the datascreen was wiped and the past forgotten. *Yet I still have reservations about Han Solo. Even so, I don't want to murder him, so he doesn't need protection.*

He realized he was attempting to rationalize why Tycho was being escorted by armed guards, and the most simple answer was because Tycho presented a threat to the Alliance in some way. The obvious ludicrousness of that idea shone like a supernova because if Tycho was a threat of any sort, no one would trust him to be teaching pilots how to fly. *Then again, he* is *assigned a Headhunter Trainer.*

"There you are."

Corran's head came up at the sound of the woman's voice. Just a bit taller than he was, but slender and walking on very shapely long legs, she entered the hangar from the corridor and stared right at him. Corran turned and looked behind himself to see whom she was addressing, but when he looked back at her, she had stopped right in front of him. "I was wondering where you were."

"Me?" Corran raised an eyebrow. "Are you sure you were looking for me, Erisi?"

She nodded confidently. Sympathy played through her big blue eyes. "I was sent to find you. The rest of us are in Down-Time, going over what happened out there."

"Not enough laughs, so you wanted me to join you?" He shook his head. "Thanks anyway, some other time."

"No, now." Erisi took firm hold of his left elbow. "We *do* want you there. So we can apologize."

Corran hesitated, covering his surprise. She sounded sincere, but she was from Thyferra and almost always in Bror Jace's company. He tried to figure out if she was setting him up, but the gentle way her short black hair lay against the nape of her long neck distracted him. "I'm not sure I'd be good company."

"You *must* come." She tugged him gently toward the corridor. "Look, we all used your data because Commander Antilles told us our exercise involved doing just that. It wasn't until we made our runs that he told each of us what had happened— what he had done to you. He ordered us to say nothing to you except to report our scores. None of us felt good about what happened and we want to make it up to you."

He nodded and started walking with her. "So how did you get the job of coming after me? You pick the sabacc card with the lowest value?"

Erisi smiled at him, her eyes dominating a delicately sculpted face with high cheekbones and a strong jawline. "I volunteered. Nawara Ven and Rhysati Ynr are trying to talk some sense into Bror and I had to walk away."

"You'd abandon a fellow Thyferran to a conversation with a Twi'lek lawyer?"

Her laughter echoed faintly through the dim corridor. Strip illumination ran along the edges of the tunnel where the floor met the walls and gave them enough light to travel by, but most of the people in front of them were shadowed silhouettes.

"Bror Jace is from a family that owns a significant portion of stock in Zaltin. His people are known for being rather haughty and obstreperous."

"I hadn't noticed."

"I would have thought you a keener observer than that." She gave his arm a squeeze. "Besides, Bror has noticed you. He sees you as his chief rival for supremacy in this squadron."

"He's forgetting the Commander and Captain Celchu."

She shook her head. "No, he's not, he's just ignoring them. As Commander Antilles said, those who have served with Rogue Squadron before are legends, and Bror doesn't think it's possible to defeat a legend. Become one, yes, but best one, never."

"Erisi, I appreciate your candor, but I'd hardly expect you to be speaking of a friend in such uncomplimentary terms."

"What gave you the impression we were friends?"

"Perhaps the fact that you spend a lot of time with him."

"Oh, that?" Erisi chuckled politely. "Better the Moff you know than the Emperor's new Envoy. I could never truly be friends with anyone who grew up in the Zaltin corporate culture. My people are with Xucphra, the true leader in bacta production and refinement. My uncle was the person who discovered the contamination the Ashern introduced into Lot ZX1449F."

"Really?"

The woman glanced sidelong at him, her face frozen for a millisecond, then she smiled and playfully slapped his left shoulder. "You! I know Thyferran corporate politics is boring, but it's the lifeblood of my people. Though there are thousands of Vratix who actually grow *alazhi* and refine bacta, the ten thousand humans who run the corporations are really the people who make bacta available to the galaxy. Since we're such a small community—and, I'll admit, a fairly affluent one—we set great store in the accomplishments of our relatives."

Corran nodded as they stepped onto an escalator that took them down deeper into the heart of Folor. "Choosing one of you from each corporate family was meant to keep things even?"

"Were that possible, of course." Erisi winked at him. "More of us would have been sent, I suspect, but strong involvement with the Alliance is a thing of fierce debate on Thyferra. Benign neutrality seems to be the course our leaders are choosing."

Playing both ends against the middle means big profits for the Bacta Cartel. "But you felt strongly enough about the Rebellion to volunteer to join it?"

"There are times one must place higher ideals over personal safety."

At the bottom of the escalator they stepped off and walked across a small chamber to a dark opening carved in smooth-melted stone. Beyond it lay a noisy stone gallery with next to no visible light—unless the bright colors of strobing neon tracery were to be considered adequate for lighting. Voices from dozens of alien throats croaked below or shrieked above the booming din of human conversation. The heavy, moist air stank of sweat; acrid, cloying smoke; and fermented nectars from hundreds of Alliance worlds and not a few Imperial strongholds.

Corran paused on the threshold of the makeshift tapcafe the Rebels had named DownTime. *If I were still in CorSec, I'd be calling for backup before setting foot in a place like this.*

Erisi, taking his hand in hers, led him into the room. As if she could see things he could not, she guided him between hologame light tables and knots of pilots and techs. Back in the corner a holoprojector had been set up. It appeared to be projecting a sporting event being broadcast down on Commenor, but the exoskeleton padding the players wore and the curiously spiked ball they tossed back and forth weren't from any game Corran recognized. Aside from a quartet of Ugnaughts sitting right at the edge of the projection ring and staring up at the towering figures, no one appeared to care about the game.

The rest of Rogue Squadron had gathered in a corner of the tapcafe. Corran spotted Gavin first—both because of his size and his nervousness. The youth stared at all the different aliens as if he'd never seen them before. That surprised Corran because he thought, with Mos Eisley being on Tatooine, Gavin would have had his fill of aliens. *Then again, I doubt the kid spent much time there. He's as green as the foam on Lominale.*

Over on the right Bror Jace and Nawara appeared to be deep in conversation. Shiel slipped past Corran and handed Gavin a mug full of a steaming liquid that smelled sweet. Lujayne, seeing Corran, smiled at him and rapped the heel of her mug on the table around which they stood.

"Corran's here."

The Bothan's reaction to his arrival appeared to be relatively apathetic, but everyone else seemed to be pleased to see him. The Twi'lek pointed toward Corran with the tip of a head tail and Bror Jace managed a tight smile. Stepping forward, the Thyferran pilot offered Corran his hand. "I want you to know I would not have flown with your data had I known. I'll be the first to sign the letter of protest to General Salm."

"Letter of protest?"

Nawara looked a bit exasperated. "Some members of the squadron feel that a protest of Commander Antilles's treatment of you is in order."

Corran looked Nawara in the eyes. "You don't think so?"

The Twi'lek slowly shook his head. "I don't think it will be effective and I believe, quite honestly, that this incident is really fairly minor."

Corran smiled. "I'm glad to see someone hasn't lost a sense of perspective here."

Bror's blue eyes narrowed. "What do you mean by that?"

"I mean, my friends, we're part of a military unit involved in an illegal insurgency against a government that controls the vast majority of planets in this galaxy. We're all volunteers here, and we've all come because we expect to win freedom and liberty for all sapient species by overthrowing the government. We're all willing to make the ultimate sacrifice if it comes to that, yet we're going to protest how one of the most decorated and revered leaders conducts training exercises? I don't think so."

Gavin gave Corran a wide-eyed look of confusion. "But what he did to you wasn't right. It was nasty and cold and meant to hurt you."

"I'll agree it was nasty and cold, but it wasn't meant to hurt me." He looked around at the rest of the squadron. "Commander Antilles had a point to make with me, and he made it. And he made one with you. Your being here like this, your discomfort with what happened, and your desire to protest my treatment means I know you're going to be there when I need you to be. And you know I'm willing to do what I need to do to make sure our squadron can do its job. If that means I go in alone or with Ooryl or whatever to get information, I do it.

"The thing we all have to remember is this: There's nothing Commander Antilles can do to us that will be worse than what the Empire has already done on hundreds of worlds. They destroyed Alderaan. They destroyed the Jedi and they'll destroy us if they can. Because of what he did today, Commander Antilles knows he can count on me, and I hope the rest of you do, too."

Erisi raised Corran's left hand above his head. "I think Corran's correct. He might not have been the best pilot on the course today, but he's probably the one who learned the most."

Lujayne stood and gave Corran a firm hug. "As the *second* worst pilot today, I say thanks—both for your skill and your wisdom here."

Corran blushed slightly, freed his left hand from Erisi's grip, and extricated himself from Lujayne's hug. "Thanks to all of you, but just so you don't think I'm this cool-headed all the time, I have to admit that I had a discussion with Commander Antilles in which he pointed out most of these insights."

The wolfman growled in a low voice. "Yelling? Punches?"

"No. Just some clear and concise conversation."

Shiel bared his teeth and Gavin laughed. Lujayne fished into her flight suit's thigh pocket and produced a handful of oddly shaped credit coins. She held them out to the Twi'lek who cupped them in both hands and smiled avariciously. He flicked at a couple with taloned fingers, then looked up and froze as if caught bloody-handed.

Corran knit his fingers together and let them rest against his belt buckle. "And those credits are for?"

"Winning the pool." Nawara carefully slipped them into his pocket. "I said you'd be reasonable."

Rhysati elbowed him. "You took reasonable because you got the best odds with that wager."

The Twi'lek looked offended. "I *hold* opinions, I don't *bet* them."

Corran laughed. "Who had 'will challenge Commander Antilles to an X-wing death duel'?"

Erisi raised her hand. "It was an even-odds bet, too."

"Nawara won by betting what was in my brain, but you bet what was in my heart." Corran pointed to the bar. "In honor of your insightfulness, I will buy you that which *your* heart desires."

She took his left hand again. "And if it doesn't have a price?"

"Then I'll buy you a drink and we'll talk about how else to make you happy."

Bror Jace bowed from the waist in Erisi's direction. "To make her happy you would have to make her family's corporation yet more profitable."

"And to do that means I'd have to be boosting the use of bacta, right?" Corran opened his hands and took in the whole of the squadron. "And since the Empire buys bacta and we'll be shooting at their pilots, I don't think that'll be hard to do at all."

10

THE SHUTTLE'S PILOT looked back over his left shoulder. "Agent Loor, you'll probably want to strap yourself in. We're coming out of hyperspace."

Kirtan began to fumble with the restraining harness, then brought his head up quickly, embarrassed that his lack of coordination betrayed his nervousness. "Thank you, Lieutenant, but I've traveled this way before."

"Yes, sir," came the pilot's oily reply, "but I'd bet this is your first time to Imperial Center."

Kirtan wanted to snap some sharp reply that would sting the man, but a sense of utter and complete disaster washed over him. He had waited for two full weeks before reporting Gil Bastra's death to his superiors. In that time he furiously analyzed and tried to expand upon any leads Bastra had offered during his interrogation. They all seemed to be dead ends, leading nowhere, but he knew, he just *knew*, they would put him on Corran Horn if he had enough time to figure out their greater significance.

In his report he had tried to stress the positive, but within hours of the report being sent on up the line, he had received his summons to Imperial Center, formerly known as Corus-

cant. He was ordered to make his way to the Imperial capital
as quickly as possible. As luck would have it—luck he in no
way saw as benign—passage had been arranged on a series of
ships with a minimum of difficulty. This last ship, a shuttle on
loan from the *Aggressor*, effortlessly carried him to his doom.

The wall of light visible through the viewport dissolved
into a million million points of light as the ship left hyperspace. Imperial Center, a clouded grey world ringed by Golan
defense platforms, seemed even more forbidding than he had
imagined. He had expected to see that the world that had become a city would be as dead and cold as the Emperor who
had ruled from it. Instead, with boiling clouds burned white
by flashes of lightning, the planet's true nature lay cloaked and
hidden, as did his future.

"Imperial Center, this is shuttle *Objurium* requesting clearance for entry on the Palace Vector."

"Transmit clearance code, shuttle *Objurium*."

"Transmitting now." The pilot turned back toward Kirtan.
"This code better be good. We're well within the range of the
two nearest Golan stations."

"It is good." Kirtan blanched. "I mean, it is the code I was
given with my orders." He started to go on to explain further,
but saw the pilot and copilot exchange a quick wink and realized he was being teased.

"Don't worry, Agent Loor, the days of the Empire blasting
one of its own shuttles apart to kill an Intelligence agent are
long past. Can't spare the ships right now, which is what makes
me a bit more secure."

Kirtan forced an edge into his voice. "And how do you
know, Lieutenant, that I am not here solely to monitor and
report on your attitudes?"

"You're not the first man I've ferried to his death, Agent
Loor."

"Shuttle *Objurium*," the comm squawked, "clearance
granted. Align course for beacon 784432."

"Understood, Control, *Objurium* out." The pilot punched

the beacon number into the navigation computer, then gave his copilot a more somber glance.

"What?" Kirtan tried to stop himself from blurting the question out, and began to brace for some stinging jibe from the pilot, but he got none.

"We're heading to Tower 78, level 443, bay 2."

"And?"

Kirtan saw the pilot's Adam's apple bob up and down. "Sir, the only other time I've been given that vector is when I had the pleasure of shuttling Lord Vader to the Emperor. It was after the disaster at Yavin."

Kirtan felt a chill slowly pour into him and move up his spine bone by bone. *Did Lord Vader fear retribution for his actions as I do? Perhaps the Emperor had meant to kill him, but Vader redeemed his life by bringing news of the existence of another Jedi to his master.* Kirtan's fist hammered his right thigh. *If I had just a little more time I could have delivered my quarry.*

Ahead of the shuttle Kirtan saw lightning flare from the clouds upward toward space. It hit and spread out, faintly illuminating a hexagonal area hanging above the clouds. "What is that?"

"Defense shield." The pilot punched a couple of buttons on his command console. A miniature model of the world materialized between pilot and passenger, then two spheres made up of hexagonal elements engulfed the world. The spheres moved in opposite directions around the world, constantly shifting, with the hexes in the upper layer covering more area than those below. "Imperial Center, for obvious reasons, has the most sophisticated system of defense shields in the Empire. A small portion of it will come down to let us in, then that section will be reinforced behind us, while another one will open below."

"Nothing can get in without clearance."

The pilot nodded. "Or out. More than one Rebel agent has been caught trying to race back out while ships are coming in. It's a gamble, but not one that pays off very often."

The copilot pushed a glowing button on the console. "We're through the first shield."

"Our next opening comes two degrees north, four east."

"Course set, sir."

"Not much longer until we're down, Agent Loor. Only thing that could go wrong now is a cloud discharging and trying to hit the upper shield through our opening."

"Does that happen?"

"Sometimes."

"Often?"

The pilot shrugged. "The power for the upper shield comes through openings in the lower shield. This tends to ionize a lot of atoms, making lightning travel that much faster along those routes. However, doesn't look like our hole served as an energy conduit very recently, so we should be safe."

Turbulence hit the shuttle as it pierced the layer of clouds. Kirtan tightened some of the belts restraining him, then clutched the back of the copilot's chair with white knuckles. He wanted to blame his growing feeling of nausea on the way the shuttle bounced down through the atmosphere, but he knew that was not its only cause. *The world beneath these clouds is the last thing I will see before I die.*

The shuttle broke through the vapor shell around the planet and the pilot smiled at him. "Welcome to Imperial Center, Agent Loor."

Despite his fear, Kirtan Loor looked out at the dark world below and felt overwhelmed by the panorama. Instantly recognizable, the Imperial Palace stood tall, like a volcano that had thrust itself up through the heart of the metropolis that dominated a whole continent of Coruscant. Towers festooned it, as if spires on a crown, and thousands of lights sparkled like jewels set in an incandescent mosaic on its stone hide. Beneath it, dwarfed into insignificance, lay Senate Hill. Its tiny buildings—raised as monuments to the justice and glory of the Old Republic—seemed frozen with fright that the Palace would grow out and consume them.

Spreading out from that central point, brilliant neon lights in all manner of colors pulsed as if nerves carrying information to and from the palace itself. Kirtan followed one river of light as it shifted from red and green to gold and blue, from the heart of the world out to the horizon. As the ship swooped lower, he saw depths to the lightstreams, where buildings had accreted, sinking the streets into twisted, broken canyons. He knew the light could not reach *all* the way down, and his imagination had no difficulty in populating those black gashes with nightmare creatures and lethal danger.

But the lethal danger I face dwells above all this. Kirtan sat back as the shuttle banked and the nose came up a bit. The pilot leveled the *Objurium* off while the copilot flicked a switch above his head. A red square appeared on the shuttle's viewport and surrounded the top of one of the palace's towers. Lights blinked around an opening far too small to admit the shuttle, even with its wings folded up.

"We can't be going there. Where will we land?"

"It looks small, Agent Loor, because we're still three kilometers away from it."

Kirtan's mouth hung open as his brain fought to put everything he was seeing in perspective. The streets below, which he had taken to be narrow tracks, had to be the size of major boulevards. And the towers, they were not slender, needlelike minarets, but massive buildings designed to house hundreds or thousands of people on each level. And the structures on the surface, they armored the planet with layer after layer of ferrocrete.

Kirtan shuddered as he realized how deep the warrens had to run on the planet, yet he doubted anyone had set foot on the soil beneath Imperial City for centuries.

It all struck him as impossible that a world could house that many people, but this was Coruscant. It was the heart of an Empire that boasted millions of known worlds. If each one required only a thousand people to deal with it and its problems, Coruscant would have to be home to billions of people.

And to see to their needs, billions more would have to be in residence, working, building, cleaning.

Suddenly he went from wondering how Coruscant could house so many people to wondering if even billions of individuals were enough to oversee the Empire. *Or what's left of it.*

The *Objurium* swept in closer to the tower. The opening appeared to be a black hole waiting to suck him down and rend him atom from atom. Though logic argued against expending the money it cost to bring him to Coruscant just to kill him, he knew that Death hovered close and would be seeking him out. He had failed and the price the Empire demanded for failure was dear indeed.

Kirtan ran a finger around his collar to loosen it. Arguing against his death, aside from the wasted expense of his travel, was a thought that proved utterly ludicrous to him. The only way he would stay alive was if he had something the person who had summoned him here found valuable. But he was just one person. The only thing he imagined he possessed that was not duplicated by ten or a hundred or a thousand other people on Coruscant was his life. *I have nothing else that is unique.*

The opening loomed close enough for Kirtan to see figures moving around in its shadows. The pilot punched a button on the command console. The shuttle's wings rose and locked up while the landing gear descended. The shuttle drifted forward, easing into the hangar, then slowly settled to the deck. It landed with only a slight bump, but Kirtan's nerves magnified it until it felt as heavy as the blow of a vibroblade on his neck.

Steeling himself for the worst, Kirtan slapped the buckle against his breastbone and slid free of the restraining harness. "Thank you, Lieutenant, for your efforts on my behalf."

The pilot watched him for a moment, then nodded. "Good luck, sir."

Kirtan pulled on a pair of black leather gloves and flexed his right hand. "Smooth flight back to the *Aggressor*."

The Intelligence agent stood slowly, letting his legs get used to the planet's gravity, then walked back from the cockpit and down the egress ramp. At the base of the ramp four Imperial Guards, resplendent in their scarlet uniforms, stood at attention. When he stepped into their midst, they turned as one and marched him toward the doorway at the far end of the hangar.

The few people Kirtan saw in the hangar did not look at him directly. Even when he turned his head, seeking to catch one of them from the corner of his eye, they paid him no heed. *Have they seen so many people come this way and not return that it is no longer remarkable to them? Or do they think undue attention paid to me would find them being drawn along in my wake?*

Being as tall as he was, he could almost see over the red dome of the guards' helmets. As nearly as he could determine, the four guards were identical in height and other physical dimensions, but their cloaks shrouded them sufficiently well that details that might have differentiated them one from another were lost. Because of that they appeared to be identical to all the holograms he had seen of Imperial Guards, with one minor exception.

Their cloaks had been hemmed with a black ribbon. In the dim light it had not been easy to pick out and its presence almost made it appear as if the guards walked a few centimeters above the floor. The officially mandated year of mourning had ended over a year previously—except, of course, on worlds where notification of the Emperor's death had arrived late or, worse yet, inspired open rebellion. Here on Coruscant that was not a problem, so Kirtan took the ribbon as a sign of the guards' continued devotion to their slain master.

They passed through the doorway and into a small corridor that seemed to extend on forever. Kirtan thought he noticed a slight arch to the floor and a tremble in the structure that suggested to him they had entered one of the bridges between the tower and the Palace proper. The close passageway had no windows and any decorations on the walls had been covered with meter after meter of black satin.

Through the far end and along another corridor, the guards

brought him to a doorway where two of their number stood. His escorts stopped when the other two guards turned and pulled open the doors before him. He stepped through them into a large room, the far wall of which was constructed entirely out of glass. A tall, slender woman stood in silhouette before it, though the backlight from the planet's surface outlined her in red.

"You are Kirtan Loor." It came not as a question, but a statement full of import.

"Reporting as ordered." He had tried to keep his voice as even and vital as hers had been, but he failed. A nervous squeak punctuated his sentence. "I can explain my report."

"Agent Loor, if I had wanted your report explained, I would have had your superiors go to great pains to extract that explanation from you." She turned slowly toward him. "Do you have any idea who I am?"

Kirtan's mouth had gone dry. "No, ma'am."

"I am Ysanne Isard. I *am* Imperial Intelligence." She opened her arms. "I rule here now and I am determined to destroy this Rebellion. I believe you can aid me in this task."

Kirtan swallowed hard. "Me?"

"You." Her hands returned to her sides. "I hope my belief is not unfounded. If it is, I will have gone to great expense to bring you here for *nothing*. Accounts will have to be balanced and I don't believe there is any way you can pay what you owe."

11

WEDGE ANTILLES SMILED when Admiral Ackbar nodded. "I think you'll see, sir, that the squadron is coming along quite well."

The Mon Calamari looked up from the datapad on his desk. "Your performance figures and exercise scores are commendable. Your people are better than some operational line units."

"Thank you, sir."

"Their level of discipline is not that of line units however, Admiral."

Wedge looked over at General Salm. The irritation in his voice matched the sour expression on the small man's face. Having come up through the ranks of Y-wing pilots, Salm had not been pleased when the Rogues staged a training attack on a full wing of Y-wing bombers. Though he had approved the exercise and had flown lead in one of the squadrons, he clearly had not expected things to go so badly for his trainees. The Rogues had lost four of their own fighters, but had destroyed all but six of the Y-wings. Salm was one of the survivors, which Wedge felt was a good thing and would have asked his pilots to leave Salm alone if he had thought of it beforehand.

Despite that, the nearly eight-to-one kill ratio had been better than even Wedge had imagined possible and had made Salm furious.

"I appreciate the General's assessment of my squadron, but these are elite pilots. I think making allowances for their high spirits promotes high morale." Wedge lifted his chin. "My people have a lot to live up to . . ."

"Right now," Salm sniffed, "they're living down to the squadron name."

"Begging your pardon, General, I think you're judging Rogue Squadron too harshly." *And it's because we made your* Guardian, Warden, *and* Champion *squadrons look as if they were* Lame, Sick, *and* Dying! The fighter pilot looked at Ackbar. "Sir, there have been no incidents, aside from the exercise in which General Salm was a willing participant, in which Rogue Squadron has done anything untoward."

The Mon Cal military leader set the datapad down. "I think General Salm has legitimate concerns about modified computer code being downloaded into his Y-wings' computers. I understand it painted your squadron crest on their primary monitor after they were shot down by your people."

Salm's eyes blazed and Wedge fought to keep a smile off his face. Gavin Darklighter had created the crest and with Zraii's help had linked a digitized image of it into the start-up and communications packages in the squadron. The crest, which featured a twelve-pointed red star with the Alliance crest in blue at the center, had an X-wing at each point of the star. Though the image was not sanctioned by the Alliance, astro-techs had started painting it on the squadron's X-wings and Emtrey had requisitioned unit patches that featured the design.

Wedge had been unable to determine if it was Corran, Nawara, Shiel, Rhysati, or some combination thereof who had talked the Verpine chief tech into adding the image to the Target-Aggressor Attack Resolution Software package, but he did know that Horn's R2 unit had done some of the code-slicing. When the TAARS package informed the downed Y-wing pilots of their status in the exercise, as Ackbar noted, the Rogue crest showed up to annoy the bomber jocks.

"I undertook an investigation into that situation, sir, and have restricted the unit's recreation time until I find out who did what in this whole thing."

Salm scoffed at that explanation. "You have arranged for your squadron to use the recreation facilities exclusively. They get more time in the gymnasium now than they ever did before, and the squadron briefing room has more recreational equipment than the Officers' Lounge here. Lujayne Forge spends more time as a social secretary for your brood than she does training."

"General, I'm building a squadron that will be given difficult missions, which means I need them to trust each other. If that means they have to be cliquish, then so be it."

Ackbar rose from his chair and walked over to where a blue globe of water hung suspended in a repulsorlift cage. The apparatus negated gravity, allowing the water to form a perfect globe. Within it a school of small fish with neon blue and gold stripes flashed this way and that. The Mon Cal studied it for a moment, then inclined his head toward Salm.

"It does not strike me, General, that your earlier complaints about the TAARS tampering involved how Rogue Squadron spends its recreational time."

"No, sir, but all of this is indicative of the difficulties the Rogues are creating. I have three squadrons of bombers training here as well as two other fighter squadrons. The morale of my troops suffers as the Rogues get rewarded for ignoring operational rules."

Ackbar gave Salm a wall-eyed stare. "Your specific complaint about TAARS?"

Salm's brown eyes smoldered. "Rogue Squadron's ability to alter Top Secret and proprietary software packages has serious security ramifications, especially with Tycho Celchu serving as the Executive Officer of that unit."

Wedge's jaw dropped. "Admiral, Tycho had nothing to do with the incident, in the first place, and second, Tycho has done nothing to show himself to be a risk."

Ackbar clasped his hands together at his back. "I agree to both of your points, but you would acknowledge that General Salm's concerns are valid?"

The Rogue Squadron's leader hesitated, never voicing the hot denial he had prepared as he heard the question. While *he* did not doubt Tycho's loyalty, he could see that taking chances was not wise. "Yes, sir."

"Good, because I am going to make an extraordinary request of you."

"Yes, sir."

"I'm making Rogue Squadron operational within the week."

"What?" Wedge felt as if he'd been snared by a Stokhli stun-net. "It's only been a month since the roster was finalized, sir. Advanced training takes six months normally—four if it's rushed. We're not ready."

Ackbar returned to his desk and tapped the datapad. "That is not what your numbers suggest."

"Admiral, you know there is more than just numbers to a unit. My people are good pilots, but they're still green. I need more time."

Salm folded his arms. "Rogue Squadron has gone into battle before with less training."

"Yes, and I lost a lot of good men and women because of it." He opened his arms and appealed to Ackbar. "Admiral, I've not even run any hyperjump exercises with these pilots."

"Ah, but I thought all the pilots were pre-screened for being astronav capable."

"They are, but . . ." Wedge was going to protest that Gavin Darklighter needed more work with astronavigation, but Lujayne had been tutoring him and reported Gavin was a natural. *Just like his cousin. Dammit, I don't like this.* "I would still prefer having time to take them through more drills."

"We would all like that luxury, Commander, but we don't have it." Salm frowned. "I'm taking my Y-wings—the wing you so neatly chewed up—operational in two weeks."

Wedge fell silent. *My people are far closer to battle-ready than Salm's. As always, the needs of the Rebellion outweigh the needs of its people—but this we knew going in.* "Admiral, can I at least run some astronav exercises to get my people working together when they come out of hyperspace?"

"By all means, Commander. In fact, I have the perfect assignment for you to use in that regard." Ackbar touched his datapad screen in two or three locations and the lights in his office dimmed. As they did so, a swirling disk of stars appeared suspended between ceiling and floor. It tipped up on edge and a green circle slowly zoomed in on Commenor, locating it just outside the dense Galactic Core. "I will be moving Rogue Squadron from here to Talasea in the Morobe system."

Even before another green circle could appear and pinpoint the new system, Wedge's eyes narrowed. "That's Coreward of here."

Ackbar nodded. "There has been much debate in the Provisional Council about how we should proceed in the war against the Empire. Much of what we have discussed has been paralleled in the conversations held by the vast majority of citizens, Rebel and Imperial alike."

"We're going after Coruscant? Imperial Center?"

Ackbar's chin fringe twitched. "We are given little choice, really, if we wish to overthrow the last remnants of the Empire—that goal being an exercise that may well take generations to complete, mind you. Many of the Moffs are adopting a wait-and-see attitude about the New Republic. Others, like Zsinj, have proclaimed themselves warlords and are doing what they can to consolidate their holdings with those of weaker neighbors. Any of these warlords could decide to turn his forces toward Coruscant and, by taking it, proclaim himself heir to Palpatine's throne."

"So we have to get there first."

"Or at least appear to be bent upon that goal, discouraging others from usurping our place in the galaxy." Salm tried to keep his voice even, but his desire to see the Rebels in power hurried his words. "These pretenders will learn that we have not labored so long just to give them an opportunity to rape and pillage whole systems."

Wedge agreed with the General's sentiment, but he knew breaking Coruscant open and taking the world would be far from simple. "It almost seems to me that an expedient alternative is to let some Moffs push themselves forward and have Iceheart deal with them."

"Your opinion was also heard in our councils. It was decided that leaving anyone to her tender mercies was a crime of grand proportion."

Ysanne Isard had risen to fill the power vacuum left by the Emperor's death. The daughter of Palpatine's last Internal Security Director, she came of age in the Emperor's court. Wedge had heard rumors that she had been the Emperor's lover for a time, but he had no way of verifying that story. What he did know was that she had betrayed her father to the Emperor, claiming he was going to defect to the Alliance. Her father was put to death immediately and it was said she triggered the blaster shot that killed him. The Emperor elevated her to replace her father and in his absence she did a remarkable job in holding the core of the Empire together.

The Mon Calamari warrior pointed to the galactic display. "From Talasea, Rogue Squadron will provide escort to ships pushing even deeper, setting up safe worlds and supply depots. You will be but one unit of many probing the central Imperial defenses."

"You want to see how hard Iceheart will hit back. Gauge strength based on speed and the nature of response?"

"Yes, as well as determining supply routes for possible disruption."

That made perfect sense to Wedge. Though space provided a limitless number of ways to get from one point to another, some simple basic rules governed how and where ships traveled. A ship attained speed and direction before jumping to light speed, and then maintained velocity in hyperspace. A ship moving fast enough could skirt phenomena like black holes, cutting parsecs off a more conservative and safer route.

Because objects with mass—stars, black holes, planets, and Imperial *Interdictor*-class cruisers—exerted influence over hyperspace, they had to be navigated around. Their presence could abort a hyperspace flight and, in the case of a black hole or a star, could spell disaster for any ship that traveled too close to them. Making a trip through hyperspace required precise calculations that took advantage of a ship's speed and mass to get it safely to its destination.

Because hazards to navigation diminish the number of calculable routes between places, trade tended to move through predictable corridors. Since traveling between stars was not inexpensive, merchants chose routes that allowed them to visit the most profitable systems along the way. These routes, including systems where ships leave hyperspace to change their travel vectors, were well known and piracy was not uncommon.

Disrupting Imperial supply routes would have a double effect for the Rebellion. Not only would it deprive Imperial garrisons of needed matériel for making war, but it would provide those same matériels to the Rebellion. While the New Republic and the Empire used different starfighters and capital ships, supplies like blasters, rations, and bacta could easily be employed by either side.

Wedge ran a hand along the edge of his unshaven jaw. "I understand the mission, and I appreciate the urgency for it. I do have a question, though."

Ackbar nodded. "Please, Commander."

"Rogue Squadron will do the job, but I was wondering if we were advanced for it because we're the unit that can do the job, or if we're being used as a symbol."

"Frankly asked." The Mon Cal's coloration brightened to

a salmon-pink on the dome of his head. "I argued against employing you this soon, but others aptly pointed out that if you were not put in place *now*, our operations might not have time to succeed. Rogue Squadron is a symbol in the Alliance and by positioning you to drive against the Empire we show we have made a commitment to liberating everyone in the Empire."

Wedge's mouth became dry. "But the only way our use can function as a symbol is if our use is well publicized. And that publicity must get out to the warlords you expect to be frightened off by our presence."

Ackbar's shoulders slumped every so slightly. "Your words are ripples of my discussions with the Council. Borsk Fey'lya is quite persuasive and he has Mon Mothma's ear in many things."

Wedge looked at Salm. "And you're worried about Tycho being a security risk!"

"Tycho Celchu did not risk his life to get the Alliance the location of the second Death Star."

"No, he only risked his life to destroy that Death Star."

Ackbar stepped between his subordinates. "Please, gentlemen, if I want petty bickering I can go to more Council meetings. It is important for you to air your grievances, but I will not have you fight and refight the same battles over and over again."

"Sorry, sir. My apologies, General."

"Accepted, Commander. I beg your pardon, Admiral."

Ackbar nodded slowly. "Commander Antilles, in an effort to minimize damage done by the public profile being given your mission, we will keep your destination secret. This means your pilots will not know where they will be stationed and they will only be told that they are going on an extended training exercise. Logistics and Supply Corps staffers have prepared lists of equipment that cover anything your unit might not carry with it on the trip. We have an Imperial shuttle that Captain Celchu will use to bring supplies on your journey."

"Nav data will be fed out to my pilots prior to each jump?"

"Exactly. You should give your flight leaders numerous routes for which they will compute navigation solutions, then you choose the appropriate one and have it communicated to your squadron at each change of course." The Mon Cal pointed at the representation of Talasea on the display and it zoomed in. "The Morobe system is a red-yellow binary and Talasea is the fourth planet in orbit around the yellow primary. The world is cool and moist with indigenous insect and reptilian life. There are mammals there as well—feral descendants of the animals brought in for an early farming colony. Your base is on the largest of the island continents. The atmosphere is thick, fog is common, but the world is safe."

"What happened to the farming colony?"

"Over the centuries most of the children emigrated to worlds where they could see the stars and didn't have to work so hard. The last group of them made the mistake of harboring a Jedi after the Clone Wars. Lord Vader destroyed them as an example. Settlement ruins are on your island but our people have reported there was nothing of interest left behind there."

"Home Sweet Home." Wedge smiled. "When are we to be on station?"

"A week from now."

"That's not much time."

"I know." Ackbar shrugged his shoulders. "It was all I could buy you. May the Force be with you, Commander Antilles. I hope you won't need it."

12

K IRTAN LOOR CLUTCHED his hands at the small of his back so they would stop trembling. "I am in your debt, Madam Director, and at your service."

"How kind of you to say so, Agent Loor." Ysanne Isard thumbed a small device. The lights in the room slowly brightened while shields descended over the windows. The rising illumination revealed the room to have a tall ceiling, with dark wooden beams curving up from the four corners to meet in an apex above the center of the floor. The walls and carpet shared the same deep blue, though a strip of carpet the same bright red as worn by Imperial Guards bordered the floor at the edge of the wall. In the far corner he saw a desk and chairs that were elegant yet far from ornate—in keeping with the general spartan nature of the room.

It struck him as odd that a large room that was all but empty could seem so decadently opulent. The only thing the room seemed rich in was wasted space. Then it struck him. *On a world that is so crowded with so many people, wasting this amount of space is the height of luxury.*

Isard's predatory pacing in the center of the room snatched his attention away from the subtle messages of the architecture and appointments. She wore an Admiral's uniform, complete with boots, jodhpurs, and a dress jacket, though the garments were red. A black armband circled the upper part of her left arm and the jacket bore no rank insignia or cylinders at all. Yet even without the external signs of rank, her intensity and the deliberation with which she moved radiated power.

Though he would have put her age at a dozen years older than his own, he found her attractive. Tall and slender, she wore her black hair long, and the white streaks descending from her temples made her seem more exotic than middle-aged. Her face appeared classically beautiful to him. A strong jaw, sharp cheekbones, a high forehead, a gracefully small nose, and large eyes were all the elements that most women would have killed to possess, or would have paid to have given to them.

Even as he catalogued all the bits and pieces of her that should have triggered some sort of lust in him—and the aura of power surrounding her was terribly exciting—fear overrode any glimmerings of carnal desire. When she looked at him, with dark brows accenting her eyes, he knew where the menace dwelt in her. One eye was ice-blue—as cold as Hoth and as cruel as a Hutt in a sporting mood. The other eye, the left one, was a molten red, with golden highlights that flashed with fiery determination. The left eye told him that any effort by him that was not fully devoted to her service would be met with the bloodless retribution promised by her cold right eye.

Kirtan shivered and she smiled.

"Agent Loor, your personal file has a number of interesting inputs. You are rated as having a visual memory retention rate of nearly one hundred percent."

He nodded. "If I read it or see it, I remember it."

"This can be a useful tool, if applied correctly." Isard's expression lost some of its hardness, though this in no way made Kirtan feel as if he were any safer. "In the report about Bastra you mentioned not using *skirtopanol* during his interrogation because he had been dosing himself with *lotiramine*. This was a precaution you learned to take because of a case on Corellia where doing just that had negative effects, yes?"

"The suspect died."

"Your report says you used the fact that the *lotiramine* masks the presence of *blastonecrosis* to confront Bastra with his own mortality. When that did not prove effective, you began conventional interrogation."

Kirtan nodded. "Sleep deprivation, protein starvation, coercive holographic and auditory illusions taken from what I knew of him. It all proved quite promising until the *blastonecrosis* began to make his whole body septic. I then initiated treatment for the condition."

"And this treatment killed him." Her eyes became mismatched slits. "Do you know why?"

"He had a reaction to the bacta used to treat him."

"Do you know why?"

Kirtan was about to offer her the explanation the Emdeefive droid had given him when Bastra died in the bacta tank, but he knew that she would not accept it. "I do not."

Isard hesitated for a second and Kirtan knew he had escaped punishment by being truthful. "What does ZX1449F mean to you, if anything?"

He instantly recognized the number, but held back his answer until he could sort out the details and put them in a coherent form. "That is the lot number of a batch of bacta that was contaminated by the Ashern rebels on Thyferra. It made its way to Imperial Center and infected nearly two million soldiers and citizens. It rendered them allergic to bacta." Kirtan frowned. "But Gil Bastra never was on Imperial Center."

"You do not know that for a fact. Perhaps he *was* here." She shook her head slowly. "It does not matter, because he could have run into that batch of bacta almost anywhere. It was ordered disposed of, and I saw to it that much of it was funneled to the black market. *That*, however, is not important. What is important is this: *Blastonecrosis* is a condition that affected roughly two percent of the people who were dosed with that particular lot of bacta. An Emdee droid would have inquired of a patient if he had been dosed with bacta in the last two years."

"But because I ordered treatment and didn't recognize the significance of the disease, Gil Bastra died."

"No!" Isard's eyes hardened. "Gil Bastra committed suicide."

"What?"

"His reports about you are in your file. Your slicer was able to excise them from the Corellian records, but not *my* records. A man is best evaluated by his enemies."

Kirtan's stomach slowly collapsed in on itself. "Those evaluations were prejudiced against me."

"Perhaps, but Bastra was amazingly perceptive. He wrote that you rely on your memory too much—trusting that retention of information can somehow compensate for an insufficient amount of analysis. Because you know so much—like the obscure fact about the fatal interaction of *lotiramine* and *skirtopanol*, you didn't look beyond Bastra's obvious line of defense to see how much deeper things had gone. If you had, you would have known about his possible bacta allergy and he might still be with us."

She slowly exhaled and tugged at the hem of her scarlet jacket. "Bastra knew you well enough to know he'd be dead soon. That gave him enough hope to feed you useless information. He held out as long as he could because he was playing for more time for his confederates to further sever ties with their past."

The Intelligence agent realized right then that the display of bravado Bastra had provided during their first meeting on the *Expeditious* had not been a false and hollow thing. Kirtan's face burned as he heard again everything Bastra had said, this time with the man's mocking tones intact and brutal. *What I had seen as my brilliance in ferreting out his errors had been him playing to my sense of superiority, leading me on after him like a nerf eager for slaughter. For two years I've been a fool.*

A revelation hit him strongly enough to make him tremble. "I've been fooled for even longer than the two years I've chased them down, haven't I?"

"Very good, Agent Loor." Isard's expression lightened slightly, as if she were on the verge of smiling, but she did not. "The responsibility for your deception is not wholly your own. Our training and indoctrination tends to make agents and soldiers believe in their own infallibility. This has proved to be a detriment to the Empire. You were not alone in falling prey to it—even the late Emperor had his blind spots."

Kirtan decided to avoid the invitation to question the Emperor's wisdom, or lack thereof, and instead followed up on his previous question. "The 'falling out' Bastra and Horn had was faked. I thought the reason for it was stupid, and assumed they were stupid for being at odds over it."

"This is even better, Agent Loor."

"I feel as if in realizing how badly I was used, I can see more depth to things."

"A blind spot is eliminated, letting you see more of what goes on around you." She ran an index finger along her jaw. "If you had read Bastra's evaluations of you instead of having them destroyed, you would have been able to come to this epiphany sooner."

He nodded confidently. "And I would have had them by now."

"And you were doing so well." Isard's face contorted into a snarl. "Don't backslide."

Kirtan blushed. "I'm sorry."

"More's the pity that you are not. You assume superiority where there is none." She folded her arms across her chest. "The Emperor likewise assumed that if he destroyed all the Jedi Knights that *his* Jedi Knight—and a handful of Force-trained special agents—would be sufficient to control the galaxy. He did not see—though I tried to warn him—the impossibility of proving that all the Jedi had been destroyed and that no other Jedi could rise against him. His obsession with the Jedi blinded him to the real threat posed by opposition leaders who are no more intelligent or remarkable than you are.

"As a result the Empire is falling apart and the Rebels are threatening to supplant the Empire with their own New Republic."

Kirtan nodded. "And you wish to restore the Empire."

"No." Her denial came cold enough to freeze carbonite. "My goal is to destroy the Rebellion. Imperial restoration can only be accomplished if the Rebels are eliminated and that can only be accomplished if we blunt their military, sorely stress their administration, and crush their spirits. These goals are interwoven and I have operatives, like you, working on all levels to bring my plans to fruition. Can you withstand the pressure of so vital a mission?"

Kirtan slowly nodded. "I can. How may I serve you?"

This time she did smile and Kirtan wished she had not. "Your target is to cut the heart out of the Rebellion. You will be the death of Rogue Squadron."

"Excuse me?" Kirtan frowned, wondering if he had heard her incorrectly. "I am no fighter pilot. I know nothing about Rogue Squadron."

"Ah, but you have the expertise I want and desire. You served on Corellia and the unit's commander is Corellian."

"Wedge Antilles, I know." Kirtan raised his hands. "But that is not to say I know *him*. I don't. I don't even know anything about the squadron."

"But you can learn."

"Yes, I can learn."

"And you shall learn." She nodded slowly toward him, then brought her head up abruptly. "You will also find you have a personal stake in this."

Kirtan aborted a wince. "Yes?"

"Our source within the squadron tells us that a friend of yours is a flight leader of remarkable skill."

One of Isard's earlier statements ran through his mind again. *A man is best evaluated by his enemies.* "Corran Horn."

"You see, you already know more about them than you thought you did." Ysanne Isard gave him an even stare. "Do you accept being the instrument of Rogue Squadron's destruction?"

"With pleasure, Madam Director." Kirtan smiled to himself. "With the utmost of pleasure indeed."

13

CORRAN FORCED HIMSELF to relax. Though Commander Antilles had cast the trip as an exercise in astronavigation and hyperspace jumping, deep down in his gut Corran thought a lot was being left unsaid. He was certain that if they had been going out on a formal patrol or escort mission Wedge would have told them so. The fact that he hadn't said anything conflicted with the mission requirement of packing up and stowing their personal gear in their X-wings. This left Corran thinking something more than an exercise was taking place.

Because of his training exercise scores, Corran had been promoted to Lieutenant and given the command of Three Flight. As an officer he had expected Wedge would trust him enough to let him know what was really going on. Even so, with his background he had great respect for security, and that put a brake on his uneasiness.

Those concerns don't matter. Getting through the drill does. Heading outbound from Folor's scarred grey surface, Corran flew lead for Rogue Squadron's Three Flight. Ooryl was back to starboard while Lujayne and Andoorni were off to port, similarly staggered front and back. Within the unit they had comm unit call signs of Rogue Nine through Twelve respectively, though for this exercise they would be operating as a semiindependent flight.

"Let's keep it close, Three Flight. Whistler will send you all our jump coordinates and speed parameters. Have your R2s double-check it, then lock the route." He checked his data-screen for the positions of the first two X-wing flights and Tycho Celchu bringing up the rear in a captured *Lambda*-class shuttle, *Forbidden*. "We follow One Flight on this leg, then Two Flight on the next one. After that we're leading, so let's be prepared."

The members of his flight signaled their readiness to jump, so Corran keyed his comlink over to the command frequency. "Three Flight ready to jump on your mark, Rogue One."

"Good. All flights, five seconds to mark."

With Wedge's reply Whistler began counting down for the five seconds. Corran watched the seconds click off the digital display. When it read 00:00 he engaged the X-wing's hyper-drive and sat back as the stars filled the viewscreen. Just as the color threatened to overwhelm him with its intensity, his snub-fighter leaped into hyperspace and moved beyond the ability of the light to abuse him.

The first leg was to take them about an hour and had them flying along the plane of the galactic dish, moving against the swirl of the galaxy itself. The course brought them in ever so slightly toward the Core, which was good because the data-bases containing information about navigation hazards got progressively better as they headed toward the Core.

And Coruscant.

Corran knew the Imperial capital was not their intended target—at least not for this flight—but he felt certain they would get there eventually. His more immediate concern, how-ever, was plotting the course for the third leg of the jump. While he had not been told their final destination, Com-mander Antilles had given him a list of twenty starting and ending points, and he had calculated the best courses he could see for making those jumps. The direction, speed, and duration of the first leg allowed him to eliminate all but two of the courses given to Rhysati for solution for the second leg and that narrowing down of ending points meant he only had two plans of his own to refine.

The first course of his, which would take the flight further along the disk and outside the most populated and advanced section of the galaxy, had been plotted pretty tightly. Several black hole clusters narrowed leeway as far as that course was concerned. He glanced at it again and decided it couldn't be refined any more.

"Whistler, bring up the course for the Morobe system."

The astromech droid hooted at him as numbers and graphics scrolled up on the screen.

"Yes, I know you did the best you could on this plotting. Freeze output there." He tapped the glass on the monitor. "At the Chorax system you have us skirting it by .25 parsecs. There's only one planetary mass in that system and the sun isn't that big. Since the Chorax system comes up so early in our leg, if you pull us another tenth of a parsec closer we should come out of hyperspace close enough to Morobe's habitable planets that we won't need to make an in-system jump to find gravity if we need it."

The astromech wailed at him.

Corran laughed. "You're correct, the data you used to compute the course indicated giving the system a wider berth, but that's because you're using *merchant* data and they're afraid of pirates and smugglers working the system. We're a squadron of X-wings. We have nothing to worry about."

With astronavigation and hyperspace jumping being so tricky a business, courses were plotted as often as not to brush by inhabited systems, even if they were inhabited by social misfits and undesirables. If a hyperdrive went out in midflight, or refused to engage after a course correction between jumps, being within hailing distance of worlds from which help could easily be summoned was a blessing. Trying to find a ship that had misjumped to some random location in the galaxy was

next to impossible—as all those who hunted after the fabled
Katana fleet had learned since its disappearance.

The first leg of the journey ended uneventfully. Two Flight,
with Rhysati flying lead, took over from One Flight and
brought the squadron around on its new heading. Just before
they made the jump to light speed, Commander Antilles shot
Corran the coordinates for the third jump.

"So, it's Morobe after all." Corran called the flight plan up
for one last time, ignoring Whistler's disgusted wail, and went
over it. The course appeared as nearly perfect as possible,
given the ships they were using. A ship capable of greater
speed could have trimmed even more distance off the run by
getting closer to the Chorax system. The greater speed would
allow it to resist the influence of the star's hyperspace mass
shadow. Without the resistance the ship would be dragged
back into realspace in the system and, more likely than not,
would be unable to escape the sun's gravitational grasp.

"Fortunately X-wings have enough power to get us
through." Corran glanced at his reactor fuel level readings.
The hyperdrives barely sipped fuel, while the sublight engines
gulped it. Running up to a lightspeed jump burned a lot of
fuel, though not as much as maneuvering through a dogfight,
but nothing they had done on their journey so far had been
that taxing on the engines or fuel supply.

*By the time we make my jump we'll still be at eighty-seven
percent of a full load. More than enough to make it to the
Morobe system and back home again.*

The squadron came out of hyperspace and Corran eased
his stick to port. "Squadron, come about to a heading of 230
degrees and depress 12 degrees. Flight plan on its way to you."
He pushed his stick forward until the X-wing's nose dipped
slightly. "Jump to light speed in five."

The jump to hyperspace for his leg seemed somehow
smoother and more effortless than the previous two. He knew
that sensation was an illusion and he wondered about it for a
moment or two. It occurred to him that the reason he was

more at ease with his jump was because he had been in control of it. Mistakes made in calculating a hyperspace jump could be fatal and Corran had never been good about putting responsibility for his life in another person's hands.

"But I don't have to worry about a mistake on this leg, since I did the calculations." A keening whistle from his astromech made him smile. "Fine. *You* did the calculations, with no help from me at all."

Whistler's hooting became more urgent. The astromech started scrolling sensor data over the cockpit screen, but none of it made sense to Corran. "There's another stellar mass in the Chorax system. That's impossible, unless . . ."

Before he could broadcast a warning to the other members of Rogue Squadron, the automatic safety cutout on the hyperdrive kicked in. The snubfighter burst through an incandescent white wall and into the outer reaches of the Chorax system.

And right into the middle of a running lightfight.

Corran threw the stick hard to port and pushed it forward. "Rogue Eleven, break up-star." He trusted Ooryl would follow him moving down and to the left, which cleared the way for the rest of the squadron to enter the system. "Lock S-foils into attack position."

He reached up and flipped the switch with his right hand. "Whistler, have you IDed those ships yet?"

The little droid shrieked urgently back at him.

"Anything you can give me." The big ship, Corran knew immediately, was an Imperial Interdictor cruiser. Its quartet of gravity well projectors allowed it to create a hyperspace shadow roughly equivalent to that of a fair-sized star. The Interdictors had proved effective in ambushing smugglers and pirates—and the presence of one of the six-hundred-meter-long triangular cruisers in the Chorax system was not wholly unexpected.

It hadn't been there to trap them, however. Running from the cruiser, which Whistler identified as the *Black Asp*, was a modified *Baudo*-class star yacht. About three times as long as his X-wing, the yacht had a broad, triangular shape to it that was softened by the gentle down-curve of the wings. It looked almost organic in origin, as if it should have been swimming through space instead of rocketing along on its twin engine's ion thrust.

Corran had seen plenty of modified yachts in his time with Corellian Security, and this one even looked vaguely familiar. Most often the yachts were modified to haul contraband. While he had no love for smugglers, he had even less for the Empire. *Enemy of my enemy is my friend.*

Whistler bleated sharply. Corran glanced at his screen, then keyed his comm. "TIEs. Squints—I mean Interceptors. Looks like a dozen of them." He looked up through his cockpit canopy and felt panic when he couldn't see with the naked eye what his instruments showed so plainly on his monitor. "Rogue One, what are your orders?"

Wedge's voice came back cool. "Engage them, but watch the cruiser's guns."

"I copy that. Rogue Ten, on me."

Ooryl double-clicked his comm, indicating understanding of Corran's order. That action seemed, like Commander Antilles's order, to betray no nervousness at all. The bitter taste slicking Corran's tongue surprised him because he'd flown against Imps in real life and endless simulator battles. He'd never been this bad before—nervous, yes, but not edging toward losing it.

Pull yourself together, Corran. His hand snaked up and touched the coin he wore. *Your squadron mates and the folks in that yacht are counting on you.*

Because the break they'd executed had taken them down, the Interdictor and its TIEs were coming in above their line of sight. Pulling back on his stick, Corran thumbed a switch that put all power in the forward shield.

"All power to forward shield, switching to proton torpedoes." A targeting box appeared on the heads-up display and Corran maneuvered the X-wing to drop the sight on the lead

Interceptor. The range indicator dropped numbers and digits as the X-wing closed on the Imperial fighter.

Easy, easy. Let yourself go, just like in training. He nudged the flight stick to the left and framed the incoming squint perfectly. The box went red and a strident beep filled the cockpit. Corran hit the trigger and the first torpedo sped in at its target.

Another torpedo streaked past him and raced toward an Interceptor. Both of the Imperial ships broke hard, but Ooryl's torpedo reduced his target to fire and scrap metal. Corran's missile missed his intended target, so he switched back to lasers and evened his shields out.

"Good shot, Ten. Scratch one squint!" Fingering the coin he wore beneath his flight suit, Corran swallowed hard, then keyed his comm unit. "Cover me, I'm going after mine."

Ratcheting the throttle up to full, Corran swooped the X-wing up on its port stabilizers, then corkscrewed down through a roll that brought him out on the Interceptor's tail. He linked his offside lasers so they fired two at a time and triggered a burst that burned armor from the Interceptor's bent wings, but failed to destroy it.

The squint drifted to the left, then came up in a roll that brought it around and over Corran's line of flight. *If he continues that roll, I'll overshoot him and he'll end up on my tail.* Corran pushed the stick to the left, making a wide turn to port that opened distance from the Interceptor, but still let the Imperial ship slip in behind him.

"Ooryl cannot get him, Nine."

"I know, Ten, not to worry."

Keeping one eye on the rangefinder, Corran kept his X-wing on the long loop. *Come on, you know you want me. If you had proton torps I'd be freespace ions, but you don't!* "Yes, Whistler, I know what I'm doing." Feeling some of his confidence returning, he shrugged. "At least I'm pretty sure I do."

The Interceptor pilot came up fast and flew in a straight line to get quickly to the same point in space where Corran could get slowly with his great loop. Seeing his prey close in fast, Corran centered and hauled back on his stick, tightening his turn considerably and jamming his body down in his seat.

The X-wing shot across the TIE's line of flight barely twenty meters behind the ball-and-wing craft. Yanking the stick to starboard, Corran rolled the fighter 180 degrees. He pulled the stick back to his breastbone, bringing the X-wing's nose up in another turn that reversed his previous course. Leveling the fighter out, he sailed in right on the TIE's tail—his long S-turn having allowed him to let it overshoot him by a fair distance.

A lethal distance. Corran lined the Interceptor up in the sights and blew it apart with two laser blasts. As pieces of the disintegrating ship whirled past him, he keyed his comm unit. "Ten, report."

"Cover Ten. Heading 90 degrees."

"I have your wing, Ten." Guiding the stick to the right he saw Ooryl's X-wing shoot ahead of him and into the ion wake of an Interceptor. The Gand's first shot struck sparks and armor from the fighter's central ball. *One more, Ooryl, and you have him!*

"Nine and Ten, break hard port! Get out of there!"

Ooryl's compliance with Wedge's order came immediately. His sharp turn took him across Corran's line of flight, forcing Corran to yank back on his stick and roll to starboard. He leveled out and started a turn to port, but Whistler's shrill whine filled the cockpit. The stick slammed back into Corran's chest, pinning him in his ejection chair as the droid brought the X-wing's nose up. Red crept into the corners of Corran's vision and the stick's pressure against his breastbone made breathing hard.

The vast expanse of the *Black Asp*'s bulk filled his viewscreen. *By all the souls of Alderaan!* A blue bolt of ion-cannon energy sizzled in and battered down the X-wing's shields. Whistler yowled and the stick went slack for a moment, allowing Corran to act.

He slapped the stick hard to port, bringing the X-wing up in a snap-roll that put the Interdictor beneath his feet. He started to pull back on the stick, to show the cruiser his stern and rocket full away from it, but he felt a tingle run through him as another ion blast partially caught the starboard stabilizer foils. The astromech's screams died abruptly and Corran was slammed against the left side of the cockpit.

Even without seeing the stars swirling around him like dust motes in a Tatooine sand tornado, he knew what had happened. The ion blast had knocked out his starboard sublight engines, leaving the pair on the port side of the ship operating at full power and without competition. This put him into a flat spin, with his stern chasing his nose, completely out of control.

But at least I'm hard to hit.

The ion blast, in addition to shutting Whistler off, had killed all his cockpit electronics and acceleration compensator. The only thing he could do, he knew, was to shut his engines down and go for a restart. Until he had some sort of power, *or until that cruiser slaps a tractor beam on me*, the X-wing would spin like a gyroscope. *Gotta power down.*

That was easier said than done. The emergency shutdown panel had been placed on the right side of the cockpit. Mashed against the opposite side by centrifugal force, it remained just beyond the reach of his outstretched fingers. Gritting his teeth, Corran levered himself off the cockpit wall with his left elbow and tried to hit the panel.

The stick slammed him back into place pinning him. Corran caught it with his right hand and tried to pry it forward. Pain radiated out from where the stick had jammed his medallion into his breastbone. *So much for that being terribly lucky.* The stick made it painful to breathe, adding one more unnecessary complication to his predicament.

A sense of urgency boiled up in him, overriding panic instead of boosting it. "Let. Me. Go!" He redoubled his effort to move the stick. It resisted at first, but Corran refused to be daunted. Concentrating with every fiber of his being, he pushed and the stick yielded. Centimeter by centimeter he forced it away from himself. *Yes, I'm free.*

Corran shoved the stick as far as it would go to the left, then used it to pull himself away from the port side of the cockpit. With his left hand on the top of the stick, he brought his elbow up, inch by inch, scraping it past various switches and knobs that had died with the rest of the ship. When his arm came up above the top of the stick, he lunged to the right, letting the stick slip beneath his armpit, and hit the shutdown panel with his right elbow.

The thrumming of the port engines died, leaving him alone with the sound of his own breathing in the cockpit. The ship still spun and showed no signs of slowing, but without friction or other resistance in the vacuum of space, it would continue to spin forever. Corran relaxed slightly in relief at cutting the engines off, and was rewarded by being bashed back against the port side of the cockpit. His helmet hit a hard stanchion, leaving him a touch dazed. Along with the spin-induced nausea, it made him hope someone *would* shoot him and end his misery.

That flash of despair lasted for a moment until another spark of pain spread out from his breastbone. *Kill us they might, but I'm not going to make it easy for them.* He slid his right hand across his chest, past the medallion and his left shoulder, and tipped three switches up. A bit farther along, he lifted a plasteel plate that covered a recessed red button, then punched that button and hoped for the best.

What he wanted to hear was the return of the engine thrum, but what he got was nothing. *Ignition circuits must be fried. There has to be something else I can do.* Without the engines, he had no power. The primary power cells and the reserve power cells for the lasers probably had enough energy in them to at least give him communications, attitude control jets, and limited sensors, but getting at it from inside the cockpit presented him a problem. *It's not like I can just land this monster and do some manual cross-wiring.*

Corran laughed aloud. "No, but I *can* manually land this thing."

He brought his left leg up and hooked a small tab on the cockpit wall with his heel. It flipped out a small bar that sat in a groove. Corran centered his foot on the bar and pumped it down. It came back up beneath his foot and he pushed it down again and again.

From the nose of the fighter he heard metallic pops and clicks. The bar was connected to a small generator that put out enough current to deploy the fighter's landing gear. Extending them did nothing to affect the spin, but the payoff Corran hoped for wouldn't come until the gear locked into place.

With a shudder he felt throughout the ship, the landing gear snapped into their fully deployed positions. The monitor in the cockpit lit up again and the stick began to feel alive in his left hand. Laughing aloud, Corran took the stick in his right hand and tugged it over to the starboard side of the cockpit. The spin began to slow.

He fingered the medallion with his left hand. Because no-power landings would be seriously harmful to most lifeforms, extending the landing gear on the fighter opened a circuit that allowed the primary and reserve power cells to drive the S-foil impeller jets for simple maneuvering and to kick in the repulsorlift drives. The power cell tap tended to be used primarily by techs for moving the ships around in repair and maintenance facilities, because running the fusion engines up for full maneuvering power in enclosed places is generally considered harmful to most living creatures.

Corran tried his restart again, with the same results as before. Diagnostics told him he'd lost one of the starboard Incom phi-inverted lateral stabilizers and the engine just wouldn't start with power levels fluctuating all over the place. *No engines, but maybe I have sensors and communication.*

He brought those systems on-line but got nothing from sensors and a lot of static covering voices on the comm. "This is Rogue Nine. I could use some help here."

Waiting for a reply, he flipped on the proton torpedo launch circuits. Without sensors, his ability to hit anything was nil, but at least he could get a shot or two off. *And I'm probably going to need it.*

Above and to starboard he saw the *Black Asp.* Rogue Squadron had regrouped to form a screen between the Interdictor and the smuggler. He couldn't tell how many Rogues were left, and the occasional glint of sunlight off TIE Interceptors' Quadanium solar panels told him a few of the squints still existed, but there seemed to be far more Rogues than there were TIEs, and that was a good sign.

The Interdictor ventured in close to the fight, its lasers and ion cannons blazing away with green and blue bolts. The energy streams filled space with tangles and knots as the gunners tried to target the elusive X-wings. Though he had been hit fairly easily, he knew his collision avoidance maneuver had kept him in one place long enough for the gunners to hit him, and that the only reason they hadn't was because he'd ventured far closer to the Interdictor than he should have.

He half heard a command crackle in over the comm, but he couldn't make sense of it. Out beyond his ship's nose he saw a series of proton torpedo launches from the X-wings. They came in at the large ship from a multitude of angles. While the power in each of the torpedoes was hardly a threat to the Interdictor, the combined damage of a volley like that was enough to batter down its forward shield. The concave energy wall glowed a sickly yellow before it imploded and Corran thought he saw several torpedoes explode against the Interdictory hull.

"Yeah, Rogues!" Corran laughed aloud. "Oh, Whistler, you're going to be sorry you missed this."

The Interdictor brought its nose up to pull the vulnerable bow away from the X-wings. It could repair the damaged shield by pumping more energy into it, but that would require the shutting down of the gravity well projectors. That, in turn, would allow the X-wings and the yacht to escape, turning the whole engagement into a draw. *If you don't count the vaped squints.*

The big ship executed a roll that combined with the loop to reverse the cruiser's course. "He's running. They've driven it off! Yes!"

His jubilance died as he realized that meant the cruiser was heading back in his direction, and the surviving TIE Interceptors were flying along in its wake like fledgling mynocks chasing a slow freighter. "Whistler, you're lucky you're not seeing this. It'll be ugly."

"Rogue Nine, do you copy?"

"I copy." Corran didn't immediately recognize the voice. "I'm on partial power. Whistler's dead and I'm blinder than a Y-wing."

"This is Rogue Null. You have squints coming your way. I mark two."

"Oh, more good news. Thanks, Null. Be my guest." Corran craned his neck to see where Tycho and the shuttle were, but he couldn't see it. "I'm naked here, so please get them off me."

"Not possible, Nine. Clear your sensors to 354.3."

"What?" Corran frowned as he saw the TIE getting closer. "I'm a sitting Hutt here."

"So you have indicated, Nine. Clear your sensors."

Corran punched the frequency code into the keypad under his left hand. "Done, Null."

"Happy hunting, Nine."

Corran's targeting display came back alive and his monitor showed targeting telemetry data from the *Forbidden*. Beyond the display Corran saw the TIEs juke to try to shuck the shuttle, but Tycho managed to keep his sights locked on the lead Interceptor, despite flying a slower, less agile craft.

The HUD went red and Corran hummed an imitation of Whistler's target tone. He squeezed the trigger on his stick twice, sending two torpedoes streaking out at the lead Interceptor. "Lead's gone, Null, give me number two."

The display flickered, then Corran nudged the X-wing around and launched two more missiles at the Interceptor boxed in red on his tactical display. So intent had the Imperial pilots been on losing the shuttle behind them, they had no chance to react to the missiles shooting in at them.

The first pilot died without being able to execute even the most basic of evasive maneuvers. The proton torpedoes blasted through the cockpit ball, ripping the craft to bits and igniting the ion engine fuel into a swollen ball of fire. The second set of missiles lanced through that fireball and blew one wing off their target. That squint careened away, somersaulting and twisting wildly through space. Bits and pieces of it flew off into the void, then it exploded brilliantly, blotting out the image of the Interdictor going to light speed.

"Great shooting, Nine."

Corran shook his head. "Greater flying, Null. I did the easy part."

"The kills are yours, Corran. Three confirmed—the best today."

The Corellian pilot shrugged. "Maybe today wasn't so unlucky after all."

"Glad you feel that way, Nine."

"Why, Captain?"

"You had the most kills. When we get where we're going, all the drinks are on you."

14

CORRAN HAPPILY POPPED the cockpit canopy seals on his X-wing after the yacht killed its maneuvering jets and the thick fog descended over the ships. At Chorax the yacht had come back and picked him up, using landing claws to capture the X-wing's landing gear. This left his ship clinging to the dorsal hull of the yacht like a dauber-wasp on the back of a bird. He didn't particularly like the situation, but it was a long walk from Chorax to Talasea in the Morobe sector and he liked the idea of leaving his fighter and Whistler behind even less than being carried into port.

He'd shut down all systems except for life support, so he had no communication with the yacht's pilot. Corran had been impressed with how smooth the landing was at the primitive spaceport. A dense fog hid almost everything, and what little he could see in the backwash of maneuvering jets seemed overgrown with dark green ivy. He saw dim shapes that resembled buildings, but most of them were covered with sufficient plant life that he wondered if the New Republic hadn't *grown* the base instead of building it.

He stood and stretched, then doffed his helmet and gloves and put them on the seat of his command couch. Vaulting from the cockpit, he landed heavily on the yacht's hull. *More gravity here than I expected.* Corran looked for a ladder to let himself down, but couldn't find one. Instead he walked along the curved wing and jumped down to the ground from the lowest point.

His knees buckled with the impact and he went down on all fours. "Either there *is* more gravity here than I expect, or that fight really wrung it out of me." As he straightened up and scraped mud from the knees of his red jumpsuit, he knew both of his assumptions were probably correct. *I'm lucky to be alive.*

A hatch opened with a hiss on the underside of the yacht and a boarding ramp slowly descended. Corran turned toward the ramp, wiping his hands off on his thighs. A Sullustan descended first, followed by an insectoid maintenance droid of Verpine manufacture. Corran nodded a salute at them, but they ignored him as they waited at the base of the ramp.

Corran assumed they were waiting for the captain of the ship—a person he had assumed to be male since very few of the independent smugglers were female. As the captain descended the ramp, Corran had his assumption exploded by his first glimpse of shapely long legs encased in boots and a form-fitting, dark blue jumpsuit. A gunbelt encircled her slender waist and long black hair fell to midback. She grabbed the ramp's forward support and swung around to face him in a carefree manner, and Corran was very taken with the smile lighting up her beautiful face.

He wiped his hands again on his jumpsuit. "Thanks for the ride back here."

She returned his smile as she shortened the distance between them. "Thanks for the save back there."

"My pleasure." He extended his hand to her. "I'm Corran Horn."

Something dangerous flashed through her brown eyes. "Are you any relation to Hal Horn?"

"He is . . . was my father. Why?"

"Because he hounded my father and had him sent to Kessel." She poked him in the chest, right where the flight stick had bruised him. "If I'd known who you were I'd have left you there."

Corran recoiled in surprise and for the first time saw the patch on the shoulder of her jumpsuit. It showed a Corellian sea-ray that had a bar where its eyes should have been. Because of the polarized thread used to embroider the black eye-bar, a little vertical white line passed through it, running side to side. *I know that crest—I knew this ship was familiar!* "This is the *Pulsar Skate*. If I'd known Booster Terrik was bringing me in, I'd have *stayed* out there."

"I can see you two have already met?"

Corran whirled around and quickly saluted Wedge. "Yes, sir."

The woman planted her fists on her narrow hips. "You didn't tell me who this pilot was because you knew I'd not have transported him, right?"

Wedge smiled easily. "I *suspected* there might have been some friction. How have you been, Mirax?"

"Paying for spare parts and fuel, Wedge." Mirax kissed Wedge on the cheek. "I've also been collecting stories about you from all over the galaxy. Your parents would have been proud."

Wedge nodded solemnly. "I'd like to hope so."

Corran's green eyes narrowed. "Sir, you realize the *Pulsar Skate* is a ship with a well-documented history of smuggling and that Booster Terrik is one of the more notorious smugglers who ever flew out of Corellia."

Corran's commander smiled. "I know all about the *Skate*, Lieutenant Horn. I was about fifteen years old when I helped replace the fusion chamber on that starboard engine. Mirax's father regularly used my parents' fueling station for repairs and refueling."

"But, Booster used to smuggle glit . . ."

Wedge cut him off with a scowl. "He also helped me track

down the pirates who destroyed the fueling station and killed my parents—pirates who destroyed it while fleeing Corellian Security and whom CorSec never caught."

"And that makes it all right?"

"No, Lieutenant, it just puts things in perspective." Wedge gave Mirax a hug around her shoulders. "Mirax isn't her father. Ever since he retired, she's been running a lot of supplies for the Alliance." He then turned and gave her a hard stare. "And Corran isn't his father, either. If he'd not made some last-minute adjustments to the course we were taking, we'd not have ended up in the Chorax system to save you."

Mirax glanced down at the ground. The anger in her expression eased slightly, aided and abetted by the color rising to her cheeks. "You're right, Wedge. I'm still bleeding off the stress of being jumped like that. The *Black Asp* came out of hyperspace right on my exit vector and gravved me in place. Someone sold me out."

Corran snorted. "No honor among thieves."

Wedge frowned at him. "More like Imperial credits buying more loyalty than the promise of Alliance credits."

Mirax shrugged her shoulders. "Some of us find those promises more safe than letting the Empire get their hooks into us." She extended her hand to Corran. "I want to apologize for my behavior, Lieutenant."

Corran shook her hand. "Apology accepted, and I apologize as well. I'm still rattled after getting fired upon by a cruiser. My R2 is down and I'm a bit worried . . ."

She smiled and some of the tension in his chest eased. "I understand. If I can help in any way."

"I appreciate the offer." Corran looked over at Wedge. "I should probably see to getting the X-wing unloaded and Whistler's getting repaired."

"In a moment, Lieutenant, I want to speak with you first." He jerked a thumb at the *Pulsar Skate*. "Mirax, do you know where your shipment was going?"

"I was supposed to rendezvous with a ship for transfer or

coordinates." She shrugged. "According to the manifest it was a lot of basic stuff for setting up a base. You could probably use most of it here."

"I don't doubt it." Wedge fished a cylindrical comlink from a pocket of his flight suit and flicked it on with his thumb. "Antilles to Emtrey."

"Emtrey here, sir. I've been trying to reach you since we landed . . ."

Wedge rolled his eyes skyward. "I'm sure you have. No time to talk now. I need you to get a salvage crew with a lift crane over here to get Horn's X-wing and R2 unit. You also need to get the ship's manifest from the *Pulsar Skate*. Find out where that shipment of supplies was going and see if you can't arrange for what we need to remain here."

"Yes, sir. As I was saying, sir . . ."

"Antilles out." Wedge turned the comlink off and shoved it deep into his pocket again. "Tycho said he didn't have any trouble with the droid on the trip out here, but why not I can't imagine."

Mirax arched an eyebrow at Wedge. "So you send him out here to talk with me?"

"Believe me, he's not the worst protocol droid on our side, not by a long shot." Wedge winked at her. "Just give him the datacard, retreat to the *Skate*, and threaten to shoot him if he comes aboard."

"Make sure you shoot twice."

"I'll remember that, Lieutenant." Mirax sighed. "Wouldn't it be easier if I just downloaded the manifest to your central computer?"

Wedge winced. "Right now he *is* our central computer."

"True, this isn't exactly Coruscant Rimward. It makes the Outlier worlds look civilized."

"I'm glad you understand." Wedge tossed her an abbreviated salute. "We will talk more later, Mirax. Lieutenant, if you'll follow me."

STAR WARS: ROGUE SQUADRON

Corran fell in step with his commander. "You wanted to say something to me, sir?"

"It's never again going to be quite like that first time." Wedge smiled. "Taking on fighters is one thing, but fighting in the shadow of a capital ship, that's enough to get to anyone." *Maybe that was the difference between this time and the others.* "I appreciate the perspective, sir."

"I also wanted to congratulate you for the way you recovered yourself out there. You were in a very difficult position and you got yourself out of it rather handily."

"It was more luck than anything else, sir. If that second blast had caught me square on, I would have been on that Interdictor and Talasea would be under assault."

"Call it whatever you like, Mr. Horn, you did well." Wedge shook his head. "Getting those two Interceptors after your systems were down was very impressive."

"As I told Captain Celchu, he did the hard part, I just pulled the trigger. If they'd broken his lock, I would never have hit them." The younger man frowned. "That brings me to a question, sir."

"Yes?"

Corran stopped and grey mist swirled between the two of them. "Captain Celchu was able to get a torpedo lock on those two Interceptors. Why didn't he shoot them himself?"

Wedge hesitated, instantly putting Corran on his guard. "The *Forbidden* is being modified for training purposes to simulate the profile of an assault gunboat. While it has the sensor package for concussion missiles, it doesn't carry any and couldn't shoot them if it did."

"Then why didn't he take them with his lasers? *Lambda*-class shuttles have lasers."

Wedge's reply came tight and laced with frustration. "The *Forbidden* does not."

Corran glanced down at the ground. "Commander, I saw Alliance Security escorting Captain Celchu around on Folor.

He's never had fully powered weapons on his Z-95 Head-hunter and you're telling me his shuttle had the lasers removed despite our travel through contested sectors of the Core? What's going on here?"

Wedge took a deep breath, then let it out slowly. "Have you told anyone else about the security escorts?"

"No, I . . ."

"Lieutenant, I want you to understand two things: First, I have the utmost trust and confidence in Captain Celchu. I have no reservations—none—about him, his service, his skills, or his commitment to the Alliance. Do you understand?"

"Yes, sir."

"Second, the matter to which you allude is a private one, concerning Captain Celchu alone. Because of it he has agreed to have limitations placed upon himself. Discussion of it is up to him, but both he and I believe bringing the issue up will only serve as a distraction to the squadron."

As if not knowing will not *distract me.* "Does this mean I can't ask him about it?"

Wedge folded his arms across his chest. "Corran, you were a law enforcement officer, so suspicion comes easily to you and trust does not. Ask yourself this question—if you could trust him to help shoot those two Interceptors, don't you think you can trust him all the way around? He didn't have to save you, but he did, knowing full well he was as dead as you were if the Interceptors turned on him."

"I see your point, sir." Corran nodded slowly. "Doesn't mean I may not ask, unless you order me not to, but I won't tell anyone else about it. And if the Captain refuses to answer my questions, I'll have to let it go, I guess. He saved my life. I owe him that much at least."

"Good."

"One more thing, sir."

"Yes, Lieutenant?"

Corran looked back toward the *Pulsar Skate*. "Back there

you mentioned that Corellian Security never caught the pirates who destroyed the Gus Treta station and killed your parents. My father got that case and worked hard on it. He didn't give up, he just didn't have your connections on the other side of the law." He swallowed hard. "I think, if my father had known about Booster Terrik helping you find them, he'd have cut him some slack and Booster wouldn't have done time in the spice mines."

Wedge reached out and slapped Corran lightly on the shoulder. "Booster clearly wasn't a Jedi, nor was he Sithspawn, and the time on Kessel got him out of the business. In a more candid moment, Mirax will probably admit the five years he spent in the dark was good for her father."

"I doubt she and I will share many *candid moments*, sir."

"Really? I think you two would get along quite well together."

"Our fathers openly hated each other, sir. Not the best foundation for a lasting friendship." Corran shook his head. "Besides, she's your friend . . ."

"But *just* a friend. More like a sister, since she stayed with us when her father was on dangerous runs."

Like a "sister" to the commanding officer, now there's incentive to get to know her. Corran smiled. "I'll take that under advisement, sir."

"Do that, Lieutenant. Having friends never hurts."

"Sir, sir!"

Both men looked up as Emtrey materialized out of the Talasean fog. *His dark color on this dim world—I don't envy the Commander trying to avoid dealing with the droid here.*

Wedge looked over at Corran and in an instant Corran knew they had been thinking the same thing. "Emtrey, good, I'll leave you to discuss the condition of his X-wing with Lieutenant Horn. Find me after that." Corran read an "if you can" in Wedge's smile as the leader of Rogue Squadron turned and walked away.

"As you wish, sir." The droid aborted a salute, then shuffled his feet around to face Corran. "About your X-wing. Sir, the damage is not that extensive."

"What about Whistler?"

"Ah, your R2 unit." The droid canted his clamshell head to the side ever so slightly. "Your Whistler will be fine. He shut himself down before the ion blast could do it—this by virtue of the near miss. I must say, sir, that I thought . . ."

"Yes, Emtrey, I appreciate that, but he'll be fine?"

"I should think so, sir, though it was a near thing."

"Near thing?" Corran asked, instantly regretting his invitation to Emtrey to explain.

"Well, sir, a power coupling was negatively polarized, precluding an auto-restart. Many would consider this a minor problem. The coupling will have to undergo thermo-reconditioning, but we have the facilities for that here since the colonists used to use agrodroids and this world has some fierce thunderstorms in the rainy season."

"Fascinating, really, Emtrey." Corran smiled easily. "You should ask Commander Antilles to let you brief the squadron on the climatology of this world." *Use me to escape the droid, will you?* "Demand it, really."

"Demand? Oh, my."

"Insist absolutely. Fifteen or twenty minutes of reasoning with him should convince him of its necessity." Corran nodded solemnly. "Now, about my X-wing. I blew a phi-inverted lateral stabilizer."

"That is correct, sir." Emtrey handed Corran a datapad. "I have downloaded the requisition forms for the part into this datapad. If you will fill them out, along with an incident report, I'll get Captain Celchu to review the forms and get Commander Antilles to sign off on them. We'll relay the information back to General Salm. We should have the part in a month or two at the most."

Corran's jaw dropped. "A month or two?"

"Provided they have the part and you don't get pushed back in the priority list."

"Priority list?"

"Yes, sir. You brought your X-wing with you and have never formally signed it over to the Alliance. To prevent individuals from using the Alliance as a maintenance depot, regulation 119432, subsection 5, paragraph 3 states 'Non-Alliance craft that are allied with or working under the command of an Alliance leader will be provided with parts and maintenance at the discretion of the commanding officer and/or the senior officer in charge of parts and supply for said craft. If said craft are damaged in any actions that were not planned or sanctioned in advance (see Sec. 12, para 7 for a list of exceptions), all damage is considered non-Alliance related and to be repaired only after authorized repairs to sanction-action-damaged craft have been completed.' Now the exceptions . . ."

"Hold it, Emtrey." Corran massaged his temples. "Is this the only way to get a new stabilizer?"

"Sir, I am conversant in the regulations of over six million different military and paramilitary organizations and there is nothing that . . ."

The pilot rapped a knuckle against the droid's black breastplate and that stopped the litany. "Emtrey, there have to be more phi-inverted lateral stabilizers in existence than we have in all the Alliance ships and stores. Z-95 Headhunters and Incom T-47 Airspeeders both use the part. There's probably a wrecked T-47 out here somewhere, in fact."

"There might be, sir." The droid rotated his head around in a circle to scan the whole area. "I'll prepare the forms requesting a general survey of the local sector."

Dropping the datapad, Corran reached out and grabbed the droid's head in both hands. He pulled Emtrey's facial opening toward him. "You're missing my point, Emtrey. Forms and requests will take time. Without that part, I can't fly. If I can't fly, I'll be stuck in this fog and on the ground and that will make life miserable for me and I don't want that. There are parts to be had . . ."

"And regulations to be observed."

"Regulations be damned!"

The droid pulled back a step and the condensation on his head let him slip away. "Sir, of all the members of Rogue Squadron, I would have thought *you* would appreciate adherence to regulations!"

Corran sighed. "Regulations have their place, but not when they hurt. Can't you just scrounge the part or something?"

The droid froze in position, the flashing light in his eyes being the only indication he was still working. The pilot luxuriated in the cessation of the droid's chatter, but it went on far longer than he'd heard before in the droid's presence. The eye-flashes became asynchronous, and this worried Corran a bit.

"Emtrey?"

The droid's eyes went dark for a moment, then his limbs and head jerked as if he had been struck by lightning.

"Emtrey?"

The eyes lit up again and Corran would have sworn they were a bit brighter. "Scrounging protocol engaged, sir." The droid bent down and smoothly retrieved the datapad. He glanced at the datapad, then shook his head. "I'll shoot a requisition up through channels, but I think I can find you something sooner than anything we get from Command. You're a pilot, and my job is to keep you flying. Consider it done."

Even the voice sounded different to Corran. "Emtrey, are you all right? Is the moisture getting to you?"

"I'm fine, sir. The moisture is no problem." One eye-light flashed on and off. "Touch of a virus, maybe, but nothing to worry about."

Did that droid just wink at me? "Are you sure?"

"Yes, sir." The droid saluted smartly. "If you have nothing further, sir, I'll get on this right away. And I'll have your gear sent around to your billet, sir."

"Thank you, Emtrey." Corran returned the salute. "Dismissed."

The droid turned sharply on his heel and walked away. Corran stared after him, then shivered.

"Ooryl did not think it was so cold here."

Corran spun and saw the grey-green-colored Gand standing behind him. *Another who blends in with this fog.* "Not cold, Ooryl, just fatigue. It's been a long day, full of surprises."

"Qrygg wanted to apologize for abandoning you." The Gand Findsman clutched his hands together penitently. "Qrygg was too busy dodging Interceptors on Qrygg's tail to see you were not there."

"You followed orders, just as I would have."

"Qrygg would give you a sign of Qrygg's sorrow."

Corran threw an arm around the Gand's exoskeletal shoulders. "I tell you what. Guide me back to my billet and let me get a solid eight hours of sleep, and we'll call it even. Will that assuage your Gand guilt?"

"Ooryl finds this acceptable."

"Good." Corran swept his left hand through the fog. "Lead on, Ooryl, and this time I promise I'll follow right behind you."

15

THE OFFICIOUS, BULBOUS officer stared laser bolts at Kirtan Loor. "I can see your orders are all properly drawn, but I have never appreciated Intelligence operatives meddling in fleet affairs."

"I appreciate your concern, Admiral Devlia, as well as your willingness to return from retirement to Imperial service, but Imperial security must take precedence at this time which, I believe you would agree, is most critical."

The little man brushed his grey moustache with a finger and his expression eased. "Just so we understand each other."

"Of course." Kirtan cared little for the Admiral's concerns, but the Interdictor cruiser *Black Asp* was part of Devlia's command. Its report of being ambushed by a squadron it identified as Rogue Squadron had brought Kirtan all the way from Coruscant to Vladet in the Rachuk system to speak with the *Black Asp*'s Captain Uwlla Iillor. He suspected a great chunk of Devlia's discomfort with his visit came because it forced the Admiral to deal with Iillor, one of the women who had risen to command to fill the gaps left in the Imperial Navy after the Endor debacle.

The Intelligence agent found himself anxious to meet Cap-

tain Iillor. He had read her file, as well as that of Admiral
Devlia and most of the senior command staff during his journey out from Coruscant. The files were a welcome departure
from tracking the various rumors about Rogue Squadron, but
her record especially intrigued him. In studying it he caught
hints of how forceful she had to have been to have risen in the
Imperial Navy as far as she got before the Emperor's death.

Devlia stood and smoothed his grey jacket over his round
belly. "And I'll tell you here and now that I'll stop any questions I think are off the mark."

"I understand that, sir." *Dream all you want, Admiral.*

Devlia led Kirtan from his spacious office down a narrow
hallway in the mansion that housed the command staff. The
Admiral preceded him into a small study that had been converted into a conference room through the addition of a big
table that dominated the room. Boxes full of datacards still
lined the built-in shelves and Kirtan judged it a larger library
than he would have expected to find on a planet like Vladet.

Devlia secured himself the chair at the head of the table,
then waved a hand toward the woman standing at the far end.
"Captain Iillor, this is Agent Kirtan Loor. He wants to ask you
some questions about the ambush."

"Yes, sir." The brown-haired woman looked at Kirtan
without a trace of the hunted look most people acquired when
told Intelligence wanted to question them. "I'll help if I am
able, Agent Loor."

Her voice had an edge to it that backed up the challenge in
her dark eyes. Kirtan assumed her lack of fear came after years
of being on the Navy's NhM track—Non-huMan. The Empire's bias against aliens and women reached an unprecedented
level of refinement in the Imperial Navy. Iillor had been sent to
serve under Colonel Thrawn and a host of other alien superior officers before she had been given a ship of her own. She
would have been stuck on that *Carrack*-class cruiser had not
the defeat at Endor made the need for competent officers so
great that the command staff's survivors reevaluated person-

nel and awarded commands according to some semblance of merit.

"I'm sure you will, Captain. I would like any reports you have filed about this action, as well as any holographic records of it, along with any communication intercepts." He walked around to the left side of the table, then turned back toward Devlia. "With the Admiral's permission, of course."

The old man nodded.

"Very well. If you don't mind, please tell me what happened."

"May I sit?"

"By all means." Kirtan smiled but remained standing. "Make yourself comfortable."

Captain Iillor sat and turned her chair so she gave Devlia her profile. "We had information that a smuggler running supplies to the Rebels was expected in the Chorax system at a particular time, and would be departing after picking up some supplies there. I sent a shuttle in to monitor the smuggler's situation while I put the *Black Asp* on the fringe of the system. When the *Pulsar Skate* started to head out of the system, I jumped the *Black Asp* in and brought my G7-x gravjectors up."

Kirtan frowned. "Intra-system jumping is a rather unusual tactic, isn't it?"

Iillor shook her head. "I've seen it used with great success out in the Unknown Sector. It worked at Chorax, too, because the *Skate* had no idea where we came from. It took them nearly six seconds to begin evasive maneuvers. I took the liberty of closing to use our ion cannons on the *Skate* during that time. Then a dozen X-wings came into the system.

"I deployed my Interceptor squadron, but none of the pilots are Academy material. They would have been eaten up, so I brought the *Black Asp* in and managed to disable one X-wing. By then, however, the remainder of them screened the *Skate* and hit my forward shield with a volley of proton torpedoes. The shield came down and I lost two laser batteries. I had to choose between reinforcing my shields or keeping the gravjectors operational. I made the former choice, recovered five Interceptors, and went to light speed."

Devlia leaned forward. "They were waiting for the *Black Asp*. They came out of hyperspace right on top of her."

Kirtan stroked his chin. "I don't see that one thing establishes the other. I see no evidence of an ambush."

Iillor's head came up. "That's what I've been telling the Admiral."

"You're both blind."

"I think, sir, with all due respect, you are making unwarranted assumptions." Kirtan began to pace around the edge of the table, passing behind the Admiral and back again. "Interdictor cruisers are *designed* to pull ships out of hyperspace. Of course, only where the route is known in advance can they be positioned in such a way that doing that is possible. In this case, since the *Black Asp* was in the Chorax system specifically to prevent a ship from *entering* hyperspace, you have chosen to discard one of its primary functions."

"Preposterous!"

Which is precisely the kind of mistake I would have made previously. Kirtan allowed himself a slight smile. "Check your thinking. If you chose to ambush an Interdictor cruiser, would you do so with a single squadron of X-wings?"

Devlia's face reddened. "Perhaps *I* would not, but *I* have training most Rebel officers do not."

"Granted, sir, yet the Rebels are not without wise leadership." Kirtan left allusions to Yavin and Endor unvoiced, but he saw by Devlia's expression the man had caught them anyway. "I might ask why the Rebels would waste their time attacking an Interdictor cruiser at all? No disrespect intended to you, Captain Iillor, or your ship, but the action of Interdictors is hardly crippling to the Rebellion. Our main battle fleets are garrisoning key worlds, like Corellia and Kuat, so even predation on Interdictors is unlikely to draw them out."

Iillor did not smile, but her nod was not as stiff as before.

"My assumption was that we had suffered the misfortune of pulling a convoy out of hyperspace, but the Admiral found such coincidence unlikely."

Kirtan smiled. "The Admiral, despite this misjudgment, is formidable enough that I should think the Rebels utter fools to operate in his command sector."

Devlia had opened his mouth to protest the first half of Kirtan's statement. The second half, which Kirtan had added as a sop to the man's vanity, killed the Admiral's comment and clicked his jaw shut.

The Intelligence agent again focused on Captain Iillor. "How did you identify them as Rogue Squadron?"

"Communication intercepts used 'Rogue' call signs. Visual data is not very good, but there is a unique unit crest painted on the S-foils. Preliminary searches correlate it with a crest said to be that of Rogue Squadron. Also the *Pulsar Skate* is a ship with Corellian connections, just like Wedge Antilles. And the pilots were hot—they took off seven of my Interceptors, with the last two falling to an X-wing that was dead."

Devlia leaned back. "Interesting, but circumstantial, as I am sure Agent Loor will agree."

"Circumstantial, yes, but persuasive." Everything she had said about the squadron that attacked the *Black Asp* did seem to point to Rogue Squadron. Kirtan doubted any other unit in the Rebellion would sport Rogue call signs, and the crest data would have to be checked. Still and all it was not conclusive. *It is, however, a start.*

"Captain, did your shuttle stay in-system and monitor the squadron for outbound vector and speed?"

Iillor scowled. "No, and Lieutenant Potin has been repri-manded for fleeing when not threatened. I do have entry vector and velocity data, and it is triangulated with the data from the shuttle."

"That's something, then."

"I will make certain you have it in time for your return to

Imperial Center, Agent Loor." Devlia stood. "Assuming you want nothing else here."

"I *do* want to speak to the pilots who flew against the X-wings as well as review any data recorded from the Interceptors that were destroyed."

"I'll see the interviews are arranged right away."

"Take your time, Admiral. The next two or three days will be soon enough."

The old man's expression soured. "Staying that long are you?"

"Longer, I suspect." Kirtan smiled broadly for the Admiral. "If Rogue Squadron is operating in this area, and I believe it is, I'll leave only after we've found them and destroyed them, and not a moment sooner."

16

IN ONLY TWO WEEKS, while the official request for a new phi-inverted lateral stabilizer languished in red-tape limbo, Emtrey found a pair of phi-inverted lateral stabilizers that the *Pulsar Skate* dropped off on its second run to Talasea. The Rogues' Verpine tech used the new parts to replace the older, damaged parts. In synchronizing them, Zraii managed to smooth things out so Corran noticed a five percent increase in power at full throttle, with a three percent reduction in fuel consumption.

Corran throttled back slightly, matching his speed to that of Ooryl. "Three Flight to lead—we're all in formation, sir."

"I copy, Nine. Stand by."

"As ordered, Lead." Corran smiled broadly in spite of himself. Back when he was with CorSec he had hated escort duty, but after two weeks on the ground he would have volunteered to go after Death Stars even if they were strung around a system like pearls on a necklace. Even during his time on the run from Corellia he'd managed to fly at least once a week, even though that was well outside the profile of the identity Gil Bastra had created for him.

He turned and looked back at Whistler. "Has Emtrey come up with any information based on his analysis of the ID Gil made up for me?"

A mournful hoot came in reply as the word "No" appeared on his display.

"Yeah, I don't like the idea of never seeing Gil again, either." He glanced at his sensor monitor. "Twelve, trim it up a bit there, you're slipping behind. Trouble?"

"No difficulty. Compliance."

"Good. Keep close. This mission should be easy enough that a nerf-herder could do it, but the other side will be shooting back, so we have to be careful."

Despite the light tone in his voice he knew things could get nasty. Alliance operatives had been conducting surveys of Core worlds to assess the political climate and determine the strength of Imperial forces protecting them. On one run back toward their operations base—known to the pilots only as "Black Curs Base," with no location specified for security reasons—they ran into the Strike cruiser *Havoc*. The Rebels went to ground on a small jungle planet in the Hensara system. They sank their ship, a modified Imperial Customs frigate, in a deep lake and lacked the equipment needed to repair damage that would allow them to move it again.

The *Havoc* grounded an Imperial walker and two scouts along with two platoons of stormtroopers. While their reported progress in searching out the Rebels had been slow, they started relatively close to the lake, so the ship's discovery was a matter of time. The Alliance had reconciled itself to the loss of the ship and had intended a covert extraction of the operatives, then the *Havoc* left the system, providing a window for repair and escape of the frigate *Battle of Yavin*.

Wedge sent the squadron the coordinates for the trip to the Hensara system. To cover the location of their base, the journey would be undertaken in three parts. The first jump, a short one, would take them to their first transit point, an uninhabited star system not far from the Morobe system. From there they would jump back out Rimward to the second transit system and back in to the Hensara system.

While the multiple jumps and changes of direction would add hours to the flight time, obscuring their point of origin was vital. The Alliance had learned that spreading out its forces meant it was all but impossible for the Empire to land a deathblow to the Rebellion. But for the efforts of a courageous few on Hoth, the Rebellion's headquarters would have been destroyed and the Rebellion along with it. Without taking precautions, they would pinpoint the location of their base and invite retaliation.

They made the first jump on Wedge's mark and came out in the fringes of the transit system all in one piece. The X-wings maneuvered around to the exit vector quickly, then had to mark time as the *Skate* and the Corellian corvette *Eridain* came about. Corran nudged his throttle back a notch, shortening the gap between him and the Gand.

The larger ships reported they were ready, so the whole convoy shot into hyperspace and came out in the second transit system intact. The course adjustment there was not as radical as the one from the first system, so they headed out quickly and arrived in the Hensara system just outside the gravitational tug of the third planet.

Corran heard Tycho's voice come through the comm. "Rogue Leader, Captain Afyon reports a clean scan of the system. You're clear for your run."

"Copy, Control. Three Flight, you fly CAP. Two and One, on me."

Corran let a low snarl resound in his throat. Flying Combat Aerospace Patrol meant his flight would remain at the edge of Hensara III's atmosphere against the possible incursion of any Imperial forces. The other eight fighters in the squadron were going to escort the *Skate* down and strafe the Imperial mudbugs and the durasteel dogs they had hunting Dirk Harkness and his compatriots on the planet. Strafing runs against ground troops—even stormtroopers—wasn't much in the action department, but it was better than skipping across atmosphere, shooting at nothing.

He shrugged. "Maybe slagging an AT-AT will sweeten Jace's disposition."

Whistler gave a stuttered chirp that sounded as close as the droid could manage to a laugh.

Corran matched it with some laughter of his own. "Jace clearly figures that because his name rhymes with 'ace' he should be one. He can't understand why TIE pilots don't just line up for him to vape them all in one pass."

Tycho's urgent comm call cut off Whistler's trilled comment. "Control to all Rogues. We have a Strike cruiser that just jumped in-system. Profile matches *Havoc*, but two fighter bays have been added. TIEs are launching."

"Three Flight, lock S-foils in attack position." Corran glanced at his sensor display. "Come to a heading of 272 degrees."

"Control here. I have thirty-six, repeat, three-six TIEs launched. Six Interceptors, six bombers, and twenty-four, repeat, two-four starfighters. *Eridain* beginning evasive maneuvers. Wait. Confirm, bombers are heading to ground."

"We copy, Control." Wedge's voice came through strong despite being nibbled upon by static. "Rogues Three and Four, the bombers are yours. The rest are ours. Keep them off the *Eridain*."

"As ordered, Rogue Leader." Corran shoved his throttle full forward. "Go all out, Three Flight. Into the middle, shoot at anything that isn't an X-wing. Call if you need help."

Under normal circumstances Corran knew that flying into the teeth of an enemy formation would have been suicidal, but odds of thirty-to-four weren't all that conducive to long-term survival anyway. Since running wasn't an option, doing what the enemy didn't expect would buy him a second or two of surprise, and that would keep him alive just that much longer.

Hauling back on his stick and canting it ever so slightly to the side, he brought the X-wing up into a lopsided corkscrew maneuver. While the jerky motion of the ship's nose meant he didn't have a flame's chance on Hoth of hitting anything, he was that much harder to hit himself. He pumped more power into his shields, then shot through a flurry of laser bolts before he penetrated the Imperial formation.

He hauled back on his stick, killing the weaving flight and arrowing his ship up into a flight of TIEs. He lined one starfighter up in his sights and let it have a quad blast of lasers. As the eyeball exploded, he cut the stick hard to starboard, then rolled out into a level line that continued his original course, with a half-kilometer cut to the right thrown in. As the TIE formation collapsed in after him, he cruised out the other side of it.

Inverting his X-wing, he pulled the fighter into a loop that brought him around in the TIEs' wake, though slightly below their formation. Keeping the nose up, he headed back in again. He picked up on a TIE Interceptor that had broken right while its wingmate had broken left. Ooryl continued on the tail of the latter squint. The other Interceptor tightened its turn into a teardrop loop designed to bring it onto the Gand's aft.

Corran's quad lasers shredded the Interceptor's starboard wing and blew apart one of the twin ion engines. The other, operating at full power, sent the squint spinning away. Corran winced in sympathy with the pilot, then drove into the middle of the TIE formation.

The X-wings plunging and wheeling through the middle of the TIEs had an unanticipated advantage in that they had a very high target-to-comrade ratio to shoot at. Moreover, because the X-wings had shields, even a shot taken in haste at another Rogue would not likely prove fatal. The same could not be said of the TIEs—one burst from their lasers could cripple or kill a fellow pilot.

Corran snapped a shot off at one starfighter and watched it disintegrate. A warning warble from Whistler and he mashed his right foot down on the etheric rudder pedal. The X-wing's stern slewed around to the left, swinging him out of an Interceptor's line of fire while pointing his nose right at the ship as it sailed past him. He punched the X-wing over ninety degrees, hauled back on the stick, then completed the inversion and dove down onto the Interceptor's tail. He sent kilojoules of scarlet energy into the ball cockpit and watched the craft explode.

"Nine, break left."

Without thinking Corran slammed the stick hard to port and caught the green highlights of laser bolts shooting through where he had just been. More red laser fire chased back along those same lines and something exploded out there.

"Thanks, Commander."

"No problem, Nine."

Corran eased his stick forward and dove down to stay clear of the mass of starfighters. With the arrival of the rest of the squadron he knew there was no way he could track all the ships and sort friend from foe. Even as he came back up he saw less laser fire permeating the cloud of fighters than there had been when the forces were less evenly matched. "So much twisting and turning going on in there, no one can find a target and stick with it long enough to dust it."

Pulling up to continue his loop around the fringe of the battle he saw one X-wing break free with a starfighter on its tail. His sensors told him Gavin was at the stick of the Alliance ship. Measuring Gavin's line, Corran rolled his craft and looped down at a tangent to it. "Rogue Five, break hard right."

Gavin's fighter rolled up on its starboard S-foil crisply and pulled away at an angle that cast doubt on the existence of inertia. The starfighter following him tried to imitate his maneuver, but neither the pilot nor craft were up to it. As the TIE rolled, Corran swooped and fired. His quad-lasers burst the spherical pod like a bubble, sending the hexagonal wings slicing off through space.

Before he could even smile, his X-wing jolted forward. His instruments indicated heavy damage to his aft shield. "Whistler, get me a lock on that TIE."

Corran inverted and dove, then pulled back on the stick to power up through a teardrop and onto the TIE's tail. Instead of being where he expected it, the TIE, an Interceptor, showed up off his port S-foil, going away at a right angle to his course. Corran stood on his left rudder, then did a snap-roll that gave him a view of the planet above his head and the Interceptor racing away from him.

Just as he feared it was going to run far enough for Tycho or someone else on the *Eridain* to blast it, the Interceptor pulled its own loop planetward and started back at him. *Head to head—he knows what he's doing.* As Wedge and Tycho had pointed out countless times in training, the majority of kills took place in head-to-head engagements. *But so do I.*

"Watch our tail, Whistler." Corran kicked his shields full forward and drove in straight at the Interceptor. The range-finder on the targeting monitor scrolled numbers off with blurred speed. His crosshairs went green and he fired, but couldn't see how much damage he'd done because of the light show produced by the Interceptor's lasers eating away at his shields.

Corran stabbed the right rudder pedal with his foot, swinging the ship around a full 180 degrees. Punching his throttle to full, he killed his momentum, then dropped the engines to zero thrust. With his thumb he popped his weapons control over to proton torpedoes and got a solid tone when he trapped the fleeing Interceptor in the targeting box. His finger tightened once on the trigger and a single torpedo shot away on a jet of blue flame.

The torpedo caught up with the Interceptor quickly enough, but the TIE pilot, confirming his possession of the skill Corran had willingly granted him before, juked his Interceptor out of its path at the last second. Unfortunately for him, his maneuvering and run at Corran had taken him to the outer edge of Hensara's atmosphere. While not particularly dense, impact with it at the speed the Interceptor was traveling proved devastating. The starboard wing shattered and the Interceptor ricocheted away in a wobbly somersault.

"Control, this is *Skate*. We're on our way back up. We have company that wants to go home."

"Good job, *Skate*. Rogue Leader, mission accomplished."

"I heard that, Control. Rogues, regroup for egress."

Corran smiled as he heard Gavin's voice over the comm. "Leader, there are two getting away."

"Let them go, Five. Flight Leaders, check your flights."

"Whistler, give me feeds on my people." A tracking chart replaced the targeting data on Corran's screen. *Nine, Ten, Eleven, and Twelve*. "Three Flight is all here."

"Control to Rogue Leader, I have a dozen X-wings in-system, two Interceptors on recovery vectors, and two deployed shuttles on pilot recovery missions."

Corran clapped his hands. "We didn't lose *anyone?*"

"Are you complaining, Nine?"

"No, sir, Commander, not at all. It's just . . ."

"Yes, Nine?"

"This is Rogue Squadron. I thought most of the pilots didn't survive Rogue missions."

"That was when there was still an Emperor, Nine." The grim tone in Wedge's voice gave way to one somewhat lighter. "I guess that's the difference. Let's head home, Rogues. This is one victory we can celebrate without having to toast dead comrades and I, for one, like the change."

WEDGE SAT WITH his back against the thick wall of the Grand Room in what had once been Talasea's Planetary Governor's Palace. The title sounded much more important than the building and room it described. Built with heavy beams made of the dark native wood and plaster slathered over wooden slats, it reminded him of the sorts of reconstructions he'd seen in museums on Corellia. *This is about as primitive as it gets.*

The incongruity struck him as he watched his pilots sitting around a couple of central tables, using their hands to describe the twists and turns they went through in what they had taken to calling the Rout of Hensara. They could have downloaded their sensor packets and played them out on the wide-screen holoviewer in the corner, but that device remained black. By telling the stories themselves they shared not only what they did—which the sensor data would have shown in exacting detail—but how they felt about it.

And in doing that they'll know they're all the same. Wedge tipped his chair back against the wall. He glanced at two Alderaanians who shared his table with him. "They did a good job out there today."

Tycho smiled broadly. "They did better than good—they were spectacular. We recorded thirty-four kills out of a possible thirty-six with no losses. If I hadn't been there, I'd think it was propaganda."

Afyon looked up from a barely touched tankard of the local lum equivalent. "You know as well as I do, gentlemen, they were awfully lucky. They may be the hottest pilots going, but vaping TIEs won't Coruscant take. That's going to take an operation that will need more than snubby jocks to make it go."

Wedge lowered his lum mug. "Captain, I've been in this Rebellion for as long as you have. I remember the fighting at Endor and I know the *Eridain* fought hard."

"I appreciate that, Commander Antilles, but it was *you* who got paraded around the New Republic as the hero who saved the Rebellion."

Tycho's blue eyes narrowed. "He did blow the Death Star, you realize, and survived the previous Death Star run."

"I know, and I know you were there, too." Afyon sat back and frowned. "Look, I'm not saying you don't deserve your recognition, and I'm not saying your people don't deserve their little party here. Strapping yourself into a fighter isn't the easiest thing to do, and more fighter pilots die than do the folks I have crewing with me, but *our* contribution to this Rebellion is just as important as yours is."

Wedge nodded slowly. "I know that, Captain, and if the *Eridain* hadn't been there today to make the *Havoc* think twice about closing with us, we would have been blind-jumping out of the system."

Afyon shook his head. "Don't take me for a stormie, Antilles, I don't believe everything I'm told. You'd have gone in after the *Havoc* itself. What's a Strike cruiser to a crew that turned two Death Stars into black holes?"

The Corellian brought his chair down onto all four legs. "The New Republic might promote me and this squadron as immortal and immune to danger, but I know better than that.

Two of us, just *two*, survived Yavin. A half dozen survived Hoth and just four of us lived through Endor. As far as I'm concerned the Death Stars lived up to their names.

"Well *now*, this squadron has to live up to its name. The New Republic is using us as a symbol because it's easier to blind people to the blood-cost of war when you get to celebrate the heroic efforts of a half-dozen people. Luke Skywalker is easy to admire and want to follow. Han Solo is a man who rose from nothing to become a hero and consort with royalty. Me, I'm the quintessential soldier who does his job very well. But what is that job? Two things: neutralizing Imperials and, the part I take most seriously, keeping my people alive."

Wedge raked fingers back through his brown hair. "It doesn't matter if we were good or lucky out there today—and I'd rather the former than trust in the latter. What does matter is that we all survived, and that's as close to a miracle as I ever expect to see in my lifetime. The key thing to remember is that I can't trust in our luck or skill. I can't allow myself to believe we were that much better than the opposition and I can't let my people believe it. If they do, they'll die taking chances they should never take."

Afyon sucked on his teeth for a second. "You're right. I guess I just remember the Clone Wars and how the 'hero' labels were handed out. You'd think a dozen Jedi and two dozen snubby jocks won the whole thing. Even all the years I spend pulling for peace—same as most of the rest of the folks on Alderaan—never dulled that feeling of injustice I had concerning credit for the war. Weird, eh, wanting peace enough to agree to disarmament of my home planet, yet still burning about getting credit for my part in a war?"

The other Alderaanian at the table shook his head. "One of the problems we all have is that we try to think of ourselves in general terms, and that smoothes over some of the inconsistencies that make us who we are. We see all Imperials as rancors and they see all of us as nerfs. The very fact that we see them as a united front is ridiculous, just the same as we're not all united—as this discussion proves."

Afyon smiled. "I've not heard that kind of philosophy since, you know, our world . . ."

Tycho nodded solemnly and squeezed Afyon's shoulder with his right hand. "I *do* know." He smiled and looked over at the knot of pilots in the center of the room. "I'm afraid this group does not inspire that much philosophy. I appreciate being able to share some with another Alderaanian."

Wedge glanced at his pilots, then tipped his chair back up against the wall as the Twi'lek stood. Nawara Ven flipped one of his brain tails around and over his shoulder as if it were a scarf, then stumbled slightly. Wedge wasn't sure if it was the cavalier way he tossed his brain tails around or the drink that made the pilot stumble. The lum brewed up by the ground crew had the potency of Corellian brandy and the piquant bouquet—according to Gavin—of a Tatooine dewback in heat.

Nawara remained almost completely upright as he wove his way through tables to where Wedge sat. "Forgive me, noble leaders, but we require your esteemed personages to act as a tribunal to adjudicate a question." The Twi'lek pressed a hand to his own chest. "Owing to my legal background, I have been appointed a neutral advocate to present the cases to you."

Wedge couldn't keep a smile from his face. "Please proceed, Counselor."

"Thank you, sir." Nawara turned back toward the other pilots. "First we have the case of the *worst* pilot in the unit. May I present Gavin Darklighter, who won this award by virtue of the fact of not getting *anything* out there today."

Easier to read than the scowl on Gavin's face was the open relief on the faces of Lujayne Forge and Peshk Vri'syk. Wedge knew the award had to sting Gavin badly, but he was young. The rest of the squadron had been willing to cut him a lot of slack because of his youth, but that latitude would last only so long. In Wedge's opinion Gavin wasn't the worst pilot by far, but his lack of kills allowed his squadron mates to rib him a little.

Nawara gestured at Gavin. "The accused will stand."

Gavin remained seated.

Bror Jace grabbed him by the shoulder of his flight suit and hauled him up out of his seat. "Here he is, the *worst* we have. Just like the TIE pilots, he got *zero* kills."

The edge in Jace's voice provoked a snarl from Gavin's wingmate, Shiel. Color flooded Gavin's face and muscles bunched at his jaw as he ground his teeth. Jace laughed and tugged on Gavin's shoulder, like a puppeteer manipulating a marionette.

The Twi'lek, seemingly oblivious to Gavin's discomfort, smiled at the tribunal. "We have determined there should be a punishment of some sort, to encourage an improvement in performance."

Wedge turned his head to face the other two members of the tribunal. "Ideas, gentlemen?"

Tycho held a finger up. "Strikes me that apprenticing Gavin to the *best* pilot, having him run errands and the like for him, might provide the perfect situation for Gavin to learn how to be better."

I like that, Tycho. Corran won't be too hard on him and the added responsibility will give Corran something to think about other than your situation. Wedge nodded. "I think that is a good idea. Captain Afyon?"

"Sure. I know I'd love to have an aide to draft the performance reports for the *Eridain*."

Captain Afyon's suggestion brought a groan from the squadron, so Wedge catalogued the threat of report preparation for future disciplinary use. "I believe, Counselor, you have your judgment rendered."

The Twi'lek bowed and straightened up slowly, then turned back to his compatriots. "Gavin Darklighter, you are sentenced to serve as aide to the best pilot in the squadron until such time as you are no longer judged the worst pilot."

Bror smiled broadly and gave Gavin's flight suit one last tug. "Good, you can start your service by getting me more lum."

Wedge frowned. "How is it that you, Mr. Jace, are considered the best pilot? You only had five and Mr. Horn had six. If we average them over the last two engagements, then Mr. Horn has four and a half, with you, Mr. Qrygg, and me each at two and a half. You fare no better when we total them."

Nawara smiled, flashing pointy peg-teeth. "You have hit upon the crux of the matter, sir. Mr. Jace argues that percentages tell the true story. He killed five of the six bombers he faced, meaning he downed eighty-five percent of the TIEs he engaged."

Gavin sat down and snarled, "And they were big, lumbering bombers—no one could have missed them."

The Twi'lek clucked at Gavin, then continued his explanation. "Mr. Horn, on the other hand, shot only six of thirty, giving him a kill percentage of twenty percent."

Wedge shook his head. "This is ridiculous. Percentages have no place in this."

"If you don't mind, sir"—Corran stood up and glared over at Bror—"I'm willing to let things be figured by percentages."

"Go head, Mr. Horn."

Corran folded his arms across his chest. "You want a real contest, Jace?"

The Thyferran raised his head and glared down at the shorter man. "It's an easy offer to be made by the man in the lead."

"I'm willing to make it even, and I'll even concede this round to you—declaring you the best pilot until our next mission." Corran opened his arms and rested his right hand on Gavin's shoulder. "What I'm willing to do is average Gavin's kills in with mine. The one he got at Chorax adds to my nine, then we split that in half. That puts us even at an average of five kills. You and I are both aces and now so is he."

"Don't do this, Corran."

The small man winked down at Gavin. "I trust you, kid. You'll do fine."

"We start even?" the Thyferran asked.

Corran nodded. "We go straight kills from here on out, or average them, your choice."

Bror raised a blond eyebrow. "You are still willing to average the kid's kills in with yours?"

The Corellian nodded again and patted Gavin's shoulder. "You willing to take the challenge?"

Wedge watched conflicting emotions ripple over Bror Jace's face. He clearly wanted to go one-on-one with Corran, to prove he was better free and clear, yet the rules Corran was offering him played in his favor. Any kill Corran got would only count half. Unless Corran excelled—killing two for Bror's one—or Gavin started on a tear, Bror would win easily. The difference between their skill levels was not significant enough to give Corran a real chance of winning.

Bror's blue eyes thinned to arctic slits. "We'll average things, just to keep Gavin in the game, but you and I can go head-to-head whenever I choose."

"I wouldn't have it any other way."

"And you and I, because we *did* have the most kills at Hensara, will share the best pilot crown until our next outing."

Corran smiled. "Done."

Wedge nodded once to Corran, then looked up at the Twi'lek. "So, by this settlement, Bror and Corran are co-best pilots, and Gavin has five kills, correct, Counselor?"

The Twi'lek nodded. "If you so agree, members of the tribunal."

The three judges agreed and Nawara smiled. "It is done, then."

"And the worst pilot is still apprenticed to the best pilot?"

Nawara nodded. "The worst pilot is still bound by that agreement."

"Good." Wedge stood and slapped the Twi'lek on the back.

"Then since Gavin has five kills to his credit, that makes *you*, with only *one* kill, the worst pilot."

Nawara's pasty complexion became ghostlike. "No appeal?"

Wedge smiled. "To you there probably is not, but the idea of a lawyer getting the sentence instead of his client has some *appeal* to me."

The Twi'lek frowned and caressed one of his brain tails. "Perhaps it *is* true that a lawyer who has himself as a client is a fool."

"Which is why you're a pilot now, Mr. Ven." Wedge laughed lightly. "Consider your sentence suspended, at least for the duration of this celebration. Today we proved how good we can be—tomorrow we go back to training to make sure we know *how* we did what we did, so we can continue doing it in the future."

KIRTAN LOOR SCRATCHED at the reddish raw patch of flesh behind his right ear. Rachuk roseola was a virus, he was told, that got to everyone who came to the world. Scratching it didn't appear to make it worse, and nothing but time made it better. It annoyed him because he found it distracting, and at this late stage in his calculations, distraction was the last thing he needed.

He pored over the data from Hensara again, correlating figures and sensor tracks with known performance parameters for X-wings. All the ships in the squadron appeared to be operating within two standard deviations of the mean of Rebel specifications. This told him that the ships were in good repair, which meant the Rebels were expending considerable resources on that squadron to keep the ships working.

That little factoid combined with the spectacular kill ratio led him to believe Rogue Squadron had been at Hensara. Visuals were of generally poor quality, but crests and fighters appeared to match those images recorded by the *Black Asp*, confirming the squadron's presence at Chorax as well. He had no objective confirmation about the squadron being Rogue Squadron, but one communications intercept had included the name "Wedge" and Kirtan thought he heard some faint trace of Corran Horn's voice in other messages. The end-for-end swapping maneuver that led to the damaging of one Interceptor had been vintage Horn, providing Loor all the evidence he needed to label the X-wings as Rogue Squadron.

Admiral Devlia had not been convinced, but he had agreed to send units out to find the squadron's base, *if* Kirtan could isolate it. Admiral Devlia had made the offer in a voice that suggested providing such information would be impossible.

It *should* have been impossible, and for most people it would have been. However, Kirtan Loor remembered a wealth of things that might be trivia to others, but proved to be useful to the search for the Rogues' base. He had to make a few assumptions about them and the force they arrived with, but his calculations could be run with a number of variables factored in, then all that data could be correlated with known system locations and Rebel preferences for bases.

Because several of the X-wings entered the atmosphere of Hensara III, they left significant traces of ionized fuel in the atmosphere. Spectral analysis of those trails provided an amount of thrust that gave Kirtan an indication of the quantity of fuel used per second of operation with sublight engines. This proved consistent with the known specifications of the X-wing. Since the performance of sublight engines had not been modified, he assumed the hyperspace engines were similarly standard.

The forces on the ground on Hensara provided some basic entry vector and velocity data for the Rebel force. Back-plotting was not terribly difficult and suggested to Kirtan that the force had begun their last jump from the Darek system. Using the fuel consumption figures for an X-wing's hyperspace engine, he was able to subtract from the weight of the ship the appropriate amount of fuel.

Thrust output, vector, and velocity data provided him with changing weights for the X-wings as they burned up fuel in their flight. The ending weight and fuel consumption seemed consistent for known performance profiles. Precluding refueling stops along the way, the amount of fuel he calculated for them determined the range to their base.

He had to assume, of course, that they had started with a full load of fuel, and the same had to be assumed for the *Pulsar Skate* and *Eridain*, as well as the *Lambda*-class shuttle at Chorax. Working out the fuel consumption and range limits for those ships had shown them to be far more fit for distance travel than the X-wings, as would be expected of larger ships, but few ships like to travel beyond range of their escorts.

Even limiting the trip to the range of the X-wings gave each flight the capability of traveling a considerable distance. He further reduced the range by assuming the Rebels would keep sufficient fuel in the X-wings for a dogfight or rearguard action to allow the other ships to escape. This cut the range roughly in half, and when given a spherical plot on a map of the galaxy for each of the squadron's sightings, the spheres intersected in a relatively small area of space.

Five hundred known systems existed in that overlapping slice of space. Kirtan discarded all truly loyal worlds from the list. He also removed the openly rebellious worlds because Intelligence had enough spies of their own in hotbeds of Rebel support to inform him if Rogue Squadron had been seen. While the Alliance was willing to draw volunteers and support from such worlds, they chose not to jeopardize them by basing operations on them.

Inhospitable worlds were shuffled onto a secondary list. While the base on Hoth had shown the Rebels were willing to hide almost anywhere, post-invasion breakdowns and evaluations of the Hoth operation showed the Rebels had trouble modifying equipment to work there. In fact, had the Rebels not been reeling from the defeat at Derra IV, they probably would have bypassed Hoth altogether.

Being the opportunists they were, the Rebels did tend to prefer worlds that already had structures on them that could be converted into installations. It appeared that the more benign and abandoned the world seemed, the more likely the Rebellion was to choose it as a base. Kirtan doubted the Rebels themselves realized they had this predilection for taking over ruins for their own use, and he imagined it had to do with a subconscious desire to renew the Old Republic. The very thing that drove them against the Empire demanded they embrace things older than the Empire to give their movement a legitimacy it lacked itself.

The final list of primary worlds contained only ten names on it. Kirtan subjected this list to the final selection process— one that had come to him as inspiration upon waking from a dream that included visions of Ysanne Isard metamorphosing into a scarlet ghost of Darth Vader.

The X-wings, in arriving at Chorax, had not expected to be dragged out of hyperspace. That meant their entry vector, if drawn as a line through space, would point out their *intended* destination. Kirtan plotted that line through his data model and then asked the computer to sort the candidate worlds according to their proximity to any world on that line.

One world had a perfect correlation with that line. Kirtan smiled. "Talasea, in the Morobe system." He downloaded his result into his personal datapad and headed off for Admiral Devlia's office. "We know where you are, Rogue Squadron. Now we will crush you."

18

C ORRAN'S EYES SNAPPED OPEN. He knew from the chill of the air and the deep darkness that it was still night. The fog drifting in through the window of the small cottage seemed to amplify the silence of the night. He knew that nothing, not light nor sound had awakened him, but he also knew something was wrong.

He glanced over at Ooryl's cot and saw it was empty. That wasn't much of a surprise. He'd learned that Gands needed only a fraction of the sleep humans did and appeared to be able to store it up for times when they could not sleep. He would have loved to know what set of evolutionary pressures had given the Gands this ability, but Ooryl remained decidedly private concerning his species and Corran hadn't pressed for details.

Corran's sense of unease didn't center itself on Ooryl. It remained a feeling that something was wrong, and this sensation was one with which Corran had a lot of experience. He'd felt it when preparing for meetings with criminals or during undercover work when his cover had been blown and enemies were waiting to hurt him. His father had nodded sagely when Corran told him about that feeling, and had encouraged him to heed it when it occurred.

He threw open his sleeping bag and shivered as the cold air hit his naked flesh. *Well, Father, I'll "go with my gut."* Corran pulled on his flight suit and discovered that its synthetic material retained the night's chill better than his flesh retained heat. He stepped into boots that were also rather frigid. He would have run in place for a moment to warm himself up, but a wave of malignancy washed over him.

Corran crossed to the cottage's open doorway and crouched in the shadows. He'd have given his right arm for a blaster, but he stored his personal sidearm in Talasea's flight center, along with his helmet, gloves, and other equipment. *In my days with CorSec I wouldn't have been caught dead without a gun of some sort. I don't even have a vibroblade. Either I'm going to be very lucky here or very dead.*

Any advantage he might have came from the basic appearance of the cottage itself. With an open doorway, unglazed windows, and sagging roof, the cottage hardly looked like the sort of place anyone, let alone pilots, would choose to live in. Unfortunately Ooryl and Corran had no choice since a windstorm had knocked a local *kaha* tree through the wall of their room in the pilots' wing of the flight center. Unpowered and barely visible from the center of the compound, the cottage might go unnoticed.

Unless someone is being very *thorough.*

The unmistakable squish of mud beneath boot alerted Corran to the presence of someone just outside the cottage. Looking up he saw the snout of a blaster carbine poke through the doorway. A left leg encased in the slate-grey armor worn by stormtroopers on commando missions followed it. The gun's muzzle moved to the right, away from Corran, and began a slow sweep of the room.

Corran exploded up from his crouch and slammed his left fist into the stormtrooper's throat. Using his own body as a weapon, the Corellian smashed the stormtrooper against the doorjamb. Hooking his right hand through the armpit of the soldier's armor, Corran spun and flung the man into the center of the cottage. Taking one step forward, Corran leaped up and landed with both knees on the Imperial's stomach.

The stormtrooper retched and vomit squirted from beneath his helmet. Corran pulled the man's blaster pistol from his holster, tucked it up beneath the trooper's chin, and pulled the trigger once. A muffled squeak accompanied the reddish light flashing through the helmet's goggle-eyes, then the body beneath him went limp.

Corran winced. *He who carries a blaster set on* kill *dies by a blaster set on* kill. He tossed the blaster pistol to the floor beside the carbine, then slid off the dead man's abdomen. He unbuckled the dead trooper's ammo belt. Tugging it free of the body, he noticed, in addition to the erg-clips for the blasters, a number of pouches, half of which were bulging. Opening one of them he saw compact silver cylinders and a new shiver ran through him.

Explosive charges! Some must already have been set.

A noise in the doorway made Corran spin. A stormtrooper stood there, staring down at him. Corran's right hand groped for the blaster pistol, but he knew he'd never make it in time. Then he noticed the stormtrooper's hands were empty and, more importantly, the man's feet were two inches off the ground.

Ooryl cast the body aside and it crumpled to the floor. The Gand took a look at the stormtrooper on the ground, then nodded once. "Ooryl apologizes for having left you undefended. Ooryl was out walking when the presence of these interlopers became apparent."

"How many?"

The Gand shook his head. "Two less. Ooryl saw four others at various points on the perimeter."

"And our sentries?"

"Gone."

"Not good. Stormtroopers travel in squads of nine—let's figure two dozen with the crew of whatever brought them here." Corran refastened the ammo belt and slung it across his body. Reholstering the blaster pistol he noticed that Ooryl had similarly appropriated his trooper's weapons. "Is your boy dead?"

The Gand nodded and rolled his trooper onto his stomach. The trooper's helmet had a blood-smeared hole in the back of it. The hole itself looked odd, and Corran knew that was because of its shape, not just the jagged outline from where the armor crumbled. *Kind of a diamond shape . . .*

He looked up. "Did you hurt your hand?"

Ooryl folded his three fingers into a fist with the wound's peculiar shape. "Ooryl is not impaired."

"Well, I am, by the night and the fog. You'll be in the lead. We have to assume the others are rigging the flight center to blow."

"No alarm?"

Corran hesitated. By rights raising an alarm would be the smart thing to do, but there were no troops to fight against the stormtroopers. Waking everyone up would be inviting them to get slaughtered as they ran about unarmed. The pilots would head toward their ships and the stormtroopers in the flight center would cut them down in seconds.

"Have to go silent on this one. We want to approach the flight center from the blind side."

The Gand nodded and led Corran out into the misty darkness. Clutching the blaster carbine to his chest, a legion of conflicting thoughts and emotions flooded through him. With each step a new plan presented itself to him. There *had* to be better ways to handle the situation than slipping blindly through the night to go hunting stormtroopers. They had every advantage over him. Not only would their armor protect them, but the helmet enhanced their vision and the built-in comlink meant they could coordinate any efforts to hunt him down and kill him.

Thoughts shifted and ambition sparked dreams of glory. He saw himself as a hero of the Alliance for foiling the stormtrooper raid, yet that dream died quickly. As Biggs Darklighter and Jek Porkins had shown, most heroes of the Alliance were made heroes posthumously, and posthumous was the most likely outcome of the expedition. This did not suit Corran, but the sense of menace radiating out through the night made it hard to deny.

At the same time the knowledge that he was surely dead provided him with a sense of freedom. His goal shifted from staying alive to making sure his friends would stay alive. He wasn't fighting for himself, he was fighting for them. He was the shield that would prevent the Empire's evil from touching them. In this idea he found a haven from the sense of doom grinding in on him.

Ooryl stopped him with a hand pressed gently to his chest. The Gand held up one finger, then pointed straight ahead. He made a fist with his right hand, then signaled with his left in a looping motion.

Corran nodded and sighted the carbine along the line where Ooryl had pointed. The Gand slipped to the left and immediately disappeared in the fog. The Corellian waited, willing himself to be able to see through the fog to his target. He knew the chances of hitting anything were minimal, and he expected to aim at the source of any blaster fire he saw. Even so, he allowed himself to believe he could feel the soldier in a hard carapace standing twenty or so meters in front of him.

A wet crunch drifted to him through the fog. Corran moved forward, carefully pushing his way through the leafy plants and curtains of tendril-moss at the fringe of the compound. About where he had expected his target to be he found the Gand crouched over a prostrate stormtrooper. The helmet looked decidedly flattened on top and now rode low enough to hide the man's throat.

Ooryl unfastened the last of the catches on the breast and stomach armor, then pulled it from the dead man's body and handed it to Corran. "You shall have exoskeleton, too."

The human pilot smiled. He removed his gunbelt and

slipped the armor on. It was much too big for him, but he tightened the flank straps as much as he could and got a vaguely reasonable fit. Adding the trooper's ammo belt to his own helped hold the armor in place, though the weight of two blasters—one on each hip—made him feel slow.

Ooryl hefted the other carbine in his free hand, then headed off into the night. Corran followed and quickly enough they came to the side of the flight center that faced away from the central compound. They made good use of the hole the *kaha* tree had made in the wall to slip back into the building. Light shone in beneath the edge of the door into the hallway and Corran took this as a good sign.

He pointed to it. "If the troopers were in this wing, they'd have killed the light because leaving it on means they'll be sil-houetted when they enter a darkened room. Gavin and Shiel are in the next room. Let's get to them."

The Gand nodded and opened the door a crack. He peered out, then waved Corran forward. Corran shut the door behind him and followed Ooryl through the next door down the hall-way. The Gand crossed to where the Shistavanen lay while Corran approached Gavin's bed. Shifting the carbine to his right hand, he crouched down and laid his left hand over Gavin's mouth.

He felt the boy start. "Gavin, be quiet. It's me, Corran. Be still."

Shiel awoke with a low growl, but after taking a couple of healthy sniffs of the air, he stopped making any noise. He sat up, then slipped from the bed and crouched along with Corran and the Gand at Gavin's bedside. "Troopers. Blood."

Corran nodded. "We have stormies here in the base. They're rigging it to explode—they're in the hangar now, I think. We have three down and we're guessing there were two dozen total."

Ooryl handed the Shistavanen wolfman a carbine. "You know how to use this?"

Shiel's whispered laugh sounded like a growl. "Death marks don't come with the rain."

Corran stripped off one of his gunbelts and shoved it at Gavin. "You can fire a blaster?"

The youth nodded, his face pale in the light from beneath the door. "Don't know if I'll hit anything, though."

"Point and shoot. And shoot. And shoot." Corran looked over at the two aliens. "Since you both can navigate in the dark, and since your coloration makes you hard to spot, I think you should head out and around to the hangar." He passed Shiel two of the spare clips from his belt. "We'll work our way in through the center here and try to attract their attention. If you get a clue to where their ship is . . ."

The hall light went out.

"Uh-oh." Gavin shucked the pistol from its holster and the power selection lever clicked.

"Leave it on kill, kid." Corran pointed to the window. "Go, you two. Flank them."

Wordlessly Corran turned and scuttled over to the door. Reaching up he turned the knob and opened it a crack. He couldn't see anything in the dark, but he did hear the squeak of hinges farther along the hallway. He touched the medallion he wore once for luck, then pulled open the door, stepped into the hallway, and fired a burst.

Two bolts caught one stormtrooper in the chest and tossed him backward into another trooper. The dead man's finger jerked his carbine's trigger, sending a line of bolts down the hallway. Corran dove to the right, slamming his shoulder into the wall avoiding them. Red light flashed back out of the doorway near the head of the hall, reminding Corran of the flare in the eyeplate of the first trooper he had killed. In an instant the Corellian knew the room contained a third stormtrooper and that at least one of the squadron's pilots lay dead in bed.

Corran's second burst knocked down the stormtrooper emerging from beneath the Imp corpse. Corran thought he went down hard enough to be dead, but the little votive fires lit in the floors and walls by the stray blaster bolts didn't supply enough light for him to be certain. Then the trooper in the room at the head of the hallway emerged and, as if the trooper's mirror image, Gavin came through the doorway of his room.

"Gavin, no!"

The farm boy triggered one shot while the trooper filled the hallway with a steady stream of fire. Corran hit his trigger and scythed the muzzle back and forth across the hallway. He heard Gavin grunt and fall behind him. His own shots cut the legs out from under the stormtrooper. The last bolt blasted through the square eyeplate and bubbled the armor at the back of the man's head.

The doors all along the hallway swung open. Nearest to him Corran saw the Twi'lek. "Gavin's down. Help him. Stormtroopers are here in the base."

Nawara Ven stared at him. "How did they find . . ."

"I don't know. The place is rigged to blow. Get everyone clear." Corran sprinted down the hallway, leaping over the trio of dead stormtroopers. He stripped the power pack from the carbine and slapped a new one into it. As he neared the hangar he heard plenty of blaster fire. The semitransparent plastic strips hung over the doorway showed a lot of shots heading out to converge on two points in the darkness, which told Corran that Shiel and Ooryl had attracted plenty of attention with their flanking maneuver. *Shooting coming from either side of the door, too.*

Corran fished one of the explosive cylinders from a belt pouch and set the timer for five seconds. He punched his thumb down on the arming button. Glancing up he located what he saw as the largest concentration of shots heading out at his comrades. *Six. Looks good to me.*

Corran stepped through the plastic curtain and let the arming button come up, starting the timer. He slid the explosive cylinder across the smooth ferrocrete surface toward the knot of commandos. *Three, two, one!*

The explosion scattered the soldiers, casting two up and over the generator cart they'd been using as cover. Before they hit the ground, Corran turned and thrust his blaster carbine at the stormtrooper hunkered down to the left of the door. The burst of laser fire burned through the torso armor, blasting the man out from behind a breastwork of crates.

Spinning, Corran sprayed scarlet blaster darts over the stormtrooper on the other side of the doorway. The shots hit him in the chest and legs, somersaulting him back through the plastic sheet and out of the hangar. Continuing his spin, Corran snapped shots off at various muzzle flashes, backing and turning, picking up speed and allowing himself to drift almost at random.

He knew he should be terribly frightened, but since he had decided he was as good as dead before, fear could find no purchase on his soul. He viewed his situation with an emotional detachment that surprised him. It allowed him to see his entry into the hangar much as he had seen diving into the cloud of TIEs at Hensara. *I can shoot at anyone—they have to take care.*

Corran's gun came up and the muzzle tracked strobing laser fire over the silhouette of a stormtrooper up on the hangar's catwalk. The trooper straightened up and twitched, then slowly began a backward spin toward the floor that Corran found incredibly graceful. His landing, which was all broken and herky-jerky, ruined the beauty of his fall and brought Corran back to the hideous reality in which he was enmeshed.

A laser bolt caught him in the right breast and pitched him into the shadows. He landed hard against a wall of wooden crates and stars exploded before his eyes when his head hit something solid. He heard wood and glass break and a gurgle of a vessel emptying. He hoped it wasn't his body emptying of blood, but the shooting pains in his chest and the fire radiating out from the wound all but guaranteed he *was* the source of the sound. A sickly sweet scent mixed with the stink of burned flesh and Corran knew he was dying.

That smells like Corellian whiskey. His mind flashed back to the endless rounds of drinks at his father's wake. Each one punctuated a toast or a testament to his father by members of CorSec, from the Director on down to Gil and Iella to the rookies his father had taken under his wing. At that time Corran had thought having such a wake would be the grandest sendoff possible. *And now I hallucinate the smell of it.*

A jolt of pain left him a moment of lucidity in its wake and Corran clung to it. His vision cleared and he saw laser bolts burning in all directions through the darkness. He tried to lift his own carbine, but he couldn't feel its weight in his hand. He decided to draw the blaster pistol, which was when he discovered his right arm wasn't working so well.

That realization came a second or two before the laser fire silhouetted a stormtrooper seeking cover nearby.

Corran willed his body to sink into the ferrocrete, but nothing happened.

The stormtrooper swept something aside with a foot and Corran heard the clatter of the carbine against an unseen crate. He tried to lever himself up with his left arm, but the pain in the right side of his chest stopped him. He found himself short of breath. *My lung. Collapsed.*

The stormtrooper lowered his carbine, giving Corran a good view of the muzzle. "It's over for you, Rebel scum."

"You, too, little stormie." Corran raised his left hand but kept his thumb pressed on the end of the explosive cylinder he'd eased from the pouch on his belt. "I die and it blows."

The stormtrooper hesitated for a second, then shook his head. "Nice try. You're holding the wrong end."

Blaster whine filled the crate-lined cul de sac and Corran flinched involuntarily. He thought flinching was a bad way to die, then he realized that the dead are seldom that vain. Above him the stormtrooper's body wavered, then buckled at the knees and crashed down beside him. The hole in the back of his armor sparked and smoked.

Wedge came running up and dropped to one knee beside Corran. "How are you doing, Mr. Horn?"

"Parts of me don't hurt that much."

Wedge smiled. "Hang tight. The stormies are withdrawing. Medic!"

"Bombs."

"I know. We're finding and disarming them."

Corran smiled and tried to take a deep breath. "Gavin?"

"Bad, like you. We're already getting set to evacuate."

"I'm as good as dead." He winced. "I'm so far gone I smell Corellian whiskey."

"You *do* smell Corellian whiskey, Corran. You're lying in a puddle of it." Wedge frowned. "The crate that broke your fall is full of Whyren's Reserve."

"What? How?"

Wedge shook his head as Emdee droids toddled over. "I don't know. Consider solving that mystery your assignment while you recover from your wounds."

19

W EDGE ANTILLES WATCHED as Gavin Darklighter and
Corran Horn floated all but lifeless in bacta tanks.
Seeing them there brought back memories of the time he had
spent in such a tank—it hadn't been aboard the *Reprieve* but
on *Home One*, Admiral Ackbar's flagship at Endor. He'd been
barely conscious during his time in the tank, which he saw as
a blessing. Being awake and thinking while being able to do
nothing would have driven him insane.

"Your pilots have improved, Commander Antilles?"

Wedge turned and blinked his eyes in surprise. "Admiral
Ackbar? What are you doing here, sir?"

The Mon Calamari clasped his hands at the small of his
back. "I read your report and found it disturbingly clinical. I
decided I wanted more information."

Wedge nodded. "There wasn't much time to prepare the
report."

"And you have never really liked datapadding."

"No." Wedge rubbed a hand over his face and discovered a
fair amount of stubble on his chin and jaw. *How long has it
been since I slept?* "You could have requested a supplemental

report, or asked me to report to you aboard *Home One* and saved yourself the trip."

"I thought of that, but I knew another report from you would be light in bytes and that you would refuse to leave your people, so I chose to save myself the annoyance." Ackbar stared through the viewport at the two men in the tank. "Besides, the tone of the Provisional Council meetings is beginning to wear on me. The fate of Rogue Squadron is important enough that I was able to slip away without being accused of running."

The Corellian looked over at his commander. "Are things that acrimonious?"

"I probably exaggerate. Politicians tend to view soldiers like their pet Cyborrean battle dogs."

"And soldiers don't like to be considered pets."

Ackbar's barbels twitched slightly. "Since we are the ones who get bitten and bleed and die, we tend to resist plans that are politically expedient but militarily suicidal." He tapped his hand against the viewport. "Is the picture of what happened there any more clear?"

"Not yet. The basics are the same—three pilots seriously wounded, one dead, and all six sentries dead. A number of others have cuts and scrapes. It should have been much worse but it looks as if the stormtroopers wanted to plant the explosives, withdraw, then arm and detonate them by remote. Had they just put them on timers we would have lost equipment and people before we found them all. A full platoon was operating on Talasea. We got all of them and captured the Delta DX-9 Transport they came in on."

"Hardly worth the cost, but a good thing, nonetheless."

Wedge nodded. "The ones we captured—two stormtroopers and all five of the transport's crew—refuse to talk. I have them in detention, isolated from each other. I've had an Emdee-oh and Emdee-one droid engaged in postmortems of the troopers we killed. With luck something will give us an idea where they came from."

"And Talasea was evacuated?"

"Yes, sir. We expect Imperials to come looking for whatever got their people, so we set up some booby traps and other surprises for whoever follows us in there." Wedge sighed heavily. "I have a list of what we left behind in case we ever have cause to go back."

The Mon Calamari nodded slowly. "What is the mood of your unit?"

Wedge turned and pressed his back against the cool transparisteel. He just wanted to close his eyes and go to sleep, and he feared he'd do just that if he *did* close his eyes. "We're all stunned and exhausted. Losing Lujayne came as a shock. She wasn't the best pilot in the unit, and not one to take chances, so none of us had her pegged as someone who would die first. Corran or Bror or Shiel were easy to picture going out in a blaze of glory—and Corran almost did. Lujayne was a fighter, so having her die in her sleep was, well, it just made it worse. She was murdered, not killed in combat, and I guess I thought we were somehow immune to that sort of ignominious death."

He shook his head. "That makes no sense, of course."

Ackbar patted him on the shoulder. "It does make sense. We know war is barbaric, but we try not to be barbaric in waging war. We hold ourselves to a high standard that demands we only attack legitimate military targets—not civilians, not medical frigates. We would like to see this honor we demand of ourselves reflected in the actions of our enemies."

"But if they were as honorable as we are, we'd not be fighting this war."

"And in that, Commander Antilles, you have the core of the whole problem." The Mon Calamari paced away from the viewport. "When will your people be out of the tanks?"

Wedge glanced down at his chronometer. "Twelve hours more for Horn and Darklighter, another twenty-four to forty-eight for Andoorni Hui. I've been told it has something to do with her metabolism, but she was hurt worse than they were, too. I want to hold a memorial for Lujayne fairly soon." He rubbed his eyes. "Gavin will be crushed—she's been helping him sharpen his astronavigation skills."

"It seems, then, nothing can be done until at least twelve hours from now."

Wedge shook his head. "Nope, we just have to wait."

"No, you just have to sleep."

The Corellian turned and looked at Ackbar. "I can rest later."

"But you *will* rest now. Consider that an order, Commander, or I will order a Too-Onebee droid to sedate you." Ackbar's chin came up as he spoke and Wedge knew he'd carry out his threat. "In fourteen hours I want to see you and your XO on *Home One*. General Salm will have arrived by then."

"If I'd known I could look forward to a dressing down by him, I'd have let the stormtroopers shoot me."

"Yes, he can have that effect, can't he?" Ackbar's mouth hung open in a silent laugh at his joke. "The purpose of this meeting is not a reprimand, however."

"No?"

"No." Ackbar's voice became calmer, yet more intense. "Someone in the Empire struck at one of my forward bases. If we don't strike back, and strike back hard, they might feel emboldened to continue such activity. I don't want this to happen. General Salm's bomber wing should be sufficient for exacting retribution."

"If you want Rogue Squadron to fly cover for such a mission, you have us."

"That was the reaction I expected from you, Commander. Now, go get some sleep."

"Yes, sir." Wedge saluted. *Sleep it is, and dreams of retribution will be very pleasant indeed.*

CORRAN WASN'T CERTAIN what was worse: the sour taste of bacta in the back of his throat or feeling like he was still bobbing up and down in the tank. To him bacta tasted like lum that had gone flat, gotten stale, and been stored in the sort of plastic barrel that lent it an oiliness that slicked his tongue. Because the blaster bolt had punctured his right lung and collapsed it, a little bacta had been circulated through the lung, bringing the fluid's cloying bouquet to his nose every time he exhaled.

Other than that, he felt pretty good. He still had a reddish spot on his chest where he had been shot. The mark on him was about half the size of the mark on Gavin. Corran realized that armor had saved his life by absorbing some of the power of the bolt—how Gavin survived taking a shot to the naked abdomen he hadn't a clue.

Gavin rolled onto his side on the next bed over. "Never done that before."

"Blunder into a lightfight or spend time in a bacta tank?"

"Neither." The youth frowned. "I didn't think I was blundering . . ."

"You weren't." Corran shook his head and swung his feet around so he could sit up. "I should have realized you didn't know to wait until I signaled the hall was clear. I didn't think, which is why you went down. It was my fault you got shot."

Gavin covered the reddish area on his stomach with his right hand. "It hurt a lot, then I guess I fainted."

"You're lucky that's all you did. That shot should have killed you."

"I know I shot back at the stormtrooper. Did I get him?"

"I don't know, Gavin. Unless you have a holo of a lightfight, trying to reconstruct it after the fact is all but impossible." Corran slid from the table and found his legs supported him with only a few minor tremors. "He and his buddies died, and that's all that counts."

"Were any of us killed?"

Corran remembered the impression of death he'd had in the corridor, but he shook his head. "I don't know, Gavin."

The med-center hatch opened and Wedge Antilles stepped

through it. His smile broadened at first, then shrank slightly. He paused and returned the hasty salutes Gavin and Corran managed. "Good to see both of you hale and hearty."

"Hearty, perhaps, sir, but hale will need some work." Corran worked his right arm up and around in a circle. "A night's rest ought to make it all right."

"And you, Gavin, how do you feel?"

"Fine, sir. I could fly right now if you need me."

"That's not necessary right away." Wedge's expression darkened. "We've abandoned Talasea and evacuated it cleanly. We got the stormtroopers and captured their transport ship. Forensic analysis of the bodies has given us a good indication of where they came from. I'm meeting with Admiral Ackbar and General Salm to consider a counterstrike against their base."

"I'm in."

"Me, too." Gavin hopped off the bed. His knees buckled, but he caught the edge of the bed and remained upright. "I want to go and repay them."

Wedge nodded and Corran knew he was getting to the worst part of the report. "In the raid we gave better than we got—but we had casualties. Six of our sentries died. You two and Andoorni were severely wounded." Wedge glanced down at the deck, then over at Gavin. "Lujayne Forge was killed."

Gavin leaned heavily on the bed. "Lujayne is dead?"

Corran sat abruptly on the floor. He'd felt her die, he knew she had died, yet he couldn't believe it any more than Gavin could. She'd always been the member of the squadron who was concerned with the welfare of the others—not just their physical welfare, but how they felt. *She formed the heart of our unit, bringing us together. There's no way she should have been the first of us to die.*

He stared down at his empty hands. *She never even collected on that favor I owed her for fixing my X-wing and now she's gone.*

Gavin shook his head. "She can't be dead. She's been tutoring me in astronavigation. She . . ." The youth balled his fists and hammered them against the edge of the table. "Dead . . ."

Wedge sighed. "It's never easy to lose a friend, Gavin."

Gavin raised a fist as if he wanted to smash it down again, but let it slowly drift back to his side. "This is the first time anyone I've known has died."

Corran raised an eyebrow. "Really?"

"He's only a kid, Corran."

"I know, sir, but his cousin . . ."

Gavin shook his head. "I've met people before who later died. I remember Mr. Owen and Aunt Beru—that's what I called them on the couple of times Biggs let me tag along when he visited Luke at the Lars farm. When they died, my father took the farm over . . ."

Wedge frowned. "I thought Luke had given it to an alien."

"Yes, Throgg was his name. He worked it for a couple of seasons, but my uncle wanted to add that farm to his holdings, so he got the Anchorhead Municipal Council to pass an alien landowner tax which would have broken Throgg to pay. My father didn't hold with his brother's tactics, so Dad bought the farm from Throgg, paying him what it was worth instead of letting Uncle Huff buy it in a tax auction." Gavin shrugged. "Growing up on that farm I could remember having seen the Larses, but I never really knew them. I was a kid, a *real* kid. They were nice to me, but . . ."

"But you didn't *know* them." Corran drew his knees up to his chest. "I understand. Still, your cousin, Biggs . . ."

"Biggs was eight years older than I was. There were times he liked having me around and times he didn't. I couldn't understand why not then." Gavin shrugged. "I've grown up since then, so I kind of understand now but, still, I didn't really know him. And not seeing his . . . him or Luke's aunt and uncle after, well, it's not like I know they're gone. I do, but, you know . . ."

"I do know." Wedge folded his arms across his chest. "I was there when Biggs died. I got hit and pulled up out of the trench on Luke's orders. Your cousin and I both knew we were really there as an added set of shields to keep Luke safe, but we didn't regret that. We knew he'd have done the same thing for us and we also knew he had to blow the Death Star. Biggs stayed there, keeping the TIEs back, and died there. And even though he died, he bought Luke the time he needed to destroy the Death Star."

The Rebel commander's eyes nearly shut as he stared off into space. "I flew with Biggs before Yavin and he was really good. It seemed like he could read the minds of TIE pilots. He knew when to break, when to shoot, and did everything necessary to stay in their ion exhaust and blast them to bits. He was proud of his record and his skill, but not arrogant."

Gavin smiled. "He had that smirk, the one he'd give you when he'd done something you couldn't."

Wedge chuckled. "I used to hate that smirk, but I didn't have it directed at me all that often. In his first mission we went against an Imperial convoy, right after they'd started assigning Nebulon-B frigates, just like the *Reprieve* here, to jump cover for the convoys. It launched two dozen TIEs at our squadron. Biggs lit and vaped five, making him an ace, but another pilot claimed his number-three kill. That kill made the other pilot an ace—I think he was on his fifteenth mission at the time. Biggs gave the guy the smirk and let him have it. And thereafter when Biggs got five of something, he'd give this guy the third one. He wasn't nasty about it, but he didn't let the guy forget."

Gavin nodded. "Biggs was like that—he'd needle you with your own little foibles until you did something about it, or it didn't bother you anymore."

"It was his way of making everyone toe the line and push themselves to be the best they could. That's why he used to get after Luke about going to the Academy. He didn't want to see anyone waste themselves when they could be doing more." Wedge scratched the back of his neck. "If he'd survived Yavin, we'd be reporting to him now."

Corran raised a finger. "Did the third-kill guy ever redeem himself?"

The curve of Wedge's smile flattened out. "The guy, Karsk was his name, Amil Karsk, took the third of five scheduled patrols for Biggs. It was an easy job—nursemaiding a blockade runner on a courier mission. It even promised a couple of days of rest and recreation. It was a plum assignment, but Biggs let him have it and was willing to call it even. That mission and that courier took Karsk to Alderaan. He was on the ground when the Death Star appeared."

"Ouch." Corran reached up and hauled himself to his feet. "Biggs was lucky he let the mission slide."

"Yeah, but luck runs out eventually." Wedge's brown eyes hardened. "Ours hasn't, not entirely, yet. I'm glad you're both back with us. I'd prefer not having to add you to the list of friends I've lost to the Empire. The list is too long already."

Gavin swallowed hard, once, then extended his hand to Wedge. "Thank you, sir. I feel like I know Biggs a bit better now."

Wedge shook the youth's hand. "Thanks for giving me the chance to remember the good things about Biggs. Too much of war is remembering the loss—the point at which people cease contributing to this life. Biggs, Porkins, Dack, Lujayne—they all need to be remembered as more than just casualties. I don't do that often enough."

Their commander glanced at the chronometer on the ship's bulkhead. "I'm due to meet with Admiral Ackbar shortly. You've got about four hours before we'll have a memorial for Lujayne and the other people we lost on Talasea. And after that, Ackbar willing and Salm being sanguine, we'll bleed some Imperials pale of luck and let our dead rest just that much easier."

20

E MTREY'S UNCHARACTERISTIC QUIET on the flight over from the *Reprieve* to *Home One* had started Wedge wondering if the galaxy hadn't changed around him while he'd been sleeping. The droid hadn't wheedled, cajoled, begged, or bored him with details about the need for him to travel to *Home One*—he just showed up and said he had things to take care of on board the Rebel flagship.

Tycho had shrugged, so Wedge agreed. The droid seemed uncharacteristically quiet, but that didn't seem sinister and really was quite welcome. As he piloted the *Forbidden* on the run over to the Mon Calamari Star cruiser he realized he'd not seen much of Emtrey during the time on Talasea, and he'd heard even less from him. He'd heard even fewer complaints about the droid, and this he took as a good sign. He felt caring for pilots was tough enough without having to worry about droids, too.

The smile on General Salm's face as Wedge and Tycho entered Admiral Ackbar's briefing room increased the Corellian's sense of dislocation with the galaxy. "Good to see you, Commander Antilles, Captain Celchu. It was very kind of you to have your M-3PO droid send that gross of new flight suits to Defender Wing. We accept your apology and look forward to working with you on this mission."

Wedge looked at Tycho, but his XO gave his head a nearly imperceptible shake. *If it makes Salm happy, do I really need to know what's going on?* "You're welcome, General. We're all on the same side, after all."

Ackbar's face shifted from Wedge to Salm and back again. He blinked, then clasped his hands together. "Clear water, gentle waves, good." The Mon Calamari seated himself and pushed a button on the chair's arm. "Our droids have double-checked the findings of the forensic team working on the stormtroopers you brought up from Talasea. They confirm the rash on three of them as being Rachuk roseola. DNA analysis of the virus shows a variation from the sequencing reported there two years ago, and given the spontaneous mutation rate, this would be the most recent strain."

Wedge nodded. "So they came from Rachuk."

Ackbar pointed to the computer-generated holographic image growing up in the middle of the group. It showed a relatively small world with a scattering of jungle islands. "The Rachuk system itself is unimportant except that its central location means a great number of ships pass into and out of it as they conduct trade. The Empire located a base on Vladet to discourage piracy and they were relatively successful in doing so. The Chorax system is within the sector controlled from Rachuk, as is the Hensara system, so it is logical to assume that the sector commander decided Rogue Squadron needed to be eliminated."

"But how did they know where we were?"

Salm's face darkened slightly. "The presence of a spy in your midst cannot be fully discounted."

Wedge glanced at Tycho but saw no reaction to the remark at all. *A better man than I not to shoot back.* "No spy at all would leave the same evidence as a very good spy—one in so deep we couldn't find it."

"That is still no reason why we shouldn't look for a spy."

Tycho shook his head. "Security at the base was tight. We had no unauthorized messages going in or out."

"That you know of."

"No, sir."

"Or," Salm smiled, "that you're choosing to report."

"General, Captain Celchu is reporting the results of checks I performed myself. There were no leaks from Rogue Squadron."

Ackbar waved the discussion away with a flip of his hand. "It is more than likely that the Empire planted a number of passive sensor devices in the buildings there after Vader killed off the colony. If such sensors gathered data and then sent it out on a delayed basis, or in a format we would not easily recognize, we would miss it. While we did have teams sweep the area, detecting passive devices is not easy."

"It also could have been blind luck."

Salm looked at Tycho. "What do you mean, Captain?"

Tycho raked brown hair back from his forehead. "Imperials tend not to be subtle. If I'd been in command and I knew where Rogue Squadron was, I would have brought in everything I had. We know Rachuk command has an Interdictor and at least one Strike cruiser that can carry three squadrons of TIEs. Since all of that didn't show up, I suspect they just sent out stormtrooper platoons to recon uninhabited systems in the sector—assuming, of course, that they have spies in most of the inhabited systems. One platoon found us and the commander decided to be ambitious and destroy us himself."

Ackbar nodded. "Another logical conclusion drawn from the evidence at hand. There has also been a fair amount of traffic by small trading ships into and out of Talasea."

"Yes, sir. Emtrey can give you the data on them."

"He already did and they all appear to be clean, Commander, but one misstatement by one crew member and your security would be compromised. Ultimately, though, the reason the Talasea base was discovered is less important than our discovery of the source of the stormtroopers. It has been two standard days since the stormtroopers died, so chances are very good that their absence has been noticed."

Wedge folded his arms. "Standard Imperial response would be to move in, secure the planet, and prevent us from using it again."

"We expect the *Havoc* and the *Black Asp* to be used to prevent Rogue Squadron from making a quick hit and run on the Talasea expeditionary force; they won't be defending Rachuk." Salm reached out and touched the holographic world. The island he selected grew up in place of the world of which it was part. As the image expanded the computer added buildings, mountains, ion-cannon batteries, and other details of military importance. Two steep mountain chains—the edges of an extinct volcano's crater—enclosed the base like parentheses. "We have other information about the locations and patrol routes of the Rachuk sector's ships. We believe Vladet should be open to a reprisal strike, and Grand Isle here is the place to hit."

Wedge took a step closer to the holographic island floating in midair. "Defense shields?"

Salm smiled and Wedge was pleased that predatory leer wasn't directed at him. "Not if they want to fire their ion cannons. The island, as you can see, is part of an old volcano. The generators are geothermal and old and not up to the strain of raising the shield *and* powering the ion cannons."

"And if they choose to go turtle instead of trying to shoot?"

The bomber pilot traced a circle around what would have originally been the edge of the crater. To the south the wall had broken down almost completely and much of the base had been built on the flat stretch of land that linked the volcano and the bay. On the north side of the crater the wall had begun to erode, but it was just a small divot compared to the gap to the south.

"The shield generator has to cover everything from the beach to the tops of the mountains. On the north side it should be possible to blast through the *mountain* and open up enough of a gap to let our bombers in. Once we're under the shield, the generators go and it's over."

It looks like it should work. Wedge rubbed a hand over his chin. "Are we hitting and running, or moving in?"

"We want to cripple Vladet so the Empire will have to move new forces in." Ackbar hit another button on the arm of his chair and the island vanished. "The Rachuk sector is immaterial at the moment, except as a symbol and a wound the Empire must stanch. We want this raid to go off in twelve hours. What will Rogue Squadron's operational strength be then, Commander?"

"I'll be down two pilots. I could give Captain Celchu Forge's X-wing."

"No." General Salm shook his head adamantly.

Ackbar opened his mouth in a smile. "What General Salm meant by this is that we will be using the *Eridain* as a command and control center. Captain Celchu will operate there to coordinate Rogue Squadron and Defender Wing. This is at Captain Afyon's request."

Wedge frowned at General Salm. *How is it that you will trust Tycho to direct* all *our forces, but won't trust him in the cockpit of an X-wing? Isn't it obvious where he can do the most damage?* "Is that acceptable to you, Captain?" He put enough of an edge in his voice that he felt certain Tycho knew he'd fight Salm if Tycho wanted to fly in the raid.

"Yes, sir. I've not logged enough time in an X-wing to be mission qualified anyway, Commander, so I'll be happy to do flight coordination and control."

Salm tugged at the hem of his blue coat. "I'll have my own flight controller on the *Eridain*. You'll work with him."

"Of course, sir."

And your man will decide whether or not to relay orders. Wedge nodded to himself. "We'll make it work."

"Good." Ackbar closed his eyes for a moment and Wedge took that as a sign of appreciation for his cooperation. "You are returning to the *Reprieve* for the memorial service?"

"Yes, sir."

"If you don't mind, General Salm and I will fly over with you in the *Forbidden* to attend ourselves."

Wedge smiled, more at the Admiral's offer than Salm's clear look of surprise. "We would be honored, sir."

"And we will honor your dead." Ackbar turned to the bomber pilot. "And you will want your Defender Wing pilots there, too, yes, General?"

Salm hesitated, then nodded. "Perhaps if we mourn together before we fly together, our units won't have so much to mourn after we hit Vladet."

KIRTAN LOOR DUCKED involuntarily as he felt the tremor rip through the soil. A muffled report reached his ears a second later. The comlink clipped to his lapel hissed with static, then calmly reported, "Four-Eighteen and Four-Twenty are down."

The Intelligence agent shivered, and it wasn't the cool Talasean night that shook him. The stormtrooper making the report had reacted as if the Rebels' little booby trap had killed droids, not people. *Of course, stormtroopers are hardly people, are they?* Brought up to be fanatically loyal to the Emperor, most of them seemed slightly distracted by his death. While this did not dull their efficiency, it did seem to make them care less about their own lives.

On Talasea care for one's continued well-being seemed to be a required skill. The Rebels had rigged up a lot of explosive surprises for whoever followed them to Talasea. *Just who that would be was not difficult for them to figure out.*

Loor straightened up. "Not that it matters how many stormtroopers die. There must be a factory that stamps them out."

He started to smile at his own whispered comment, but a cold dagger of fear plunged into his guts. Two stormtroopers in white armor emerged from the fog like wraiths risen from the grave. They stopped directly in front of him, but neither one bothered to crane his neck back to look up at Loor's face. "Agent Loor."

Kirtan nodded and did his best to wear a mask reminiscent of pictures he'd seen of Tarkin. "Yes?"

"Priority message relayed from Vladet. You are ordered to return to Vladet immediately and await further orders."

"What does that idiot Devlia think he's playing at?" Kirtan had been furious when he learned Devlia had sent a single stormtrooper platoon to check Talasea. He had recommended using a probe droid and then following it with a full-scale attack. Devlia had ignored his recommendation and had sent stormtroopers because they were, in his words, "a renewable resource." The same could not be said for probe droids.

Nor could it be said of stormtrooper transports. Kirtan stared down at the stormtrooper. "Send a message back to Admiral Devlia and tell him I will return to Vladet when I am finished with my survey of this base."

"Sir, the message came from Imperial Center, not Admiral Devlia."

He purposely, slowly, raised his head and stared off above the white domes of their helmets. He knew his efforts to hide his shock and fear were useless. *I suspect stormtroopers smell fear the way animals do.* "A ship has been sent for me?"

"You're to take one of the shuttles, the *Helicon*, directly to Vladet. It is waiting for you in the landing zone."

"Thank you for relaying the message." His voice carried no conviction with it. "Carry on."

The two stormtroopers marched off through the swirling mist, leaving Kirtan to be assaulted by cold air outside and cold dread inside. *Iceheart must have already gotten my message about this fiasco. If she's looking to place blame for this disaster, it won't be on my head.* He forced himself to smile and bolstered his effort by visualizing a trembling Admiral Devlia. "Tremble you shall, little man. In ignoring me, you have angered my mistress and I suspect her anger can be decidedly lethal."

———

THE SEVEN CASKETS lay atop a repulsorlift platform, each one draped with white cloth to which had been affixed a blue emblem. For six that emblem was the Rebel crest. Lujayne Forge's shroud bore the Rogue Squadron crest with one of the dozen X-wing fighters cut away. The caskets had been laid out in the center of the starboard fighter bay aboard the *Reprieve*, with Lujayne's in the middle.

Directly behind them stood all the members of Rogue Squadron save one. Andoorni Hui had been allowed out of the bacta tank for the duration of the ceremony but she was still too weak to stand unaided. She lay back in a hoverchair, her dark eyes half-lidded and her limbs nearly lifeless. She looked, to Wedge, the way he felt inside—all crushed down by the squadron's loss.

Behind the pilots stood the techs and crew who had been evacuated from Talasea. Flanking them were the men and women of Salm's Defender Wing, as well as some of the crew and medical personnel on the *Reprieve*. The gathering reminded Wedge of the assembly held on Yavin 4 to honor Luke, Han, and Chewbacca for their destruction of the Death Star. *I only wish this occasion were as happy a one as that had been.*

Wedge stepped out from between Admiral Ackbar and General Salm, looked down at the caskets, then back up again. "Over seven years ago many of our brethren were gathered together in the aftermath of a great battle to commemorate the heroism of our friends. None of us thought, at that time, of how desperate our situation was, or how long our battle against the Empire would continue. The future was, for us, the next minute or hour or day or week. Life expectancy, especially among pilots, was measured in missions and seldom were multiple digits involved in the calculations.

"At that gathering, on Yavin 4, we were able to celebrate our victory as if, with the destruction of that one terrible weapon—the first Death Star—we had brought the Empire crashing down. We knew it wasn't true—we knew we would abandon Yavin shortly thereafter—but for that time we were able to forget how desperate and difficult our fight for freedom would be.

"We could forget how many more of our friends would die pursuing the common dream of freedom for all people, all species, within the galaxy."

Wedge swallowed hard against the lump thickening in his throat. "That dream still lives. Our fight continues. The Empire still exists, though its strength ebbs, its tenacity slackens, and its grasp on its worlds weakens. Dying though it is, it can still inflict death and these, the bodies of our comrades, make that fact abundantly clear.

"I will not tell you that Lujayne or Carter or Pirgi or the others would want you to keep fighting, or that your fighting will make their sacrifice worth it. That's trite, and our friends deserve more than trite. They have given up what we fight to preserve. Our duty, and their silent charge to us, is to continue to fight until the Empire can never again strip life from those who want nothing more sinister than freedom for all."

He stepped back, then nodded to a technician near the launching bay's external port. At his signal the repulsorlift platform gently rose and floated toward the vast opening. The ranks of pilots and ground crew parted to let the bier drift past, then closed up again as the platform entered the magnetic containment field around the external port. Once outside the ship, the platform dropped away from beneath the caskets and they hung there, surrounding by stars and vacuum.

The technician used a tractor beam to impel the caskets, one by one, on a gentle course toward the red dwarf burning at the heart of the star system. *Off on a final convoy . . .* As the white shrouds picked up the sun's red highlights, the string of seven caskets took on the appearance of laser bolts, traveling in slow motion, on a looping arc that would stab them into the distant star.

Ackbar rested a hand on Wedge's shoulder. "It is never easy to let your people go."

"No, and it never should be." Wedge gave the Mon Calamari a firm nod. "If it is, then we've become the enemy, and I'm not going to let that happen."

21

CORRAN'S FIRST GLIMPSE of Vladet after coming out of hyperspace revealed a blue ball streaked with white and stippled with dark green. "I think we ought to take it and keep it, Whistler. It looks a lot more pleasant than Fog-world ever did."

The astromech piped agreement, then brought the tactical screen up on Corran's monitor.

Corran glanced at it, then keyed his comm. "Three Flight is negative for eyeballs." He raised his left hand and flipped a switch above his head. "S-foils locked in attack position."

"I copy, Nine. Stand by."

"Standing by, Control." Ahead of him, speeding in at the planet, two of Defender Wing's Y-wing squadrons flew with an escort of four X-wings each. Because his flight was two ships shy of full, he and Ooryl were assigned to Warden Squadron. Champion, with General Salm flying lead, and Guardian squadrons were to go in first and soften things up so Warden, with its "understrength" defenses, could sweep through unmolested.

From the briefing Corran knew the base on Grand Isle would be no match for two squadrons of Y-wings. In addition to two laser cannons, the Y-wings sported twin ion cannons and two proton torpedo launchers. Each ship carried eight torpedoes, which meant either of the squadrons packed enough firepower to turn the lush, verdant landscape of Grand Isle into a black, smoking mass of liquid rock.

"Rogue Nine, continue to follow Two Flight, then orbit at Angels 10K."

"As ordered. Call us if you need anything."

"Will do, Control out."

Corran thought he caught a hint of his own frustration reflected in Tycho's voice. The orders he had just given Corran were being relayed to the members of Warden Squadron by Salm's own controller. The dual command chain was supposed to guarantee good command and control during the operation, but Corran doubted it would do anything of the sort. *In CorSec, when we were working a joint operation with Imperial Intelligence, the dual control became* duel *control, and that didn't work well at all.*

The ride down through the clear atmosphere got a little bumpy, but having a little resistance to fight with the controls felt good after six hours of doing nothing during the hyperspace run. Corran leveled the X-wing out at ten kilometers above the surface of the planet. "Control, Three Flight on station. Can you send me tacvisual from below?"

"Here you go, Nine. From Rogue Leader—returning the favor."

Corran's cheeks burned as he recalled his sensor data being used by the rest of the squadron on Folor. "Relay my thanks."

The visual feed from Wedge's X-wing showed four Y-wings swooping in at the northern face of the volcano's crater. From about a kilometer out, each of the slow craft launched a pair of proton torpedoes, then peeled off. The blue balls streaked out toward the mountainside. They exploded against it at a point where the abundant rains had already eroded and weakened the rock.

The rippling series of explosions cast smoke, rock, and burning plants into the air. The visual feed went vector, with green grids representing the land hidden by the smoke. Where there had been a gentle, curved dip in the crater's rim there now existed a sharp, jagged rift that looked as if some titanic vibro-ax had been used to chop the rock away. As Corran watched, the gap grew larger and he suddenly realized it was because Wedge was going in.

"TIGHTEN IT UP, DEUCE." Wedge's X-wing plunged through the smoke. "Mynock, make sure Control is getting a topo-scan of this trench."

The smoke cleared almost instantly, showing him a bristle of shattered volcanic rock a dozen meters off each wing. *Wide enough for the bombers, but not much room for error.* He nudged his throttle forward, distancing himself from the Y-wings following in his ion wash, and emerged from the split rock faster than any prudent pilot would have flown.

The laser shots from a quartet of TIE starfighters illuminated the air behind him as he came into the crater beneath the shield's protective dome. He immediately inverted and dove toward the base of the crater. Wind whistled from the S-foils. He rolled 180 degrees, filling his cockpit canopy with sky and pulled back on his stick to level the X-wing out.

The astromech behind him shrieked a warning.

"I know, I have two eyeballs on my tail." In the vacuum of space the presence of two TIEs behind him would have been very serious because their superior maneuverability made them difficult to shake. In atmosphere, however, their less-than-aerodynamic design and the turbulence produced by their twin engines' exhaust meant they had significant yaw problems. This made them no less deadly in a dogfight, but it did open up a myriad of strategies for dealing with them.

"Deuce, help here."

"On my way."

Bror's voice crackled through Wedge's helmet. "Three, on me. I have them."

Okay, time for me to gouge at least one of the eyeballs. Wedge brought the left wing up at forty-five degrees, then feathered his throttle back. The lessened thrust and atmospheric drag slowed him enough that his X-wing slid fifty meters down and twenty to the right.

The TIE pilot tried to follow him and remain at his back, but the hexagonal wings killed the sideslip. The drag slowed the TIE considerably, and it started to dip toward the jungle carpeting the crater floor. The pilot did the only thing he could to avoid a stall and crash. Diving his ship, he picked up speed and shot ahead of Wedge's X-wing, but not so far in front to allow Wedge to sideslip left and come in behind.

Not that I wanted to do that anyway. Wedge punched the left rudder pedal down and slewed the fighter's stern around to the right. Goosing the throttle straightened the ship out, then Wedge's crosshairs spitted the TIE and burned green. He hit the trigger and the quad lasers converged to blow bits of TIE fighter all over the Grand Isle landscape.

"Vaped one."

He saw a smoking TIE slam into a crater wall. "You're clear, Leader."

"Thanks, Deuce. Report, Three."

Nawara Ven's voice seemed tinged with some disgust. "Four got a pair. Island is blind to my sensors."

"Rogue Leader to Control, Champion is clear to run."

"Relaying that message now. Nine sends thanks for the feed."

Wedge smiled. He would have preferred to have Corran more involved in the action, but resistance was expected and until they could bring a new pilot in for Lujayne Forge, his flight would be vulnerable—in spite of the skills both Corran and Ooryl exhibited. General Salm had suggested leaving Three Flight to oversee Warden Squadron—Defender Wing's least experienced squadron. They'd all get mission experience, but nothing too life-threatening.

"Control to Rogue Leader, Champion and Guardian squadrons beginning their runs."

"I can see them, Control."

Through the gap lumbered the Y-wings. Never an elegant craft, they appeared to have the atmospheric flight characteristics of something between a TIE starfighter and a big rock. All of the Y-wings dove to pick up speed, but they leveled out with little apparent trouble and started in on their strafing and torpedo runs.

They may be slow and awkward, but Salm's pilots do know how to do their jobs!

"Control to Rogue Leader, we have trouble."

"Go ahead, Control."

"Two ships. *Carrack*-class cruiser and a *Lancer*-class frigate are in our exit vector. *Eridain* is beginning a withdrawal."

Wedge felt his stomach begin to fold in on itself. "Control, confirm *Lancer*-class frigate." *They're rare, maybe this is a mistake. Please, let it be a mistake.*

"Confirm *Lancer*-class frigate. Orders?"

Lancer-class frigates had been the Imperial Navy's solution to the problem of snubfighters and the threat they posed to capital ships. All of 250 meters long, the boxy ships were studded with twenty gunnery towers, each one sporting a Seinar Fleet System Quad laser array. With its speed, which was exceptional for a big ship, and those weapons, the *Lancer*-class ships were rancors amid a nerf herd. While the *Eridain*'s turbolasers could have driven it off, the *Carrack*-class cruiser outgunned the blockade runner, leaving the *Lancer* free to pounce on the fighters.

The X-wings were fast enough to elude the *Lancer*, but there was no way the Y-wings could outrun it or fight it. The *Lancer*'s guns made it the equivalent of eighty TIEs. Wedge glanced at his fuel monitor. He didn't have enough fuel remaining for a long fight with the *Lancer* and the run home. *I don't have enough fuel to let the* Eridain *run for help.* The best chance the Y-wings had was for the X-wings to engage the *Lancer* while they ran.

Before he could reply to Tycho's request for orders, General Salm's voice came over the comm. "Rogue Leader, screen Warden and Guardian squadrons and get them out of there. Champion will buy you the time."

"Negative, General. Champion *will* die that way, Rogue *may* die if we hit the *Lancer* and you break out."

"I'm making this an order, Antilles."

"Rogue Squadron takes its orders from Admiral Ackbar, General."

"Rogue Leader, this is Nine."

"Not now, Nine."

"Commander, I know how we can get the *Lancer*. Worst case, we lose one ship."

"What is he babbling about?"

"Easy, General. Go ahead, Nine."

"Ships have to close to two and a half klicks to get a firing solution for a proton torpedo. The Y-wing getting that close to the *Lancer* will be vaped. An X-wing can get in and send targeting data to the Y-wings, increasing the range for their solution. Same thing Captain Celchu did in the *Forbidden* at Chorax. The proton torps will home for thirty seconds, which means they can hit a target at just over fourteen and a half klicks. That will keep them safe from the *Lancer*."

Wedge frowned as he worked through Corran's plan. *A weaving X-wing might be able to get in close to the* Lancer.

General Salm saw the flaw in the plan at the same time Wedge did. "A weaving X-wing won't be able to get a targeting lock on the *Lancer*, Antilles. This is nonsense."

Corran's voice came back strong. "The X-wing doesn't need to get a targeting lock, he just needs to get in close. The Y-wings will be targeting the X-wing's homing beacon. Time it right, put the *Lancer* between the missiles and the X-wing, and you can scratch one *Lancer*."

"That just might work." Wedge pulled back on the X-wing's stick and started up toward space and the waiting Imperial ships. "I'll make the run."

"Negative, Antilles."

"General . . ."

"Rogue Leader, this is Nine, outbound. Release Warden Squadron to me."

Salm's fury sizzled over the comm. "Under no circumstances! Stop now, Rogue Nine."

"Release the squadron to me. I'm outbound and I'm going to play tag with that *Lancer*."

"This is treason, Nine." Salm's voice cracked with anger. "I'll have you shot."

"As long as it's Warden Squadron that's doing it, I don't mind a bit. Nine out."

"Antilles, do something!"

"He's got the altitude, General." *And the attitude.* "Release the squadron to him." Wedge let a deep breath out. "Then form Champion up on me, just in case his run doesn't do the trick."

CORRAN KEYED HIS COMM. "Okay, Wardens, this is how we become heroes. Link your torpedoes so you'll be shooting two. You'll shoot them on my mark. Timing is critical here—go too early and you won't hit anything. Go too late and I'm . . . look, just don't go too late. Ten, I need you to match their speed and don't let them get any closer than eight and a half klicks from me. And not much farther either. My homing beacon will be on 312.43. Use that as the frequency for the target lock on the torpedoes."

"Got it, Nine."

"Control, Nine here. Be prepared to scatter the Wardens

with evasive maneuver plots in case the *Lancer* gets aggressive once the torpedoes are away."

"On it, Nine. Good luck."

Corran's hand strayed to the medallion he wore. "Thanks, Control. Nine out."

"Okay, Whistler, we have our work cut out for us." The pilot hit switches that pumped the full output of the fusion engine into propulsion. He ran all shield power to the forward shields. "I'm going to be trying to weave in at that monster. I want you to route my stick commands through a randomizer that adds or subtracts portions of five degrees in all dimensions from my commands. Don't let the *Lancer* get out of a twenty-degree cone of my nose, but in that cone I want to be jumping around, got it?"

The droid replied with a sharp, affirmative whistle.

"And at the *Lancer*, I want to invert and pull a tight loop scraping right over the top of its hull and down the other side. We should be going away at ninety degrees to our current line and back toward Vladet's atmosphere." Corran sighed. "If we make it that far."

Whistler squawked reprovingly.

"Sorry to get you into this." Corran punched the console button that enabled the droid's ejection system. "Maybe your next pilot won't be so stupid."

The green light above the button went out.

Corran hit the button again. "And maybe your next ship won't have shorts."

The light died again.

The pilot turned and looked back at the droid. "You got a death wish?"

Whistler brayed derisively at him.

"I am *not* looking at taking all the glory for myself." Corran swallowed past the lump in his throat. "Thanks for hanging in. My father died alone. Doing that doesn't recommend itself."

The droid gave him a scolding whoop.

"Okay, you do your part and I'll make sure we don't die."

Corran looked at his scanner. Sensors put him eighteen klicks out from the *Lancer*. "Whistler, check my math. At full power I'll do six klicks in the time it takes the missiles to catch me. That means they have to shoot when I hit the six klick mark. They have to be inside fifteen klicks from the *Lancer*. Looks like we're all lined up and ready to go."

The droid chirped triumphantly and a countdown clock started in the upper corner of the sensor display. "Nine to Wardens, forty, four-oh, seconds to launch."

"Whistler, cut in the randomizer when I hit two and a half klicks from the target." The *Lancer*'s weaponry, because it was taken from TIE bombers, suffered the same range limitations as the fighters. "Also map how the towers are working and send that data back to Control and Rogue Leader. If the *Lancer* has any weak points, any guns that aren't shooting well, they need to know."

The timer counted down to ten seconds. Corran rubbed his medallion one more time, then settled his right hand on the stick and smiled. "Here goes Rogue Nine, following the unit's tradition of accepting suicide missions with a smile. Wardens, on my mark. Five. Four. Three. Two. One. Mark. Launch torpedoes!"

The comm came alive with fire reports. Corran couldn't make sense of the babble, but as the clash of voices died, he did hear "Warden Three, torpedoes away."

He glanced at the timer, which had started scrolling off seconds until impact. *Two seconds late. Probably not a problem.* "Whistler, you want to kill the volume on the missile lock warning siren? I *am* aware they're incoming."

The background noise in the cockpit died. He watched the seconds slowly count down. It seemed to take forever for him to pass from the launch point to halfway in on the *Lancer*. As his ship streaked in he could see strings of green laser bolts begin to stretch out toward him. They began to curve and curl as the gunners tried to track his ship. The closing speed made all of their initial shots go long.

Twelve and one-quarter seconds from impact, Whistler brought the randomizing program into play and Corran felt the stick begin to twitch. A tiny spark of fear ran through him as he imagined he had lost control of the ship. In its wake he found a calm that felt all too familiar from the last night on Talasea. *Well, I didn't die then. Maybe, just maybe . . .*

Easing the stick back and to the left he tossed the X-wing into the weave. Wave after seemingly solid wave of green laser energy lashed out from the *Lancer*, yet his snubfighter sliced through the troughs and curled around the crests, flirting with their deadly caresses. Light flashed against his shields, partially blinding him, but those glancing hits neither slowed nor deflected him.

There was no missing his target. The *Lancer*-class frigate— Whistler identified it as the *Ravager*—swelled into a hard-edged, spiky rectangle with an up-bent prow and a bulbous engine assembly. Green backlight from the quads splashed color over the ship's Imperial-white exterior. Corran nudged the X-wing in line, more or less, with the ship's middle deck, then the X-wing whirled out of his control.

In compliance with the instructions he had given Whistler before, the droid rolled the fighter hard to starboard. The stick bashed Corran's right hand against the side of the cockpit, but before the pain could begin to register, the stick tore itself free of his grasp and smacked him solidly in the chest. With the stick pinning him back in his command chair, Corran could only look up and watch the *Ravager*'s hull blur as it flashed past.

The torpedoes had been within half a second of catching the X-wing when it snapped up and around the *Ravager*. While fully capable of making the same maneuver the fighter had, because of their greater speed, the torpedoes needed more space in which to make it. Even as they started to correct their courses to follow Corran, they slammed into the *Lancer* and detonated.

The first half-dozen explosions produced more energy than

the shields could absorb. The shields went down, leaving the frigate open to the rest of the torpedo swarm. Blast shields buckled and transparisteel viewports evaporated as the torpedoes detonated. Titanium hull plates went molten, flowing into globules of metal that would harden as perfect spheres in the frozen darkness of space. Decks ruptured and the growing fireball at the center of the ship consumed atmosphere, equipment, and personnel with a rapacious appetite.

All but two of the torpedoes fed into the roiling plasma storm raging in the heart of the *Ravager*. In bisecting the ship, the torpedoes cut all power and control links between the bridge, in the prow, and the engines at the stern. Automatic safeguards immediately kicked in and the engines shut down. All laser fire from the *Ravager* died and the stricken ship keeled over. It began to lose a tug-of-war with the planet below and slowly tumbled down into Rachuk's gravity well.

Corran, in an X-wing sprinting away from the Imperial frigate, could see none of the damage the torpedoes did to the *Ravager*. He stared down his sensor monitor and smiled as the sensors reported, line by line, the deaths of twenty-two torpedoes that were following him.

Twenty-two? But there should have been twenty-four. He pried the stick off his chest. "Whistler, where are those last two missiles?"

The sensor array shifted. The torpedoes had shot under the *Lancer*, reacquiring his beacon when he cleared the frigate's far side. *Almost here. I have to break hard!*

The stick twitched and jerked of its own accord. Horror trickled electricity through Corran's guts. "Whistler, cut it out!"

The stick still bucked and fought against his grip. Corran realized, in one painfully crystal-clear moment, that in having used the indefinite pronoun *it* in his last command he had made a mistake equal in magnitude to still having all shield energy in his forward arc. He started to rectify both of those errors, but the proximity indicator reporting the location of Warden Three's torpedoes told him his time had run out.

22

K IRTAN LOOR'S SHUTTLE came out of hyperspace a second before the spread of proton torpedoes hit the *Ravager*. Hanging nearly ten kilometers above the distant *Lancer*, all Kirtan saw was a cone of green laser light stabbing off into space, then a brilliant light dawning at the base of the cone, illuminating the frigate in which it burned. Subsidiary blasts surrounded the ship with fire, then it slowly started to drift away as escape pods shot in all directions away from it.

"What in Sith happened there?"

The shuttle's pilot shook his head. "I don't know, but I'm reading a Corellian blockade runner out there and a number of Alliance fighters. I'm taking us in to the *Expeditious* now!"

The fear in the man's voice almost overwhelmed Kirtan's sense of mission. "While you're running, Lieutenant, get me as much comm chatter captured as you can. I want all of it. Do you have any survey probes? Launch one."

"Sensors are telling us all we need to know about the dead frigate, sir."

"Not it, you moron, launch it at the runner and the fighters." Only because he couldn't fly the shuttle did Kirtan refrain from throttling the pilot. "If you had lasers for brains you couldn't melt ice with them."

"Probe away." The pilot glanced back at him. "Anything else, or can I land us on the *Expeditious* and get us out of here?"

"Are the fighters a serious threat to us?"

"Probably not, they're all too far away, but I don't want to chance it."

"Very well, do your docking maneuver, but keep data flow constant from that probe."

"As you command, my lord."

Kirtan ignored the mocking tones in the man's voice and sat back to think. The tiny rocket probe would provide little solid data. It was designed to be used to sink into a planet's atmosphere and provide a shuttle with wind and atmospheric data that would affect flight and landing. It also had basic communications scanning capabilities and some visual sensors that might provide him data about the blockade runner and the fighters.

All of that would only confirm what he knew inside already. The fighters, or part of them at least, were from Rogue Squadron. Their need to strike back after the raid on their base was obvious, as was the Rebellion's need to punish Admiral Devlia for daring to strike at them.

Kirtan pressed his hands together, fingertip to fingertip. "Lieutenant, is there any signal from Grand Isle?"

"Automatic warning beacons and faint homing locators from TIE wreckage."

Good, then Devlia got what he deserved.

Kirtan had assumed Rogue Squadron and the Rebellion would exact retribution for the raid even before he had deduced its location. This was why he had wanted a mechanical probe to be followed by a full-scale assault. Destroying Rogue Squadron would have hampered Rebel operations in the Rachuk sector and clearly would have prevented the loss of the

Ravager, as well as Grand Isle. *If it had been done my way Admiral Devlia would be a hero instead of just dead.*

Kirtan closed his eyes and summoned up all the information he had about troop strengths and locations in the sphere of space that surrounded Coruscant. Corellia and Kuat both were located in the most thickly populated portion of the galaxy and were heavily defended because of their shipyards. Their sectors had limited Rebel activity, largely because of the Imperial presence. The Rebels, while arrogant enough to think they could destroy the Empire, were not stupid. Hitting the Empire where it was strong was not a good way to win the war.

Sectors like Rachuk were weak links in the perimeter, but were not the keys to winning the galactic civil war. Industrialized warfare called for the destruction of a force's ability to wage war. Conquering primitive worlds that produced very little of what contributed to the war effort was not a way to do that. The ease of delivering forces to strike at Rachuk from other Imperial garrisons meant it would be difficult to hold, therefore he assumed the Rebels would not try to hold it.

By leaving it in our hands we have to devote forces to holding it, further diluting our strength.

The ideal choice for a Rebel strike would be in a sector of space where travel was limited because of black holes, clouds of ionized gases, and other gravitic anomalies that made hyperspace travel unpredictable and dangerous. It would also be outside the most solidly inhabited areas of the galaxy to minimize the amount of support the Empire could devote to it, but it wouldn't be so far outside that same area that the Alliance, which also drew a lot of support from the Empire's populous worlds, could not supply and support it.

From his encyclopedic memory Kirtan dredged up the names of a dozen candidate sectors, and he knew there had to be four times that number that he did not know about. He purposely refrained from allowing himself to select a target. *Assuming the veracity of a working hypothesis is the sort of mistake that caused Gil Bastra's death. I cannot afford another such mistake.*

The pilot flipped a switch on the shuttle's command console and the wings retracted. The *Lambda*-class shuttle settled down on the dorsal hull of the cruiser. Retraction clamps clicked into place. A tremor shook the shuttle as the docking tunnel bumped the ship from below and formed an airtight seal around the shuttle's exit ramp.

Kirtan freed himself from his restraining straps. "Lieutenant, download all the feeds and probe data onto separate datacards, then wipe this ship's memory."

"Yes, sir."

Kirtan left the cockpit and descended the ramp into the *Expeditious*. Captain Rojahn greeted him with a curious light in his eyes. "Welcome back aboard, Agent Loor. Your timing was rather precise. We were not waiting long."

"I don't imagine the *Ravager*'s crew has the same perspective on our timing you do."

The shorter man shook his head, then adjusted his grey cap. "Perhaps not. We might ask them about that if we are allowed to recover escape pods."

" 'Allowed' to recover them?"

"Most are going toward Vladet, but some are heading out into space. They probably assume the Rebels will take the world." Rojahn shrugged his shoulders. "I would recover them, but I have strict orders to head out to the Pyria system the moment I have you aboard."

The Pyria system was one of the candidate systems Kirtan had pinpointed. Borleias was the name of the inhabited world in that system. The Empire maintained a small base there overseen by General Evir Derricote. It was unremarkable, except that it was on his list of target systems for the Rebels.

Kirtan raised an eyebrow. "The orders came from Imperial Center, from Director Isard?"

Rojahn nodded. "There are sealed orders awaiting you in your cabin."

Kirtan thought for a second, then nodded. "Take us out of this system. If we pick up some escape pods before we jump, I have no problem with that. You will have to plot an evasive course to our destination. If the pods can concentrate themselves in our exit vector, they are all yours."

The Navy captain smiled. "Thank you, sir."

"No thanks are needed, Captain. We are all in this together." Kirtan refrained from smiling despite the feeling of power growing in his chest. *I trade time for loyalty—something I did not know to do on Corellia. With every lesson I learn I become more deadly to the Rebellion.*

Finally he did smile. *And the more deadly I am to the Rebellion, the more useful I become within the Empire. That usefulness translates into power, and in the Empire, power is the very stuff of life.*

23

C ORRAN PUSHED HIMSELF back on his bunk, leaning against the bulkhead and drawing his knees up. "What brings you guys here?"

Rhysati, sitting down at his feet, frowned. "We just heard you were confined to quarters and could be facing a court-martial. How are you doing?"

The Corellian shrugged. "I'm fine."

Erisi Dlarit brushed black bangs away from her face as she sat on Ooryl's bed. "Aren't you angry? To be treated like this, after what you did."

He hesitated before answering her. Upon their return to the *Reprieve* Wedge had pulled him aside and said General Salm intended to bring him up on charges of insubordination, disobeying direct orders, and pirating a squadron of bombers. Wedge had said he thought he could get the charges quashed in light of how things went at Vladet, but until then he wanted Corran to consider himself confined to quarters. In disciplining him in private, he gave Corran the chance to keep the matter private until it was adjudicated.

"I guess I'm not angry." Corran was surprised to hear himself saying that, but he didn't feel the throat-constricting rage that had characterized how he felt after his father's murderer was turned loose without so much as an arraignment. "General Salm has no choice but to prefer charges. What I did was pretty stupid and very risky—and I put one of his squadrons in jeopardy."

The Twi'lek let one of his brain tails drape itself over Rhysati's shoulder and lightly stroke her throat. "If the General didn't report Corran's actions, military discipline would break down. Any pilot with a crack-brained scheme—not to characterize what you did as crack-brained, mind you—could disobey orders and, most likely, get himself killed."

Erisi leaned forward with her elbows on her knees. Corran noticed that her flight suit was unzipped far enough to give him a fair view of her cleavage. "But Corran didn't get himself killed . . ."

Corran smiled. "But it was a near thing. One of the pig-drivers shot his torps late. They lost my signal, then picked it up again when I was heading away from the *Ravager*. When I noticed they were coming after me I realized that Whistler hadn't killed the jiggle program he had running to randomize my flight as I headed into the *Lancer*'s light. I wanted to break hard, but he had me locked in on a twenty-degree cone, so all I could do was fly straight."

"Then how did you . . . ?" Even a puzzled frown couldn't detract too much from Erisi's beauty.

"I told Whistler to cut *it* out. I was thinking the jiggle code when I said *it*. Whistler, being a bit more direct in his problem solving, just cut the homing beacon the torps were using to track me. They lost their target, couldn't reacquire it, and exploded. The second or so it took them to do all that took me outside their blast radius."

Rhysati smiled and gently patted Nawara's brain tail. "Well, we're happy your R2 unit takes such good care of you. And I, for one, want to thank you for doing what you did out there. That *Lancer* would have killed a lot of us if we had tried to take it out the normal way."

The Twi'lek nodded. "The traditional Rogue Squadron way—leaving bits and pieces of X-wings scattered around."

The blue-eyed woman from Thyferra frowned at Nawara. "We have a new tradition now, and Corran's action is a glorious part of it. We've had three missions and we've lost none of our pilots—and this when Commander Antilles told us our first five missions would kill a bunch of us off."

"Erisi, we *have* lost a pilot." Corran scratched at his chest where he'd been shot. "We almost lost three more on Talasea. Don't start thinking we're invulnerable. The missions we've had so far have been relatively simple."

"I know that, Corran. I don't think of us as leading charmed lives." Her eyes tightened slightly, but Corran sensed no ire in the changed expression. "In reading about the unit's history, it has always flown well on simple missions. Even so, our kill rates and repair rates are better than ever before. I don't doubt we'll have missions that will push us to the limit, but if statistics have any truth in them, we've not been burning up all our luck on our missions."

"Speak for yourself." Corran winked at her. "At the Bank of Luck, I've hit my credit limit."

Nawara jerked a thumb at the cabin's closed doorway. "Well, there's a wing of bomber jocks willing to make payments on your account. Right now they're settling for buying the Rogues a couple of rounds down in the recreation center."

"They're toasting Bror for picking up two eyeballs over Grand Isle." Rhysati rolled her eyes. "They'd rather be buying drinks for you."

"He's the hot pilot from the run. Two is more than I got."

Erisi frowned at him. "But you got the frigate."

Corran shook his head. "No I didn't."

"What?"

The Twi'lek explained. "If Corran had so much as shot one laser burst at the frigate, then he would have gotten a piece of the kill, but fractions below a half are not recognized as being worthy of being recorded. Warden Squadron got the frigate— Corran is able to verify it, but he gets nothing for it."

"That's not fair." Erisi looked from Nawara to Corran and back again. "He should get credit for the kill."

"Erisi," Rhysati began, "if you're shooting at some squint and he jukes and your shots illuminate an eyeball, would you want the squint to get credit for your kill?"

"I see your point, but I do not think it is fair."

"I'll survive it." Corran shrugged. "What's not fair is the three of you spending time here with me when you should be downstairs having fun and billing it to Defender Wing. Go on, have a good time."

Rhysati stood and slipped an arm around Nawara's waist. "We'll be going, then. We'll let the others know you're doing fine."

"Thanks."

Rhysati looked at Erisi. "Coming?"

"In a minute."

"All right."

The two of them left and the hatch slid shut, then Erisi crossed the narrow room and took Rhysati's place at the foot of the bed. All of a sudden it seemed to Corran that the cabin, which was none too big to begin with, had become much more close and tiny. He would have used the word "intimate" to describe it, but the way Erisi laid a hand on his knee gave him the impression she had that word in mind as well, and for some reason that made him feel a bit uncomfortable.

"Corran, I just wanted to let you know that I felt . . . feel I owe you a debt it will be very hard to repay. When the report of a *Lancer* being in our exit vector came through I knew . . ." Erisi hesitated and pressed her free hand lightly against her throat. "I knew I wasn't going to make it. I'm not the best pilot in this unit and I was certain I would die fighting against the frigate. And then you did what you did and I felt as if a great crushing weight had been lifted from me."

She shook her head, bringing dark bangs down to half hide

her blue eyes. "I know this is sudden and . . . well, I just feel very *close* to you now." Leaning forward, she rested both her hands on his kneecaps and laid her chin on top of them. "Do you know what I mean?"

"Yeah, probably better than you think."

She blinked her eyes, then smiled. "You feel it, too?"

"I've felt it." Corran sighed. "A huge hunk of what you're feeling comes from the downside of the emotional spike you hit during the run. I know what that's like. In CorSec I was partnered with a woman, Iella Wessiri. She was pretty— not as pretty as you are, but no Gamorrean either. We raided a glitterstim dealer's warehouse and a rather nasty lightfight erupted. One guy had me centered in his sights when she took him out. I'd thought I was dead and she saved me.

"In the immediate aftermath of that I thought I was in love with her—or in lust, at least. Before then we'd just been friends, like you and I are. Maybe there were some core sparks of something but nothing we'd noticed or acted on. And that night, well, we both felt it."

"What happened?"

Corran scowled. "The Imperial liaison officer took the two of us into custody for debriefing. Two days later we saw each other again. The heat of the moment had passed and we laughed about it, but never did anything. That fear, and having been so closely brushed by death, made us want something positive to counteract it."

"Is that bad?"

"No, it's not bad, Erisi." Corran shifted around so he sat beside her and held both of her hands in his. "It's also not genuine. And, I must admit, I'm not sure about the wisdom of getting involved with someone inside the unit."

"Rhysati and Nawara don't seem to have trouble with it."

"I know, and I think they're good for each other."

Erisi raised his right hand to her mouth and kissed his palm. "I think you may be right, Corran, but I need to ask you something. You said you and your partner had sparks at some basic level, and that led to your attraction to her. Do we have those sparks?"

"Perhaps, I don't know." Feeling uncomfortably warm, Corran tugged at the collar of his flight suit. "For the past several years, both before and since leaving CorSec, my emotional life has been a bit unstable."

"Is there someone else? Do you still care for your partner?"

"No, there's no one else, not Iella, not anyone."

Erisi pursed her lips for a moment, then nodded. "I accept what you're saying." She stood and stretched languorously. "Of course, you don't know what you're missing."

Corran let out a deep breath, then rose from his bunk. "I wish I didn't. Right now, though, I'm exhausted enough that I'd be no good to either one of us."

She laughed and kissed him lightly on the mouth. "Corran, I really *do* appreciate your concerns over my feelings." Erisi backed away from him toward the opening hatchway. "Have sweet dreams."

She turned in the open hatchway and came face-to-face with Mirax Terrik. The smuggler's daughter smiled politely. "Excuse me, I didn't realize I was intruding."

"Not at all, Miss Terrik." All the warmth drained from Erisi's voice. "I was just leaving so Lieutenant Horn could get some rest. He's confined to quarters and I don't believe that order allows *civilian* visitors.".

Mirax tapped the datapad riding in a sheath on her left forearm. "I have permission to visit from his commanding officer. We can check with Emtrey if you wish."

Erisi looked back at Corran and he would have preferred being under the *Ravager*'s guns again to her stare. "It's okay, Erisi. I'm sure Miss Terrik won't be staying long. Thanks for the talk."

"You're most welcome, Lieutenant." Erisi turned and nodded curtly to Mirax. "Miss Terrik."

"Later." Mirax watched Erisi walk away, then added under her breath, "*Much* later." Turning back around she caught

Corran staring after Erisi. "Flyboys—all you think about is sex."

"What?"

She shoved the plastic case she was carrying into his stomach none too gently, then walked past him into the cabin. "The smallest smuggling hold on the *Skate* is bigger than this."

"The *Reprieve* wasn't built for pleasure cruising or smuggling. I'm looking forward to grounding at a new base." Corran stepped back out of the hatchway and let it close. Hefting the box he asked, "What's this?"

Mirax flopped down on Ooryl's bed. "Wedge said you might be down—but then he didn't realize the bacta queen would be here. I figured you might like some stuff from home so I got this little package together." She shrugged. "I intended it as something of a peace offering, I guess."

Corran sat on the edge of his bed and undid the case's two latches. He opened the box and smiled. In it he saw a half-dozen datacard issues of magazines from Corellia, as well as two tins of spicy, smoked nerf and a bottle of Whyren's Reserve whiskey.

"Wow. This is more stuff from Corellia than I've seen in the past two years."

Mirax rolled up on her right side and rested her head on her right hand. "Below the whiskey is a *ryshcate*. I had to substitute some ingredients but I think it turned out pretty good."

Corran pulled the whiskey bottle out of the case and set it down beside him. Beneath it, wrapped in clear plastic, sat the dark brown sweetcake that was traditionally reserved for birthdays, anniversaries, or other celebrations of momentous occasions. "Last time I had *ryshcate* was after my father died, after the funeral. Where'd you find the *vweliu* nuts to put into it?"

"Around."

"Around?"

"Yeah, around. There's a thriving black market in Corellian goods out there. A lot of us are out here and with the

Diktat in place the Imps still control our space. This means we have a big demand with a restricted supply, so it pays to move the merchandise." She scowled at the hatch. "That blasted protocol droid of yours has—er, had—two *cases* of Corellian whiskey and has been doling it out to me in one and two bottle lots. I could have gotten an old Customs ship to replace the one that got left in that lake in the Hensara system for the whole case, but he's holding back on me. Getting two bottles out of him cost me a hyperdrive horizontal booster and a case of l'lahsh mixes that came from Alderaan before it died."

Corran raised an eyebrow. "Emtrey had the whiskey?"

"I got two bottles from him. One's beside you and one's in the *ryshcate*." She sat up and their knees almost touched. "You going to arrest the droid for smuggling?"

"No, just let him off with a warning, I guess." The fighter pilot smiled. "Do you want some of the *ryshcate*? You made it, so you should have some of it."

She hesitated, then nodded her head. "A small piece, but only if we can think of a reason to celebrate."

"How about being alive?"

"Good enough for me."

Corran punctured the plastic wrap with his thumb and broke a corner off the moist, flat cake. He split it in two and handed her the larger of the pieces. In keeping with the tradition he said, "We share this *ryshcate* in the same way we share our celebration of life."

"To the celebration of life."

They each bit into the cake and Corran clumsily caught crumbs in his left hand. The cake itself was delicious. The sweetness softened the woody bite of the whiskey, and the *vweliu* nuts just melted in his mouth. He swallowed and smiled. "This is wonderful!"

"Even if it was made from smuggled ingredients?"

"Even more reason to eat all the evidence." He shook his head. "As a peace offering, I can't think of anything better."

"Good." Mirax stood and ruffled his brown hair with her

hand. "When this Alliance finally gets around to going after Coruscant, I'll make another *ryshcate* and you can carry it to whoever thinks they're in charge. Make the war shorter."

"This *ryshcate* might have been able to turn Darth Vader into a Jedi again, but I'm not sure it would work on old Iceheart." He set the case on the bed. "Sure you don't want more?"

"Thanks, but I need to go back to the *Skate*." She looked at her datapad. "I have about six hours until I pull a run Coreward."

"Are we going to fly cover for you?"

"Nope, I'm using my wits and guts to get me through."

Corran frowned. "No slight intended, but isn't that dangerous?"

Mirax shook her head. "I've been ambushed *once* and you Rogues have been ambushed *twice*. Right now I suspect traveling without you might be a bit safer than traveling with you, but this is a simple run anyway." She kissed him on the cheek as the hatch opened. "Thanks for your concern. See you when I get back."

The hatch eclipsed her as it closed. It struck him that while he had been relieved when Erisi left, he wished Mirax had stayed. He knew he didn't lust after her—though she didn't surrender much, if anything at all, to Erisi in the way of looks. With her, because of their common world of origin, he had a connection that he and Erisi would never share. Even the fact that their fathers had been enemies somehow strengthened the bond between them.

He shook himself. "Snap out of it, Horn. You're fixing on her the way Erisi fixed on you. Booster Terrik's daughter and Hal Horn's son might be able to be friendly enemies—maybe even friends—but nothing more than that. Remember, first, last, and always, she's a smuggler. There'll come a point when you're not cost effective and she'll cut her losses."

He heard his words and knew there was a lot of truth in them. He also heard a lot of his father in them, and that gave him pause. He popped the other half of his piece of *ryshcate* into his mouth. *There are better things to do with my mouth than give voice to speculations that dishonor her gift. We can be friends and* will *be friends. Out here, with the Empire cutting us off from our home, what we have in common is more important than any differences that might drive us apart.*

24

WEDGE'S FEELINGS ABOUT the briefing on *Home One* had started bad and quickly went to worse. It hadn't helped that he had no time to pull Admiral Ackbar and General Salm aside to work out some sort of compromise on Corran's case. *Leaving him hanging is more of a disservice than disciplining him.* Given the Admiral's apparent distraction with the briefing, Wedge assumed he would get no chance to make a case in support of Corran.

Though he was a Commander, he was the most junior officer in attendance at the meeting. He recognized several people besides Admiral Ackbar and General Salm but by no means knew who all those in attendance were. He noticed a knot of four Bothans—a General, two Colonels, and one Commander—up toward the front of the room, but could not name any of them. Clearly, though, they were in charge of the briefing—a point made abundantly clear when the junior officers moved through the room, downloading information from their datapads into those of the other officers.

The Bothan General took the podium at the front of the room and the lights above his audience dimmed. The Bothan's white fur became almost dazzling and his golden eyes appeared to be made of liquid metal. Wearing an Alliance Army uniform and clutching a telescoping silver pointer in both hands at the small of his back, he began speaking in a soft voice that did not lack for intensity.

"I am General Laryn Kre'fey and I am now going to brief you on the mission that will open the way to Coruscant for our valiant forces. If you will look to your datapads, you will see the basics on the installation we are to hit. You do not need to know where it is right now, but suffice it to say possession of this base is the key to the Imperial Core."

Wedge did his best to follow the briefing. The world— codename Blackmoon—was normal and habitable, not unlike Endor save that it had no native lifeforms akin to the Ewoks. Initial survey teams, sent out under the Old Republic, had rated the world poor in mineral or otherwise exploitable wealth. A small base had been created there because the system proved useful as a plotting point for runs to the Corporate sector and beyond, but being a crossroads in space was insufficient to spur much growth and commerce. Other than some experimental attempts at development—all of which failed when exotic research no longer earned generous investment tax credits under the Empire, the world was left largely alone.

"The Empire did expand the base and provide force shield projectors but only so the Rebellion would not find it an inviting target for transition into a sanctuary so close to the Core." General Kre'fey gestured with an open hand. "The base also supports four heavy ion cannons and has two squadrons of TIE fighters available to it."

Wedge frowned. The defenses struck him as odd—too much for an out-of-the-way world, but too little for a world that would put them perilously close to Coruscant. Vladet, a sector headquarters, had only had four TIEs on the ground, two ion cannons, and a set of shields, but not enough power to bring both cannons and shields on-line at the same time. Wedge didn't get the feeling that Blackmoon was some sort of Imperial trap, but he did think it was tough enough that the

Imps on the ground might be able to summon help from other worlds nearby and hold on until it arrived.

The Bothan General went on and described his proposed mode of attack. It consisted of using the *Emancipator*—one of two Imperial Star Destroyers that had been captured at Endor and repaired by the Alliance—to batter down the shields. General Salm's Defender Wing would then go in to pound the Imperial facilities and defenses, with Rogue Squadron keeping the TIEs away from the bombers. Once ground resistance had been weakened, troop transports would land Alliance troops and complete the conquest of the world.

General Kre'fey concluded, "I expect to be operational in two weeks, with conquest completed within fifteen standard days from now."

General Salm looked past Wedge to Admiral Ackbar. "This plan is already approved?"

Ackbar, who had a silver Mon Calamari Admiral—Ragab of the *Emancipator*—on his other side, wore a pained expression on his face. "Yes, General Salm, this plan . . ."

Kre'fey interrupted him. "Forgive me, Admiral Ackbar, but I believe I can answer that question myself." The Bothan brushed the white fur on his face with his left hand, bringing the fur down to a point at his chin. "Yes, General, the Provisional Council has approved this plan. Would you be objecting to their exercise of wisdom in this matter?"

"I would never do that, General Kre'fey, but two weeks to prepare for an assault is a very short time."

"If your pilots are not up to it, General, there are other Y-wing squadrons in the fleet."

"My people will be ready."

No love lost between those two. Wedge raised his hand. "If I might, I do have some questions about the operation."

The Bothan opened his hands indulgently. "Please, proceed, Commander."

"The deflector shields—your report shows them vulnerable to bombardment when they are projected far enough to cover nonessential satellite facilities on the ground. What if the commander just shrinks the diameter of the coverage?"

"It would not matter. The base has insufficient generating capacity to bring up shields that could withstand our bombardment."

"Even if the ion cannons are not on-line?"

That question brought a moment's hesitation before it was answered. "It would make no difference."

Wedge didn't like the faint confidence in Kre'fey's voice. The success of the operation was predicated on bringing the shields down. While Wedge didn't want to think General Kre'fey was being stupid, his reliance on bombardment from space seemed remarkably shortsighted. The Imps had chosen to use a ground assault on Hoth to bring the shields down. While bombardment had worked elsewhere in the past, the Hoth solution seemed to work the best. And the presence of ion cannons on the ground meant the ships doing the bombarding could be disrupted, slowing their schedule and raising the specter of help coming in from another system in time to beat back the assault.

He raised his hand again.

"Yes, Commander Antilles."

"I don't see a breakdown of the TIEs on Blackmoon. Are they eyeballs, squints, dupes, or brights?"

The Bothan's eyes hardened. "I beg your pardon?"

General Salm translated. "He wants to know if the fighters are TIE starfighters, Interceptors, bombers, or advanced models."

"Ah, starfighters mostly, and some others." Kre'fey looked around the room for other questions, but no one had any. "To maintain operational security you will not be given the actual coordinates of your destination until you head out. The simulation packages you are given will fill your needs for detailed information. Ysanne Isard has stepped up her counterintelligence efforts against us and without surprise, this mission will suffer."

Without surprise, our *people will suffer.* Wedge shook his head. "I don't like this."

The Bothan General's eyes narrowed to golden crescents. "Your likes and dislikes are immaterial, Commander. The Provisional Council has approved this plan, and that is enough."

The Corellian pilot bristled at the rebuke. "They may approve of it, but they're not going to be flying this mission, General."

"But *I* will be there, Commander, in the first transport, leading the way down to take Blackmoon." Kre'fey's nostrils flared as if he were sniffing about for prey. "I trust you do not doubt Bothan courage."

How could I when you Bothans take every opportunity to remind all of us that your *people captured the location of and information about the second Death Star?* "No, sir, I do not. I trust you do not doubt the courage of my people. They'll do the mission, but I feel I have an obligation to them to make sure they're going to come home from it."

Kre'fey's lip curled in a sneer. "An obligation you have acquitted so well in the *past*, Commander Antilles."

Wedge felt a fist tighten around his heart. The faces of all the friends and comrades he had lost throughout the Rebellion flashed through his mind. It struck him that each one of them had become posthumous heroes specifically to allow idiots like Kre'fey the opportunity to make *more* Rebels into *posthumous heroes.* The ranks of the dead seemed endless, and inside a heartbeat the fire Wedge would have turned on Kre'fey was snuffed by the void that had claimed those he remembered.

Ackbar stood abruptly. "I believe, General Kre'fey, that Commander Antilles's concerns are valid. I am surprised your normally painstaking precision in matters of intelligence gathering has been allowed to flag here. If you will, you have told us the hour the tide will be high, but some of us need to know the minute and the second. You have it within your ability to provide us this information and you will."

The Bothan glared at the Mon Calamari. "Or?"

"Or I will see fit to cancel the operation."

"But the Council approved it."

Ackbar's chin came up. "The Council is a political body that makes political decisions. Unlike a battle where the outcome cannot be reconsidered, political decisions can be recalled and revised endlessly. The Council did decide that a move toward Coruscant needed to be made, and your assault met the parameters they set forth. This does not mean it is the *only* plan that might do that."

"We shall see whether or not this assault goes forward, Admiral. I will distribute simulator packages to all the commands so they may begin training."

The Mon Calamari rested his fists on his hips. "You'll get that data, or I shall destroy all your simulator packages myself."

The Bothan nibbled his lower lip, then nodded to his staff. "Fine, we will get you the information you want, *if it is obtainable*." He snapped an order in Bothan to his aides and they trailed him from the room.

The room emptied rather quickly, leaving Wedge, Salm, and Ackbar alone before the illuminated podium. The Mon Calamari lowered his head and peered down into Wedge's face. "You have my sympathies. That was uncalled for."

Wedge still felt like he'd been gutshot. "Why is it that everyone gives the Bothans credit for locating the second Death Star and announcing the Emperor would be on it? Has everyone forgotten the Emperor lured us to Endor to exterminate us? The Bothans were had, yet they wear their deception like a badge of honor."

The Mon Calamari nodded slowly. "I have heard others voice your opinion—mostly those in the Council who have found themselves between a Bothan and some mote of power. Bothans would tell you that the Emperor only conceived of the ambush *after* the information was stolen and he became suspicious. We only have the Emperor's word that he fooled the Bothans and while Luke would never knowingly lie to us, I cannot trust the Emperor in anything."

Wedge sat forward and scrubbed his hands over his face. "I'm sure you are correct, Admiral. I guess I just see that doubt as the shadow lurking behind the unbridled self-confidence the Bothans exhibit. They may have been right about the Death Star, and Kre'fey may be right about this Blackmoon, but if he isn't, lots of people will die."

"I share your concern, Commander. You will get your information."

The Corellian nodded. "Can you tell me where this Blackmoon is anyway?"

Ackbar hesitated. "Need to know, Commander, and right now you don't need to know. Before you go, however, you will have all the data you need. The Blackmoon system is located in a dense sector, with limited ways in and out. Computing astronav solutions will be simple since there are so few. It makes ambushes easier, too, so the information will be provided when you need it, not when you want it."

Wedge mulled that over, then nodded. "I do understand the need for security. I don't like the limitations it imposes, but I understand them."

The Mon Calamari's mouth opened in a low chuckle. "We have progress. You'll be moving from the fleet to a world called Noquivzor and you will stage from there. Several other units will join you there, including Defender Wing." He clapped his hands together. "So, I imagine you would like to discuss the charges General Salm will bring against Corran Horn?"

Wedge sat back up. "If we're going to be living together I think it would be for the best. Do you concur, General?"

Salm nodded his head. "I agree, but let's save the trouble. Forget the charges."

"Excuse me?"

The balding bomber pilot held his hands up. "If I push for a court-martial of Horn for his actions, I'd be a fool and he'd sit out this assault on Blackmoon." Salm's brown eyes contracted with disgust. "I still think the whole of Rogue Squadron is out of line, but I think things are going to go badly at Blackmoon. With Horn and the rest of your pilots there, maybe things won't end up becoming the nightmare that I'm afraid is going to haunt me for the next two weeks."

25

THAT GENERAL DERRICOTE managed to refrain from sweating in the steamy atmosphere of Borleias did not surprise Kirtan Loor too terribly much. The good General was toadlike enough in his demeanor that the Intelligence officer imagined it saved him from melting in the heat and humidity. The bloated, lumpen commander of Imperial forces in the Pyria system fitted his face with a smile—the abrupt curve of his mouth imitated by the sweep of the two chins jiggling beneath it.

"I am pleased to see, Agent Loor, that the past week and a half here on Borleias have not appeared to have taken their toll on you." The man pressed stubby-fingered hands against the dark wood of his desktop. "You found everything you needed for your survey of our defenses?"

Kirtan nodded once, then froze and stared down at the Imperial officer for a second without saying anything. He waited, silent and unmoving, until the corners of the man's smile began to quiver. "My security review proved satisfactory. Everything is as it should be here at the installation. Your shield generators are in good repair, your two squadrons of TIE fighters are being maintained at a high level of readiness, and your training schedule has your pilots logging enough time for *twice* their number."

"Preparation is the price for constant vigilance, Agent Loor." Derricote's voice remained blasé, but his bovine, brown eyes began blinking a bit more rapidly than they should have normally. "We are here to stop the Rebellion, so we must be prepared."

Kirtan smiled easily, then leaned forward on the man's desk. "And you are prepared. You have done very well to keep this base secure, and in fact, your computer security is tighter than anything I have seen outside Imperial Center itself. You also work harder than any other officer I have seen since the Emperor's death."

"I am all for the Empire."

"You are all for *yourself*." Kirtan tapped the datapad built into the man's desk. "I took the liberty of visiting your office when you were not here and I pulled the secret files from your datapad. You truly are an artist. You duplicate requisitions, append intricate routing tags to them, and send them off to multiple commands, each of which believes you are under its care. You have successfully drawn enough fuel and ordinance to maintain *four* squadrons of TIE fighters. Since only two are here, I have to assume the others are at the Alderaan Biotics site."

"I don't know what you're talking about."

"I sincerely doubt that, General. I have read your file. You studied at the Imperial Naval Academy, but concentrated on biological and botanical subjects. While you are fully qualified to oversee a military installation such as this, you are *uniquely suited* to making the Biotics site operational again." Kirtan smiled. "And profitable?"

Derricote's face became ashen, but his smile did not fully erode. "This has not been unanticipated, Agent Loor. I *do* have resources."

Kirtan raised himself to his full height, then looked back down at Derricote. "This does not surprise me, General. The

Alderaan Biotics hydroponic facility was barely more than a tax loss for the parent corporation before the tax laws changed. It was abandoned to the care of maintenance droids and forgotten. Then Alderaan was *disciplined* and the market for goods from Alderaan blossomed. My conservative estimate, based on data about twelve months old, is that if you've been operational for two years you should have cleared two million credits."

"We have been at our fullest production capacity for only fifteen months, but our overhead is low, so we have actually made 2.75 million credits—though much of this is tied up in inventory maintained off-world."

"Your overhead is low because the Empire is subsidizing your operation."

The General steepled his fingers. "Think of it as *our* operation."

"I could think of it as *my* operation, General." Kirtan folded his arms across his chest. "I do not think I could hold it for long, however. In going back over your security system I noticed evidence of what could have been Alliance tampering with holonet messages."

Derricote's eyes grew hard and he sat up straighter at his desk. "Bothans. They make runs at all holonet communications. I feed them data and it keeps them happy."

The edge in the man's voice surprised Kirtan, as did the physical transformation. Just by sitting up and raising his chin, Derricote had shifted from being a noodle-spined sycophantic failure to the sort of man who could engineer the deception that made his covert agricultural enterprise possible. *He showed me what I wanted to see so I would underestimate him.*

Derricote touched the screen on his datapad. "Frequency of hits and length of contact is up. Should I correlate that to your visit, Agent Loor, or shall I just assume the Alliance and Empire taking an interest in my little home is a coincidence?"

Kirtan's eyes narrowed. "The Pyria system is one of a number that fits a profile for being a conduit into the Core for the Alliance."

"It fits because they don't know about my defenses."

"Two more squadrons of TIE fighters will mean little to them."

"Ah, so there are some things you *don't* know about Borleias. Imagine that." Derricote smiled. "I tell you what, son: You leave the defenses here to me. You're an Intelligence officer, not a military genius."

Kirtan pointed to the General's private datapad. "I saw nothing in there to indicate you're a military genius, sir."

Derricote tapped the side of his head with a thick finger. "That's because I'm smart enough to know that the only data that is safe is the data stored up here. I've anticipated a move against Borleias ever since I found the Biotics station in working order, and I've planned accordingly."

The Intelligence officer heard the confidence in the man's voice and isolated another component in the tone he used. *Eagerness.* "You're looking forward to this."

"I may have my business on the side here, Agent Loor, but I *am* a loyal son of the Empire." The large man shrugged. "Besides, I was at Derra IV. I learned to enjoy killing Rebels there, and have formed my plans here to make Borleias just as deadly to the Alliance."

"A *convoy* died at Derra IV, General. A laudable event, but it was not a military force." Kirtan shook his head. "You'll get their best here, including Rogue Squadron, I do not doubt."

"Their best or their worst, it does not matter." General Derricote smiled easily. "They're expecting to snuff a candle here at Borleias, but when they come, they'll get burned by a nova."

C ORRAN'S X-WING CAME out of hyperspace in the shadow of the *Emancipator*. The Imperial Star Destroyer's daggerlike profile stabbed deeply into the image of the world he knew only as Blackmoon. Beyond the *Emancipator* he saw the *Eridain* and two modified bulk cruisers. The *Mon Valle* was home to Salm's Defender Wing while the *Corulag* was the launching platform for the eight assault shuttles that would ferry down the Rebel ground troops.

The *Emancipator* remained in position to safeguard the fleet's exit vector from the system. While none of the briefings had supplied Corran the name of the system and world, he did know jumping out would be difficult. General Kre'fey, in giving them a final briefing, had emphasized the need for security concerning the operation and had promised that while they did not know the name of the world at which they were going to fight, future generations would, and would laud them for having been there.

At the time Corran had thought Kre'fey had enough confidence to take the world by himself, but that failed to banish the bad feelings he had about the mission. The briefings had all been longer on morale building than they had on facts.

While the simulator runs had let everyone get comfortable with their roles in the assault, something just felt *wrong* as far as Corran was concerned.

Keep your eyes open and fly your best—that's all you can do right now. Whistler brought up Corran's tactical screen. "Rogue Leader, I have no enemy ships on scan, but the base does have a shield up."

"Thanks, Nine. Rogues, form up to escort Defender Wing." Wedge's voice came cleanly through the speakers in Corran's helmet. "Fly high side on the *Emancipator*."

Corran pulled back on his stick and kicked the X-wing over in a lazy roll that brought him up above the Star Destroyer. All at once the capital ship started pulsing out salvo after salvo of turbolaser and ion cannon shots. Red bolts would merge into sheets of energy burning down through the atmosphere to slam into the Imperial base's shielding. The bloody-red color would soak down into the shield, obscuring the installation beneath it.

As it faded to pink, a cerulean blanket of ion cannon energy would drop over it. The blue fire fragmented and sizzled over the energy dome with hundreds of lightninglike tendrils. Some of them bled off the dome and buildings outside its sanctuary exploded and melted. The surrounding jungle began to burn, ringing the base with fire. *Makes for a perfect target, though the fire will make flying tough down there.*

"Whistler, get me a general track on air currents groundside. Also monitor the size of the shield. When it shrinks, it's coming down."

WAVE AFTER WAVE of energy poured down through the rising column of smoke. The energy slammed into the shields with a thunder crack that sent vibrations deep enough to shake the command bunker where Kirtan stood. The relentless pounding had made him flinch at first and fear for his life, but now the sounds merged into one unending rumble. The few working monitors in the command center showed satellite views of the attacking fleet and the fiery circle on the planet's surface.

Derricote turned toward Kirtan. "Hard to believe anyone could survive down there, isn't it?"

The Intelligence officer nodded. "It does tax credulity, General."

"And the Rebels are so ready to be credulous." The military man looked over at one of the technicians at the shield controls. "Status, Mr. Harm."

"Still at one hundred percent, sir."

"Good. Begin a step-back in random percentages of power—randomize from seven. When you hit seventy-five percent, cut to fifty. When their salvos slacken, go down to twenty, then five, then zero."

Kirtan felt fear trickle through his guts. "You are confident they won't level this place? They took Vladet down to the foundations."

"Which is why we are below the foundations, Agent Loor."

Kirtan cringed as a particularly powerful blast shook the ground. "I trust you know what you are doing."

"As you have no choice, I appreciate your confidence." Derricote rubbed his hands together. "The Rebels want this place to use for future operations, that's the only reason they're attacking. If they want it, they're going to pay my price to get it."

WHISTLER'S SQUAWK MADE Corran focus on the tactical screen. The shields over the base had begun to contract. As they began to come down, the *Emancipator* slackened off with turbolaser fire and concentrated on using the ion cannons. While they did slightly less damage than the lasers, if the shields came down unexpectedly quickly, an ion salvo wouldn't destroy what General Kre'fey intended to capture.

Corran brought his X-wing in beside Warden Squadron and killed his thrust. "Three Flight on station."

"I copy, Nine. Stand by." Tycho's voice clipped off abruptly as the flight controller switched channels.

Corran flipped his comm unit over to the tactical frequency he shared with his flight. They still had not gotten a pilot to replace Lujayne so Three Flight remained one pilot light. That was just one element of the operation that Corran didn't like. He knew pilots were not easy to come by, but he knew Tycho could have easily flown Lujayne's X-wing, and he thought the man would be a lot more valuable in a fighter than inside the *Eridain* directing traffic.

"Ten, Twelve, we hold here." Corran glanced at his tactical screen. "Their shields are failing fast. We'll be going in next."

Whistler's triumphant bleat heralded the collapse of Blackmoon's shields. Corran started to smile, but something nagged at the back of his brain. He couldn't identify it, but it nibbled away at his smile and started bile burning in the back of his throat. He keyed his comm. "Control, Nine still shows the enemy to be blind."

"Got it, Nine. Rogues, stand by." An uncharacteristic hesitancy echoed through Tycho's words. "Rogues, this is direct from General Kre'fey. You will escort the assault shuttles down to the planet."

"Say again, Control?" The disbelief in Wedge's voice resonated through Corran. "Defender Wing is ready for its sweep."

"Rogue Leader, Kre'fey sees that as an unnecessary delay. The Y-wings have been ordered home. You are to escort his shuttles in. Resistance on the planet is ended."

"Control, what about the ion cannons?"

"If they could have shot, they would have done so by now." General Kre'fey's voice growled through the comm channels. "Resistance is ended. It is time to claim our prize."

Static punctuated the silence that followed Kre'fey's declaration, then Wedge came back on the frequency. "Rogue Leader to Rogue Squadron, form up to screen the escorts."

Corran's stomach flip-flopped. "I don't like this."

"Nine, this channel is for military use, not opinions. Let's save commentary for the debriefing." Wedge's voice lost some of its edge as he continued to speak. "And let's fly well enough that there *is* a debriefing."

"That's my intention, Rogue Leader." Corran eased his throttle forward and hit a switch. "S-foils in attack position."

The *Emancipator* rose away from the planet, taking up a position so it could screen the force from any interloping Imperials. Corran felt even more naked as it withdrew. While the Star Destroyer was not built to deal with starfighters, its overwhelming firepower could interdict TIEs and perhaps even destroy their launching facilities on the ground.

Of course, Kre'fey would forbid them from doing that, since he wants the real estate intact. Corran's sense of unease grew as he closed with the boxy assault shuttles dropping away from the *Corulag*. The eight shuttles each carried forty commandos and would make three round-trips between the planet and the *Corulag* to bring the whole force down. Though they were slow, the shuttles were sufficiently armed to hold TIEs at bay long enough so the Rogues could pick them off.

His tactical screen still showed nothing in terms of fighter opposition. The base's shields were down. The operation seemed to be going better than expected and that realization started a cold chill working up Corran's spine. He knew it was silly for him to feel fear when everything seemed normal, but part of him couldn't accept the good fortune.

His left hand pressed unconsciously to the medallion he wore. *Things were going this perfectly when my father died. We anticipated trouble, found none, and I relaxed. He died because I relaxed—I watched it happen and I did nothing. I didn't see it coming, but it did, just like it will here. What is wrong here?*

The answer to the question came to him a nanosecond before the first azure ion bolt lanced up from the ground and hit the first assault shuttle. The blue energy snared the *Modaran* and enmeshed it in a web of electrical discharges. Flashes of silvery light marked explosions in the weapons system and engines. With smoke pouring from a dozen hatches, the shuttle began a slow rolling tumble through the atmosphere and the ground below.

It never hit the planet. A full kilometer above the ground it crashed into a renewed energy shield. The shuttle exploded. Bits of debris struck sparks from the shield as they skipped across its surface.

Whistler wailed out a warning. The tactical screen showed multiple fighter contacts heading up out of launch tunnels around the shield dome perimeter. It also reported that while the shield had grown no larger in diameter, its power level was two hundred percent higher than before, easily half again more powerful than possible, given the power generation estimates in the briefings. *All that and ion cannons, too.*

"Control," Wedge ordered, "pull the transports out, now!"

"Rogue Leader, you have multiple fighters. Two squadrons, eyeballs and squints."

"Got them, Control. Rogue Squadron, keep the Imps off the shuttles."

Corran shook his head. "Seven shuttles, two dozen Imps, and eleven X-wings. Piece of *ryshcate*."

Whistler's mournful keen matched Corran's feelings more than his words. He keyed his comm. "Three Flight, hang together. Squints are coming our way."

"Ooryl has them, Nine."

Andoorni likewise reported in. "Twelve has acquired targets."

Corran punched up a graph and had it overlaid on the track of the incoming Interceptors. *Coming at us rather obliquely. Their funeral.* "Three Flight, switch to proton torpedoes and lock a target in. If they want to play . . ."

A trio of ion blasts shot up from the planet's surface. One sliced in at Three Flight, cutting through the vector the squints should have been using to engage the X-wings. The second hit the *Emancipator* and played out over it like a thunderstorm on a prairie. The third lanced up at one of the shuttles, but never reached its target. Corran saw the blast diffuse ever so slightly, as if it had hit a shield, but its dissipating ball left no debris behind.

"Two, report."

Dead air answered Wedge's call.

"Rogue Leader, we have no contact with Rogue Two."

Damn, Peshk caught that one. He's gone.

"Full evasive, Rogues. Control, get the shuttles dancing."

"Stay alert, Three Flight." Corran's aiming reticle went red and a target-lock tone filled his ears. He tightened on the trigger and launched a torpedo at an approaching Interceptor. Switching to lasers, he linked all four, then picked another target. As his torpedo hit the first, he flashed into range on the second and let it have a full burst of laser fire.

The glare of lasers against his shields hid the results of his shooting, but Whistler reported one Interceptor destroyed and another damaged. In seconds he shot past the line of Interceptors, then hauled back on his stick, rolled, and dove back in at them. The squints, reduced from eight to six, split up into flight elements and moved to engage single X-wings. As two started to circle around toward him, Corran inverted, dove, and came back up and around to go head-to-head with them.

He boosted power to his forward shields, then pulled a snap-roll that stood the X-wing on its port S-foil. That narrowed his profile and allowed the first volley of laser fire from the squints to pass on either side of himself. At the last second he selected a proton torpedo and let it fly at point-blank range. Even though it never got a solid target lock, it nailed the lead TIE dead on and tore it apart.

Corran nudged the stick and shot through the center of the fiery explosion. Clear on the other side he lost the Interceptor's wingman, but a more immediate problem captured his attention. "Twelve, break to port, now!"

Andoorni's X-wing juked left, but the squint riding her exhaust stayed with her.

"Break harder, Twelve. Climb."

"Not do. Lateral stabilizer gone."

"Weave, Twelve."

The Rodian started her X-wing in the corkscrew maneuver and the Interceptor's first shots went wide of their mark. Then the aft end of the ship came back around and the squint's fire ripped up through the engines. Fire blossomed on the right side of the ship, shredding the S-foils. A second later the whole fighter shook and its skin split from the inside out. Argent flames burst free, converting the ship into a miniature sun, then the roiling ball of gas collapsed into its own black hole.

Bloodlessly Corran vaped Andoorni's killer. Part of him wanted to cheer at having exacted revenge for her, but he overrode those emotions. He could no more allow himself to luxuriate in the death of an Imp than he could afford to mourn his comrade. There would be time for that later—*if there is a later*. Anything that distracted him from the job at hand would kill him, so he pushed it all away and concentrated on the battle around him.

"Three Flight, shuttle *Devonian* has four Interceptors inbound."

"Ooryl copies, Control. Ooryl has them."

"I'm on your back door, Ten."

The Interceptors had re-formed into two flights and had selected one of the assault shuttles as a target. Ooryl brought his X-wing in behind the lead pair and throttled back to match their speed.

"Ooryl using torpedoes."

"Shoot straight, Ten."

The TIEs broke formation and split out in four directions. "Ten, go to lasers, they must have lock-threat warning systems." A fighter with that equipment would provide the pilot with an indicator light when another ship had a torpedo lock on him. By jinking sharply it was possible to break the lock before the torpedo was launched. The Interceptor pilots ahead of them clearly knew their business. Only very good pilots survive to become veterans in TIEs, making them far deadlier than the pilots the Rogues had yet faced.

Corran rolled the X-wing up on the starboard stabilizers and started the long turn that would bring him in behind one of the squints. Whistler anxiously hooted a warning about another Interceptor moving to swing onto Corran's tail, but the pilot did nothing to lose the fighter. He pressed his attack, sharpening the arc of his turn to trim distance from his target.

Whistler became more insistent and Corran smiled. "Kill thrust." As the droid complied with that order, Corran punched the right rudder pedal with his foot. That swung the aft end of his ship up, a maneuver that further corrected his course for the ship in front of him. It also provided a tantalizing broadside shot for the squint following him.

"Counterthrust, now."

Whistler brought the engines back up to power as the X-wing's aft completed its 180-degree arc. The engines thrust against the line of the ship's flight, effectively killing its momentum and, for a split second, freezing it in space. For the barest of moments it lay dead in the sights of the Interceptor.

But the Interceptor pilot had already begun his roll and turn to keep his guns trained on where the X-wing *should* have been. Corran feathered his left rudder pedal and tracked the nose of his fighter along the squint's flight path. The quad lasers loosed two bursts of red darts that perforated the port wing and stabbed through the cockpit.

That Interceptor slowly spiraled out of control. More ion bursts from the planet coursed through the dogfight. The *Emancipator* took two more hits and the *Mon Valle* took another. Corran didn't see any more fighters get hit, nor shuttles, but a string of green laser bolts slicing across his flight path distracted him.

"Ooryl hit!"

Corran punched the throttle and whipped the X-wing up and over in time to see his wingman's ship break apart. "Ooryl!"

The X-wing disintegrated. The engine pods spun off in different directions and the cockpit canopy exploded into a million glittering fragments. He saw Ooryl float free of the stricken ship, and saw the Gand wave his arms. Corran hoped it was more than random reflex, then a piece of the fighter's S-foils sliced through the pilot's right arm, taking it off above the elbow. The body began to tumble through space, but it remained otherwise unmoving.

"Control, Ten is extra-vehicle. Get someone down here to get him."

"Nine, *Emancipator* reports the zone is too hot for rescue operations."

"Convince them, Control."

Wedge's voice came on to the frequency. "Control, I have Three and Eight EV. We need help here."

"I'm on it, Rogue Leader. It'll be done."

Three and Eight, that's Nawara and Erisi! Two dead and three more out of the fight.

A new voice came through Corran's headset. "Control here, Rogues. Good news: Your rescue's on the way. Bad news: We have two squadrons of squints coming in from planetary north. ETA two minutes. Shuttles are heading to hyperspace now."

Corran watched as the assault shuttles started the runs to light speed. The *Corulag* had already vanished, as had the Y-wings, leading the way out of disaster. Two ion blasts caught the *Mon Valle*, stopping it dead in space. The *Eridain* was beginning to move and the *Emancipator* had begun to drift toward planetary north but, in doing so, oriented itself for entry into hyperspace as if Admiral Ragab could not decide whether he was going to run or fight.

Run. No reason to stick here.

A sharp whistle from his astromech made Corran invert his ship and dive. A pair of squints flashed past, then one exploded as Rogue Four shot by on its tail.

"Thanks, Four."

"Thanks for playing bait, Nine."

The remaining TIEs broke away and headed toward the incoming fighters flying over the planet's polar cap. "Do we pursue, Rogue Leader?"

"Negative, screen our people until pickup."

Corran keyed his comm. "Rogue Leader, two squadrons of squints against a half dozen of us is going to be ugly."

"Nine, if you can't handle your four, I'll take them."

Corran ignored Bror's jibe.

"Trim it, Rogues. We're here protecting our own." Wedge's voice carried a confidence with it that buoyed Corran's spirits. "Focus on your mission and let the rest take care of itself."

"Control to Rogues. Squint ETA is thirty seconds. EV Three is recovered."

Corran smiled and looked up. In the distance he could see the white triangular hull of the *Forbidden* motionless in space. The pilot had brought the ship in close to where Nawara Ven had been floating, then used a rescue tractor beam to pull the pilot inside the emergency hatch in the hull.

The Corellian brought his X-wing up and around, then flew toward where Ooryl hung in space. "Ten is here, *Forbidden*."

"Thanks, Nine, I have the coordinates. On my way."

Corran blinked. *That's Tycho's voice.* "Cap, is that you?"

"Guilty, Ten. You have four squints closing on your position. Deal with them before I get there, please."

"You got it." Corran shivered. The only thing he could think of that was more stupid than engaging four Interceptors with a single X-wing was flying an unarmed shuttle into a hot zone to pick up pilots. A smile slowly crept across his face. *It's only stupid if we die doing it, otherwise it's heroism.* "And I can be a hero today."

Corran jumped his throttle full forward and shunted laser energy into his engines. That pushed his speed up toward maximum. Adjusting the stick and tapping the pedals he made his ship jump, cut, and dive. He flipped his weapons over to torpedoes and tried to get a lock on the lead squint, but it juked out of his sights. The others took shots at him, but his evasive maneuvers made them miss.

His fighter flew past them and two of the Interceptors started loops to come after him. Their turns took them high and away as they throttled up to match his speed. Increasing their speed meant their loops became wider than they might have preferred. *They outnumber us enough that being a bit sloppy can't hurt.*

Corran chopped his throttle back to half and pulled his X-wing through a tight turn. "*Forbidden*, paint one with a missile lock."

Punching the throttle full forward, Corran shot his ship back along the vector that had carried him through the squint formation. One of the Interceptors broke off on its run at the shuttle, so Corran concentrated on the other. He centered the ship in his aiming reticle and waited until he got a missile lock. When the reticle turned red, he hit the trigger and sent a proton torpedo speeding out toward the Interceptor.

The Interceptor pilot juked up and starboard, which pulled him out of the shuttle's forward firing arc. While that maneuver would have carried him away from any torpedo the shuttle had launched, Corran's missile had to make little more than a minor course correction before it hit. The torpedo cored through the Interceptor's ball and exploded, spitting shrapnel out in all directions from an incandescent cloud.

Knowing he was pushing his luck, Corran rolled the X-wing and dove after the first Interceptor the *Forbidden* had scared off. Throttling back he tightened a turn and came up inside the arc of the squint's loop. With a flick of his thumb he snapped weapons control over to lasers. The squint began to juke and twist, but Corran stayed with him.

Whistler screeched a warning about the return of the other two Interceptors, but Corran ignored it. He triggered one burst of lasers and clipped one of the squint's wings, but it sailed on. Pushing more power to his engines, Corran started to close with it, but the astromech whistled insistently at him.

The pair of Interceptors had closed to inside a kilometer and were firmly on his tail. "Nine here, I could use some help."

"I'm on it, Nine. Ten on the way. Break to port on my mark."

Ten? That's Ooryl, but not his voice. What's going on?

"Mark."

Left rudder, then a snap-roll onto the port stabilizers pulled him wide out of his previous flight path. He saw blue bolts shoot back toward the ships following him and for a half second Corran felt utterly disoriented. Blue beams meant ion cannon shots, but the planet had been behind him, not in front of him. And the ion cannons on the ground wouldn't be shooting at TIEs in any event.

"You're clear, Nine."

Corran brought his ship around and suddenly everything became clearer. Defender Wing's Y-wings dove and climbed through the dogfight, blasting away at Interceptors with wild abandon. What the slow ships lacked in grace they made up for in sheer firepower. Their entry into the fight destroyed or disabled a half-dozen Interceptors.

"They're running!"

Salm's voice came through the comm. "No celebrations. With them clear the ion cannons will open up again."

"*Forbidden* to Control, I have all EV pilots."

"*Forbidden*, you are clear to hyperspace."

Four ion blasts from the planet stabbed up and again struck the *Mon Valle*. The modified bulk cruiser began to break apart. Escape pods shot out from around the bridge and away into space, while the rest of the ship began to slowly drift back down toward Blackmoon.

"I hope it hits the installation."

"Control to all fighters, you are clear to hyperspace."

"Control, does *Eridain* need cover for getting the escape pods?"

"Negative, Rogue Leader, they're on our way out and the Interceptors are heading home."

"Thanks, Control." Wedge's voice seemed filled with weariness. "Back to base for us, Rogues."

"Got it, Rogue Leader." Corran took one last look at Blackmoon, then pointed his fighter toward the stars. "Back to base for *most* of us he means, Whistler. Two months of prep and in ten minutes the squadron is cut in half. Someone made some very bad mistakes here, and our friends paid for them. Never again."

27

CORRAN STARED OUT the window of the Noquivzor base recreation center. Rolling hills and treeless plains stretched out for kilometers in all directions from the building. Gentle and warm breezes washed in waves over the golden grasses and tickled the back of his neck. *If Erisi weren't over in the med center floating in her family's finest stock, I'd take her on a long walk out there and just enjoy the countryside. As beautiful as it is, though, it's hard to think of enjoying anything right now.*

He forced himself to smile as a man in an infantry uniform set a mug of lum down on the table in front of him. "Thanks, Lieutenant."

The man nodded. "Call me Page."

Corran shoved the chair on the other side of the table out toward Page. "What's the lum for?"

"Drinking usually." Page sat. "Me and my people were on the *Devonian*. You and your wingman scattered the squints coming in our direction. We owe you."

The pilot lifted the mug and drank a mouthful of the fiery ale and let it burn its way down his throat. "I appreciate the drink, but you'll have to buy one for Ooryl when he comes out of his bacta dip."

Page nodded. "Gladly. How badly was he hit?"

"Lost half his right arm. The suit shut down around the wound so he didn't suffocate, but he got very cold." Corran put the frosted mug down and shivered. "Bacta is for exposure—all the EV pilots are getting a dunking, though none of them are as bad off as Ooryl. The Emdees don't know about prosthetics for him—they've never done Gands before and don't have appropriate limbs to use for replacements."

"Rogue Squadron got hit hard."

"Two pilots dead, three EV, and one was flying wounded."

"I heard about him, the Shistavanen."

"Very tough individual." Corran nodded. "Shiel wasn't going to report for medical care but Gavin forced him to go. Net result, we're at two-thirds strength, but only if we can find X-wings to replace the ones we lost. If not, we're below fifty percent."

The infantry officer looked around the crowded, above-ground pavilion, then leaned forward and lowered his voice. "This mission was vape-bait from before Kre'fey ordered the Y-wings home."

"No kidding." The pilot glowered at the mug. "About a second before the cannons took the *Modaran* apart I realized that just because the cannons hadn't shot didn't mean they *couldn't* shoot."

"That occurred to all of us, I think, except for General Kre'fey. He was blind to that possibility." Page shook his head. "We all knew he wanted Blackmoon so the Council would give him command of the Coruscant invasion. In three weeks the planet's orbit takes it through an annual meteor shower. I wanted to use that as cover to bring my commandos in to do a ground recon of the base. We would have taken the ion cannons down."

"That makes sense. Why didn't he approve it?"

"The world's only moon—the Blackmoon that gave the

system its codename—would be in our entry and exit vector. It would act as a natural Interdictor cruiser, which could make things a lot more dangerous."

Corran shrugged. "The ion cannons made things dangerous enough, thanks."

"No kidding." Page smiled. "We would have taken them down. *And* we would have found the base for those squint squadrons that came in late to the fight."

"The Bothans didn't even know they were there."

The infantryman winced. "And they should have. They're very good at worming their way into Imperial networks."

"So this time they failed." Corran hesitated as an idea occurred to him. "Or records of those forces aren't part of the official garrison."

Page frowned. "What do you mean?"

"Working with CorSec I was involved in a sweep of a smuggler's headquarters. She was very sharp and had always distanced herself from glitterstim stores, so we couldn't pin anything on her. This one time, though, we found a couple of kilos of glitterstim in a warehouse she owned. She said she knew nothing about it and accused us of planting it. Turned out that she *didn't* know anything about it. The glitterstim had been skimmed from shipments by one of her aides and hidden there until he could find a way to move it himself."

"You're saying the Empire doesn't know those Interceptors were there?"

"A squadron is a rounding error for Imperial bookkeepers." Corran leaned forward, resting his elbows on the table. "And the Bothans didn't know about whatever power source was used to boost the shields back up after we took them down. Whoever is in charge of wherever Blackmoon is might be running some operation his Imperial masters know nothing about."

Page nodded slowly. "The data on the covert operation is kept away from the Imperials, so the Bothans had no way of discovering it."

"Not without being on the ground."

"We had intel on the vislight from the galaxy, but we got jumped by the IR and UV." Page rapped his knuckles on the plasteel tabletop. "If we'd been given proper background on Blackmoon, we might have been able to guess at the kind of information we really needed."

"I understand the need for operational security—but you can bet now the true location of Blackmoon won't be declassified until we're all dead and gone."

Page nodded. "Still, the simulations of an assault are only as good as the databases from which they are constructed. Bad intel gets people killed."

Corran ran a hand over his face. "Well, now we have an inkling of what we don't know about Blackmoon. At least two squint squadrons and a power generator are hidden there somewhere—hidden from us *and* Imp officials."

"The information in the official Imperial survey files is clearly useless."

"Right. And that means . . ." The chirp of the comlink on the table cut off Corran's comment. He picked it up and opened the channel. "Horn here."

"Emtrey here, sir."

"Something wrong with Ooryl?"

"No, sir."

"Is Erisi coming out of the bacta?"

"No, sir."

Corran frowned. "Then why did you call me?"

"Sir, Whistler asked me to inform you he has completed the calculations of the wind currents you requested."

"Wind currents?"

"On Blackmoon, sir. He said he has found some very interesting things."

"We'll be there in a second. Horn out." Corran looked up at Page. "It may be raising the shields after the base had been strafed, but I'm up for learning a little more about the world we just ran from. How about you?"

"I had friends on the *Modaran.* I didn't like seeing them die."

"Good, let's go." Corran shot him a smile. "Maybe, just maybe we can find a way to go back in and make the Imps pay."

WEDGE WASN'T CERTAIN he had heard General Salm correctly. "Did you just say it was just as well that we failed to take Blackmoon?"

Salm nodded slowly and pointed with a glass of pale blue Abrax cognac at the datapad on his desk. "Intelligence reports that the Imperial Star Destroyer-II *Eviscerator* left the Venjagga system on a course that would have put it in at Blackmoon within six hours after we launched our operation. Its six squadrons of TIEs would have matched our fighters and the *Eviscerator* would have pounded on the *Emancipator*. Chances are very good we would have lost our strike force *and* Blackmoon."

The Corellian's jaw dropped. "The mission was a go with an Impstar-Deuce within six hours of the target? How did that happen?"

"I don't know. Iceheart has been shifting some resources around, and some Admirals move them even further to avoid her control. It could be the *Eviscerator* was moved at random."

Wedge frowned. "Or Iceheart anticipated where we were likely to strike."

"Or"—Salm looked at Wedge over the rim of his glass— "someone told Iceheart where we were going to be."

"Tycho was in the dark about our destination as the rest of us were—and he was out there without any lasers or torps pulling in EV pilots."

Salm held up his open hand. "Easy, Commander, I wasn't accusing your XO. I don't trust him, but I know he was innocent this time."

"You checked the monitor logs on him?"

"I checked the logs on *everyone*. There were more call-outs than I like, but nothing incriminating. Now *I* didn't know where we were going before we pulled out, so I assume no one else did, but there are always leaks." The General set his cognac on his desk, then walked over to the small bar in the corner of his quarters. "Would you like a drink, Commander Antilles?"

"I'd prefer it if you'd call me Wedge."

The smaller man seemed to consider that for a moment, then he nodded. "Very well, Wedge. A drink?"

"How old is the Abrax?"

Salm smiled. "I don't know. My aide obtained it from the black market so your guess is as good as mine. The bottle does have Old Republic tax holograms on it, though."

Wedge shrugged. "I'll chance it, then, thanks."

The General poured him a generous dollop of the aquamarine liquid. "Please, be seated."

The General's quarters were as sparsely furnished as his own, with munition cases and old ejection seats being about the best thing available to use as tables and chairs. Salm's liquor cabinet had been built out of a plasteel helmet case with foam inserts to keep glasses and two bottles safe. Wedge appropriated one of the ejection seats and raised his glass of cognac. "Thank you for coming to our rescue out there."

"Defender Wing pays its debts."

Glasses clinked as they touched and both men drank. The liquor's spicy vapors opened up all of Wedge's nasal passages. He let the liquid pool on his tongue for a moment more, then swallowed it. A warmth started in his belly and pulsed out to ease some of the fatigue in his limbs.

The General hunched forward, cupping his glass in both hands. "I want to ask you what you intend to put in your report about what I did out there."

Wedge made no effort to cover his surprise. "You saved my unit. I thought I might recommend review for the Corellian

Cross. Since I'm not your commanding officer I can't put you in for it, but . . ."

Salm shook his head. "That's not what I'm talking about."

"What, then?"

The man's brow furrowed. "I disobeyed a direct order to leave the system."

Wedge blinked in confusion. "If you had returned to the *Mon Valle*, your entire wing would have been killed."

"We know that now, but we did not know that at the time the order was given." Salm swirled the cognac around in his glass. "General Kre'fey and I had often been at odds with each other—you may have gathered that from the briefing. I felt, when he ordered me out, that he wanted to rob me of any credit for the operation. I started us on an outbound vector, but came in close to the *Emancipator* so I could claim its mass prevented us from making the jump to light speed. I didn't want to leave and closing with the Star Destroyer made for a convenient excuse, but datafeeds from the onboard computers will reveal the truth."

"And so you were in position so the *Emancipator* could screen you from ground sensors *and* the incoming squints." Wedge shrugged. "If I'd been given that order and thought of that trick to let me stick around, that's what I would have done."

"I know." Salm stood and began to pace. "That's the problem, Commander Antilles: What I did is *exactly* what you would have done."

"It worked."

"It doesn't matter that it worked. I'm not you. My people are not your people." Salm's face became a mask of frustration. "The only thing that keeps my people alive out there is rigid adherence to discipline, and this discipline is instilled through consciously constructed drills that build them into a unit. My people lack the native talent in your squadron, but we make up for it because we cover for one another and watch out for each other."

"As you watched out for *my* people."

"Yes, I did that, but only by disobeying an order from a superior officer. And you have to write it up that way."

Wedge shook his head. "I don't want to see you taking slugs for something that wasn't wrong."

"But that's not up to you, Wedge. You can excuse something one of your pilots does, but only Ackbar and the High Command can forgive me for this mutiny." Salm tossed off the last of his cognac. "So, don't give the Admiral a single byte report—tell him what happened."

"What, and pretend I understand it?" Wedge sat back in the padded chair. "Interceptors came out of nowhere and the base suddenly developed more power than even the worst case allowed. If the *Eviscerator* had showed up and dumped two wings' worth of fighters into the battle, we would have lost all our ships. With the Star Destroyer-II in the area, of course, Blackmoon won't fall."

"You're probably right, though the presence of an Impstar-Deuce is not insurmountable." Salm splashed some more cognac into his glass. "Stripped of their fighters, they are vulnerable to TRD."

Wedge waved away a refill and smiled. TRD was Alliance slang for Trench Run Disease, or the tactics that had destroyed the first Death Star. The Empire had developed *Lancer*-class frigates to prevent TRD from claiming any capital ships. While attacks by snubfighters had proved relatively insignificant in hurting Star Destroyers, TRD was something Imperial officers feared and took great pains to avoid.

"Fine, I'll head out with my half-dozen pilots and we'll vape the *Eviscerator*'s TIEs so you can waltz in and give it a dose of TRD."

"It would be my pleasure, Commander, but High Command is going to want a lot of questions asked and answered about Blackmoon before more operations are conducted in that sector of space."

A tone sounded at the door, but before Salm could say anything, the door retracted and Corran Horn rushed in, followed closely by an infantry Lieutenant. "Commander, you wouldn't believe . . ." The enthused smile on Corran's face died as he saw Salm.

Both men snapped to attention. "Begging the General's pardon."

"At ease, Lieutenant Page, Lieutenant Horn." Salm clasped his own hands behind his back. "What's the meaning of this?"

Corran's gaze darted back and forth from Wedge to Salm. "Emtrey just said Commander Antilles was here, sir. He didn't mention these were *your* quarters, sir."

Salm looked at Wedge. "Your officers barge into your quarters uninvited?"

"Not so far. Perhaps, General Salm, I need to institute some of the discipline you were speaking about earlier." Wedge stood and gave Corran a hard stare. "News of our compatriots in the medical unit?"

"No, sir."

Wedge could see Corran was fit to burst. "This had better be good, Mr. Horn."

"Yes, sir." Corran looked at Salm. "With the General's permission."

Salm nodded. "Proceed."

Corran's smile blossomed again. "If we want Blackmoon, we've got it."

"What?"

The junior officer nodded. "Whistler, my astromech, collected a lot of data while we were out there and has been running it through the programs he used to analyze smugglers' bases so CorSec knew where to hit them."

Salm's face hardened. "This is an Imperial base, not some bandit's hideout."

Page shook his head. "Begging your pardon, sir, but the droid found a lot of parallels to smugglers' bases, and that gives us some new options. Whistler also pinpointed Black-moon from a star chart and is pulling up more data than we were given in our briefings. It can fall."

Wedge shook his head. "Good work, gentlemen, but there's an Imperial Star Destroyer Mark II we have to figure into the scenario. That changes everything."

Salm held a hand up. "Perhaps not, Commander."

"No?"

"Not entirely." Salm folded his arms. "Who knows about this information you have?"

Horn thought for a second, then answered, "As nearly as I know, just Page, my R2, the unit's 3PO, and me."

"I want you to confirm that. You two are hereby sworn to secrecy. If any word about this gets out I'll have you flying solo missions against Ssi-ruuk strongholds, got it?"

"Yes, sir."

Wedge smiled. "Being a bit lenient there, aren't you, sir?"

"Perhaps I am, but I think they know I'm serious." Salm smiled confidently. "Now let's see what you have, gentlemen. Blackmoon was picked as our best, closest step to Coruscant yet. No reason we should abandon our quest if we don't have to."

28

KIRTAN LOOR RAISED a hand to ward off the dust storm raised by the shuttle's landing jets. The *Sipharium* settled down easily, its landing lights strobing brightly in the Borleia-sian evening. The hum of the engines filled the air, drowning out the sound of the gangway being lowered from the belly of the ship.

The Intelligence agent smiled at General Derricote as the base's commander crested the stairs to the landing platform. "Come to see me off? I'm honored."

Derricote returned the smile. "Your visit was not as oner-ous as you might imagine, Agent Loor." The older man held a bottle out to him. "A memento of your visit."

Kirtan took it. "Corellian whiskey, Whyren's Reserve, no less." He looked closely at the cap and the holographic tax seal. "It looks genuine. Is it, or have you prepared this so I can poison myself and eliminate a problem for you?"

Derricote opened his hands. "If you want to open it and lumguzzle, I'll join you. It is genuine, and quite costly, but I have connections that make it possible for me to obtain it. It's not poisoned because it is given by way of thanking you. Had you not come here the Rebels might have taken me by surprise.

I think the result would have been much the same as it actually turned out to be, but one can never know. Your use of influence to transfer a squadron of TIE starfighters from the *Eviscerator* until my fighters can be replaced was also appreciated."

The General's openness surprised Kirtan. "You do not feel my being ordered back to Imperial Center is a threat to your operation here?"

Derricote shrugged. "I am too much a realist to imagine I could keep this operation secret forever. I trust you will use your knowledge of it to your own gain, which means I will not be sacrificed casually. This operation, of course, has uses. I would think that Ysanne Isard would find it more valuable than any object lesson she could provide others by destroying it and me."

The man's eyes hardened. "Besides, if I saw you as a threat, you would have died during the Rebel attack."

Truly spoken. Kirtan nodded slowly. "I accept your gift in the spirit in which it is given." *But I will have it tested before I drink.*

"I hope, also, you will view this invitation in the spirit in which it is given." Derricote spread his arms wide to encompass the planet. "The Empire is dead. What will rise to replace it, I don't know, but the Core will be heating up and Imperial Center is going to be roasted alive. Rebels, warlords, either could do the job. Old Borleias here, it's been through its time of fire. I'll be here when Imperial Center isn't. If you need a haven when things break apart, remember that I'm here."

Kirtan brought his head up. "Thank you, General. I *shall* remember you. I hope I won't have to avail myself of your invitation, but if I do, I know where to find you."

"Have a good trip to Imperial Center, Agent Loor."

Kirtan raised the bottle in a salute. "Until we meet again."

WEDGE FELT A GIDDY anticipation in his belly the like of which he'd not known since Endor. He glanced over at General Salm.

The man sat on the other side of the briefing table with his eyes closed, nodding to himself as he rehearsed what he would say to Admiral Ackbar. The plan they'd concocted over the last week *could* work, but it was risky and highly time-dependent.

The door to the briefing room opened and Ackbar entered the room. He nodded to both men, then settled down in the chair at the head of the oval table. "What have you woven together?"

Salm smiled and punched keys on his datapad. The small device fed information to the holographic projection disk in the center of the table and a starfield began to sparkle and slowly spin above it. "We have found a way to take Blackmoon."

The Mon Calamari sat back. "I do not recall your having been told which world Blackmoon was."

Wedge shook his head. "We weren't. As per orders, coordinates were downloaded to and erased from all of our astromechs and navigational computers before and after the operation. Unfortunately for operational security, one of my unit's astromechs has a special criminal investigation and forensics circuitry package. It gathers evidence and, in this case, included a star chart of the area in it."

Ackbar's barbels quivered. "Something will have to be done to correct that situation."

"Agreed, Admiral, but this droid in Commander Antilles's squadron has provided us with invaluable information that points out why we lost the fight and how we can take Borleias."

"And more, sir." Wedge pointed at the starfield. "Computer, isolate the triad."

The starfield grew and stars bled out of the edges of the image. In the center three stars intensified in radiance and faint green lines stretched out to link them. A small arrow pointed down and away from the lowest point of the triangle indicating the direction of the Core and Coruscant.

"These three systems are, in descending order, Mirit, Venjagga, and Pyria. The center one, Venjagga, is home to the *Eviscerator*. It is using Jagga-Two as a base and is there to protect the concussion missile production facilities. While the output is considered small by Imperial standards, the fact that the world is actually producing missiles makes it worth protecting."

Salm indicated the uppermost system, the one on a virtual straight line with Borleias. "The Mirit system is home to Ord Mirit. The Empire abandoned that base shortly after Endor and shifted the garrison all the way over to Corellia to help hold the shipyards there. Ord Mirit is really too far away from anything substantial for us to use it as a base, as we have done with Ord Pardron. Still, it is part of the sector the *Eviscerator* is tasked to defend."

"Finally we have Borleias." Salm hit a button on his datapad and the starfield dissolved into the image of the planet. "When we were there before we discovered the estimates of power generation for the planet were low by at least half and two squadrons of fighters—Interceptors no less—showed up without warning. All of the data we had about the planet had been stolen from Imperial files by Bothan slicers. Unfortunately for us, that information was incomplete."

Wedge nodded. "We went back and pulled old data files on Borleias and they've provided the answers to questions that were never asked before the first operation. Back before the Empire existed, Alderaan Biotics set up a research facility on the far side of the planet. It included a geothermal generation station *and* a local spaceport. Because everything was located in the northern part of the planet, the facilities were built underground to avoid complications from the harsh winters. A series of scan surveys of the planet would be required to locate the sites from space."

"What Commander Antilles says is true, sir—and the effort to locate these bases from space would have revealed our interest in the planet to the Empire."

The Mon Calamari acknowledged Salm's comment with a nod. "Why was there no information about this place in the Imperial files, General?"

"The facility was shut down years ago. We suspect that the current base commander, Evir Derricote, refurbished it and has it operating to produce goods—foodstuffs mostly—that are sold to the refugee Alderaanan population via the black market. At the very least his Imperial superiors would see this as giving aid and comfort to the enemy, so hiding knowledge of it from them makes sense."

"So you suspect this facility and its generator was the source of the power used to reinforce the base's shields?"

"Yes, sir." Wedge pointed to a faint red line linking the military base and the Biotics facility. "A tunnel that runs about one and a quarter kilometers beneath the surface of the planet links the two facilities. There is a rift valley where a ferrocrete conduit links the tunnel one side to the other. This is the weak link—the generator is too deep to blow with proton torpedoes and destroying it makes no sense if we intend to take the planet."

Ackbar nodded, then tapped his lower lip with a flipperlike hand. "If you sever the connection with the military base, you bring us back to the original Bothan estimates of the defenses. If we bring our ships back in, we should be able to bring the shields down as we did before. We could take the base, but then the *Eviscerator* would come and destroy it."

Salm shook his head. "Not if the *Eviscerator* arrives too late. Our plan is this—we stage a feint at Jagga-Two. The *Emancipator* and the *Liberator* arrive in-system, just at the outer edge of the gravity well created by the seventh planet, a gas giant. They deploy my Defender Wing and another wing of fighters, matching the *Eviscerator*'s complement of TIEs. The *Eviscerator* will deploy its fighters and move out behind their screen to engage our ships.

"Even at full speed, it will require two hours for our ships to engage each other. Our snubs won't be traveling at full speed, and our Star Destroyers will be pulling back. It will appear to the *Eviscerator* that we're running from it or, at the very least, are reluctant to engage it. When the *Eviscerator* moves into position within the system to engage us, our ships will go to light speed. The Star Destroyers will head for Ord Mirit while the fighters will head for Borleias. The *Eviscerator* will be unable to follow our Destroyers immediately because of its position in the system and the presence of planets that act as natural Interdictor cruisers."

Ackbar's eyes half shut. "Then the *Eviscerator* goes to Borleias."

"Without her fighters?" Salm shook his head. "The TIEs cannot enter hyperspace by themselves the way our fighters can. They will have to be recovered and that will take time. Borleias can take care of itself, and the feint at the Venjagga system will be obviously intended to keep the *Eviscerator* away from Ord Mirit."

The Admiral gave Salm a wall-eyed stare. "Why would the captain of the *Eviscerator* believe there was anything of value at Ord Mirit?"

Wedge smiled. "We were thinking that there are some Bothan slicers who seriously want to redeem themselves. We want them to plant information in the Imperial networks that suggest a newly discovered, previously secret facility on Ord Mirit may possess the key to finding the *Katana* fleet."

He felt a shiver run down his spine as he saw the effect of his words on Ackbar. The *Katana* fleet had once been real enough, but back before even the Clone Wars it had passed into legend. Over a hundred ships that were slave-circuited together, the fleet had jumped into hyperspace and had never been seen again. With the Empire crumbling, possession of that fleet would make its owner *the* power in the galaxy. If the Alliance found it, the New Republic would become invincible. If an Imperial officer found it, a new Emperor would be born.

"No sane officer could truly believe the *Katana* fleet could be found." Ackbar's mouth gaped open in a grin. "But no sane officer could refuse to take the chance that it could be found. The *Eviscerator* would have to go to Ord Mirit and Ord Mirit is, what, twelve hours at flank speed to Borleias?"

"Add the four from Venjagga to Ord Mirit and we have sixteen hours at the very least to take Borleias." Wedge nodded solemnly. "The beginning of the raid on Borleias will be very simple. Rogue Squadron goes in and blows the conduit. Going in and coming out we expect to attract a lot of attention because while we're fighting, Lieutenant Page and his commandos, as well as a number of similar units, are going to use the conduit to get into the Borleias base and disable it. They'll also hit the Biotic station's spaceport. If they do it right, the TIE pilots sent up to engage us won't know there's been a change in ownership until they come home. Once the commandos are down and in, my people head out home."

"The arrival of my Defender Wing and the other fighters from Venjagga will provide the Borleias base with enough of a distraction that Page's people can take things down in short order, without having to damage anything we'll need to use to defend the base."

Ackbar's barbels twitched. "Security will need to be very tight for this return to Blackmoon."

"Yes, sir, but we have some advantages here. Derricote won't think we'll be coming back because the moon is in position to block our escape route. We are preparing a simulator package that hides the identity of our target. The run across the lunar surface will be disguised as a run through an asteroid belt, leading our people to believe we're moving against a ringed planet." Wedge smiled. "This time our pilots will not know where they're going, but they won't be in the dark about what they will face when they get there."

The Mon Calamari nodded. "You will have to hide your location from your XO."

"I know, so does he. He's not part of the operation, so he accepts not knowing."

The Mon Calamari stood slowly. "I think this plan is a

good one, and can be made better. I do have one concern, however. It concerns your Rogue Squadron, Commander Antilles, and the commandos."

"Sir?"

"If the operations are launched simultaneously—and I must assume they will be so an alarm raised by the *Eviscerator* will not put Borleias in a heightened state of alert in time to disrupt your effort—there will be at least four hours before we have more forces arriving at Borleias. Flight suit life support lasts for three hours. Anyone left behind will die."

"I know that, sir."

"Do your people know that?"

Wedge shook his head. "They will before they go. I've got six operational ships. This will be a volunteer mission."

"And a very bold one." Admiral Ackbar nodded solemnly. "Let us go over it again and guarantee the gain will be worth the likely cost. Right now I believe I could sell it to the Provisional Council, but some modifications will make this a certainty. And if things go well, the way to Coruscant will finally lie open to us."

29

CORRAN HALF HID his face behind his left hand, daring only to stare at the floating hologram of the mythical world of Phenaru Prime with his left eye. Aside from the addition of an asteroid ring, an ocean where the southern continent was, and some adjustments to the coastlines, it looked exactly like Borleias. The computer-projected world slowly spun above the cylinder in the well of the pilots' briefing room. It looked calm and almost peaceful, especially without the air-current overlays Whistler used to project onto it.

As peaceful as it looks, it's not where I want to die.

Wedge continued his briefing. "Our objective is a ferrocrete pipe roughly four meters in diameter and forty meters long. It's reinforced and has suspension cables helping to support the weight. A single proton torpedo should be able to destroy it, but we're not sure how well it's going to show up on the targeting computers. If we get a lock, it's likely to be at point-blank range."

Nawara Ven stroked the tip of one of his brain tails. "Run up this rift valley and hit something the third of the size of an X-wing, without the benefit of a targeting computer? That's impossible."

Gavin shook his head. "That's nothing. Back home in Beggar's Canyon . . ."

The youth's voice trailed off as Wedge raised an eyebrow in his direction. "I don't think *any* pilot from Tatooine ever found a mission tough, especially when it involves racing through a canyon."

"Well, the target's not really that small, sir."

Corran laughed. "It is the size of a reclining Hutt, give or take a couple of meters. The conduit can probably move faster, too."

Even Wedge laughed at the comment, but Corran knew it wasn't because of the weak humor in his statement. Everyone in the room, the nine surviving pilots from Rogue Squadron and Tycho Celchu, knew the mission being presented to them was difficult. Their laughter came from the nervous tension of staring death in the face and knowing death was likely to win this one.

"The real sticking point on this mission, people, is time-over-target. We'll be coming in and using a meteor shower as cover for our insertion to the atmosphere. This means we'll have to maneuver through the asteroids to get into Phenaru and get out again. We also have a long run up to light speed so we can make the jump out of the gravity well. All this means we've got a half hour over the target. If we burn too much time and fuel fighting, we don't get out."

Bror Jace scratched at the pale stubble on his chin. "That's cutting it rather fine, isn't it? The valley run should take a third of that. If only six of us are going in, that's one pass per flight element."

"He's right, Commander." Rhysati frowned. "Can't we get auxiliary fuel pods for our T-65s?"

Wedge glanced over to where Emtrey stood. "Last check of our inventory didn't show we had any and a check of the Alliance requisition system shows a backlog of requests. That's what you said, wasn't it, Emtrey?"

"Yes, sir." The droid raised a hand and tilted his head to the side. "However, sir, we now have some."

"What?" Wedge frowned. "I thought you characterized requisitioning them as an exercise in futility."

"I did, sir." The droid shrugged in a most un-mechanical manner by bobbing his head up and down on his neck. "I saw we needed them, so I scrounged 'em."

"Scrounge?"

"They cost a couple suits of the stormtrooper armor we had left over from Talasea, the cold weather gear we are not using here on Noquivzor, and some spare parts for which we have little use."

The squadron's commander stared at the droid for a moment. "How many did you get?"

"A half dozen."

Wedge shook his head. "All that only got you *six* auxiliary fuel pods?"

"Sir, when scrounging merchandise you can get it fast, in good condition, or cheap: pick two." The droid's clamshell head righted itself again. "They're here and Zraii is ready to fit them on ships. He's fitting them with a quick release so you can jettison them when they're empty. It'll kill the drag when you're fighting the squints. These pods give you half again the time-over-target."

Forty-five minutes sounded like forever, and in some ways it was. In atmosphere the engines gobbled a lot more fuel than they did in space because of the friction and drag. X-wings were a better fighter in atmosphere than TIEs, but the two squadrons on the ground outnumbered the Rogues four to one. *Long odds and we ran through the last of our luck on the previous visit to Blackmoon.*

Rhysati raised a hand. "Any defenses in the rift valley?"

Wedge shook his head. "None that we know of, but it's possible there are some. Whoever goes in first has got to be careful. First run probably won't nail the prize."

"I can believe that." Corran scratched at the back of his neck. "Are Page's folks coming down while we make our runs?"

"If they were, Lieutenant, the answer to that question would be classified." Wedge hesitated for a moment, then nodded. "It's a logical assumption to make, though. Regardless, any of us who gets left behind will be in severe straits—out of fuel and out of luck long before the assault for which we're doing the prep work will hit."

Bror Jace slowly nodded. "This is a suicide mission."

"No, I want it to be anything *but* a suicide mission. The facts do point to this being very dangerous." Wedge folded his hands together. "We've got six ships and eight pilots. I'm sorry, Ooryl, but without a proper prosthetic fit, I can't consider you healthy enough for this mission."

Corran's wingmate sagged a bit in his seat. The Emdee droids had fitted him with an odd device that capped his stub with what looked—and smelled—like a boiling pot of bacta. Below it a rudimentary prosthetic arm ended in a pair of pincers that snapped open and closed. "Qrygg offers apologies for Qrygg's failure."

"Your feelings are understood, Ooryl." Wedge folded his arms across his chest. "Three of you are fit to fly but you don't have a ship. We do have Lujayne's X-wing ready to go. If all of you volunteer for this mission, I'll choose one of you at random to fly that ship. If anyone else opts out, you're up. Do you all want to go?"

All three of the pilots nodded.

"Emtrey, randomize a choice here."

The droid hummed for a moment. "Nawara Ven."

Shiel growled and Erisi shrugged in Rhysati's direction.

Wedge smiled. "Welcome aboard, Mr. Ven. You'll fly with Mr. Jace, assuming he volunteers."

The Thyferran shot a quick glance at Erisi, then nodded. "It shall be my pleasure to bring glory to the Thyferran people as their representative on this mission."

"Mr. Darklighter, this isn't Beggar's Canyon . . ."

"I know, sir. It's bigger and this won't be for fun." Gavin smiled slowly. "I'm in."

Wedge looked over at Rhysati. "And you, Ms. Ynr."

"Someone has to break up the boys' club."

Wedge turned to Corran. "Need I ask?"

"You want to know if I'm willing to fly to an enemy-held planet where I'm to race through some eroded ditch and pop a sewer pipe with a proton torpedo while Interceptors are swarming around, and do all this with no hope of rescue if I slip up?"

Wedge's reply came cold and calm. "That's what I want to know."

Corran's mouth soured and his stomach tightened. Despite Gavin's protest, Nawara Ven had been correct—the mission was impossible. Performing any *one* of the feats mentioned might have been possible, but doing them all would push every pilot to his or her limit. Failure by some was inevitable—only who and how many were in question.

They all knew that. They knew it as well as he did, yet each one of them had volunteered without a second thought. The mission needed doing, and they were going to do it. It wasn't a question of survival, but a question of how best to make certain the mission succeeded. Each of them decided they were up to the task and now it was up to him to come to the same conclusion.

"Overwhelming odds, tough target, scant chance of survival—business as usual for Rogue Squadron." Corran nodded. "I'll go on one condition."

"Go or stay, Mr. Horn, no special deals."

"Then think of this as a tactical consideration." Corran sat forward and rested his elbows on his knees. "I'm first into the valley."

Wedge shook his head. "That position's already filled."

"You need a wingman, Commander." Corran jerked a

thumb at the other pilots. "They've had practice using someone else's telemetry to make a run, I haven't. We'll make the
first run together."

Wedge looked away for a moment, then back at Corran.
"Glad to have you with us, Mr. Horn. Shiel, Ms. Dlarit, you'll
work with Captain Celchu and provide opposition for us while
we do the simulator runs on the operation. You'll have to do
your best to kill us before we go. If you can't, maybe, just
maybe, we'll be able to come back and thank you for your
hard work."

C ORRAN LEANED AGAINST the body of the simulator and gave Wedge a weak smile. "We got it that time, boss, but only just barely."

"That last cut is very sharp. Banking is the only way to make it, but leveling out for the torpedo shot is tough."

The junior officer nodded. The one time he had tried to make the last turn to the target by applying rudder and skidding around the turn, his X-wing slammed into a canyon wall. Making that turn and escaping a crash required very fine manipulation of the throttle. He could do that, but by the time he had negotiated the turn and recovered, he was past his target.

"I like the idea of popping up over the last turn and gliding on down in, but that might attract some of the TIEs the bacta boy is lighting up."

"I agree that going up and out of the valley to avoid that last turn is probably the most simple way of handling the problem, but we go in first to provide the data for others to make their runs. Mr. Jace and Mr. Ven will decide if they want to hop past the last turn or go through the valley."

Bror Jace came out from around the corner of Corran's

simulator with his wingman. "Valley, I think, unless our fuel estimates are lower than expected because of dogfighting."

Corran winked at him. "Don't worry, we'll keep them off you while you squirm your way into the tunnel."

"I'll do the job."

The Twi'lek laid a hand on Bror's shoulder. "We'll do the job."

Wedge smiled. "Only because our near misses will weaken the structure for you."

"Of course, Commander." Bror looked at Corran. "Even clean misses must ionize the air and do some harm."

The Corellian Lieutenant levered himself away from the simulator. "Last I looked, I've hit more targets than you."

Gavin and Rhysati joined the group. "If not for me not holding my end up, Corran would be winning your contest, Bror."

The Thyferran waved that comment away. "Corran has one more kill than I do. If this simulation is at all accurate, I will eclipse his mark by three kills."

"So it's just you and me, head-to-head?"

Bror looked down at Corran. "Just you and me. Head-to-head. As it has always been."

Wedge stepped between them. "At ease, gentlemen. Let me remind you of two things. First, Gavin's got the best record for hitting the tunnel, which means the second flight didn't do so well. Second, that tunnel is our target, not all the eyeballs and squints flying around."

He rested a hand on each man's shoulder. "I've not discouraged this contest because there's no way to stop you from keeping score. It's given you a competitive edge which is good— neither of you has allowed the other to become complacent or bored. A bored pilot gets overconfident, careless, and, rather quickly, *dead*. And, in spite of planning and promoting this difficult mission, I don't want to see any of us die."

Wedge took a step back and folded his arms. For the barest of moments he looked far older than his twenty-seven years. Corran saw the weariness as Death's fingerprints. *Death's never gotten Wedge, but it's been close enough to leave marks on him. There's undoubtedly a nightmare for every pilot Rogue Squadron has lost, and I bet he runs through them far more regularly than he'd like.*

The squadron commander forced a smile onto his face. "Back when I first welcomed you to this squadron I told you that most pilots die during their first five missions. We were very lucky in our first three, but it all caught up with us on the run at Blackmoon. Looking at the numbers there is no reason to assume it will go any better for us this time."

Corran nodded and fought the shiver coursing up his spine. In the first run they had eleven ships to take against Blackmoon's fighters. They engaged two squadrons then and would likely face that much opposition this time. While the best pilots in Rogue Squadron were going in on the mission, fuel considerations limited their ability to perform.

"I want you people to know I've flown with the best the Alliance has to offer. Luke, Biggs, Porkins, Janson, Tycho, all of them. I don't feel their lack here. This isn't a Death Star we're going after, and this mission doesn't have that sense of urgency. That's because back then we were fighting for the very survival of the Rebellion.

"The fact is, though, this mission is just as important as either of the Death Star runs." Wedge glanced down at his hands, then back up. "This time we're fighting for the future of the Rebellion and all the people who want freedom from the Empire. That's a lot less immediate than what we fought for in the old days, but in many ways it's far more noble a goal."

Corran smiled in spite of himself. The nagging sense of doubt and doom that had been grinding away at his consciousness didn't go away, but it became muted. Wedge's words muffled it. Fear and insecurity were issues about *himself*, but their mission was about others. He was going off to make the future a bit brighter for people like Iella Wessiri and her husband and Gus Bastra and his family. *And even folks like Booster Terrik.*

The realization that this blow struck at the Empire would make life easier for the sorts of criminals he and his father and grandfather used to hunt didn't tarnish the mission. He'd never believed the "virtuous bandit" myth most criminals like to wrap around themselves—raiding the affluent to give to the destitute was a pattern often claimed, but he'd seen no evidence of it. Still he couldn't deny the contribution of folks like Han Solo or Mirax Terrik to the Rebellion. And how could one compare the minor evil of a Hutt with the grand evil of a government that would conceive of, build, and utilize weapons that could destroy planets?

If we cap the wellspring of evil, cleaning up all the little puddles it leaves behind will be that much easier.

Wedge looked at all of the pilots. "This mission isn't going to be easy, but I know we can do it."

Corran nodded to him. "If it was easy, it wouldn't be a Rogue Squadron mission."

"And if it wasn't given to Rogue Squadron," Bror added, "it would have no chance of being accomplished."

"If ego could power shields, you'd be invincible." Wedge shook his head. "You've got twelve hours to kill before you hit the line. No drinking and definitely get some sleep. You can't use the holonet for obvious security reasons, but if you want to record some messages for friends and family and leave them with Emtrey, he'll see to their disposition in the worst case. Get going, I'll see you at 0800 on the line."

"We'll be there, Commander." Corran tossed him a quick salute. "Nervous as Sithspawn in the glow of a Jedi's lightsaber, but ready for whatever the Empire throws at us."

WEDGE WATCHED HIS pilots walk away and saw both Shiel and Erisi catch up with them. He turned and smiled at Tycho. "Nice flying in the sim. You wouldn't have bagged me if that belly pod hadn't slowed my climb."

The Alderaanian pilot shrugged. "Fifth time's the charm."

Wedge pointed toward the retreating knot of pilots. "Do they ever seem like kids to you—kids who shouldn't be in this at all?"

"Gavin, yes, and Ooryl because of the insular life he's led. The rest of them only surrender a year or two to us."

"I know that, but it seems like the Emperor's death was the end of an era. They've all joined *after* the New Republic was established. Before that we were outlaws fighting the legitimate government. Now we're a movement that is bringing freedom to countless worlds." Wedge shook his head. "Sometimes I think they've joined us because of the romance of the Rebellion's having struck a blow against the Empire. We brought down Darth Vader, killed the Emperor, and destroyed the Death Stars."

Tycho brushed a lock of brown hair from his forehead. "I hope you're not heading toward the idea that they don't really know what they're getting into. I seem to recall hearing that same speculation about the new pilots in the squadron before Endor. Back then you saw the destruction of the first Death Star as what marked the end of an epoch."

Wedge had memories flood back. "Yeah, I guess I did think about that then, didn't I? The situation was different, though."

"No it wasn't. Look, Wedge, none of us have been through all you have. I joined up after Yavin, so I've been here for a long time, but for me Biggs and Porkins and the others are just legends. For you they're memories—friends you've lost." Tycho threw an arm across Wedge's shoulders. "These guys have lost friends, too. There's not a one of them that doesn't know the odds of surviving this run are about . . ."

Wedge held up a hand. "Don't give me odds. You know Corellians have no tolerance for odds."

"Which is why you so willingly play sabacc."

"And why so many of us are part of the Rebellion."

The two of them laughed aloud and Wedge felt a lot of his

tension bleeding away. As he wiped tears from his eyes he saw an Alliance Security Lieutenant come walking over. "Yes, Lieutenant?"

"Forgive the intrusion, sir, but I just wanted to remind Captain Celchu this area is restricted when he's not actually involved in an exercise."

"That's all right, Lieutenant, he's with me."

"Yes, sir." She glanced anxiously back toward the doorway. "I'll wait out there."

"I'll be along presently, Lieutenant."

Wedge frowned. "I'll take responsibility for Captain Celchu, Lieutenant. You're dismissed."

"Sir, my orders come from General Salm."

"I know. Log your protest with him."

"Yes, sir."

Wedge looked over and saw a frown on Tycho's face. "What's the matter?" He glanced at the Security officer's retreating form, then back at his friend. "Have you become involved with her? Did I break something up here?"

Tycho shook his head. "No, nothing like that. She's very nice, and lived on Alderaan for several years, so we can talk about places we'll never see again. *And* she works with two enlisted men, one of whom watches me all the time. I do find her intriguing, but I'm not of a mind to begin a new relationship without knowing if the old one is over or not."

"I can understand that." Wedge recalled the woman Tycho had fallen for a couple of years earlier. She worked in Alliance Procurement and Supply and spent most of her time on covert missions directing operations on enemy worlds designed to liberate matériels from the Empire. Because of the importance and sensitivity of her work, learning anything about her from Intelligence was impossible, and Tycho's status raised that difficulty level by an order of magnitude.

Tycho poked a finger against Wedge's breastbone. "I think you're changing the subject on me to avoid the real issue that prompted your earlier question."

Wedge raised an eyebrow. "Oh, and that is?"

"You're afraid you're getting too old for what we've always told ourselves is a young man's game."

"If you think that, you're as confused as a Gamorrean placed between two full mugs of lum." The Corellian frowned. "First off, you're a year older than I am."

"Nine months."

"Which is rather close to a year, my friend."

"True enough, but years aren't the only measure of time." Tycho tapped the rank insignia at the collar of Wedge's flight suit. "You're a Commander. Luke was a General before he abandoned his rank. Han Solo and Lando Calrissian are Generals. Most of the officers who have been with the Alliance for as long as you have are at least Colonels."

"You're only a Captain, Tycho."

"And there I will stay, if Salm has anything to say about it."

"Well, I've had my say about my rank, and I'm happy where I am. I like leading a squadron."

"I know that." The Alderaanian shrugged and folded his arms. "You can't help but wonder, though, if refusing those promotions was the right decision to make or not."

"True." Wedge looked up at his friend. "So, *am* I too old to be doing this?"

"Wedge, over the last four months I've flown against—and shot down—every one of the kids you have going on this mission. So have you." Tycho let a low chuckle rumble from his throat. "If you're too old for this, the New Republic might as well give up now. Barring a squadron of Jedi Knights winging their way in here, you're the best we've got. That may not impress you, but there are plenty of Imp pilots out there who don't sleep the whole night through because of dreams about you being on their tails."

31

CORRAN SMILED AS Erisi caught up with the group. "You did well in the sim, Erisi."

"It felt strange trying to shoot you down."

"Emphasis on *trying*." Bror flashed a predatory grin at her. "You had no more success than they will tomorrow."

Nawara Ven glowered at his wingman. "If you *have* found a way to shunt ego into your shields, I wish you would share it with me."

Rhysati shook her head. "Just have him expand his shields to cover us all. There's ego enough there."

Bror turned to Corran. "The mewing of our inferiors grows tiresome, don't you think?"

The Corellian's mouth hung open for a second. He wasn't certain if he was more surprised with Bror's put-down of the others or his own elevation into Bror's peer group. "I wouldn't call it 'mewing' and I don't see them as our 'inferiors.' Everyone here has worked hard and come through a lot. Gavin and I have both been wounded, as has Shiel, and only you and Rhysati have avoided personal or ship damage. We might have a few more kills than they do, but things will average out over time."

The Thyferran looked thoughtful for a moment, then nodded. "That is something to consider, certainly. And I did not mean my comment as a slight against any of you, though clearly it was taken as such. I respect you all and believe you all capable of more. I will be honored to fly with you tomorrow."

"On that note . . ." Nawara Ven bowed his head to his companions, allowing his brain tails to hang down over his shoulders. "I shall see you all in the morning."

"Wait a moment." Rhysati held her hand out to him. "I'll head off, too. Get some sleep—we'll need it."

Gavin smiled, then stretched and yawned. "I want to record a message for my parents. Biggs never got the chance and that kind of ate at Uncle Huff."

Corran winked at the kid. "You'll make them proud, Gavin."

Bror bowed slightly. "I, too, shall record a message for my parents."

They all departed, leaving Corran alone with Erisi. "Well."

"Well, indeed, Corran." She reached out and took his left hand in hers. "I wish I were going with you tomorrow."

"We'd be thankful for the help." Corran allowed her to gently pull him along toward the accommodations she shared with Rhysati. "Given how things are working out, you may be lucky that you're not going."

"Don't say that." Her voice dropped to near a whisper and a tear formed in the corner of her right eye. "Worse than dying on this mission will be surviving it here. If the mission fails, if you don't come back, I'll be left wondering if I could have made a difference."

"Dying out there might be less emotionally trying, but I don't think it's the lesser of two evils here."

She brushed the tear away. "You're correct, of course, and I'm being selfish." Erisi stopped and turned to face him. "Doesn't it bother you that you don't even know the name of the world where you could die?"

Actually, I do know the name of the world. Wedge and I

are the only ones, though I don't think that makes this mission any easier. "To be honest, Erisi, I hadn't given it that much thought. The Imps there want me dead, and I don't feel too friendly toward them, either. *Where* we end up fighting isn't all that important to me."

"It's important to me." She began walking again. Her hand moved up to the inside of his elbow and guided him forward. "If things go badly I thought I would visit or make sure a memorial was raised. I . . ."

Erisi's voice broke and Corran felt a shudder run through her. "Hey, Erisi, it's all going to be fine. Remember when the Commander warned us that we'd never be able to be greater heroes than the folks who have already died in service to Rogue Squadron?"

"Yes," she sniffed.

"Well, he was wrong. We *can* be bigger, but only by living longer and doing better than they ever did. As he was saying just now, in those days they fought for survival. We're fighting for the future. If we do this right, Biggs and the rest won't be remembered as Rogue Squadron's greatest heroes, but the *predecessors* to Rogue Squadron's greatest heroes." Corran gave her a strong smile. "I'm planning on sticking around to make that prediction come true."

Erisi smiled, but the corners of her mouth trembled. "You probably will do that, Corran. I hope it is so. I just wish I knew where the rest of you were going. You aren't the least bit curious?"

"Maybe for my memoirs, sure." Corran reached up and wiped tears from her cheeks. "They'll declassify the operation in fifty years or so—just in time for me to include the location in my autobiography."

"Even if I had to wait fifty years, I'd have a memorial built for you." Erisi paused before the open door to her quarters. "Corran, you know Rhysati isn't going to be coming back here this evening. You can stay here, if you wish."

"I shouldn't, Erisi."

"Are you certain?" The disappointment in her voice twisted into forced levity. "Think of it as a chapter for your memoirs."

"I have no doubt it would take two chapters." Corran sighed heavily. "I'm afraid I'd get no sleep. *That* would kill me. I'd die happy, but I'm afraid our compatriots would not."

Erisi nodded slowly and looked down. "I understand."

I've got to be insane. I've said "no" to one of the most desirable women I've ever met. Corran smiled. *Of course I'm crazy, I volunteered to go back to Borleias.*

"Why the smile?"

Corran stroked her cheek. "I was thinking you're ample incentive for me to do everything I can to return."

Erisi leaned down and kissed him on the mouth. "Then if you do not return, I shall feel horrible for the rest of my life."

"I can't have that, can I?"

"Certainly not." She kissed him again, then slowly pulled away from him. "Sleep well tonight, Corran Horn, and fly the best you ever have tomorrow."

The door to her quarters closed and Corran turned to backtrack to the hallway leading to the billet he shared with Ooryl. *Though with Ooryl staying in the med station so they can monitor his arm, I'll be all alone.*

A jolt of fear ran through him and he almost turned around and went back to Erisi. Since his father's death he had spent a lot of time alone. It wasn't that they had been in each other's constant company, but just knowing he could speak with his father, and that his father would understand his problems, meant he didn't have to face them without help. Unlike most of the folks he knew, he got along well with his father. They had their occasional fights, but nothing that ripped apart the fabric of their relationship. That relationship, strengthened by mutual grief when Corran's mother died, weathered all adversity and just grew stronger.

They'd always been like paired banthas yoked to the same gravsledge. Together there had been nothing they could not accomplish. He realized that since his father's death, he'd been trying to go forward as much as possible, but without his father being there, he had a hard time figuring out exactly which way *was* forward. Gil Bastra had tried to help him out, and had been very effective, but since leaving CorSec, Corran had been without a moral compass. *Actually, I've had the moral compass, but I was so used to checking it against my father's feelings on things, that I'm not certain it's still calibrated correctly.*

Deep down he knew his father would have supported his decision to join the Rebellion, but his approval would have been harder to earn. Corran felt fairly certain he could have earned it, too, but death prevented him from knowing his father was still proud of him. He knew his father would have thought the mission to Borleias was stupid and needlessly dangerous, but he would have also been one of the first to volunteer for it.

"I guess, old man, you really aren't gone." Corran fingered his medallion. "I've got your sense of duty and your good luck charm. Definitely puts me ahead of the game."

Corran opened the door to his quarters and hit the light switch. He'd already unzipped his flight suit from throat to navel before he noticed the blanket-shrouded lump on Ooryl's bunk stir. "How did you get in here?"

Mirax sat up and scooped long locks of black hair out of her face. "Your Gand friend let me in."

"Where did you run into him?"

"Med-station. Coolant pump went in the *Skate* and flooded the ventilation system. My droid is locking it down, but I got a lungful. He was there and recognized me. The Emdees declared me healthy, but I couldn't go back to the *Skate*, and with you staging for an operation, there's scant free space here. Since he's staying with the doc droids, he offered me his billet." She yawned. "I agreed since I assumed you'd be spending the night with the bacta queen."

Corran blinked at her. "You did?"

"I saw the look she gave you when I showed up on the *Re-*

prieve. She could teach the average Hutt a thing or two about possessiveness."

He didn't like the smug tone in her voice. "You must have gotten more coolant than you thought."

"How do you plot that?"

"I'm here, aren't I?"

"Hey, Corran, I'd be the first to say Hal Horn's boy was smarter than Erisi is pretty."

"But you thought I'd be with her."

"Everyone makes mistakes, and you'd have been making one if you'd stayed with her."

Corran shot Mirax a wry grin. "She's possessive and you're, what, being *protective?*"

"There are only so many of us out here, Corran." Mirax plucked at the shoulder of her sleeveless tunic. "She wouldn't be good for you."

"And who would? You?"

"In your dreams, CorSec."

The look of surprise on her face coincided with the remark's sting in his heart. He wouldn't have thought so automatic a response, tossed off with the speed of a reflex that had been well exercised, could have bothered him. In his previous career he'd heard the same line delivered hundreds of times, with more and less vehemence, by every creature that ever tried to get its mouth around Basic words. He'd shrugged it off without really hearing it more times than he could count.

The surprised expression she wore told him that she hadn't meant to speak without thinking. She seemed to be second-guessing her comment as much as he was wondering about the effect it had on him. *The automatic dismissal hurts because I expected to merit something more than that. And she shot back so sharply because I dared suggest she wouldn't be better for me than Erisi—and her own reaction surprised her!*

Corran crossed over and sat at the foot of Ooryl's bunk. "Look, Mirax, it's been a long day and tomorrow is going to be tough. I meant no offense."

"I know. I was picking on someone in your unit. I'm a little mad at the Thyferrans right now. The price of bacta is going up—they're blaming an Ashern attack on a processing plant. I used to turn a tidy little profit on shipments, but I can't raise the money to buy a lot. I'm left running foodstuff and parts, which is not the way to get rich."

"I wish I could help."

"Sure you do." She shook her head, all the while smiling. "If I wanted to kill my father I'd send him a holo and tell him Hal Horn's son said he wished he could help me make some runs."

"Somewhere in orbit between Corellia and Selonia my father's ashes are trying to recoalesce to stop me." He smiled and patted her blanketed knee. "I do mean it, though."

"I believe you. Wherever you're going tomorrow, if you run into anyone on the ground who can sign an exclusive import/export deal, think of me and get it on a datacard."

"If I'm on the ground tomorrow, the only thing that will get exported is me, and I'll be exported to Kessel."

"I'll make you a deal on the spice you dig up."

"You're all heart."

She drew her knees up and hugged them to her chest. "It's going to be nasty, is it?"

"About the only thing we have going for us is that they don't know we're coming."

"That's something, then." Mirax reached out and touched the medallion he wore. "Is that what I think it is?"

"I don't know. It was my father's good luck charm." Corran took it off and passed it to her, complete with the gold chain. "It's a coin in a collar that lets me put it on a chain. My father used to keep it in his pocket, but I lose things too easily like that. So what is it that you think it is?"

Mirax turned it over and back in her palm and peered at it closely. "It's a Jedcred."

"What?"

She frowned. "Jedcred is what my father used to call them;

it comes from Jedi credit. It looks like a coin but was really a commemorative medallion struck when a Corellian Jedi became a Master. A dozen or so would get minted and distributed to family, close friends, the Jedi's Master, and favored students."

Corran raised an eyebrow. "How do you know so much about it?"

She smiled sweetly. "Have you forgotten, my dear, that I make my living by bringing that which is ordinarily rare to those who want it? Collectibles like these can fetch a fine price, especially since the Emperor cornered the market on Jedi Knights. How did your father get it?"

"I don't really know." He thought for a moment. "I know my grandfather liaised with the Jedi, to coordinate their actions with CorSec and had a good friend among them, but that was back before the Clone Wars. I guess this guy was someone he knew. He did say the only Jedi he knew well died in the Clone Wars."

She handed it back to him. "I hope it's a better luck charm for you than it was for the Jedi whose face is on it."

He refastened it around his neck and relished the sensation of its weight against his breastbone. "You're not alone in that hope." He stood and smothered a yawn with his hand. "Sorry, that's not from talking with you."

"I know. It's late and the day's been exhausting."

"I'll get up early to record some messages, but right now I need my sleep."

"So do I."

"I'm just going to go over there and lie down."

"So I imagined." Mirax lay back down and pulled the blanket up under her chin.

Corran walked over to his bed, sat down, and kicked off his boots. He started to pull off his flight suit but stopped when he noticed she was watching him. "I thought you were going to go to sleep."

"I am, but I was just wondering . . ."

"Yes?"

"Do you think you'll be warm enough tonight?"

Corran peeled his flight suit down to his waist, then snaked it down over the lower half of his body. Her question sounded innocent enough, but the inflection in her voice filled it with all sorts of innuendoes and invitations. Visions of the two of them entwined together in his bed flashed through his mind.

He was tempted. In her arms he could find sanctuary from the loneliness and fear he felt, but what *they* would be doing *he* would be doing for himself. *That wouldn't be right.*

"Yeah, Mirax, I think I will be warm enough."

"Oh, good." Mirax smiled at him as he pulled his sheets over himself. "I just thought I'd ask."

"Thanks." He hit the light switch and the room went black.

"Corran?"

"Yes?"

"Are you sure you'll be warm enough?"

"Quite sure," he said, regretting each syllable.

"Good." Mischief shot through her voice. "Then you wouldn't mind tossing me your spare blanket, would you?"

"Not at all." He laughed lightly and tossed the blanket from the foot of his bed off into the darkness. "Good night, Ms. Terrik."

"Sleep tight, Mr. Horn. Tomorrow will be all clear skies and easy shots for you."

32

WEDGE PRESSED HIS thumb against the datapad screen offered to him by the Verpine tech, Zraii. "Thanks for getting the auxiliary fuel pods on so quickly. It's going to mean a lot on this mission."

The insectoid technician buzzed something at him, prompting Wedge to smile and nod, since he had no idea what the tech was saying. He assumed it had something to do with the ablative sheaths fitted over the nose of the X-wings. It would burn off as they entered Borleias's atmosphere, giving the snubfighters the appearance of meteorites burning up on entry to observers on the ground. "A very good job, Zraii."

Over the top of the tech's head he saw Mirax walk into the hangar with Corran. She gave him a kiss on the cheek, then the pilot ran off toward his own green and white X-wing. Mirax watched him go, pulling a Rebel-issue flight jacket more tightly over her shoulders.

Mirax and Corran? Perhaps opposites do *attract.* It struck him that their attraction to each other seemed as improbable as that of Princess Leia to Han Solo. The thought caused a sinking feeling in the pit of his stomach. *If they have as many ups and downs as those two . . .*

Mirax walked over to him and watched him through slitted eyes for a second. "Are you borrowing trouble, Wedge?"

"Are you reading my mind?"

"Huh?"

"Nice coat—looks better on you than it does on Corran."

Mirax smiled, but didn't blush. "We're friends. Ooryl offered me his bunk last night and I accepted. Corran and I talked. Nothing happened." She glanced to the side and noticed Erisi's approach. "It's a good thing Corran doesn't snore—I was able to get *some* rest."

Wedge shook his head. "We're heading out, Mirax. I left a message behind for you and your father, if I don't make it back."

"You will, Wedge. You've gobbled up the best the Emperor had to offer—no reasons to imagine the crumbs will choke you." Mirax gave him a hug and a kiss on the cheek. "I'll see if I can find enough paint to be able to decorate your T-65 with the new kills."

"Thanks, Mirax." He turned to Erisi. "You have something for me, Ms. Dlarit?"

"Mission Control says Case Green is in effect."

"Good. We're clear to go." Wedge whistled loudly and circled his right hand over his head. The Rogue Squadron pilots looked at him for a second, then pulled themselves into their cockpits. "Sorry you're not going with us, Ms. Dlarit."

"Not as sorry as I am. May the Force be with you."

Wedge smiled. "Thanks. Stay out of danger, the both of you." He pulled on his helmet and climbed up into the X-wing's cockpit. He strapped himself into the ejection seat, then punched the ignition sequence into the computer. The engines came up with only a trace of a whine. He closed the cockpit canopy, then glanced behind himself.

"Are you ready, Mynock?"

The R5 unit beeped at him and Wedge projected a trace of fear into the reply's tremolo. *Wouldn't be a mission if we didn't feel that way.*

"Rogue Leader to Mission Control, requesting liftoff clearance."

"Control to Rogue Leader, you and your squadron are clear for takeoff. Be strong in the Force. And shoot straight."

"As ordered, Tycho. See you in ten hours."

"I'll be waiting."

Wedge gave Tycho's silhouette in the control center's window a thumbs-up, then he slowly cut in the repulsorlift drive. The X-wing rose from the ground and, with a light foot on the rudder pedals, turned left toward the hangar door. Easing the throttle forward he applied thrust and started out. He let his nose dip a bit to give himself a better view of the area through which he flew, retracted his landing gear, and cruised out into the open.

All around him the golden savannahs of Noquivzor spread out, the long grasses teased by gentle breezes. His ship seemed immune to the wind, just as it was immune to the peace of the planet. Off in the distance brown specks flowed together into a dark flood as a mossy-horned herd of wildernerfs invaded the valley. In one huge tree, the only one visible to Wedge, a pride of taopari waited for the prey to drift closer before they would start their hunt.

Tycho was right—I'm not too old for this game. I have, however, been playing it for far too long. When I get back, I'm going to get out and walk across these plains and drink in a little life, a little peace. He nodded slowly. *It's no good to keep fighting if I allow myself to forget* why *I'm fighting.*

Corran's voice crackled through the helmet speakers. "Rogue Squadron assembled, sir."

Wedge brought the nose of his fighter up. "Thank you, Rogue Nine. Full speed to the jumppoint, people. We've got an appointment to keep and it won't do for us to be a minute late." Wedge punched his throttle full forward, leaving windwhipped grasses and roiling clouds as the only sign he had been on the planet.

And Noquivzor erased those traces effortlessly.

———

Mirax shivered and hugged her arms around herself. As she turned away from the hangar opening, she saw Erisi staring ion bolts at her. *Now I know why I felt cold.* She put her arms through the sleeves of the jacket and pulled it taut at her waist so Corran's name tape could be read over the breast pocket. "I think they'll do fine."

"I *know* it." The Thyferran glared at her. "Of course, your antics with Corran could doom the mission. He needed rest."

"And he got it." Mirax met Erisi's stare openly. "Corran and I are friends, nothing more. His father knew my father."

"His father *hunted* your father."

"And got him, so you can rest assured that nothing could develop between us."

"Good. See that it doesn't."

The implied challenge got beneath Mirax's skin. "And if I don't?"

Erisi's blue eyes sparked anger. "You are a smuggler. I have it within my power to see to it that you never are able to handle bacta shipments. I can guarantee that anyone who wants to handle bacta shipments will never deal with you. In short, I can end your career here and now."

The Thyferran's expression eased, but the energy in her eyes did not diminish. "Conversely, you can be rewarded for leaving Corran alone. The very influence that I could bring to bear against you can be made to work for you. We can be friends, and you will find that a very good thing."

Mirax killed the desire to haul off and smack the smug grin from Erisi's face. *She was adrift in space and isn't on a mission with her squadron—she's bound to be muddy in her thinking.* "I'll take that under advisement. Even *if* I felt something more for Corran, well, I make my living selling all sorts of things I might like for myself. In fact, I should be seeing to business right now. If you will excuse me."

"Of course." Erisi smiled sweetly, but it failed to cut the venom in her eyes. "We'll speak again."

Mirax mirrored her smile, then stalked off toward the *Pulsar Skate*. She headed up the gang-ramp and sniffed the air for traces of coolant. She smelled nothing, which should have made her happy, but the abbreviated conversation with Erisi left her uneasy. *And*, she realized, *it's because of more than the imperious way she spoke to me.*

Mirax had learned to handle all manner of client attitudes toward her, but that had been easy since it was business, not personal. Erisi was giving her orders concerning her personal life. She even threatened business pressures to make Mirax change her personal life. While what Erisi offered was indeed very tempting, the practical result would be that Mirax would be selling a piece of herself and that was something she had long ago vowed never to do.

She wanted to convince herself that her upset came from the principle of the whole thing, but she couldn't dismiss the nascent feelings she had for Corran. It wasn't love—of that she was pretty certain—but it *could* have moved toward it. At the very least Corran represented something from her past that provided an illusion of constancy to life.

She knew she could have hated him as easily as liked him, and she'd expected more negative feelings for him, but they just weren't there. In bringing him the *ryshcate* and the black-market goods she'd expected an angry reaction from him. That would have been reason enough to think poorly of him, but he'd been gracious in accepting the gifts. She'd started to soften toward him that night, which is why she fled.

Mirax admitted to herself that she'd accepted Ooryl's offer to get another shot at kindling negative feelings. She'd been prepared to sleep with Corran, and hate him in the morning if he'd seduced her with some "and tomorrow I may die" line. The fact that he hadn't tried to seduce her, and had deftly side-stepped invitations to keep her warm in the night, confirmed what she had known all along—he was a bit more complex than the stereotypical CorSec officer.

She shivered. *I don't need or want involvement with* anyone, *much less the son of the man who sent my father to Kessel. I also don't want some bacta queen ordering me around.*

Her head came up as she realized her Sullustan pilot had spoken to her. "What?"

Liat Tsayv, the mouse-eared pilot, chittered at her again.

"No, I don't know where we're going because I don't know what we'll be hauling."

The Sullustan canted his head to the side and muttered reprovingly.

"Well, for your information, I *didn't* sleep with a pilot, *and* even if I *had* slept with him, he isn't the unit's quartermaster. Have you thought of pulling a unit want list from Emtrey? No?" She pointed at the communications console. "Do it now."

Liat punched up a comm frequency, then squeaked and squealed through a headset. Mirax hit another button and a holographic list featuring icons and dual buy/sell prices grew up from the holoplate in the middle of the *Skate*'s cockpit. She scanned the list quickly and saw most of it was military equipment, which was paid for with promises and brought a very low profit margin into the equation. Still, she was willing to bring it in provided she had some high-value cargo to make a run worth her time.

The consumer goods list began and she found it much more promising than the military list. Then some odd products started showing up. "Liat, ask for confirmation on the prices for fifteen through twenty-five inclusive."

The Sullustan complied with the order, then nodded and rubbed his hands together greedily.

"Damn, this is not good." Mirax smacked her hands together. "Tell the droid we'll buy *all* he has of fifteen through twenty-five. Yes, *all*."

Liat chirred angrily.

"I know we can't fit it all in here. Negotiate an exclusivity contract with him. Give him whatever he wants. A partnership even. Just do it." She snatched a comlink from the recharging port in the cockpit wall. "When you have it locked, call me. I'll be out looking for Wedge's XO. We have a problem, a big problem, and if I can't head if off, I've got friends who are on their way to die."

33

WEDGE KEYED HIS COMM as the squadron came out of hyperspace and prepared for the second and final leg of their run into the Pyria system. He adjusted the power output for the comm so the signal would become weak and garbled outside the kilometer sphere in which the ships moved. Even though the comm would scramble the transmission and make it all but impossible for the Empire to decrypt, he wanted to take the further precaution of making the signal all but impossible to pull in.

"This is Rogue Leader. There is one final refinement to our plans that you should know about. There is no system code-named Phenaru. We're going back to Blackmoon." Wedge waited for comments and protests, but only silence came in over his headset. He took that as a vote of confidence in him by his people and that brought a smile to his face.

"The mission as simulated was exact with the following exception—the simulated run through the asteroid belt to get into the planet was based on a run through the canyons on Borleias's sole moon. We come into the system behind it, swing around on its surface, and take a direct shot at the nightside of the world. The moon is what will make leaving tough, but coming in it will shield us from unfriendlies on the world. Cometary fragments are causing meteor showers, so planet-based detection stations should have a hard time picking us up. Any questions?"

Bror's voice growled through the speakers. "You're saying, Commander, we're getting another shot at the squints who escaped us last time?"

I was under the impression we *were the ones who escaped last time* . . . "That's about the size of it. And there will be friendlies in the area, but not in fighters and they'll be mute. Our mission is to hit the conduit and get back out. The fuel limitations are exactly what they were in the simulator." Wedge hit a button on his console. "Speed and coordinates for the jump to hyperspace sent now. We'll be three hours to Borleias, so use the time to review the run."

The squadron went to light speed and Wedge checked his fuel level. Given mission parameters, distance from the moon to target, and expected fuel consumption rates he was in fine shape. On the run from the moon to Borleias he would begin burning fuel directly from the belly pod and begin to use it to refill what little fuel the escape from Noquivzor and the hyperspace jumps had burned from his main tank. The double duty would allow him to drain the pod more quickly and jettison it shortly after the end of the run to the target. The others would be following the same procedure, though the second and third flights would ditch their pods before they began valley runs.

Wedge felt confident his people would succeed in destroying the tunnel. That would allow the commandos, who were arriving in the system from a different direction and at a different time, to get in and do their jobs before Defender Wing arrived. The exact timing of the commando operation had been kept from him, though Ackbar had said that if his people could help, it would be appreciated. He took that to mean the commandos and their arrival would overlap with Rogue Squadron's operation, but the only help the Rogues could realistically offer would be to scatter the local fighters, and that was something he knew he could not possibly prevent his people from doing anyway.

"We're good, we're trained, and we know we have to succeed." Wedge smiled and brought up a visual simulation of the valley run. "With a little luck and a lot of heart, there's nothing that can stop us from succeeding."

"But, Captain Celchu, you *must* tell me where they are." Mirax waved a datapad at him. "I think the mission has been compromised."

Tycho shook his head. "It's impossible."

She jerked a thumb at the door to his quarters. "Sure, and the Security officers standing guard over you told me it was impossible for me to speak with you, but I'm here aren't I?"

"There are degrees of impossible, I guess." Tycho raked fingers back through brown hair. "The thing of it is that I can't tell you where they're off to—I don't know."

"How's that?" Mirax watched him carefully. "You're the unit's Executive Officer. You *must* know."

"Sorry."

"Who does know?"

"Here? Emtrey."

"Get him here."

"Ms. Terrik, I know you're a friend of Commander Antilles, and I know he sets great store by you, but . . ."

Mirax held a hand up. "Look, I wouldn't be here except that I think their mission has been compromised and they may be walking into a trap. Get the droid here, because I think he's part of it. I'll explain by the time he gets here, and if you don't like the explanation, kick me out and send him on his way. Please. I don't want your friends and mine to die."

"All right. Please, sit down." Tycho fished a comlink from his pocket. "Captain Celchu to Emtrey, please report to my quarters. This is urgent."

"On my way, Captain."

Mirax sat in a simple canvas campaign chair and cleared a stack of datacards from the proton torpedo crate Tycho used as a low table. She set her datapad down. "Do you have a holoplate to project data?"

He shook his head and scooped another pile of datacards from the table to the foot of his bed, then sat down beside them. "I've got a good imagination. What have you got?"

She glanced at the datapad and organized her thoughts. "Right after they jumped out of this system, I had my pilot pull a trade list from Emtrey. It has a lot of military items and some black market stuff. There were new additions to the normal list and all of those products were native to Alderaan. They've become quite rare over the last five years, but all had ridiculously low sell prices."

Tycho's blue eyes narrowed. "It's not like they're being made anymore."

"Right." She leaned forward for emphasis. "Get this—none of them had *buy* prices. I've seen enough people price their goods over the years that this pattern tells me Emtrey has uncovered a source for these materials that means he's getting them for little or nothing. Now since no one in Rogue Squadron has mentioned finding or recovering some lost trove of Alderaanian goods, and this list is current, I'm thinking the droid is projecting the availability of products following this mission."

Tycho sat back and scowled. "I can see how you made that assumption, but . . ."

"Couple it with this: There's been a rumor floating around about a new source for Alderaanian goods, but the prices have been prohibitively high. I assumed the Empire was releasing stockpiles to soak up credits being held by Alderaanian expatriates, denying the Rebellion a source of needed money. If there *is* a source, be it an Imperial storehouse or something else, I think Rogue Squadron is headed toward it. And it doesn't take much brains to see such a place would be a prime target for the Alliance, given how many Alderaanian nomads would love another piece of their world."

"Count me among their number. Such a storehouse would be an inviting target for a raid, and a logical site for an Imperial trap." Tycho rubbed his hands over his face and sighed heavily. "This doesn't look good, does it?"

"I've arranged to take all of these items that Emtrey can provide, so the list is clear right now. No one else can get access to it. No one else knows of it, as nearly as I know, so the leak should have stopped there."

"Still, there *is* a chance that the information could have gotten out."

"Exactly." Mirax popped up out of her chair as the door opened and Emtrey came in.

"Good morning, Captain Celchu, Ms. Terrik. How may I be of service?"

Mirax grabbed the droid's left arm. "You have to tell me where Rogue Squadron is going."

"I'm afraid, Ms. Terrik, that information is classified. Neither you nor Captain Celchu are authorized to know that information. To provide it to you would be to compromise . . ."

"Emtrey, that list you gave me this morning already compromises the location."

"I'm afraid that's impossible."

Tycho boosted himself up off the bunk. "Where are you getting the Alderaanian goods you're offering for sale?"

The droid twitched and the tone of his voice shifted slightly. "If I reveal my sources, you'll cut in on my action. No way."

Mirax stared incredulously at the droid, then turned back toward Tycho. "Can you believe this?"

"No, in fact, I can't."

"I'm just protecting my profit margin here."

"Emtrey, this is a matter of life and death."

"Sure it is, Ms. Terrik, the death of my business."

Tycho stood abruptly. "Emtrey, shut up."

The droid looked at him strangely, tilting his head. "I wasn't saying anything, sir."

"His voice has changed."

"I notice." Tycho's eyes narrowed. "Shut up."

"I beg your pardon, sir."

"Shut up."

The droid's arms snapped to its sides so quickly that Mirax lost her grip on him. The clamshell head canted forward, making the droid bow its head until its chin touched its chest. At the top of its neck, previously hidden by the head, Mirax saw a glowing red button.

"What's going on, Captain?"

Tycho half shrugged. "I'm not certain, really, but the droid is in a wait-state, it seems. I discovered this little trick when I was ferrying him to the Talasea system and we came across your ship. We were in combat and he wouldn't stop nattering. I ended up yelling at him to shut up and after the third time, this happened. He remains like this until roused. What's important right now is that until we hit the red button and reset him, he's little more than a remote with access to all Emtrey's memories."

"That's dangerous for a droid doing military work."

"It's not a standard modification for obvious reasons. There are a number of things odd about this droid, not the least of which is the voice shift when you start to press him on requisitions. I can check that later, though. Right now this override should get us what you want. Emtrey, I require the name of the system in which Rogue Squadron will be operating."

"Pyria system, Borleias, fourth planet, one moon, home to an Imperial fortress and various failed and abandoned industrial and agricultural ventures." The voice changed slightly. "Location of agro-manufacturing facility for Alderaanian agricultural products with high covert trade value."

Mirax's blood ran cold. "Emtrey, the list of products available from that facility—how many people have had access to it?"

"Yours was the only access, Ms. Terrik."

"Could a copy have been made by a slicer without your knowledge?"

The droid did not reply for a second or two. "Impossible to determine an answer to that question."

Mirax looked over at Tycho. "The Empire could have been warned. We have to do something."

"What? If we send a message out it could warn the Empire they're coming as easily as it warns our people of an ambush."

"So we go there. I can get us there fast. Maybe even before they arrive."

"And have our presence tip the Empire about the raid?" Tycho shook his head. "Any comm message could be intercepted, even if we are in-system and try to tight-beam it to them. That's no good."

Mirax balled her fists and hammered them against her thighs. "We have to do something. We can't just sit around and do nothing."

"Yes, but what we do has to be the right thing." Tycho slowly smiled and reached for the button on the back of Emtrey's neck. "And I think I know what it is."

34

WHEN THE SQUADRON reverted to realspace, the dark craggy ball hanging in space before them reduced Borleias to a slender blue-green crescent streaked with white. The moon's thin atmosphere blurred Borleias's image, making it beautiful—which was definitely *not* how Corran had remembered it. Corran inverted his X-wing, then reached up with his right hand to hit the switch that brought his S-foils into attack position. Ahead of him Wedge's X-wing similarly spread its wings, twisting around and bearing down on the moon.

The X-wings maintained comm silence as they leveled out and skimmed the black lunar surface. Corran brought his snubfighter in behind and to the left of Wedge's fighter. With their scanners in passive mode to avoid detection, they'd only register threats that had scanners up and seeking targets. As a result visual scanning by pilots and astromech droids became the primary defense against ambush.

"Not that much should be here." While the simulations had represented this run as threading their way through an asteroid ring around a planet to remain hidden, all the parameters used were taken from Borleias. As nearly as they knew the Imperials had not stationed fighters or remote detection units on the moon. Still, that possibility did exist, so the squadron did all it could to keep their presence a secret.

Volcanic glass teeth lined gaps in crater walls. They reflected scant little starlight, but strange shapes did appear in silhouette against the starfield. Whipping along at near maximum speed in the pitch-darkness of the moon's nightside did seem reckless and foolish, but no more so than the rest of the mission. They raced through the blackness, heading toward a point on the ever-changing horizon.

When the horizon appeared as a white crown, Wedge's X-wing pulled up and shot away from the moon. Down on Borleias the moon only appeared to be half full and the Rogues made their approach against the background of the moon's dark side. They plunged down into Borleias's gravity well. They let the planet draw them in, but before they hit the outer edges of the planet's atmosphere, Corran brought his ship around in a looping turn to starboard and inverted to have Borleias's dark face above him.

Pulling back on the stick, he eased the fighter's nose into the atmosphere. The ablative shell Zraii had applied to his fighter began to glow red, then came apart in a shower of sparks that momentarily blanketed his cockpit canopy. Once the fiery cloud passed, he pulled back even more on the stick and started a sharper descent into Borleias's night.

The ablative shell had given his ship the appearance of yet one more of the Versied meteors streaking through the night sky. Corran checked his scanners and had no indication of hostile sensors directed at him. *Entry is clean.* Glancing at his instruments, he came around to a heading and chopped his speed back so he would reach the rendezvous point exactly on time.

Flipping a switch, he engaged the fuel pod pump so it would start to refill his onboard fuel tank. A red-lined error message scrolled up on his main screen. "Whistler, the T65-AFP pump isn't working. Is there anything you can do?"

A negative hoot replied to his question.

Corran shrugged. *I have to run with the pod a little longer. No big deal.*

Suddenly Nawara's voice crackled over the helmet speakers. "Leader, twelve, repeat one-two, eyeballs coming in from the west, angels ten. On intercept for run. Patrol formation."

Corran felt his stomach clench. *Lucky bastards.* He smiled. *Or* very *unlucky.*

"Two Flight, Three Flight, pounce on them. Nine, we're to the deck and in. Are you ready?"

"Telemetry feed started, you are lead." Corran tightened his grip on the stick and shoved the fighter over into a steep dive. "This is it, Whistler. Keep your domed head down and enjoy the ride."

WEDGE FLIPPED HIS scanners into active mode and swooped his X-wing into the narrow end of the rift valley. The computer used muted greens to impose holographic highlights on the canopy that corresponded to the terrain outside. Nudging the stick to port and starboard he sliced his craft through the sleeping canyon. He rolled up on his port wing to slip through a narrow passage, then noted that behind him Corran had remained level to make the same run.

"No need to be fancy, Nine."

"Yes, sir." Corran's voice drifted off for a second. "Lead, I have two hostiles coming in behind us."

Wedge hit a switch on his console. "Power to rear deflector shields."

"Done."

"Mynock, bring up data on the trailers." The monitor flashed images of two TIE starfighters. *We should be faster than they are maneuvering through atmosphere here, but I'd rather they weren't there.*

Wedge keyed his comm. "Four, we have two down here. Can you help?"

Bror answered immediately. "Negative, Lead. Our plates are full, and long-range scans indicate squints coming in."

"Copy, Four." Wedge frowned. The intervention by Interceptors was not good. If both of the squadrons that showed up at the end of the last battle were to scramble against Rogue Squadron, no one would make it home. *But that's not the objective of this mission—blowing the conduit is.*

"Nine, push your speed."

"As ordered."

The X-wings came out of the canyon leading into the rift valley. To the right grassy plains stretched out through the darkness. On the left a striated escarpment rose up nearly a thousand meters. Its craggy surface reflected enough moonlight to let Wedge see Corran's X-wing in silhouette as the fighter drew almost parallel to his port stabilizer. Twenty-five kilometers farther on the valley narrowed again and five kilometers beyond that point lay their target.

Verdant laser bolts sizzled past, splitting the space between the Rebel fighters. Wedge juked up and to the starboard, while Corran's ship sank out of sight on the left. Rolling his ship and letting it move back toward the center of the valley, he saw one TIE dive, its lasers gouging up great chunks of the valley floor in front of Corran's jinking X-wing.

Wedge hauled his throttle back to half power and pulled a hard turn to port. Punching the throttle forward again, he rolled the ship onto its right S-foil and yanked it back in another hard turn. Leveling out to the left, he slipped into the aft wash of the TIE that had been on his tail. His finger tightened down on the trigger and scarlet laser fire exploded the Imperial fighter.

"Nine, report."

"Go, Lead, punch it. I'm coming behind."

"Status."

"I'll be good to go in a second."

Kicking the X-wing up on the starboard stabilizers, Wedge stabbed his fighter into the narrow northern end of the valley.

A brilliant flash of light painted shadows against white rock with skeletal clarity. The X-wing bucked a bit as the explosion's shock wave caught up with it, but Wedge's steady hand kept the fighter clear of the canyon walls.

"Nine, what was that?"

"Fuel pod exploding."

"One more time."

"Misses on the deck kicked up debris that hit my belly pod and I had a slow leak. I jettisoned it. The tank exploded and the guy behind me got an eyeful."

Wedge looked at his fuel indicators. His fuel pod was still a quarter full. "Fuel status."

"I'm okay."

"How much?"

"Three-quarters." Anger in Corran's voice transmuted into resolution. "Enough to do the job."

"Copy." *One run, then you're out of here, Corran. You're into your reserve.* Wedge clicked his weapons control over to proton torpedoes. "One klick, arming two."

"Got it. Armed two. Is that light up there?"

Wedge slowly nodded. "Be alert. Power to forward shields." Banking hard starboard he brought the fighter around the final turn before the run to the conduit. Yanking the stick to the left he snap-rolled the X-wing level, then hit the right rudder pedal and started the fighter skidding to the left. Laser bolts exploded against his forward shields.

He pulled the trigger, sending two proton torpedos sizzling out, but even as he did so he knew they would miss high. As they exploded against the canyon walls beyond the ferrocrete tunnel, Wedge snapped his repulsorlift drives on and bounced his fighter up and out of the canyon. Jamming his throttle full forward, he hauled back on the stick and shot skyward.

He saw the flashes of two more explosions below him as he rocketed away from Borleias. "Nine, report."

"Mine went low. That was a Juggernaut assault vehicle down there providing that fire."

"And it looked like they were reinforcing the conduit."

"I saw that. I nailed a ferrocrete mixer."

Wedge checked his scanners. "We have a squadron of Interceptors headed in our direction."

"What do you want to do? I'm good for another run."

"Another run would be suicide, Nine, and you don't have the fuel to play."

"Sir, I'm good for another run."

Wedge shook his head. "You're heading home while you can still get there."

"No."

"That's an order, Nine, not an invitation to debate." Wedge could feel Corran's disappointment. *It's exactly what I felt when Luke ordered me out of the trench on the first Death Star run.* "Get clear, Corran. You can't do any more good back there."

Dejection filled Corran's voice. "As ordered, sir. What are you going to do?"

"Blowing the conduit is our mission and the others can't break off to do it." Wedge Antilles slowly smiled. "What the Imps have set up there will stop almost any pilot. I'm going to remind them that in Rogue Squadron we don't take just any pilot."

35

KIRTAN LOOR FUSSED with the hem of his tunic and adjusted his cap with a tug on the bill. He wanted to feel confident about his recall to Coruscant, but he did not dare allow himself that indulgence. His mission had been the destruction of Rogue Squadron. While half of it had died at Borleias, the other half lived, with Wedge Antilles and Corran Horn still flying. In fact, the unit had amassed a considerable list of kills while it was his to destroy, so he could not imagine Ysanne Isard would be in a pleasant mood.

He cracked a smile. *I cannot imagine her* ever *being in a good mood.*

The door to her office slid open and Kirtan's smile died. Isard again wore her scarlet Admiral's uniform, complete with the black armband on her left arm. Her hair had been drawn back and fastened at the nape of her neck with a black clasp. She gestured invitingly, but the mannerly nature of her greeting only played through her hand. Her mismatched eyes prophesied doom, but he thought it might be deferred instead of immediate.

"Please, Agent Loor, do come in. I trust the journey from Borleias was not too tiring."

He shook his head, doing his best to hide any trace of fatigue. "I apologize for not being here sooner. My original agenda was disrupted, hence the week's delay in my arrival."

"I know about it. Another operation demanded some resources that I had planned to use for your return." She casually waved away concern over the delay—something Kirtan found mildly annoying since she had caused it *and* his week on Toprawa. "I trust you spent your time on Toprawa well?"

"Well?" Toprawa had been a Rebel transfer point for the stolen data about the first Death Star. As punishment for their complicity in the Rebellion, the population saw its world reduced to a pre-industrial state where banthas were the swiftest form of travel and fire was the highest level of energy production available to the native people. Imperial forces lived in gleaming citadels that remained lit like beacons throughout the night, becoming visible monuments to what the people of Toprawa had lost through their perfidy.

"You studied their suffering, yes?" Her dark brows arrowed together. "You saw what they have become."

Kirtan swallowed hard. "I have seen, yes. They are wretched and pathetic."

"And you witnessed one of their festivals?"

He nodded slowly. The "festival" involved a company of stormtroopers driving a cart laden with sacks of grain into the center of a village. To receive the grain the villagers were required to squirm on their bellies, worming their way forward, all the time weeping and wailing lamentations over the Emperor's death. Food was doled out based on some trooper's belief in the sincerity of the mourning. Kirtan had no doubt that many of the people had come to believe they truly did regret the Emperor's death.

"Those people, Agent Loor, conspired with the Emperor's murderers. They have learned that their actions have consequences, and they regret their past disloyalty." Her eyes tightened at the corners. "In their previous arrogance they dared believe the Empire was superfluous and could be replaced.

Now they know this is not true. All that is good in their lives comes from the Empire. They have been shown the truth and now live for a chance to be allowed back into our brotherhood."

"I saw. I remember."

Isard's harsh expression slackened slightly. "I recall your visual retention rate."

Toprawa must have been meant as a lesson in contrition. Kirtan raised his chin slightly, exposing his throat. "Madam Director, I regret deeply not having completed my mission."

"You do?" Isard opened her hands and surprise widened her eyes. "How is it you believe you have failed?"

"You sent me out to destroy Rogue Squadron." Kirtan's head twisted slightly to the side. "I have failed to do this."

"It is true that Rogue Squadron still exists, though for how much longer is in serious debate. The attack on Borleias hurt them badly. Your report made this quite apparent." She smiled and Kirtan had to suppress a shudder. "More important than that was the information you provided about General Derricote's private enterprise on Borleias. You could not have hidden it from me, of course, since it was key to the defense that sent the Rebels away without a victory."

Kirtan Loor bowed his head to her. "I am glad you were pleased." As he looked back up her expression changed again and it did not speak to anything even approximating pleasure on her part. It also missed mild discomfort by a wide margin, turning his mouth into a desert and his stomach into a home for a Sarlacc.

What did I do? When he swallowed his larynx scraped in his throat as if both were made of stone. *What did I fail to do?*

"I had expected something more of you, Agent Loor. Can you imagine what that is?"

He shook his head. "I cannot."

"No, indeed you cannot. And do you know *why* you cannot?"

"No."

Her hissed words echoed through the nearly empty chamber. "It is because your imagination has atrophied to the point of lifelessness. Recall, if you will, what Gil Bastra thought of you."

Kirtan's face burned. "He felt I relied on my retention of knowledge too much and used it to compensate for a lack of analysis. I remember this, and I *have* tried to change my ways. I had done an analysis of probable Rebel strategies and I isolated a number of worlds where I felt they would strike after they hit the Hensara system. And I was right, because Borleias was on that list."

"And how did you come to be at Borleias?"

"You sent me there."

"I sent you there." She held her right hand out to her side, then brought the left hand into the same position with a similar gesture. "Therefore you concluded?"

"That your analysis of Rebel strategy paralleled mine, hence you sent me to Borleias."

She brought her hands together, interlacing her fingers. "You began analysis, found what you thought was corroboration for it, and then, instead of further testing your analysis and this corroborating evidence, you stopped thinking. Consider the utter absurdity of your conclusion."

"What?"

"Kirtan Loor, are you so simpleminded as to assume that if I could predict where the Rebels were going to strike I would send *you* and you alone to be there and observe their attack? I assure you, I do not think so highly of your martial skills."

The Sarlacc in his stomach grew restless and began gnawing its way free of his belly. *Borleias should have fallen, and did not only because Derricote had hidden resources available to defend it. If she were able to predict where the Rebels would show up, she would have opposed them with significantly greater force and have struck a solid blow against them.*

"From the beginning, Agent Loor, the difficulty with the Rebellion has been in locating them. Since the Emperor's death, they have been able to spread out and diversify their bases, making them more difficult to destroy. Your effort against the base at Talasea was commendable—had Admiral Devlia not been stupid, Rogue Squadron might have been eliminated. The importance of that example, however, is to show you the vast problem we have had in finding the Rebels we want to kill."

Ysanne Isard clasped her hands at the small of her back. "Borleias is but one of two dozen worlds that provides the Rebels access to the Core worlds and even Imperial Center herself. Defending against those attacks is nearly impossible and utterly ridiculous if one bears in mind that the destruction of the Rebellion is the only way the preservation and restoration of the Empire can take place. This I *do* have utmost in my mind, and it is this consideration that sent you to Borleias."

Kirtan concentrated for a moment. *The only thing I did at Borleias was discover Derricote's covert operation. But if she had known about that previously she would have dealt with him herself.* "You sent me to spy on General Derricote?"

Isard nodded almost mechanically. "He has skills that are useful to me. The fact that he had managed to repair and make operational the old Alderaanian Biotics facility indicated that his skills had not atrophied. After I received your report I sent for him, and left my own people in charge of Borleias. In fact, he is here, now."

"My passage was delayed because you used ships meant for me to fetch him away."

"Very good, Agent Loor. Your report indicated he had the resources needed to resist a casual invitation. The arrival of a Super Star Destroyer proved enough to convince him to join me here. I have my people safeguarding his operation for him, tightening defenses and the like."

His facility is held hostage against his cooperation. Kirtan closed his eyes for a moment, hoping all the confusion and conflicting thoughts in his mind would sort themselves out.

They did not. He opened his eyes and saw her studying him

as a scavenger would study carrion. "Forgive me, Madam Director, but I've lost track of your mission for me."

"Your mission, Agent Loor, is the same as it has always been—destroy Rogue Squadron. The fact that I choose other missions for you from time to time should not deflect you from your primary duty."

"Then you will be sending me back out into the galaxy to pursue them?"

"No, you will remain here and work with General Derricote."

Kirtan opened his mouth and started to ask a question, then closed it. He watched her for a moment, then bowed his head. "As you wish, Madam Director."

"No, as it must be." She turned away from him and faced the windows that looked out over Imperial City. "There is no need to send you in their pursuit. You see, soon enough, they will be here. And when they are it will be quite the welcome you have prepared for them."

"Get going, Nine. Defend yourself if you can't run, but get out of here." Wedge rolled his fighter to give himself a final look at Corran's X-wing. "You've done good."

The other pilot gave him a thumbs-up. "I'll be waiting for the rest of you to get outbound."

"See you then." Wedge pulled the X-wing back over past vertical and saw the planet descend to fill his canopy. While the four proton torpedoes he and Corran had loosed at the conduit had not destroyed it, the burning ferrocrete mixer did mark the target rather nicely. Knowing surprise had been irrevocably lost, Wedge brought his fighter down in a spiral that put him five kilometers out from the target at just under four klicks altitude.

As Han once told me, "Stealth and subtlety work well, but for making lasting impressions, a blaster does just fine." He brought his X-wing around on a heading that paralleled the valley, dropped the nose so it pointed at the fire burning in the distance, and started his dive. *I definitely want this to be a lasting impression.*

Green laser bolts from the Juggernaut vehicle lanced up through the night at him. Mynock whined, but Wedge just dropped the fighter below the line of fire, or bounced up above it, constantly forcing the gunners to adjust their sights up and down or side to side. *Shooting at a fighter means you have a lot more movement to account for. Very few land vehicles can dance around this much.*

And none of them can do what I have in mind.

The range-to-target indicator on his console scrolled meters off by the hundreds as he dove in on the conduit. A peace washed over him despite the Imperial fire being directed toward him. He knew he wasn't slipping into some Jedi trance—as much as he admired Luke he knew he'd never master his friend's mystical skills. The sense of serenity seemed born of a conviction that he had to succeed in destroying the conduit and, more importantly, a lifetime of experience that told him the forces on the ground couldn't stop him.

One kilometer out from the target, Wedge pulled his throttle back and reversed the engine's thrust. As the Juggernaut's laser batteries brought their beams together to burn him from the sky, the X-wing dropped like a rock. In virtual freefall, it hurtled down toward the canyon floor. The Juggernaut's gunners, perhaps believing they had in fact hit the fighter, or perhaps horrified at its uncontrolled descent, stopped shooting.

Not that it would have mattered. A hundred meters from the ground Wedge clicked in the repulsorlift engines and their whine drowned out Mynock's terrified scream. The fighter's fall ended abruptly in a bouncing, bobbing hover barely five meters from the canyon's sandy floor. Dust billowed up around the X-wing and the lasers in the boxy Juggernaut's forward turret began to track down. Behind the vehicle, visible in the red and gold light of the burning mixer, stormtroopers and masons began to scatter.

Running his engines to zero thrust, Wedge ruddered the X-wing's nose in line with the Juggernaut and pulled the trigger on his flight stick. A single proton torpedo jetted out at the assault vehicle. The coruscating blue energy projectile pierced the Juggernaut's windscreen. It immolated the cockpit crew and melted its way into the vehicle's main body. There it detonated, swelling the Juggernaut with energy and rounding out its sharp corners before blasting it apart. Armor shrapnel sprayed throughout the area. It made the X-wing's shields spark for a moment, but through them Wedge could see the aft end of the vehicle tumble back up and over the conduit to fall on the other side.

Its burning hulk silhouetted the conduit.

Wedge thumbed his weapons control over to lasers and pulled the trigger. Using the rudder pedals he rocked the fighter back and forth, peppering construction vehicles and plasteel forms with scarlet energy bolts. Scaffolding collapsed and semifluid ferrocrete oozed from burning forms. Stormtroopers darted back and forth, seeking any cover they could find. He made no attempt to target them specifically—using a starfighter's weapons to kill an individual was akin to using a lightsaber to trim loose threads from a garment. It would do the job, but there were easier ways that were far more economical.

He switched back to proton torpedoes and armed two. Focusing his aiming reticle on the ferrocrete pipe, he hit the trigger, then punched power to the repulsorlift drives to vault his ship into the air.

The paired torpedoes blasted into and through the conduit in a shower of sparks. Ten meters beyond the pipe itself they exploded, igniting a rogue star right there in the canyon. The shock wave rocked the fighter. It disintegrated the pipe, shearing it off at both ends, then rolled on with such force that it snuffed the fires burning in the vehicles. The canyon walls shook, starting rocks and dust tumbling down. The explosion's harsh glare gave Wedge one last glance at the complete destruction of the target zone, then the fireball imploded, plunging the canyon into complete darkness.

He allowed himself the hint of a smile. "Conduit's gone. Now we start working on *my* objective."

Wedge punched his throttle full forward and jettisoned his empty fuel pod. "Rogue Leader here. Mission accomplished."

"Four here, Lead. All eyeballs blinded, all Rogues are safe. Squints and Rogues inbound your position." Bror's voice stopped for a moment. "We'll be there before they are."

"Time to head home, Rogues. Let's outrun them." Wedge brought his fighter around on a course that would link up with the other four fighters in the squadron. "Nine is leading the way out and will report trouble."

"Negative, Lead." The anxiety in Nawara's voice sank like ice through Wedge. "I've checked. Nine is nowhere on my forward scan."

ANGRY WITH HIMSELF, Corran considered violating Commander Antilles's order and shadowing him anyway. That thought survived about as long as Peshk had in the first fight for Blackmoon. *He's right. Your fuel reserves are down. He's given you a mission, and you're to complete it. Head out and make sure the run is clear.*

"Whistler, boost my sensors. I want as complete a picture of the theater here as you can give me. Full threat assessments."

The astromech droid chirped happily. His first list of fighters showed only three eyeballs left in the dogfight with Rogue Squadron. A full squadron of squints was inbound, but their threat assessments were in decimal points. They were no threat to him, and scant little threat to his squadron mates. While he could not ignore them, there was no reason they would interfere with his run out of the system.

The numbers on two of them climbed slightly higher. "What's with those two?"

Whistler splashed a tactical display on Corran's monitor. Two of the squints had broken off to run a flyby and possible intercept on a body moving through the atmosphere. The numbers Whistler used to describe that falling object showed its fall to be controlled, and Corran was fairly certain that little fact would not have been lost upon the TIE pilots.

"Whistler, do you think they're closing on one of our assault shuttles?"

A crisp note answered him as Whistler tagged the shuttle as the *Devonian*.

"Yeah, I thought so." Yanking his stick back to his breastbone, Corran brought the snubfighter over in a big loop. "Page, you're going to owe me big time for this one."

The droid tootled at him with low tones.

"Yes, I do know what I'm doing. If I let my dive drive me instead of burning up fuel, we'll be fine." Corran eased his throttle back. "And, no, I don't want you to calculate the odds on this. I've never asked for the odds before, and I don't want them now. Odds only matter when you're engaged in games of chance, and if Page's people are going to have any chance, this can't be a game."

Corran's dive was bringing him high, hot, and on an angle at the rear arc for the Interceptors. He focused his attention on the second squint. He couldn't switch over to proton torpedoes because a target lock would warn them of the threat they faced. If he was going to succeed, he needed things to be fast and that meant the first Interceptor had to die on his first pass.

Just over a kilometer out, Corran pushed his throttle forward and leveled out to come straight in at the Interceptors. *A bit more angle and maybe I can get both of them at the same time.* He switched his weapon over to lasers and linked them so they would fire in tandem. He dropped his targeting crosshairs on the rear ship and when they flashed green, he pulled the trigger and kept it down.

Four pairs of red energy darts perforated the slant-winged Interceptor. The first hits on the right wing started the ship rolling, then it jinked up into Corran's line of fire. Four laser bolts converged, puncturing the cockpit and filling the interior of the ship with fire. A roiling explosion blasted the squint apart and forced Corran to roll and dive to avoid the worst of the debris cloud. Snapping back to his previous orientation, he looked up at where the other Interceptor should have been.

He didn't see it, but before he could even begin to wonder if it had somehow died, too, laser fire carved into the strength of his aft shield.

Great, all I need is some Sithspawn hotshot pilot in that squint! He reinforced the aft shield, rolled, then hit the left rudder and slewed his ship around to try to give him an angle on the Interceptor. He couldn't see it on his forward or rear scope, so he hauled back on the stick and started a climbing loop.

The Interceptor appeared dead-center in his aft scan and again laced his aft shield with green fire.

Who is this clown? Corran came over, rolled up onto the port S-foil, then chopped his throttle back and let the X-wing drop toward the planet. "Whistler, comm to one klick radius. Tell the transport to go to ground as soon as possible because this guy is good. I want room to operate."

A harsh whistle stung him. A question appeared on his display.

"Yes, of course I'm better. I'm toying with him. Now reinforce those shields and hang on."

The Interceptor began to close on Corran's tail. Pulling back on the stick, Corran leveled his ship out and the Interceptor swooped in behind him. The Corellian waited until the Interceptor closed to five hundred meters, then sideslipped his ship to starboard. Hitting hard left rudder and bringing his throttle back up, his X-wing's nose swung back toward the squint.

Though more maneuverable than their vertically winged predecessors, the Interceptor's broad wings still gave them yaw problems. The squint's sideslip came slow and presented Corran with a wonderful target. His first shot hit solidly on the starboard wing, lasing two angry holes in it. The squint began to roll and Corran shot again, but the scarlet bolts shot fore and aft of the ball cockpit.

The Imperial pilot finished the roll and dove. Corran kicked the X-wing up on the port S-foil and dove after the Interceptor. The pilot in front of him let his ship jerk and juke back and forth, but the drag from the damaged wing's solar panels made all moves to the right quicker and harder to recover from.

Corran dropped his targeting reticle just to starboard of the stricken fighter. The Interceptor drifted to the right and he fired. The lasers took the right wing clean off. The squint immediately whirled off into a flat spin to port, uncontrolled and unrecoverable. Corran pulled up before he saw the Interceptor crash and part of him hoped the pilot had the intelligence to eject before he died.

He glanced at his monitor and angled his ship onto an intercept for the rest of the squadron's outbound course. "Nine to Rogue Leader, I'm still here."

He heard plenty of anger pulsing through Wedge's reply. "You're supposed to be leading, not following, Nine."

"Copy, Lead. I was getting clear, but two squints made a run."

"So you made a run."

"Avenging General Kre'fey." Corran figured Wedge would catch the reference and realize the Interceptors were closing on a transport when he picked them off. He looked at his fuel indicator. "Lead, I have a problem."

"I know, Nine, your astromech just answered an inquiry I sent."

The Twi'lek's voice broke into the frequency. "Lead, another dozen squints have launched and are following the wave behind us."

"Lead, this is Four. Let's stay. It's only twenty-two of them."

"Lead, Five here. I'm game."

Corran smiled. "Thanks, guys."

"Quiet. This isn't a democracy and what we *want* to do doesn't matter. We have orders and others are depending on those orders being obeyed." Static filled the speakers for a moment, then Wedge spoke again. "We *do* have some leeway in obeying them, though. Change in plans. We'll go sunside and draw the Imps with us. Nine, you will go in on the dark side and go to ground. The atmosphere is thin, but your life-support equipment can concentrate it enough for you. If you can avoid them, we'll be back for you."

"I'll do my best, Lead." Corran brought his X-wing into position with the rest of the squadron. "Four, how many did you vape?"

"I got six. You?"

"Three, if we count the one in the canyon."

"It counts, Nine. Unconventional, but it counts."

"Thanks, Commander."

Rhysati broke into the conversation. "What did you do, Nine?"

"It's complicated. I'll explain it later." Even as he pronounced the word "later," it turned to dust in his mouth. "I'm only at seventeen. You're plus two on me, Four. I'm going to count the ones I get on the dark side in our contest."

"I would not have it any other way, Nine."

Nawara Ven spoke. "Nine, Gavin's an ace now."

"Never doubted it for a minute. Good going, kid." Borleias's moon loomed large overhead. "Welcome to the club."

"Ten seconds to break, Rogues. Nine, don't feel you have to be a hero."

"Have to be? I'm a Rogue. I thought hero came with the territory."

"It certainly does, Nine. Break now."

Corran banked off to the left as the rest of the squadron went right and filled his aft sensor scope. "Later, my friends."

If there was any reply it didn't make it over the horizon to him.

Corran throttled back and took the X-wing down close to the lunar surface. He cut off his comm unit and flipped his sensors over to passive mode. "Okay, Whistler, it's just you and me. Let's find us a hole to crawl into. No, not one to hide in, but one to ambush out of. The Commander knew as well as we did that this split wouldn't fool all the Imperial pilots. They'll come for us eventually. I've never had a desire to die alone, and taking a bunch of them along will suit me just fine."

37

*A*S CERTAIN AS *taxes and as slow as paperwork they come.* With his X-wing nestled in a frozen lava tube on the side of a volcano, Corran watched as paired Interceptors flew search patterns over the lunar surface. They'd pushed enough power to their sensors that even with having them focused directly downward, enough energy bled off to register on his passive receptors.

Whistler had detected differences in the energy signatures of each sensor unit and had isolated a dozen different Interceptors. *That means ten squints didn't make it back from their pursuit. Given that the Rogues had only fifteen minutes to play, that's very good work.*

He reached up and tapped the transparisteel at the rear of his cockpit. "Whistler, they've been at this search stuff for nearly half an hour. Have you got the solution worked up yet?"

The droid piped a jeer at him.

"Hey, just asking." Corran started his engines and shunted power to the weapons control. He armed two proton torpedoes. "Ready when you are."

A countdown clock appeared on his console and slowly started running down. The squints continued their back and forth grid search pattern, moving ever closer to his position. From the second he saw what they were doing he asked Whistler to time the runs. They remained constant for speed and duration, which told Corran the pilots had done exactly what he would have—they programmed the search pattern into their navigational computers and let it run on autopilot.

Which means we know where they'll be in thirty-five point three seconds. He nodded grimly. *I'm dead, but you'll be dead sooner, and that's a bit of a victory, to be sure.*

It occurred to Corran that he was angry about dying. That emotion seemed, on the surface, to be rather logical, but emotions rarely were. Had someone described his current situation to him and asked him how he'd feel, he would have told them he'd have been scared out of his wits. The fact was, however, that the anger overshadowed the fear.

He took a deep breath and forced himself to relax. *Fear and anger aren't right here.* He knew that going out to bring the Interceptors down just so he'd take more of them with him when he died was wrong. He didn't know if the pilots were clones or volunteers or conscripts or mercenaries—and who they were didn't really matter. The only reason he had for fighting against them was the same one he'd had for going after the squints down on Borleias.

I want to stop the Empire from taking lives. I'm not an avenger; I'm here to protect others. He smiled. Somehow it seemed right that he, son and grandson of men who protected others in CorSec, had followed them into CorSec and had ended up here, with the Rebellion. His life, his father's life, his grandfather's life, had all been devoted to safeguarding others. *And now the guys on the ground and Salm's bomber jocks will get protected.*

The timer went to zero.

Corran hit the trigger.

Two proton torpedoes streaked out from the launch tubes on either side of the X-wing. Because they were programmed to reach a certain point at a certain time, Corran did not need a target lock on the pair of squints flying past. A kilometer separated them from the X-wing and the torpedoes went from launch to target in under half a second.

The first torpedo stabbed through the closest Interceptor and detonated. The explosion vaporized the squint, reducing it to its component molecules. The second torpedo actually overshot its target, but went off when it reached its programmed range. The blast crumpled the starboard wing. The Interceptor began to roll through a tight downward spiral, then slammed into a basalt monolith and exploded.

Shoving the throttle forward, Corran held the stick steady as his snubfighter shot from the lava tube. Once clear he hauled back on the stick and climbed. He saw other Interceptors break their search patterns, but none of them immediately moved after him. *Their sensors are still oriented toward the ground.*

He flipped his weapons controls over to lasers and set them on quad fire. It would slow his overall rate of fire, but a solid hit was a kill and he needed all the help he could get. Inverting the X-wing he took a quick look at the Interceptors as he flew past the volcano's crater. Spotting a pair of targets moving toward where the first squints had gone down, he rolled the fighter up on the starboard S-foil and came around in a wide curve.

He dove and leveled out in a small valley between the volcano and a meteor crater. Climbing at the last second, he rose up over the broad lunar plain and sent two bursts of laser fire into the belly of a squint. The starfighter obliged him by melting into a metallic fog that instantly condensed and rained down on the moon.

Whistler hooted proudly.

"Darned right, Horn pulls ahead of the bacta boy." Corkscrewing his ship into a weave, Corran avoided the retribution of the squint's wingman. He leveled out for a second, then cut the fighter hard right. Ninety degrees from his original track, he leveled out again, then climbed and did a wing-over to port that pointed him straight back at the Interceptor that had tried to stay on his tail. Corran rolled, shot, melted some armor from the squint, and broke hard right again.

He shook his head in response to Whistler's question. "No, I didn't think I killed it. Burned him a bit, though."

Corran rolled the X-wing through inversion and hit the left rudder to again carry himself back across his own trail. Green spears of laser light crisscrossed through the moon's thin air as the Interceptors converged on his ship. Whistler toted nine up on the monitor and made the closest ones flash red on the screen. Static hissed through Corran's helmet as occasional hits weakened his shields, but energy shunted from lasers reinforced it quickly enough.

He glanced at his fuel indicator. "As much as we could teach them something about flying, it's time we change some of the rules here." He broke left and climbed, then came over, inverted, and pointed his fighter at the volcano's cone. "We'll see if these guys are such hot stuff in the place where hot stuff used to spew!"

The astromech droid splashed a message on the console.

"Yes, inviting them into the caldera will be fine. The enclosed area will hurt them more than it does me, just like it hurt the TIEs that Wedge nailed on Rachuk." Corran brought the fighter down into the crater and throttled back to zero thrust. He cut in the repulsorlift engines and powered them up so he hung suspended in the middle of the obsidian arena.

As he pointed the fighter's nose toward the sky, he glanced at Whistler's reply to his earlier statement. "Yeah, nine to one odds are hardly fair."

The X-wing shook violently, as if a titanic child had grabbed it in an invisible fist. Whistler hooted anxiously and Corran felt his stomach turn inside out. *Tractor beam! It's all over.*

The astromech droid wailed piteously.

Corran read the message on his console and shook his head. "Hey, it's not your fault. Your telling me the odds isn't why they evened them." He brought his torpedo control up again as the first Interceptors streaked over the lip of the volcano's crater.

"Sensors forward, Whistler. Time to remind them that trapping a Rogue doesn't make him dead, just deadlier."

38

LOCKED IN THE SILENCE of hyperspace, Wedge glanced back over his shoulder and frowned. "Are you absolutely certain about the timing on this search pattern thing?"

Mynock spun his head around and bleated imploringly.

"Fine." The droid's numbers indicated that a standard Imperial square-klick search pattern would take two and a half standard hours to scour the dark side of the moon. *If Corran managed to stay ahead of them and slip over to the light side, then they'd have to search it, too. That means he could still be hiding from them. If not* . . . Wedge glanced at his fighter's chronometer. *If not, they found him a minimum of an hour and a half ago.*

Frustration balled Wedge's hands into fists. He knew they'd done everything they could within mission parameters to help Corran. The first set of ten Interceptors had caught up with them because they had throttled back and waited. The five Rogues had easily dispatched their foes, but the dogfight took them to critical fuel levels. They went to light speed, leaving a dozen squints to hunt for Corran.

At the first transit jump he'd ordered everyone to spend the trip into Noquivzor working up plans to go back and get Corran out. For the past three hours he'd put together a rescue operation and had figured out all sorts of contingencies depending upon what intelligence they could get from Borleias. Defender Wing would not yet have arrived at Borleias by the time the Rogues landed at Noquivzor, but there was an outside chance that Page's people could have some news and have tapped into the Imperial holonet to deliver it.

That was a long shot, but getting information from the holonet was not. Borleias would certainly have reported being under attack, and that report might contain details that would indicate Corran's status. The second he reverted to realspace he'd have Emtrey search out the latest information from Borleias. *I need to know what to expect when we go back.*

His core plan was risky, and he knew Ackbar would never approve it. The mission risks had been pointed out in advance. Corran had volunteered to go. He would be missed, but jeopardizing other people to effect a rescue that probably would not work would be foolish.

As much as he knew Ackbar would be right in pointing all those things out, he also knew he couldn't abandon one of his people. *I've lost too many friends to the Empire not to do everything I can to save others.* He knew his insistence on Tycho Celchu's inclusion in Rogue Squadron was just such a rescue. He smiled wryly. *And saving him from Salm was tougher than pulling Corran out of Borleias ever will be.*

At Noquivzor the Rogues could be refueled and head back out inside a half hour. He assumed their return trip would actually go off in an hour because he recalled that being the minimum amount of time techs needed to put the lasers back in the *Forbidden*. With Tycho flying the shuttle and the X-wings as escort, they'd be more than a match for the dozen Interceptors in the Borleias system.

Dozen? I'll bet Corran will leave us half that number.

Wedge sat back for a moment. He realized he thought of Corran as *Corran*, not Lieutenant Horn. The distance he had placed between himself and Corran had collapsed in on itself.

He'd purposely chosen to distance himself from all the new recruits to maintain authority over them. As loose as Rogue Squadron was, that detachment was necessary if they were to follow him.

Even so, he suddenly realized, he had insulated himself from them for his own protection. Having lost so many friends, having felt the pain of their deaths, he had been reluctant to let anyone else get close. Not befriending them meant he could blunt the pain of seeing them die. He regretted Lujayne Forge, Andoorni Hui, and Pcshk Vri'syk dying, but he had not been as deeply hurt by their deaths as he had when Biggs or Porkins or Dack had died.

Emotional distance is armor for the heart. That armor was necessary because without it the overwhelming nature of the fight against the Empire would crush him. After seeing how many had been slain, it would have been easy to assume all was for naught. *But if we did assume that, the Death Stars would be ravaging planets and the Emperor would still rule the galaxy.*

Corran had earned the friendship Wedge felt for him, and not just through his skill in an X-wing. He had taken to heart the things Wedge had told him about becoming part of the unit. Corran had clearly known that to go after the Interceptors closing on an assault shuttle was to be left behind. He had made that choice because it was really no choice at all. *The rest of the unit would have made the same choice, too.*

And they'll want to go back to get Corran. By jumping straight from Noquivzor to Borleias, without making a side jump first, they could reach the world in under three hours. Doing that would expose Noquivzor to discovery by Imperial forces, but Wedge expected Page's people to be giving them other things to think about. Even so, a jump to the outer edge of the Borleias system and then another jump in closer would bring them out of hyperspace from a direction that would hide their point of origin. *I hope.*

A green button started blinking on the command console.

Wedge punched it and hyperspace melted into the Noquivzor system. He immediately keyed his comm. "Rogue Leader to Emtrey."

"Emtrey here, sir. I have an urgent message for Bror Jace."

"It's not as urgent as my orders, Emtrey. Get Zraii set up to refuel us and get techs mounting lasers on the *Forbidden*. An hour from now, at the most, we're heading back out."

"Yes, sir."

"And contact Intelligence. I want any holonet data coming out of Borleias."

"Yes, sir." The droid sounded agitated. "Sir, we do have some information from Borleias."

"You do?" Wedge's heart started to pound inside his chest. "What is it? Is it about Corran?"

"Yes, sir."

"Give it to me."

"It's a hologram."

Wedge frowned. "Have the computer mash it to two dimensions and send it."

"You may want to wait, sir."

"Emtrey!"

"Transmitting now, sir, at your request."

The monitor resolved itself into an image of Corran Horn. Wedge shook his head. *What?*

"If you're seeing this, Commander Antilles," Corran said solemnly, "I know I was left behind . . ."

39

CORRAN POPPED ONE proton torpedo off and watched the lead Interceptor evaporate. Thumbing his weapons control over to lasers, he started to track the next TIE. The tractor beam limited his ship's range of motion, but a heavy foot on a rudder pedal started turning him in the right direction. *Just a bit more . . .*

The Interceptor exploded as red laser bolts ripped through the cockpit.

Corran looked down at his hand and couldn't recall having hit the trigger.

More laser fire transformed another TIE into a fireball. *What in the Cloak of the Sith?*

Whistler started hooting frantically.

Corran hesitated, not comprehending, then flipped his comm unit back on as his fighter began to rise through the volcano, picking up speed.

". . . repeat, is your hyperdrive still operational?"

He recognized the voice. "Mirax?"

"Yeah. You ready to get smuggled out of here?"

"Hyperdrive is a go."

"Key it to my signal."

"Whistler, do it."

Corran didn't afford himself the luxury of looking back at the ship that had tractored his fighter—the forward view had more than enough to entertain him. Borleias's moon was receding quickly into the starfield, as were the squints. Green lancets of laser fire reached out toward him, but they splashed harmlessly against his shields. His return fire scattered the TIEs and one more fell prey to *Skate*'s gunner.

Whistler piped a warning at him, then the starfield stretched into columns and they entered hyperspace. A second or two later they came back out again at a point well below the Pyria system's elliptic plane.

"Corran, bring your fighter around and come up into the hold."

"Gladly, *Skate*" He complied with the order and found his twelve-and-a-half-meter-long fighter fit snugly in the hold. He waited for Mirax to repressurize the hold after closing the loading bay doors, then he popped his cockpit canopy open and vaulted from the X-wing. He landed on the deck with a thump, then smiled as the hold hatch opened.

"Permission to come aboard, Captain Terrik."

"Promise you won't tell my father?" Mirax smiled and strode boldly across the deck to him. "He'd die if he could see an X-wing with CorSec markings in the belly of his ship."

"And if my father hadn't been killed years ago, having my ship here would have gotten him, too." Corran enfolded Mirax in a hug. "Your secret is safe with me."

"Likewise, Corran."

He didn't let his arms slacken until he felt her hug loosen first. "And I commend you on your shooting. You popped three Interceptors in no time."

Mirax pulled away from him and pointed toward the hatchway. "He did it, not me."

The silhouette in the hatchway shrugged. "The *Skate* is a fairly stable gunnery platform. And the squint pilots weren't the Empire's best."

Pulling off the helmet, Corran crossed the hold and offered the man his hand. "Still and all, Captain Celchu, it was superior shooting." *With skills like that, I can't imagine why you're not flying with us. Commander Antilles said not to ask, and now is not the time, but I want to know the answer.*

Mirax patted Corran on the back and let her hand linger there for a moment—a sensation he relished. "Come on up to the bridge. We'll go to hyperspace and get back to Noquivzor before the others do."

"We will?"

Mirax slapped the nearest bulkhead. "The *Skate* can push .6 past light speed—not as fast as the *Falcon*, but definitely better-looking. With our speed we can trim time off the trip back to Noquivzor and fly a course that's shorter. We'll beat them by an hour, just as we did getting here."

Corran frowned. "But how could you get here since no one was supposed to know where here was? Commander Antilles didn't tell the others until our second jump."

The smuggler smiled sweetly at him. "Not my fault you talk in your sleep."

Tycho laughed as he followed Mirax into the *Skate*'s cockpit and dropped into one of the jumpseats. "Mirax discovered a possible security breach. We arrived and went to ground on the dark side of the moon. We monitored Borleias control traffic and didn't notice unusual activity down there, so we maintained comm silence when the squadron arrived."

Corran sat down behind him. "If you told us you were there you might have alerted the Imperials."

"Exactly." Tycho said. "Since the squadron was running with weak comm system transmissions, we couldn't hear what Wedge had planned when he went sunside, but we figured things out from Imperial intercepts—the Verpine droid here has slicing skills that broke the Imp scrambling quite quickly. We stayed hidden when the squints started to search, assuming we'd break and run when they reached the volcano."

Mirax looked back at Corran. "Then you arrived with them on your tail, we grabbed you and pulled you out."

Corran chuckled as he strapped himself into the seat. "I thought I was dead."

"I imagine that is what the rest of the squadron will be thinking when they reach Noquivzor." Tycho slapped Corran on the knee. "Won't they be surprised?"

"Yeah, I imagine they will." Corran's eyes narrowed. "And I've got an idea which means we can have some fun with them."

Mirax tapped the console and smiled at her Sullustan pilot. "Get us going, Liat, and fast, too. The *Pulsar Skate* will be the first ship ever to smuggle a man back from the grave, and I mean for us to do it in record time at that."

40

"... ON BORLEIAS'S MOON," Corran's image continued. "I know the decision to leave me behind wasn't easy."

Wedge's eyes narrowed. "... *on Borleias's moon?*" *How could he have known? Wait a minute!*

"I want you to know I harbor no ill will concerning my abandonment. To prove this to you, I pried some Whyren's Reserve away from Emtrey and a *ryshcate* should have finished baking by the time you land."

"Wahoo!" Gavin's voice echoed through the comm.

Wedge keyed his comm. "Horn, if you aren't dead, you will be."

Corran's image broke into laughter. "I'm happy to see you, too, Commander. Welcome home."

WEDGE SAT BACK in his chair and held the half-full tumbler up so the light from the center of the recreation room made the amber liquid in it glow. Its chemical warmth, aided and abetted by seeing Corran alive and unhurt, had chased the chilly dread from his belly and melted the stress in his shoulders and neck. Putting his feet up on the table, he actually began to relax for the first time in conscious memory.

In retrospect Corran's message *was* rather funny. He watched his green-eyed lieutenant cut the warm *ryshcate* and hand it out to the other pilots in the squadron. They were all giddy with their success and his survival. Wedge knew they all had been as horrified as he had when the message began to play in their cockpits, but no one was more relieved than he had been when the truth of it was revealed to them.

As jokes go, Corran, it was good. You'll pay *for it, of course, but it was good.*

Wedge glanced sidelong at Tycho. "I can't believe you let him send that message."

The Alderaanian shrugged. "The shocked expression on your face was even better than I imagined it would be."

"I won't forget that, Captain Celchu."

"Besides, I can't wait to see how you're going to get back at Corran." Tycho took a swallow of his lum. "I trust you'll make it good."

"You can be assured of that." Wedge sipped a little more whiskey and let it sit on his tongue for a moment. Sucking air in through slightly parted lips let the crisp, woody aroma fill his head, then he swallowed and smiled. "Corran comes back from the dead and I understand you were resurrected, too. Three squints?"

Tycho nodded solemnly. "Two were at point-blank range—Emtrey could have shot them. The third was at range—decent shot."

"Of course, the Alliance Security team is a bit upset at having been detained in your quarters."

"No, they weren't very happy when we took them prisoner." His Executive Officer winced. "The problem was we had a possible security leak, but explaining everything we would have had to explain would have made it impossible for us to get to Borleias in time to warn you, *if* that's what we needed to do."

"Easier to ask forgiveness than permission." Wedge chuckled. "I was planning the same sort of thing for the return trip to Borleias. You've got the security problem under control?"

"I think so. Locking this thing down will mean a lot of time being spent with Emtrey."

"Put Corran on it."

Tycho shook his head. "Eew, that's nastier than even I as sumed you'd be."

"Well, leading a unit isn't a young man's game, after all." Wedge swung his feet to the floor and set his tumbler on the table as Corran approached with two pieces of *ryshcate.* "Smells good."

"Mirax made it." Corran handed the other piece to Tycho. "Corellians use it for celebrations."

Wedge hefted his piece of the sweetcake. "Getting you back from Borleias is worthy of celebration, as is having the Alliance's hottest new pilot being a member of the squadron."

Corran looked surprised. "Me?"

"No." Wedge smiled past him at the man arriving late to the celebration. "Congratulations, Bror Jace. The trio of kills you got on the Interceptors following us out of the Pyria system puts you at twenty-two kills. You beat Lieutenant Horn by one."

The Thyferran beamed, his blue eyes alive with pride. "Thank you, Commander." He glanced down for a second, then accepted a piece of the cake from Mirax. "This is good news and helps offset what I have just heard."

Wedge set his cake down next to the glass of whiskey. "And that is?"

"The message waiting for me was from Thyferra. My great uncle, our patriarch, is dying. The Emdees give him two weeks at best. Even bacta cannot cure old age."

"I'm terribly sorry, Mr. Jace, Bror." Wedge glanced at his XO. "Tycho, can you . . . ?"

"No problem, Wedge." Tycho stood up. "Compassion leave won't work, but if we send our pilot home on a recruiting run, I think the diplomatic corps will back us up. You'll be on your way as soon as you can pack your X-wing, Mr. Jace."

"Thank you."

Corran offered Bror his hand. "I'm sorry to know your uncle is ill. I'm also sorry to lose to you, but I'm not sorry about how well you did."

"Nor I about your performance." Bror pumped Corran's hand. "I would give you another chance at such a contest, but I do not want even the slightest hint of division within this squadron."

"I concur." Corran nabbed a small piece of cake from the serving tray on the table and popped it into his mouth.

Everyone followed Corran's lead and as he chewed, just for a second, Wedge felt himself back on Yavin 4, catching a hasty last meal before he and his friends went off to attack the Death Star. He knew it wasn't the taste of the *ryshcate* that brought the memory back—on Yavin 4 there had been no time and no ingredients to create something so indulgent. *No, it's the sense of unity that takes me back. The core spirit, it was there before Rogue Squadron was ever formed. It was the squadron's soul and it's still here. This is Rogue Squadron, not reborn, just continuing as it should.*

"I'd like to offer a toast, my friends, if I may." Wedge raised his glass and the others joined him. "To Rogue Squadron, to the friends we've lost, the battles we've fought, and the utter fear our return will bring to our enemies."

EPILOGUE

Kirtan Loor dropped to one knee before Ysanne Isard's life-size hologram. "Please forgive my disturbing you, Madam Director, but you said you wanted to be informed immediately on any developments."

She frowned impatiently at him. "I have seen General Derricote's requisition request for more Gamorreans. Has there been a breakthrough?"

"I am not certain."

"But you approved the request."

"Yes, Madam Director." Even though she was projecting her image from her tower office nearly three kilometers above and away from his cramped workspace, the distance did not insulate him from her ire. *Somehow her eyes seem to project venom through the holonet.* "You will forgive me, Madam Director, but General Derricote is still upset about the loss of his facility on Borleias. He said you promised him it would be returned to him if he completed his work within your parameters."

"And so it shall. The Alliance stewardship of Borleias will be of little consequence in the grand scheme of things." Isard's image stared hard at him. "So, there is no breakthrough with Derricote?"

"None to my knowledge, Madam Director."

"Then what would have prompted your call to me, Agent Loor?"

"Our agent in Rogue Squadron has provided us with some useful information. Rogue Squadron will be moving to Borleias and the base will become a major staging operation for a move Coreward."

Isard tapped her teeth with a fingernail. "This was not unanticipated."

"It was also reported that the best of the new pilots, Bror Jace, will be returning to Thyferra to visit his family." Loor reached back and pulled a datapad from his desk and glanced at it. "Given the precarious balance of loyalists and Rebel sympathizers on Thyferra, it seems to me that having a hero of the Rebellion visit will not be a good thing. Since his course of travel has been communicated to us, I have prepared orders for the Interdictor cruiser *Black Asp* to intercept and destroy him."

"Very good thinking, Agent Loor." Isard nodded slowly, her eyes focusing distantly. "Amend the orders to have him taken alive if possible. I have a facility that is most successful in convincing ardent Rebels they really should be on our side. I have room at Lusankya for this Jace. He will prove *very* useful in the future."

"I have the intercept set for a system where enough smuggling goes on that the *Black Asp*'s presence makes sense. An increase in general interception activities will hide our foreknowledge of Jace's course."

The ruler of Coruscant looked quizzically at him. "Do you truly think so?"

"I do not follow your meaning."

"Don't you think your Corran Horn will be suspicious?"

He thought for a moment, then bowed his head. "He will be, but he is not so single-minded that he cannot be distracted."

"That concurs with my reading of his datafile." She smiled slightly. "But it would take information of sufficient import to distract him, yes?"

"Yes, Madam Director."

"Good." She clasped her hands behind her back. "I have let slip the information that you killed Gil Bastra."

"What?!"

"And it includes data that suggests you are, in fact, here on Imperial Center."

Kirtan's jaw dropped. He'd seen Horn angry more than once, and knew the man to be relentless in pursuit of those who had slain other members of CorSec. Horn had even found a way to capture his father's killer, the Trandoshan bounty hunter Bossk. Kirtan had taken great delight in releasing Bossk, citing the Trandoshan lack of manual dexterity to explain why Hal Horn had been killed in a spray of blaster fire meant to kill the smuggler to whom he was speaking. Since Bossk was working under a valid Imperial warrant, Hal Horn's death was an unfortunate bit of collateral casualty.

"Madam Director, didn't you say the Rogues would be coming here, to Imperial Center?"

"Indeed, I believe I did." Her smile grew. "And I believe my prediction will be proven true."

"Then Horn will come here."

"And will be looking for you." Isard licked her lips. "More distraction from his main mission for Lieutenant Horn, and more motivation for you to succeed in Rogue Squadron's destruction."

In this case I'm *not sure those ends justify the means at all.* "I see, Madam Director."

"I'm sure you do, Agent Loor. Spare me future reports about General Derricote's tantrums. I want results, and I want them to be successful results."

"As you will it, Madam Director," he found himself saying in the darkness resulting from her termination of the communication.

He rocked back and sat on the floor. For a half a second he longed for a return to the days when he and Horn were adversaries at CorSec. They had hated each other, especially after the Bossk incident, but the tension had not yet become lethal. Then he realized he harbored no real fear of Corran Horn's retribution. *His success would mean release from* her *clutches. If he knew that, of course, Horn would find a way to clone me, so he could have the pleasure of killing me and forcing me to work for Ysanne Isard forever!*

"Yes, he could be that cruel, but he would hold himself back. Therein is his weakness." Kirtan Loor grabbed the edge of his desk and pulled himself upright. "Here on Imperial Center, in Isard's domain, I have neither the compunction nor need to restrain myself. Do come to Coruscant, Corran. Bring your friends and your hidden enemy with you. Imperial City is undoubtedly the last place you ever thought you'd visit, and I will do all I can to make certain it *is* the *last* place you visit."

ACKNOWLEDGMENTS

The author would like to thank the following people for their various contributions to this book:

Janna Silverstein, Tom Dupree, and Ricia Mainhardt for getting me into this mess;

Sue Rostoni and Lucy Autrey Wilson for making it so easy to work in this universe;

Kevin J. Anderson, Timothy Zahn, Kathy Tyers, Bill Smith, Bill Slavicsek, Peter Schweighofer, Michael Kogge, and Dave Wolverton for the material they created and the advice they offered;

Lawrence Holland and Edward Kilham for the X-Wing and Tie Fighter computer games;

Chris Taylor for pointing out to me which ship Tycho was flying in *Star Wars VI: Return of the Jedi*;

My parents, my sister Kerin, my brother Patrick and his wife, Joy, for their encouragement (and endless efforts to face my other books out on bookstore shelves);

Dennis L. McKiernan, Jennifer Roberson, and especially Elizabeth T. Danforth for listening to bits of this story as it was being written and enduring such abuse with smiles and a supportive manner.

Read on for an excerpt from

ROGUE SQUADRON: WEDGE'S GAMBLE

BY MICHAEL A. STACKPOLE

1

EVEN BEFORE HIS X-wing's sensors had time to scan and
identify the new ship, Corran Horn knew it was trouble.
That knowledge was not based on the ship's unscheduled, un-
announced reversion to realspace in the Pyria system. In the
month since the Rebel Alliance took the planet Borleias from
the Empire, more ships than Corran cared to remember had
popped in for a quick survey of the place. Some were on diplomatic missions from worlds that had already joined the New
Republic coming to inspect the latest conquest of their forces.
Other ships had been sent by the rulers of planets who wanted
to separate fact from propaganda before they decided if they
wanted to shift allegiances in the galactic civil war.

Still others had been Imperial vessels on reconnaissance
missions, and a goodly proportion of the rest were Alliance
ships with legitimate business in the system. All of them had
to be checked out, and the hostiles discouraged, but the patrols had produced no serious incidents or fatalities. This
spawned a complacency among the pilots that was not conducive to long life, but even Corran had found it hard to keep his
edge when no serious threats presented themselves.

The new ship's arrival slashed away his peace of mind like

a vibroblade. The sensors reported a modified freight cruiser that had started life as a Rendili Star Drive ship—not in the *Neutron Star*-class of bulk cruiser, but something roughly a quarter that size. That in no way made it remarkable or unusual—dozens of ships built on the same design had been through the system since its conquest. The name, *Vengeance Derra IV*, followed the naming convention common among New Republic ships of recalling some event in the course of the civil war. It had even entered the system on the course and at the speed the Rebels had dictated for freighter traffic.

Still, something is not right here. During his brief career with the Corellian Security Force, hunting down smugglers and other criminals, he'd learned to trust his gut feelings about things. His father, Hal, and even his grandfather—both Cor-Sec officers themselves—had encouraged him to follow his instincts in dangerous situations. The sensation frustrated him with its elusiveness, as if it were no more tangible than the faint scent of a flower teasing his nose and defying identification.

It's enough that I know something is odd. Exactly what *isn't important at this point.* Corran keyed his comm unit. "Rogue Nine to Champion Five, you handle the challenge. Wait here with Six. I'm going to go out and do a flyby."

"I copy, Nine, but we are supposed to expedite all shipping in this area. They aren't in the challenge zone yet."

"Humor me, Five."

"As ordered, Nine."

The system patrols had been broken up to cover four zones around the planet of Borleias. The plane of the ecliptic split the system up and down, with sun side and out splitting it core and rim. Corran and two Y-wing pilots from General Salm's Defender Wing had up-and-out, which was by far the busiest sector because the planet's moon had moved out of it and sun-ward two days previously.

"Whistler, see what you can do about boosting our sensors to pick up any anomalous readings from that freighter."

The green and white R2 astromech blatted harshly at him.

"Yes, fine, there's likely to be lots of things wrong with that freighter." Corran frowned as he nudged his throttle forward and the X-wing started off toward the freighter. "I was thinking about inappropriate weapons or other odd things."

As Corran's fighter came in closer he began to get a visual feed on the ship. All of 150 meters long, it had the gentle curves of smaller ships, or the larger Mon Calamari warships. The bridge was a bulge on the top of the bow that tapered back and down into a slender midship. Two thirds of the way back toward the stern the ship's body flared out again to accommodate the star drives. A communications array sat right behind the bridge, and quad laser turrets bristled off the bow and in a ring around the middle of the ship.

Whistler splashed a report on the ship onto Corran's primary monitor. It was a Rendili Star Drive's design, from the *Dwarf Star*-class of freighter. It shipped roughly fifteen hundred metric tons of equipment, ran with a crew of four hundred, and had nine quad lasers as well as one tractor beam that could be used to pull salvage into the belly storage area. The guns and carrying capacity made it a favorite for shorthaul traders who were willing to work in areas of the galaxy where authority had broken down, or Imperial entanglements could be a problem.

"Champion Five here, Rogue Nine."

"Go ahead, Five."

"I challenged the *Vengeance* and it answered with a code that is good."

That surprised Corran because he couldn't shake the feeling that something was wrong with the ship. "Did they get it on the first try?"

Five's comm unit didn't filter the surprise out of his voice. "No, second pass. Why?"

"I'll tell you later. Stay where you are, but get someone to lift from Borleias in an assault shuttle. You and Six be ready for trouble."

"As ordered, Nine."

Whistler chirped an inquiry at Corran.

"Yes, I think it's exactly like the doubletaker case." Back on Corellia he and his partner, Iella Wessiri, had investigated a series of burglaries where things had been stolen from houses, but there were no signs of forced entry. All of the security systems were manufactured by different companies, and installed and monitored by different agencies. The key to cracking the case was that the ROMs used in the security systems all came from the *same* manufacturer. An employee had sliced the code that got burned into the chips so when a particular password was used on the locks, the system would spit out the correct password. On the second try the thief would enter the correct code, get in, and rob the place.

The Y-wing fighters the Alliance used were old, but still vital, and most of them were a patchwork of new and old systems. Spare parts were not easy to come by, and whatever were available were used quickly to keep the fighters in service. It was conceivable that a sensor/comm unit integrator had been fitted with odd chips that gave away codes when checking them. Arranging for such things would not be beyond the Empire's Director of Intelligence, Ysanne Isard, especially if it would help prevent the Rebel Alliance from taking Coruscant away from her.

Corran punched his comm unit over to the frequency the freighter was using. "*Vengeance Derra IV*, this is Lieutenant Corran Horn of Rogue Squadron. Stop now. Stand by for boarding."

The freighter did not even slow, much less stop. "Is there a problem, Lieutenant?"

Corran shifted the targeting crosshairs of his heads-up display over to lead the freighter, then sent a quad burst of red laser fire across the ship's bow. "*Vengeance*, stand by for boarding. There will only be a problem if you make one."

"Standing by."

The freighter began to roll to port, exposing its top toward

Corran's ship. *Not good.* "Five and Six, prepare proton torpedoes. Link fire and lock on the freighter."

"Nine, they've done nothing."

"Yet, Five, yet."

Swinging up and around from the belly of *Vengeance*, four TIE starfighters raced in toward Corran's X-wing. Without waiting for them to start shooting, he slapped the stick to the right and brought the fighter up onto its starboard S-foil. The TIEs started their own turns to port and began to dive, anticipating his escape maneuver. Corran punched his left foot on the etheric rudder pedal, skidding the stern of his ship to starboard, then shot off straight in the opposite direction from his pursuit.

"Nine, we have two TIE bombers deployed."

"Five, fire on the *Vengeance*, then take the dupes. I've got the eyeballs. Let Borleias base know we have trouble." He knew the Y-wings would have little trouble outflying the dupes—pilot slang for the double-hulled bombers. If he could keep the TIEs occupied, they wouldn't be in any position to harass the Y-wings. If the missiles the Y-wings launched at *Vengeance* were enough to take down the forward shields, the freighter's captain would have to think about running, which would distract the TIE pilots, since without him, they were stuck in the Pyria system.

Lots of ifs there. Time to make some of them certainties. He used a snap-roll to bring the fighter up on the starboard stabilizer again, then dove into a long loop that took him down to where *Vengeance*'s bulk hid him from the TIEs. Rolling his ship and applying some rudder, he arrowed straight in at the freighter. This put him in position to watch as the quartet of proton torpedoes launched by the Y-wings nailed the ship's bow. Each missile exploded against the shields like a star going nova.

The astromech droid whistled up a requiem for *Vengeance*'s bow shield.

Corran tightened on the trigger and sent a quad burst of

fire toward the ship's bridge. Without waiting to see if it hit or did damage, he barrel-rolled to port, moving toward the middle of the freighter, and pulled back on the stick to bring the fighter's nose up. His targeting crosshairs hung just above the horizon of the freighter's hull.

A TIE starfighter, shying from the series of explosions against the forward shield, streaked over the freighter's edge and right into his sights. Corran triggered a quad shot that caught the eyeball on the port side quadanium steel armored solar panel, slicing the hexagon into a dozen or more pieces. A secondary explosion suggested a failure in one of the ion engines that the fighter's subsequent careening off through space confirmed.

Corran rolled up on the left stabilizer foil and drifted to port for a heartbeat before snapping over onto the starboard S-foil and hauling back on the stick. The maneuver allowed him to evade the fire coming in from *Vengeance*'s lasers. It also put him on the vector the TIE had used coming in over the freighter's hull. Adding a bit more to the starboard roll and pulling back on the stick again took him out past the ship's damaged bow and let him swoop in on the tail of another TIE.

The eyeball broke back left, but Corran rolled his ship through a corkscrew that kept him on target. He fired twice. The first quad shot missed, but the second tagged the ball cockpit full on. The lasers blew through the engine, then an explosion ripped the fighter apart. Corran dove into and flew through the expanding ball of incandescent gas, then rolled and dove again.

"Five, report."

"One dupe dead, one sleeping."

Corran laughed aloud. "Nice shooting, Five. Good thinking." The Y-wing pilots had shown the presence of mind to engage one of the bombers while using their ion cannons. The weapons were inferior in power to lasers, but they had the advantage of knocking out a ship's electronics by overloading the electrical system. The ion cannons could render a ship inoperable, allowing the pilot to be picked up later.

Chances are, though, this Imp pilot will kill himself to avoid capture. Still, the ship might teach us something.

"Nine, the freighter is turning to run. Do you want help with the eyeballs?"

"Negative, Five."

Whistler scolded him with a harsh blatty sound.

"It's not that I think I'm that good, Whistler, it's that I know they aren't." Refusing assistance to deal with enemies that outnumber you was usually ascribed to unending egotism or terminal stupidity, but Corran had a third reason in mind. The Y-wing pilots, while enthusiastic and decently trained, were insufficiently experienced in dogfighting to be much help to him. If they entered the fight, he'd have to worry about hitting them. Without their intervention, his only possible targets were Imperial ships, and that fact gave him some freedom.

"Nine, we'll take *Vengeance*."

"Negative, Five, definitely negative." *If they go in on the freighter it will pick them apart.* "Hang off there and try for torp locks on the TIEs."

Glancing at his sensor displays, he marked the positions of the Y-wings, then rolled his ship and dove. Angry green laser bolts slashed through the blackness in front of him, but neither of the TIEs' shots hit. The sensors reported the last two eyeballs had just pulled through a crisscross maneuver and were looping up and around to make another pass on him. That told him the last two pilots were good enough to have survived more than one fight in their ships.

They rolled through their double-helix maneuver and Corran shot through the center of their spiral. Rolling out to the right he cut in front of one, inviting a hastily snapped shot. The TIE pilot took it, splashing lasers against the X-wing's aft shield. Ignoring Whistler's shrill shriek, Corran reinforced the rear shield, then rolled and began a dive.

The eyeball rolled and started after him. Corran chopped

his throttle back, then rolled and dove sharply. He remained in the dive for a couple of seconds, then rolled again and climbed. Rolling back out onto his original course, he popped in behind the TIE that had previously been on his tail and took a shot of his own.

The eyeball juked at the last second, so the four laser bolts only clipped the top of one of the solar panels. The TIE starfighter began to whirl away, but it never exploded. Damaged as the ship was, it would be an easy target to follow and finish, but the last TIE sprayed laser fire against the X-wing's shields, giving Corran a more immediate threat to deal with.

Because it was coming in from the left, Corran rolled right, then cruised down through a diving turn that aimed him back along its inbound course. The TIE looped up, then rolled and came down through an inverse loop to cut across Corran's tail. Corran let the X-wing sideslip right, but not before the eyeball had taken a shot at him. Whistler screamed, then a bank of lights started flashing on the fighter's command console.

Sithspawn! My shields are down. Corran stomped on the right rudder pedal, swinging the X-wing's nose in that direction, then rolled up on the port stabilizer and pulled back on the stick. As the ship started to climb, another snap-roll to the left broke it off at right angles to the climb and away from pursuit. "Whistler, get the shields back up, fast."

A counter appeared on his main screen and began counting down from one and a half minutes.

"Not good, not good at all."

The major advantage an X-wing had over a TIE starfighter was shields. The two fighters matched each other in speed and the TIE actually had the edge in maneuverability. Shields allowed the X-wings to survive more hits during a fight, and in dogfighting, the goal was surviving to the end and beyond. Corran felt he could outfly the TIE pilot, but engaging in combat while naked was not something that made him feel at all confident.

He punched the throttle to full and pushed the fighter

through a series of twists and loops that carried it away from the TIE, but no closer to the Y-wings. Time seemed to be passing very slowly to Corran, with each second on the counter seeming to take a minute to click off. The TIE pilot seemed content to circle around, trying to close with Corran, then he broke off and streaked in toward the Y-wings, coming up from beneath them.

"Heads up, Five. Invert, you have incoming."

The Y-wings executed the flip in good order as Corran allocated power that would have normally gone to shields over to propulsion. That provided him a bit more speed, which let him close the gap with the eyeball.

"Nine, I have missile lock."

"Shoot, Six, shoot."

The Y-wing let a proton torpedo go at point-blank range, but it shot past the eyeball and would have hit the X-wing had Corran not rolled fast. "Break outside, Champions!"

The Y-wing pilots complied with Corran's order, but did so slowly. The TIE spun in on Champion Five, pouring verdant laser bolts into its shields. The Y-wing pilot continued his roll and dive, and the TIE corrected to follow him, allowing himself to fly a level arc as he pursued his quarry.

You're mine, now. Corran eased back on his stick, millimeter by millimeter centering the Imperial fighter on his targeting crosshairs.

Whistler shrilled a warning.

Behind me? Who? He glanced at his sensors and saw the other TIE closing in on him and he wanted to break away. *Can't, Five is history if I do.*

Corran hit his trigger, tracking ruby energy darts along the TIE's flight path. Even as he saw the lasers hit the eyeball's wings and cockpit, he braced for the other TIE's lasers burning through his ship. He saw his target explode and knew, as green laser bolts scythed down toward his ship, he was a dead man.

He prepared himself for nothingness.

He was not wholly disappointed.

Nothing happened.

Corran rolled left and climbed. "Find him, Whistler."

The droid gave back a negative report.

"What about *Vengeance?*"

Whistler reported it had gone to lightspeed.

At least we're clear there. Corran felt a shiver run down his spine. His left hand rose up and, through the fabric of his flight suit, touched a gold medallion he wore. *It appears all my luck has not run out.*

"Five, Six, what happened to the other eyeball?"

"I got him, Nine."

"With what, Six?"

"The missile I launched."

It took Corran a second to make sense of the reply, then he remembered the missile that had almost hit him as he had come in on the TIE starfighter. "Six, you were aiming at the *second* TIE?"

"Yes, sir, Lieutenant. Did I do something wrong?"

Corran wanted to yell at him about choosing targets that have a higher threat factor—by virtue of being closer and, therefore, more likely to hit their target—but he stopped before he gave in to temptation. "Not wrong, Six, but it could have been more right."

"Yes, sir," came a sheepish reply that remained full of nervous energy. "Next time, sir."

"Yeah, at least we can all be thankful there will be a next time."

Whistler tootled triumphantly as the X-wing's shields came back up.

Corran smiled. "Yes, I do appreciate your shaving seven seconds off the estimate, Whistler." He keyed his comm unit. "Five, Six, mark the coordinates of your sleeping dupe, then we head in. We'll have reports to fill out but the fact that we *can* fill them out means this has been a very good day."

THE STAR WARS LEGENDS NOVELS TIMELINE

BEFORE THE REPUBLIC
37,000–25,000 YEARS BEFORE
STAR WARS: A NEW HOPE

c. 25,793 YEARS BEFORE *STAR WARS: A NEW HOPE*

Dawn of the Jedi: Into the Void

OLD REPUBLIC
5,000–67 YEARS BEFORE
STAR WARS: A NEW HOPE

Lost Tribe of the Sith: The Collected
Stories

3,954 YEARS BEFORE *STAR WARS: A NEW HOPE*

The Old Republic: Revan

3,650 YEARS BEFORE *STAR WARS: A NEW HOPE*

The Old Republic: Deceived
Red Harvest
The Old Republic: Fatal Alliance
The Old Republic: Annihilation

1,032 YEARS BEFORE *STAR WARS: A NEW HOPE*

Knight Errant
Darth Bane: Path of Destruction
Darth Bane: Rule of Two
Darth Bane: Dynasty of Evil

RISE OF THE EMPIRE
67–0 YEARS BEFORE
STAR WARS: A NEW HOPE

67 YEARS BEFORE *STAR WARS: A NEW HOPE*

Darth Plagueis

33 YEARS BEFORE *STAR WARS: A NEW HOPE*

Cloak of Deception
Darth Maul: Shadow Hunter
Maul: Lockdown

32 YEARS BEFORE *STAR WARS: A NEW HOPE*

**STAR WARS: EPISODE I
THE PHANTOM MENACE**

Rogue Planet
Outbound Flight
The Approaching Storm

22 YEARS BEFORE *STAR WARS: A NEW HOPE*

**STAR WARS: EPISODE II
ATTACK OF THE CLONES**

22–19 YEARS BEFORE *STAR WARS: A NEW HOPE*

**STAR WARS: THE CLONE
WARS**

The Clone Wars: Wild Space
The Clone Wars: No Prisoners

Clone Wars Gambit
Stealth
Siege

Republic Commando
Hard Contact
Triple Zero
True Colors
Order 66

Shatterpoint
The Cestus Deception
MedStar I: Battle Surgeons
MedStar II: Jedi Healer
Jedi Trial
Yoda: Dark Rendezvous
Labyrinth of Evil

19 YEARS BEFORE *STAR WARS: A NEW HOPE*

**STAR WARS: EPISODE III
REVENGE OF THE SITH**

Kenobi
Dark Lord: The Rise of Darth Vader
Imperial Commando 501st

Coruscant Nights
Jedi Twilight
Street of Shadows
Patterns of Force

The Last Jedi

10 YEARS BEFORE *STAR WARS: A NEW HOPE*

The Han Solo Trilogy
The Paradise Snare
The Hutt Gambit
Rebel Dawn

The Adventures of Lando Calrissian
The Force Unleashed
The Han Solo Adventures
Death Troopers
The Force Unleashed II

The STAR WARS Legends Novels Timeline

REBELLION
0–5 YEARS AFTER
STAR WARS: A NEW HOPE

Death Star
Shadow Games

0

STAR WARS: EPISODE IV
A NEW HOPE

Tales from the Mos Eisley Cantina
Tales from the Empire
Tales from the New Republic
Scoundrels
Allegiance
Choices of One
Honor Among Thieves
Galaxies: The Ruins of Dantooine
Splinter of the Mind's Eye
Razor's Edge

3 YEARS AFTER *STAR WARS: A NEW HOPE*

STAR WARS: EPISODE V
THE EMPIRE STRIKES BACK

Tales of the Bounty Hunters
Shadows of the Empire

4 YEARS AFTER *STAR WARS: A NEW HOPE*

STAR WARS: EPISODE VI
THE RETURN OF THE JEDI

Tales from Jabba's Palace

The Bounty Hunter Wars
  The Mandalorian Armor
  Slave Ship
  Hard Merchandise

The Truce at Bakura
Luke Skywalker and the Shadows of
  Mindor

NEW REPUBLIC
5–25 YEARS AFTER
STAR WARS: A NEW HOPE

X-Wing
  Rogue Squadron
  Wedge's Gamble
  The Krytos Trap
  The Bacta War
  Wraith Squadron
  Iron Fist
  Solo Command

The Courtship of Princess Leia
Tatooine Ghost

The Thrawn Trilogy
  Heir to the Empire
  Dark Force Rising
  The Last Command

X-Wing: Isard's Revenge

The Jedi Academy Trilogy
  Jedi Search
  Dark Apprentice
  Champions of the Force

I, Jedi
Children of the Jedi
Darksaber
Planet of Twilight
X-Wing: Starfighters of Adumar
The Crystal Star

The Black Fleet Crisis Trilogy
  Before the Storm
  Shield of Lies
  Tyrant's Test

The New Rebellion

The Corellian Trilogy
  Ambush at Corellia
  Assault at Selonia
  Showdown at Centerpoint

The Hand of Thrawn Duology
  Specter of the Past
  Vision of the Future

Scourge
Survivor's Quest

NEW JEDI ORDER
25–40 YEARS AFTER
STAR WARS: A NEW HOPE

LEGACY
40+ YEARS AFTER
STAR WARS: A NEW HOPE

ABOUT THE AUTHOR

MICHAEL A. STACKPOLE is the *New York Times* best-selling author of more than fifty-five novels, including *I, Jedi* and *Rogue Squadron*. He's won awards in the realms of podcasting, game design, computer-game design, screenwriting, editing, graphic-novel writing, and novel writing. He lives in Arizona and frequently travels the United States attending conventions and teaching writing workshops.

michaelastackpole.com

Twitter: @MikeStackpole

ABOUT THE TYPE

This book was set in Sabon, a typeface designed by the well-known German typographer Jan Tschichold (1902–74). Sabon's design is based upon the original letter forms of sixteenth-century French type designer Claude Garamond and was created specifically to be used for three sources: foundry type for hand composition, Linotype, and Monotype. Tschichold named his typeface for the famous Frankfurt typefounder Jacques Sabon (c. 1520–80).

A long time ago in a galaxy far, far away. . . .

STAR WARS™

Join up! Subscribe to our newsletter
at ReadStarWars.com or find us on social.

 StarWarsBooks

🐦 @DelReyStarWars

📷 @DelReyStarWars